Praise for Gage and the Winter Saga

I don't know how to explain how special these books are. Gage has achieved something many authors only dream of: creating something truly lasting. The world he's crafted is unique and memorable. Winter's Legacy somehow transcends its predecessor (which is no small feat). These books break the mold and stereotype of every genre, and I would recommend them to absolutely anyone.

— MEGAN STOCKTON - AUTHOR OF ...AND NOBODY KNOWS IT BUT ME

I can honestly say Gage is one of the best writers I've freshly encountered in the last 20 years.

— S.P. SOMTOW - WORLD FANTASY AWARD WINNING AUTHOR OF THE BIRD CATCHER

WOW is Greenwood's approach original. I love what Winter's Myths had to say. It's so rare that I read something that feels special to me... and Winter's Myths felt special.

— JONATHAN EDWARD DURHAM, AWARD WINNING AUTHOR OF WINTERSET HOLLOW

Dear gods and goddesses, save me from this train wreck.

— GAGE GREENWOOD - AUTHOR OF
WINTER'S MYTHS AND WINTER'S LEGACY

Winter's Legacy

WINTER'S MYTHS
BOOK TWO

GAGE GREENWOOD

TANNER'S SWITCH PUBLISHING

To Dad and Gail,
For always making me proud to be myself.

Introduction

Winter's Myths was a difficult book to write, and not just because it's a weird genre-blender. I had to really focus on the writing and avoid flourishing any of it. The characters who capitalize the POV throughout most of the book don't know what anything is, so I had to avoid metaphors or overly descriptive text. After all, how can someone compare an object to a stargazer lily when that person has never seen the sun before, let alone a flower. Making it more difficult, the main character not only held the POV for most of the book, but he was also a storyteller!

I had to create an entire mythology, build a world, all from the mind of a person who calls guns "boom weapons," and cars "metal wagons." I took liberties, of course. Winter probably wouldn't know the difference between an oak and an elm, but occasionally during his mythologies, I might have referenced a black oak. Each time I did this, I justified the decision, thinking it made for a better reading experience.

In Winter's Legacy, I had to justify a lot more. In this book, the mythologies come from a variety of places, including a nine-year-old child, one who has the same language limitations Winter had in book one. Initially, I tried to keep Candlestick's tales to her voice, but ultimately decided it would be more enjoyable for the reader if I didn't. Don't get me wrong, the stories are still hers, and the focal points in the stories are what would matter to her, but the language used to describe them was all my own. If her tale talks extensively about a rock, then you know that rock means something to Candlestick, regardless of it being written above her descriptive abilities.

In other words, I chose to write her myths the way you might see them in a movie. A character begins telling a tale, and the picture cuts to that story. The viewer then watches the story as the director of the movie wants us to see it. It's still the character's story, even if she doesn't own an IMAX camera.

I think taking these liberties makes for a better book, and I hope you agree. If not, feel free to toss the novel at my head the next time you see me.

Thanks for reading,
    Gage

MOTEL

Storytellers

The group gathered around the fire. Flecks of embers sprinkled upward like a reverse winter storm. They'd grown accustomed to a nightly story from their orator, a ritual of happenstance. Caged inside a dim cave, they needed something to break up the daily monotony. While the speeches came like clockwork, they were always different. They gave the group something to look forward to; something they couldn't predict.

The orator tucked her arms around her torso and smiled. The group returned the warmness with their own grins. She cleared her throat. "Imagine your god, or whatever you believe in, as a storyteller. You, the characters in their wild tales. Whether they are a fair god or not depends on who you are. Your life may be filled with trials, pain, suffering, anxiety, hardship, and change. Still, even with all of that, there are rules to the universe.

"Your storyteller may love to throw stones at you as the action rises, but you know the stones. You've played a part in the story long enough to understand the system. Your god has an imagination, but he knows how his tale should flow. There will be no diabolus ex machina in his stories. So, despite the pain and suffering you may face, you find comfort in knowing how to play your part.

"But now, imagine your storyteller up and leaves before ending his tale. Imagine someone new takes the mantle and finishes it. This new person, even knowing how the story flowed before, will tell it differently. They have different outlooks, views, designs. Suddenly, the pain and suffering you had once known, changed into something new, something horrific, something you can't fix or fight against. With this change in speaker, everything is a diabolus ex machina. Everything." The orator stopped and scanned the crowd. Their eyes changed from excited to confused.

"The rules of the universe only exist because the author set them in place. No storyteller can replace them exactly as intended because no two authors are alike." She paused, waiting for a response. The group waited for her to say more. An unspoken battle brewed between the speaker and her listeners, one where both sides wished for the other to break the silence. Seconds ticked by like thick honey falling from a comb. Finally, a hand raised.

"Yes, Abraham," Dance said, pointing to the ice giant.

"You started by saying 'imagine your god, or whatever you believe in,' but, obviously, we all believe in gods. We all found out our dad was a god. And, I don't know if you remember, but just a short while ago, we went to war with gods. So, we all believe in gods. Seems unnecessary to start that way."

Dance smiled, but before she could answer, Miley Cyrus jumped in. "Yeah, that part didn't make sense to me. We are literal demigods, so Abe's right."

Laura Jane Grace snapped her fingers. "Oh, I get it. Dance was trying to show us how bad storytelling can get."

Dance shook her head. "No, no. I was just trying to start with some dramatic flair."

"It was really bad," Laura Jane Grace said.

Miley nodded. "Agreed. Besides, what the hell was that all about? You're supposed to give us pep talks. We've been locked in this cave for a long time waiting for Kevin Bacon to come back and, to be honest, I don't think he is and I'm starting to go crazy."

The group collectively nodded in agreement.

Dance put her arms up, telling them to settle down. "I can still do a pep talk. I had two reasons for saying what I just said. One, I thought you all might like something a little different."

Abraham Lincoln raised his hand but didn't wait to be called on. "No, we just want the usual feel-good inspiration."

"And two, I feel like something has changed. Don't you? Do you feel it too?"

The group turned to each other, seeing how the others felt.

Miley scratched her head. "I guess I do feel different."

Dance nodded. "See? Something is different. I think our storyteller is gone."

Abraham raised his hand, and again, didn't wait for Dance to call on him. "But, if we are just characters in his story, and our storyteller is gone, wouldn't that mean we would also be gone?"

Dance shook her head. "No. Kevin Bacon said something to me once. 'If the identity of the maker is in the making, and he has nothing left to make, he ceases to be. In that sense, we are his gods.' I think that's part of it, but more so, I think the stories are living on in someone else's mind. If I told you a story, and I died, the story would still exist because of you."

Laura Jane Grace pulled out a cigarette and lit it. "Mumbo Jumbo."

Miley tapped Laura's arm. "Pseudo intellectualism."

"Yup."

Abraham stood up, bumping his head on the ceiling, a lesson he failed to learn in the weeks they'd been stuck in the cave. "So you're saying we're only still alive because our story has been passed down? If the people who know the story don't keep telling it, we will only live as long as they do?"

Dance shrugged. "I think so. I don't know."

Miley looked around, her pupils shifting left to right, floor to ceiling. "But if your story was correct, the rules should change, right? Something weird should happen. Like, the new storyteller sees things just a little differently, so our world could get really weird. The roof could just blow off this cave."

Dance's tendrils wrapped around her as if making a protective shield. "I guess."

They all looked up, waiting for the ceiling to explode. Only the sounds of their ragged breath and the crackling fire existed in the cave. Fear, and maybe a little excitement, brewed. What would the new rules look like? Would they be wonderful or horrid?

A smile wormed up one side of Laura Jane Grace's face until she broke into a laugh. "Nothing. We're all worried about nothing. Even if Dance's idea is true, I don't think much will change."

A title card dropped from out of nowhere:

WINTER'S MYTHS 2: EVEN WINTERIER

The group all turned, staring at the magic letters floating in the air.

"What the fuck is that?" Miley asked.

"Did letters just fall from the sky?" Abraham asked.

"Winter's Myths 2: Even Winterier? What does that mean? Is Winterier a word?" Laura Jane Grace moved closer to the letters, examining them.

As they all moved toward the word 'Winterier', something clanked, and they turned, startled.

Abraham looked down as the letter Y in MYTHS spun around on the floor. "Sorry, I touched it. They're kind of fragile."

"Why?" Dance asked.

"Yes. Y." Abraham pointed to the felled letter. "Good job, Dance. You know your letters."

"No. I meant why did you touch it?"

"Because there are literal letters floating in the sky. Aren't you curious what they feel like? Kind of spongy, by the way, if you were wondering."

Laura Jane Grace said, "Well, I guess you were right, Dance, but what the fuck does this mean?"

Miley slid her finger around a letter, careful not to knock it over as Abraham had. "I think it's the title of our story. Well, the new version with the new storyteller."

"It's a really bad name," Laura Jane Grace said.

The letters crumbled, dissipated, and spiraled upward like the ember flecks of the fire behind them. A new title card dropped out of nowhere:

WINTER'S MYTHS 2: WINTER'S LEGACY

Miley's top lip curled. "Still hate it."

Let Me Die

THREE DAYS AFTER WINTER

Candlestick shivered. The glow disc came and went, came again. Three times? She lost count. She licked her lips, and an iron taste lingered. It hurt to open her mouth. Each time she did, her skin split, a tiny rip, but painful. Her fingertips throbbed, red skinned and raw. None of it hurt as bad as her toes and nose.

She kept moving, following the river which ran past the motel, or so she thought. Maybe it was a different river? She shadowed it for over a day, then tried in the other direction for a day and a half. No motel. It didn't make sense. She called for her sister and father, for Brian and Corey, for Kevin Bacon. No one answered.

Her belly growled and Lion whimpered, worried for her, but also for himself. She would die soon without something to eat. Could she eat pines and leaves? Sticks? She didn't know.

When the fire disc rose, the heat offered some relief, but not much, and it wouldn't come back for hours. The glow disc was still perched high above the treetops.

Her body urged her to stop with tightened muscles and shivering bones. Her eyelids pulled down, anchored by the cold and stress. Lion stayed strong despite his hunger. She hoped he'd catch a small animal for himself. She'd feel better if at least one of them could survive this, but Lion, loyal to the bone, stuck to her side, unwilling to live without her.

Candlestick tilted and lost her balance. Her arm landed against a tree trunk and she accepted the crutch. She rested her head against the tree, closing her eyes for just a moment. Her heart rate slowed, too slow, weirdly slow.

Lion rubbed his snout against her leg, whining, as if begging her to stay awake, but she couldn't.

She slid down the trunk, curling into a ball with her butt rested on a thick root. Sleep came. She fell into it, traveling through a whirlwind of blackness. Dreams of mother's smile came. The grin grew unnaturally wide, creeping up her mother's cheeks until they split the skin. Blood dripped down both sides, marrying under her mother's chin.

She shot up, her heart rate accelerating like a newly oiled generator, whirring against her ribs.

Lion licked her face.

"You woke me up."

He whimpered.

"Leave me alone." She pushed his face away from hers. "Please, just let me die," she cried. It was a weak cry. She didn't even have the energy to bawl. "I just want to die."

Lion leaned his snout forward, and she pushed it away again. "I'm sorry, buddy. I can't. Everything hurts. I am scared. I need my dad. I need my sister."

Lion gave her his snout again, and once more, she shoved it

away. "Enough!" she yelled. "If you really wanted to save me, you would have led me in the right direction. This is your fault."

Lion cowered and took a few steps back.

"I'm sorry. I didn't mean that." More tears. "I just don't know what to do and I'm so hungry."

Lion moved his paws in slow, cautious steps until he reached her, then he put his front paw on her chest.

She wrapped her bitter, chapped fingers around it and coughed. Was her family out looking for her? How could she have gotten so lost? She wondered if her father had survived. She knew it unlikely, but stranger things had happened. It seemed whenever the world turned against them, some bit of magic protected them like her loyal Lion.

The surrounding trees shook. She laid her head down, her cheek smooshing on the cold, hard earth. The shrubs rattled, rustled. The ground under her cheek vibrated. Screeches came from all around. Her vision grew blurry as a chilly breeze forced water from her eyes. Long, black poles smashed into the ground in front of her.

The lampposts.

Maybe they heard her prayers and came to kill her swiftly. One of them leaned down, its bright face blinding her as it came face-to-face with her.

"Kill me," she pled.

It snarled.

"Do it."

It screamed, and molten light flecks dribbled into the dirt.

"Please, kill me."

It's long, lanky hand rushed to her cheek, and she blinked, waiting for impact. But it stopped short, extended one of its claws, and rubbed its icy blade down the contours of her face. It snarled again and pressed the back of the talon to her forehead and pushed. It jolted her, shocked her to her core.

What was it doing?

It made the move again and her head jerked back. "What are you doing? Kill me."

It released a low grumble and pushed her head again.

More tears came down her face. "Why?"

Two more lampposts standing near, watching this unfold, screeched as if speaking to one another, and they stormed off, disappearing into the thick brush and charcoal night. The one in front of her wrapped its claw around her upper arm and lifted it.

"Stop it," she said.

It did it again.

"Stop it. Leave me alone."

The ground trembled as the other two returned. They leaned down around the first, the three of them staring at her.

She lifted her head. "What?"

One stretched its tendril-like arm out and dropped a fistful of red spheres. The other repeated the action, dropping a dead furry little animal. She sat up, understanding. The red things burst in her hand as she squeezed and shoved them into her mouth by the handful. She devoured them, the most wonderful tasting thing in the world.

With a mouthful of food, she pat Lion and pointed to the dead thing. "Eat," she said.

The animal listened.

Realization washed over her. This new awakening sent a shock wave of hope and power through her muscles, strengthening her. She stared at the monsters. How much would they do for her?

"Make me a fire, please."

The one who kept her awake screeched. The three creatures separated, kicking sticks, slashing their claws at fallen twigs until they'd made a pile. One beast pushed its neck out until its face rested half a foot above the pile. Molten light dribbled onto the sticks, igniting them.

More rustling came from behind her. She turned to see a shape hovering beyond some brush, creeping, as if too shy to show itself.

"Come out," Candlestick said, coughing from overusing her throat.

It gurgled and stepped forward. A husk.

"How many of you are there?"

The woods came to life, the leaves dancing from all directions until dozens of husks surrounded her.

Now that they stood around her, she didn't know what to say, so she shoved another heap of the red things in her mouth. They burst on her tongue; a sweet blast of flavor that made her tongue tingle and her glands salivate.

One lamppost roared and the rest ran away. As Candlestick sat near the fire, the husks closed in until they hovered around her like a living shelter. A female husk bent down and rested her head on Candlestick's shoulder. Another did the same on her other side. They rubbed her back.

She cried again, this time with relief. A wonderful wave of pinpricks danced up her skin and a million goosebumps appeared on her flesh. It felt so good to be protected, and not the way someone wanted to protect her, but in the way she needed them to.

A few minutes later, a lamppost returned, swung its arm out, and a giant horned animal flopped to the ground, gored by the lamppost's claw.

She stared at it. The monster screeched, and a group of husks moved on the dead animal, ripping it apart. A few of them gathered hunks of meat and stabbed them with sticks. When they finished, they held the chunks over the fire and whispered. "Cooooooook."

The meat sizzled over the flames. The smell made Candlestick's stomach grumble. It pulled at her, begging her to rip the meat from the sticks and devour it, but she ignored it, waiting for her meal.

As her dinner darkened and smoked, she thought about her sister and her father. She thought about her mother, whose features dimmed in Candlestick's mind, her prominent facial structure blurring in the distance of time. She worried her father's face, the scar on his cheek, and the splayed blades of his facial hair would vanish someday, too. Maybe Violin would become a nondescript silhouette of a tall, skinny girl, nothing more. Her thin brows and penciled nose, her bony shoulders and bad breath, just flecks in the wind. Fragile things ready to blow away with the weather.

She'd cried so much over the past series of days. She cried until her chest hurt and her throat turned raw. No more. She'd forget the past and focus on surviving. Her mother had once told her to never mourn. Move forward, erase the dead from her mind. She tried to keep this lesson when her father brought them to Earth, but it had proven easier to think than to execute.

She would never give up trying to find her family, but she'd also never allow her love for them to weaken her. Survival was all that mattered. Candlestick was alone. But as her monsters made her dinner and provided her with warmth, she knew she'd never be alone again.

Hope is a Noose

Brian watched Violin cross the parking lot toward the woods through the smeared window of room five. As she passed the small garden her father planted, now his resting place, she kissed her hand and pretended to drop it into the loose soil.

Brian had asked her where she wanted her father buried, and when she told him in the garden of the sister seeds, he balked, but she had a point when she said they couldn't eat crops from the same soil soaked with her dad's blood.

For the past three days, she woke and went into the woods with a gun in hand, chasing ghosts. The men who murdered her father were already dead. She killed one of them, the rest ripped to shreds by monsters. Still, she hunted.

She searched for her sister, for monsters, for anything to fill the growing chasm in her soul. Brian saw the change in her, something deeper than mourning. Violin had lost all sense of purpose, and he didn't know how to fix it. He yearned to have the words she needed to hear, but alas, he was not her father. No one was, not anymore.

Corey came out of the bathroom behind Brian, a burst of hot shower steam breaking into the crisp motel air.

"What's she up to?" Corey asked.

"Same as every day."

"Should we try to talk to her again?"

Brian nodded and frowned. "Nah, let her come to us when she's ready. We've made it clear we are here when she needs us."

"You're concerned, though."

"How could you tell?"

Corey came up behind him, his breath hitting Brian's shoulder in warm bursts. "Because you're staring out the window instead of paying attention to the man in the towel behind you."

Brian laughed and turned. "I'm sorry. I miss you."

He placed his forehead on Corey's stomach and wrapped his arms around his partner's lower back.

"What are we going to do now?" Corey asked.

Brian shook his head. "I have no idea. I can't sleep well. This place feels like a ghost, a memory."

"And unsafe."

"And lonely."

They separated, and Brian turned back to the window in time to see Violin approaching their door. She knocked.

"That was fast. Yesterday she was gone for three hours," Corey said.

Brian opened the door and Violin walked in. Without a word, she sat on their bed. They stared, waiting for her to say something, but she only gazed off at the wall. The scar on her face was still prominent, and the bruising around it painted her entire forehead purple. Marks left by a cruel boy who learned not to mess with Winter's children when Violin stabbed and shot him.

Corey broke the silence. "Brian and I are going to go look for your sister again in a little bit."

She nodded, still staring off into another world. "I'll come with you. I have been checking for tracks when I go into the woods, but I haven't seen anything. It's like she vanished."

"She'll come back, or we'll find her." Brian sat next to her.

"Don't do that."

"Do what?"

"Pretend that hope makes magic. You can't just say things and make them true. My sister has been gone for days. We will probably never find her. Someone might have killed her. Maybe her monsters turned on her. Who knows?"

"I know you've been through a lot, but we can't just give up hope."

"Hope is a noose, a gift given to the goddesses by humankind."

She walked to the wall and rubbed her thumb on the television screen.

"What's that from?" Corey asked.

"From my father's stupid fairy tales. A lot of good they did. Those childish stories gave me hope, and I foolishly watched my father's last breath, thinking a god would run through the woods to save him. I waited and waited. That was the last bit of hope I will give to this world." She stormed out of the room and before slamming the door said, "I'll be waiting for you in my room."

Corey changed in the bathroom while Brian stared at the wall, imagining Violin sulking on the other side. It gnawed at him. The world stopped making sense a long time ago, but he always fought for control over his life. Seeing his friend in pain and knowing nothing could fix it felt like someone spading out his guts.

After Corey finished getting ready, they packed some weapons and knocked on Violin's door. They overheard her crying while they waited for her, but chose not to bring it up, letting her keep her emotions as private as she liked.

They followed the small stream across the road from the

motel, searching for tracks as they had done every day since Winter died. Violin assured Brian and Corey that Winter taught his children to find the nearest source of water and follow it if they ever got lost. Candlestick, above all else, obeyed.

Brian doubted Candlestick listened. The area surrounding the stream showed zero signs of tracks. He'd brought this up once, but Violin insisted they follow the river. Corey suggested they split up, but Violin's eyes grew wide and she pled with shaky breath for that not to happen. She didn't mind going off into the woods alone, but didn't want Brian and Corey to, probably worried they wouldn't return.

"Look," Violin said, pointing.

"Holy shit." Brian ran to the patch of blackened sticks where a fire had once burned. Less than a day old, Brian guessed. Especially since he was certain they'd been here just yesterday.

They examined the spots, searching for tracks to follow.

Brian sighed. "There's nothing. No tracks. The only explanation I can come up with is that she is purposefully disguising them."

"Why would she do that?" Violin asked.

Corey looked up at the sun, squinting at its power. "She wouldn't. It makes no sense."

Violin's eyes watered. "Maybe she doesn't want to be found."

"Of course she does. She loves you." Brian pulled on the strap of his rifle, still examining the dirt for something they missed.

"She was scared and confused and angry. I know how she's thinking because I've been her. She's still young and makes rash decisions. I know she will regret it because yes, she loves me, but right now, she probably wants to shun every living thing."

"She's too young to be out on her own, even if she was raised by survivalists." Brian kicked some loose gravel into the stream.

"Yes, which is why we must find her."

"We still have plenty of daylight. Let's keep moving," Corey said.

Violin shook her head. "No. Let's go back to the motel and gather some food. This could be a long journey."

She headed back, not giving them a second glance or a chance to discuss it. Brian chased after her. "Wait. Let's think this through. If we turn back, we're just giving her more time to get ahead of us. She's been gone for days. We need to get to her quickly. Let's just keep following the stream."

Violin shook her head, still not turning back to them. "We don't need to follow the stream. I know where she went."

"Where?"

"Home. We are going home."

Cassius

Candlestick threw up, her stomach unable to handle the rapid change in diet. Despite the new warmth and nourishments, she struggled to adjust. Her head throbbed; her muscles ached. Tiredness weighed on her as if Kevin Bacon's hand pressed into her chest. She slept for hours, woke and nibbled on food, slept some more.

Lion cuddled with her, the husks worked to keep the fire going, the lampposts brought her meals. She ate what she could, but still, her body refused to recover. Every minute of sleep or sitting stationary by the fire felt like a wasted moment toward finding her family. She worried a new threat would push them out of the motel and they'd be lost forever, or worse, maybe they'd just give up waiting for her.

She coughed up mucus, red-stained from the food. Her stomach had little to offer her gagging, just bile and forest fruits. She'd given up on trying to eat the horned animal meat because each time she did, it came right back up. Her people were not made to eat meat.

After getting the gagging fit out, she lay in the dirt, face pressed against its rough surface. A husk stood at the other side of the fire, staring at her.

"What are you looking at?' she asked.

It crept around the fire, its leathery skin bending in the waves of heat. "I hug you?"

She wiped puke from her chin. "No. I don't want hugs. I want my family."

The husk bent down, tilting its head and squinting. "I not family?"

The breath pouring from her nose kicked up some loose dirt. "I don't mean to insult you. I meant my sister and father."

The husk put its hand on her hair. "Viiiiiiiolin?"

"Yes. Violin."

The husk nodded. "Husk understand."

It stood and moved toward a pile of the red things she'd been eating and put them in its cupped hand. When it brought them to her, she turned her head away.

"No. whenever I eat, I get sick."

"Candlestick must eat. Stomach will settle." It touched her belly. "Needs practice."

The husk smiled and seeing its creepy face attempt to make a warm gesture made her giggle. The husk responded with its own laugh, and the two chuckled for different reasons, but at the same time, in a unified way that expressed friendship. Sometimes, simultaneous happiness is all people need to feel connected. It doesn't matter the cause.

Candlestick wasn't happy. She was miserable, but she accepted the fleeting seconds where she forgot about the pain she felt in her body and brain.

She sat up and ate the red things, nibbling off the flesh before gnawing at the juicy insides. They made her hands and face sticky and her stomach turn, but the taste going down was out of this world. After she finished the handful, she pat Lion, who slept well, his belly full and steady.

Candlestick understood the husks and lampposts were doing all they could to protect her, and would do anything she told them, but the idea of asking them for help made her uneasy. They were too willing to do whatever she asked and something about that made her feel abusive for taking advantage, but she needed them.

Without her father and sister to guide her, she wasn't prepared for the world. What food was edible and what was poison? What would she do if people attacked? She'd trained with her community on how to fight and defend herself, but she was still a child and could do little against grown humans.

Her sister! How could she have not considered it sooner?

"Come here."

The husk walked to her, dragging its feet like a scared child.

"What is your name?"

The husk smiled, and its eyes twinkled, surprised by the kindness. Candlestick had realized she'd been looking at the husks like animals in the woods, one horned beast was just like the others. But the husks were individuals, each with their own personality, and therefore, she needed to treat them as they deserved.

"My naaaaaame Caaaasssssiiiuuuusss."

When the husks whispered, they dragged their words. She found it grating. "Please don't be shy around me. Speak up."

She remembered her uncle telling her the same thing during her training. *Speak up and stand tall, even when you're afraid. Especially when you're afraid.*

The husk scrunched his elongated face. "My name Cassius."

"Cassius. What a lovely name. I've heard it before somewhere." She beamed, hoping she didn't lay it on too thick.

"Thankful," he nodded.

"Cassius, I need a favor. Will you find my sister for me? Will you guide her back to me?"

Cassius's face went through a range of emotions, from worried to confused to something she couldn't quite place, but she felt belonged somewhere between honored and deceitful.

"Cassius do what Candlestick ask. Always."

She put her hand on his, and he used his other to rub her arm. "Cassius thankful."

She nodded. "Candlestick thankful, too."

He stood and walked away. As she watched him disappear into the forest, she wished she could follow him, but lacked the strength. After he was out of sight, she threw up again, wondering if she'd die from lack of nutrition.

Changing Faces

Candlestick say. Casssssiuussssss Do.

Cassius obey.

Casssiussssss find sister. Do as told. Then Casssssiussssss disobey.

On way, he scuff tracks. Sister no find Candlestick.

Cassssssiuusssss hide tracks.

Go to motel.

As told.

Cassius see sisssssster at motel. See something else. Man in woods. Watching Vioooolin.

Strange man. Man in woods wear mask. Fake face. Look like Candlestick father. Not him. Fake face.

Cassssiussss lose focus. Violin leave with friends. Finds firepit! Cassssiussss stupid! Make footprints disappear. No make firepit disappear. Cassssiuss fail. Cassius no want Violin find Candlestick.

Violin go back to motel. Cassius follow. Man with fake face follow. Cassius no like fake face man. Fake face man evil.

Violin and friends go inside motel. Cassius goes behind. Finds gasoline. Pours gasoline on door. Violin no find Candlestick now.

Cassius turns to fake face man. Snarls. Cassius hate fake face man. He watch. Cassius whisper, "leeeeeeaaaaaavvvvveeeee."

Fake face man no listen. Watches.

Cassius must do plan. Cassius light match. Drop match. Make flames. Flames grow. Fake face man smile. Cassius no like smile. Give Cassius shiver.

Fire get big. Sissssster scream. Friends sssssscream. Cassius protect Candlestick. Violin die now.

Cassius leave. One last look at fake face man. Fake face man watch Cassius. Grin. Scary, bad man. Look like Candlestick dad. Not good man. Bad man. Evil man.

Protected

Human voices came from the forest. Candlestick shot up, dizzy and tired. She spoke with her mind, telling her monsters to vanish. She'd bring them back to kill the humans if needed, but she thought it best to see how it played out first. Part of her wanted it to go awry, to release some pent-up rage on some bad people, but she also missed having someone to talk to that spoke in full sentences.

Two people, a man and a woman, came through the clearing. They were older, like Candlestick's grandma, but less sharp than the woman who helped raise her. They wore nice clothes, unmarred by a life of survival. As soon as they hit the clearing, an aroma of random flowers and chemicals hit Candlestick's nose.

The couple jolted back at the sight of Candlestick, then chuckled.

"Hello, dear," the woman said.

Lion lunged forward, but Candlestick spoke to him through her thoughts. He spread his front feet forward and rested his head in the dirt. He stuck his butt in the air, as if still ready to pounce, but accepted Candlestick's orders. The couple flinched at first but settled when the dog did.

"Hello," Candlestick said, less authoritative than she desired. Her uncle always told her to speak loudly and confidently, to make people worry about her strength before they even knew her.

"Are you out here alone?"

She looked around, not liking the question. How should she proceed? Should she convince them she was with a group, scare them off? What were they up to? What tricks were up their sleeves? Her father told her humans always had a plan, always ready to hurt.

"I am alone." There was no point in pretending she had a group of humans with her, but she had lied, hadn't she? She wasn't alone. She had an army of monsters by her side, hiding in the atmosphere.

"Oh, you poor girl. How did you end up out here? Do you want to come with us to our house? We have food and can warm you up."

She looked around again, a reaction to a lifetime of having others to answer for her. All she found was space. She'd need to answer for herself now, a welcomed change.

For a moment, she worried about leaving her spot. Cassius would return with Violin and Candlestick wouldn't be there. But she quickly remembered she could order Cassius to find her through her mind, and he'd have to obey. She worried for her health. If these people could provide any kind of food outside of red spheres, she needed to go.

"Yes," she said. "Can my dog come?"

The woman shrugged and glanced at the man, who offered no objection, and Candlestick followed the couple through the woods, away from the river. They asked her questions about how she ended up there, but she eluded them by pretending to be confused.

"I'm not sure."

"I don't remember."

If the humans believed she, too, was human, they may not want to harm her. She would welcome food and shelter until she regained her strength. The husks and lampposts provided, but they could only offer subpar provisions. She yearned for a good night's rest.

They reached a clearing where a small house stood. The brown wood was stained with green patches.

"I like the green color on it."

"Oh, that's just overgrown moss and lichen. Stains the wood," the man said. "It was done intentionally. Makes it look authentically rustic."

The man helped Candlestick tie Lion to a tree, which she almost argued against, but decided not to fight the humans just yet. They entered the house and Candlestick's jaw dropped. It was beautiful, and much larger than it appeared from the outside. A big stone structure in the middle of the room housed a ripping fire that spread its warmth throughout. The smell of cooking food wafted into her nose; unfamiliar food. From scent alone, she knew she would love its taste.

"It smells so good in here." She looked around, taking it all in, the cleanliness and the wide-open space. The dead animal heads on the wall.

"That's my roast, got it slow cooking. Should be just about done. I gotta tell you, when Dale and I saw you out there, I damn near had a heart attack. You poor thing."

She said that many times, "poor thing." Candlestick didn't understand it. She wasn't a thing and they did not know what she'd been through enough to feel sorry for her. What was wrong with a girl in the woods?

They sat by the fire and ate roast. Candlestick tried to learn to use silverware the way the humans did. She'd picked up a little from Brian and Corey, but these new humans were more dainty, more refined. They used their thumbs more and held their upper arms in straight lines as they picked food from the plates.

She didn't trust these people but, for now, she played nice. Humans always meant to harm, but if she let them think her guard was down, they'd feel superior and she could get a few enjoyable meals out of them before having to defend herself.

"This is a nice place," she said.

Dale sucked a piece of meat into his mouth. "This little thing? It's okay. This was just something we bought to rent out online. We made it look rustic and homey. Spend time away from the hustle and bustle in your very own cabin in the woods. It made us a small fortune, too."

Candlestick nodded and picked at some soggy vegetables on her plate. She was starved but worried the food would send her vomiting again. "So, why are you here and not your house?"

Dale laughed. "We lived in the city! Dangerous, in other words. So, we fled here. Occasionally, I sneak out and get stuff from our house when we need it, but otherwise, we've just holed up in here. Thing about this place is it has a nice generator, runs on propane. We not only have tanks and tanks of it, but we are not too far from the local propane company. I can load some into my truck with nothing more than a fifteen-minute drive. Luckily, no one else has thought to do the same yet. Or, maybe they have, but haven't wanted to come all the way out here."

Candlestick smiled, not really understanding most of what he said.

After dinner, Candlestick snuck some roast outside and gave it to Lion. When she came back in, the woman was cleaning off their plates and putting them into a cubby under the counter.

"What's that, ma'am?"

The woman gave her a double take. "You can call me Barbara. What's what?"

"That thing you are closing?"

Barbara closed the door on the cubby, hit a few buttons, and it whirred to life. "This is a dishwasher. Have you never seen a dishwasher?"

"No. Does it actually wash dishes?"

Barbara laughed. "Where did you come from, a cave?"

Candlestick giggled with the woman, though she didn't understand the joke. In her short time with humans, she learned they let their guard down if she pretended they were funny.

Barbara dropped her head to one side. "You have bags under your eyes. Come with me."

She wiped her hands on a rag and led Candlestick to a small room with wood walls. Besides a dresser and a thin bed, the room was bare. It didn't even have a door.

"You can sleep in here. Why don't you rest up?"

Candlestick flopped onto the bed and stared at the ceiling in the dark. She created faces from the dark rings in the wood. Abe Lincoln, Ice Giant. Rapture the Raccoon. Dance and her crops.

She worried about her stomach, but so far, the food stayed down.

The couple made noises in different rooms, coughing, walking, clicking lights on and off. Eventually, the noises died down and the lights stayed off. Still, Candlestick remained awake. Her eyes begged to shut. Her body joined the pleading. Her mind, however, fought for her to keep alert. No door. Strange humans.

The people were nice, though. Maybe they were good humans. Why would they waste their food on her if they meant her harm?

But...

How foolish of her to trust them. Why was she trying to

make sense of it? She didn't need to understand their ways. They'd deceive her in the end. They always do.

Her eyes burned, water building in them. She tossed a little, hoping some physical comfort would defeat the mental unsettling.

Something scratched at the window. In the blackness behind the glass, she made out a blurred shape. A husk. Her heart jumped, hoping it was Cassius. It wasn't.

"Sleeeeeeppppp," it whispered.

"I can't," she said.

"Weeeeeee fix it."

"You will guard me?"

It nodded. "Leeeeetttttt usssssss iiiiinnnnn."

She closed her eyes, pressing her eyelids together tightly, straining every muscle, including her brain, if such a thing was possible. When she opened them, a group of husks stood in the room with her.

"Thank you. I'm going to sleep now. Stop the humans if they try anything," she said to them.

They nodded in unison.

She drifted off into a magical sleep, floating into a dream world with ease. When she woke, hours later, refreshed and invigorated, she stared at the ceiling for a while. For the first time in forever, Candlestick felt rested and comfortable. She no longer saw faces in the wood, but instead, saw a map of stars, one that led to home. She hoped Cassius would return to her soon with good news or her sister beside him. She spoke to him, letting him know where to find her. He didn't respond.

She sat up and stretched. After her senses returned, her brow furrowed. It was too quiet.

Where did they go?

She crept into the living room and leapt backward, stumbling into a wall, bumping her head on a frame surrounding an animal head. The living room's floor was streaked with red.

The Husks were sprawled across the floor, licking up guts and gore.

"What did you do?" She covered her mouth and bit back a scream.

One husk looked up, craning its neck as if confused by her question. He had rivulets of red from mouth to chin. "Weeeeee proteeeectedddddd."

A Few More Minutes of Precious Life

Smoke billowed into the room from under the door. The front wall creaked. Flames broke through the window. There was nowhere to go, walls all around them. The door and window, nothing more than bright orange flames.

Violin stepped back into the bathroom and lay on the floor. She almost prayed to Kevin Bacon, but what good would that do? To hell with him.

She cupped her hands over her head and pressed her face into the tiled floor. A cloud of smoke formed above her.

Something hissed in the other room, and Brian shouted, "Through there! Go! Violin, let's go!"

She looked up, seeing the two men hopping through the window, now devoid of flame. A white foam layered the window frame and the floor in front of it.

She crawled forward, hacking as the smoke penetrated her lungs.

Corey came to the window, tilting away from the flames on the door and wall. He reached his hand in. "Come on," he said to her.

But as she made her way around the bed, the flames bent toward the window, pushing Corey back.

"Violin!" he shouted.

Water filled her eyes from the smoke, and from the realization her father had spoken the truth before he passed. Brian and Corey were proof the humans were okay. They risked flame and death for her; they never faltered, never asked for anything in return.

Yet, hadn't she been exactly what she faulted humanity for? Hadn't she weighed their purpose in her life based on what they could do for her? Everything she criticized humans for, she was.

She crawled forward, bursts of heat forcing her back. She prepared for death, had faced it many times, but death by fire terrified her. Panic set in. Her breath turned to rapid hyperventilation, which only increased the burning in her throat as smoke came into her lungs.

The fire spread, covering the front of the room, giving her no chance to escape. As the raging mass burned through the front wall and crept toward her, Violin slid back into the bathroom, cornering herself, but giving herself a few more minutes of precious life.

Wood cracked and snapped. A piece of roof collapsed into the living room. Brian and Corey screamed to her from outside but she could no longer understand their words over the harsh, volatile sounds of burning.

She grabbed a towel and shoved it into the crack under the door, trying to prevent the smoke from coming in, but it wormed its way through the side and top of the door, a losing battle.

~~She~~ breathe and coughed up black goop onto the white floor. She realized she would probably die from suffocating on smoke before the flames burned her flesh. She wasn't sure which was more horrifying.

Something latched onto her foot, gripping it tight, and she

screamed. She turned her head to see what it was, but the smoke blocked her vision. Before she could lift her head enough, the mysterious grip pulled her backwards, away from the fire. She thought Brian or Corey had found their way through, but then she moved through a wall, a fully intact wall, as if she were a ghost.

She found herself in the kitchen. The fire hadn't reached the kitchen yet, so her lungs took in a nice, clean gasp of air, but the thing pulling her didn't stop and, again, she went through a wall.

Violin's body scraped against cement as she landed outside in the bright, sunny afternoon behind the motel. She curled into a ball and coughed up black phlegm. After hacking until her face turned red, she turned to see her savior, only to find the shadow of a man in a pink shirt trudging toward the river. Before he vanished, he turned to her, a quick glance. Her muddled mind saw only her father's face, but the truth of the man's identity snuck through when she caught a scar dripping down the left side of his face.

She tried to yell for him to wait, but all she could muster was another coughing fit.

The flames rose above the motel. She'd long given up on the place, but seeing it burn to the ground reminded her how close they'd come to something special. She thought about her father and the peace that entered his eyes when the generator turned on and he saw his daughters smiling and laughing, and Candlestick and Lion walking the perimeter with joy on their faces.

All of it smoldered and crumbled like wood on a stove. Her community, dead in a few days. Her first home on earth, taken within minutes. Their shelter on the road, destroyed by monsters with a few powerful slashes. Now the motel, another piece of her life, wiped away with one wave of the hand by an unknown and uncaring god.

She coughed, her lungs still raw and hot.

Corey and Brian turned the corner. "Violin! How did you get out?"

They ran to her and hugged her, crying with relief.

She stared at the motel, watching the fire eat it, death hungry for her, chasing her, killing everyone within reach to get its meaty paw on her soul.

Brian gripped her upper arm. "Come on. We should move away from the building. Corey already brought the car onto the road."

She nodded, unable to look away. Another coughing fit came over her. More black phlegm dripped from her mouth.

"Jesus. Let's get you far away from here."

He helped her walk because she kept getting dizzy spells and more hacking fits. When they reached the Subaru Outback they'd been using, Brian and Corey eagerly hopped in, but Violin leaned against it and turned back to the motel, watching it burn.

"Come on," Corey said. "Let's get out of here."

"No. I need to see this." She stared at the flames until her eyes blurred and saw only a singular orange entity eating away her memories, her hopes, her belief they could start a family there, a new community under her name. She saw Jane and Sheila, Frank and Winter, their bodies engulfed in the bright force devouring each room.

After the front side of the building was gone, she turned toward the woods out front where her father's body slept forever, and said, "Goodbye, Dad. Thanks for trying."

She hopped in the backseat. As the car sputtered off, she saw a figure break through the forest edge into the parking lot. As quickly as it came, it was gone again. Was it the man who saved her? Had she really traveled through walls?

She shook off the thought. Fire had surrounded her. She had

breathed in deadly smoke as she approached death. Surely she imagined it in her traumatic state, right?

A Friend?

Candlestick scrubbed the gore from the rug, holding back tears. "Could you try to be neater next time?" she shouted.

Next time. Why would she say that? These humans had done nothing wrong. The husks killed them for no reason. Even the monsters she created feared humans so deeply they couldn't comprehend them as anything but a threat.

Maybe they were right? She'd doubted her family, her community, her entire childhood, because her sister planted stupid hope in her brain. Look what it got them? Abandonment, death, nothing but pain.

Lion licked her face and she giggled. At least she could let her dog into the house now that the humans were dead. What kind of stupid rule was it that an animal had to stay outside? Awful humans concerned more for furniture than companionship. Maybe the husks were right to kill them, but she couldn't stop herself from crying at the sight of their shredded bodies.

"Husks. Here now," she called.

A few husks entered the room. "Take these bodies and bury them out back."

The husks listened.

Candlestick dropped her rag, sighing. "I don't want to do this anymore."

She sat up straight and rubbed Lion's fur, staring at the remaining chunks of innards and blood still staining the rug.

"When you're done with the bodies, clean up this mess," she yelled.

As she played with Lion, the dog danced in circles, happy for the attention. "Brian and Corey taught me a few things about food. Maybe I should learn to use the kitchen. These people left us enough so we can stay here for a bit if I learn to make it. Hopefully Cassius will be back soon with news on my sister. Maybe she can come here with Corey and Brian and I can take care of them for once."

She went to the kitchen sink and washed her hands, a pink stream swirling down the drain. She checked the fridge. She'd learned about fridges and their usefulness from Brian and Corey. She was back to thinking maybe humans weren't so bad. This, of course, reminded her of the pieces of dead ones in the other room. She cried again.

The fridge had a lot of stuff in it; Candlestick recognized almost none of it. She grabbed a package of yellow strips and ripped it open, smelling the thin yellow squares. She waved it in front of her face, and it flopped and flailed like a flag in the wind. "What are you?"

She read the package, trying to sound out the word, but she hardly knew how to read. She ignored the larger word "Ameri-can," knowing it would take too long to sound out. "C. H. Chaaa. Chaaaa. Two E's. Eeeee. S. E. Sssss. Cha. Eeeeee. Ssssssss. Cheese."

She remembered the word, again from Corey, when he went

on a tangent, lamenting about all the wonderful products made by cows. *Cows.* THAT was a funny word. She would love to see a cow. They must look silly.

She giggled and took a little bite, trying to decide if she liked or hated it. Lion tiptoed into the kitchen, his paws making a scritch-scratch as they moved across the brown-tiled floor.

"Would you like to try some cheeeeeeese?" She ripped a piece off and tossed it to him.

Lion gulped it down in a single bite and lifted his head, whimpering for more. She tore the package open and tossed him slice after slice, feeding herself a few as well. She decided she hated the taste, but also wanted to keep eating it. It was both gross and addicting.

The top shelf of the fridge housed several bottles, but only one caught Candlestick's attention. An orange bottle with pictures of fire and weird plants on the front. She read the letters but didn't bother trying to sound them out: BIG BINGO'S FLAMING HOT JALAPENO SAUCE.

She opened the bottle and tipped it, letting the liquid hit her palm. Only a single drop fell from the top, so she rocked it until a small puddle of orange built along the creases of her hand. She licked it. It tasted nice for a second before it turned her mouth to fire. She spit gagged.

Lion whimpered as she keeled over, coughing out the fiery taste.

She ran to the sink and leapt up, putting her mouth to the running water, filling it, but the water did little to ease the pain in her mouth and lungs.

She kept gulping the water, praying for relief as sweat built on her forehead. Her lungs heaved for air.

She coughed and coughed, pressure building in her skull. Finally, the heat dissipated. She drank some more water, breathed the air. Lion stared with curious eyes. She patted him.

"That was delicious," she said. "I will try that again some time."

As she scoured the fridge for more things to try, Cassius walked in. It took her a second to recognize him. Once she did, she tried to convince herself it wasn't him because he was alone and Candlestick didn't want to handle that.

"What did you find?" she asked.

He shook his head.

"You didn't find the motel?"

"Cassius find motel. Cassius no find sister."

"They weren't there?"

The husk shook his head again.

"They left without me?" Tears formed in her eyes. "They wouldn't do that."

"Violin no wait for you. Violin think of Violin."

Something knocked on the front door. Candlestick jumped in surprise. Lion barked.

"Is that a dog? Dale, did you finally let Barbara get a dog?" A woman asked from outside the door.

Lion barked louder. Candlestick's eyes widened. "Shit. People are here for Dale and Barbara. What do we do?" she asked Cassius, who smiled at her.

"Kill," he said.

The humans knocked again. "Barbara, come on, let us in. Did you leave the spare key in the back?"

The figures walked by the windows in front, coming around to the side door, which the other husks had left open.

"Shit. What do we do?"

Before she could plan, the figures landed on the threshold of the side door: an older man and woman, around Barbara and Dale's age, and a young girl, Candlestick's age. They stared at Candlestick. Lion growled. Luckily, Cassius had disappeared.

Candlestick hadn't finished cleaning the blood and guts from the rug, and these folks could see it from their viewpoint. They stared with wide eyes, surprise knocking their jaws to the floor. The little girl smiled and waved.

"Mama, look. Uncle Dale and Barbara have a friend for me."

Candlestick smiled. *A friend?*

The Importance of Kite and Key

Violin sat in the back with the window down, allowing the fresh air to blast into her face as Brian drove down the highway. She packed the music player she'd gotten from the woman at the supermarket, but left all her bags in the trunk, so she enjoyed the whipping of wind instead. Her hacking fits occurred less frequently, but she struggled to take deep breaths and her lungs still itched.

"Why are the roads so clear?" Brian asked.

Violin ignored the question. She thought there were open stretches of road during her family's trek, but she had to admit, it appeared more open than she remembered.

They sped along, not a car in sight. They reached the Tanner's Switch Supermarket truck, where her family holed up before the lampposts destroyed it. The truck stood alone, a mangled mess of metal on the side of the road. No other cars were around.

"Stop," Violin said.

Brian slammed on the brakes and skidded to a stop.

She stepped out of the vehicle, looking both ways down the road.

Brian and Corey exited the car and stood beside her. "What's up?" Corey asked.

Violin pointed to the pieces of truck. "My family stayed in this truck. The lampposts attacked us in it."

Brian stepped closer to the pile of metal. "Jesus. You guys really went through a lot."

"It doesn't make sense," she furrowed her brow and stepped this way and that.

"What doesn't?"

"The truck was surrounded by cars. They were all over. This entire section of road was car after car, and when we walked down the road, there were dozens more all over the place."

Brian gripped the gun tucked into his pants. "Are you sure this is the same place?"

She tilted her head. "I'm positive."

Corey followed as she walked around, searching for something that could provide answers. "So, someone took all the cars?"

She shook her head. "No way. Most of the cars had crashed into one another. It's impossible that all of them would work enough to take away. Some of them were in pieces, destroyed. Even if someone could have gotten them out of here, why would they take all the little broken pieces?"

Brian sighed. "Just another fucking thing about this world that makes little sense. Let's get out of here before we find out what did it."

"Wait. What is that noise?" Violin asked.

Corey and Brian stopped to listen, then turned to each other with frowns. "I don't hear anything," Corey said.

Violin lifted her chin. "You don't hear that? It's like a faint roaring. Not like an animal; something else."

Brian scrunched his face and pushed his head forward. "Do you mean the beach?"

"The what?"

"The ocean?"

"The what?"

Corey put his arm around Brian, "I think we need to show her."

Brian shook his head. "Sometimes I think about all the things you missed underground, and there's so much I forget about. You've never seen the ocean. You have to see the ocean."

"We don't have time for field trips. I know my sister moved away from the river to get home. We should get there as quickly as possible."

"It'll take no time at all, and we're driving to your home. Candlestick will be walking. We're going to get there way before she does." Brian gave her a grin that reminded her of Candlestick when she was excited about something. The last time she saw it was when Candlestick met Lion.

They hopped back in the car and turned off the highway onto a bumpy, dirt road.

"This wasn't my favorite beach. It got too crowded and the people were loud, but I don't think we'll have to worry about that now," Brian said.

"Brian and I came here for the fireworks on the fourth one year. It was the worst crowd of weirdos I've ever been around."

Violin eyed them back and forth as their conversation ricocheted off each other from the front seats. She chuckled, which turned into a cough, causing Corey to turn to her.

"Are you all right?"

She shook her head. "Yes, very much all right. I need to laugh, even if it hurts."

"What's so funny?"

"You two being excited about a memory and forgetting I don't know what the hell you're talking about."

They joined her in laughter. Brian said, "Fuck, Corey she's never seen a firework."

They pulled into a parking lot and exited the car. Brian led them down a dirt road and around some bushes. When they reached the other side of the plants, a series of wooden houses came into view. They were propped up by gangly wooden legs.

The sound Violin heard from the highway was louder now, giant roars. Each time it came, she flinched a little, but knew not to worry too much. Corey and Brian wouldn't drive into danger. "So, what is it? What's the noise?"

Brian pointed toward a hill of sand. "It's right over those dunes."

As they reached the top of the dunes, Violin lost her breath. For a brief moment, she thought she was seeing sky collapsing into earth, but quickly realized she was looking at a large body of water. It was humongous, beautiful, and terrifying. It came up in waves and crashed into the sand, leaving behind a frothy necklace.

"Is it safe?" she asked.

"Do you know how to swim?"

She shook her head.

"Then, no. But you can go closer. It won't go much higher up the beach than it is right now. See where the sand gets darker? That's about as far up as it'll come."

A new wave crashed into the shore, and despite her preparing for it, she flinched again. "Where does it lead?"

"What?"

"This water. Where does it go?"

Her friends chuckled, and Corey pointed out toward the horizon. "Well, if you look closely, you can see Block Island out there.

It's just a small island where rich people lived. I had a friend who owned an art studio there, Milicent. She was sweet."

Brian stepped in. "But this is the Atlantic, so it leads to a lot of places. As big as it looks from here, it's much, much bigger."

Her eyes filled with water. "It's humbling. We have this much water to drink?"

"No, you can't drink it. It's not that kind of water."

"There's more than one kind?"

He nodded. "Indeed."

"I'll bet we could make one hell of a hydro-generator for it though."

Corey shrugged. "You'd know that better than we would."

She lifted fistfuls of sand and let it drain through her fingers. "Tell me stuff about Earth. I want to know more."

Corey and Brian sat on each side of her. "What do you want to know?" Corey asked.

"The trivial stuff."

Brian lifted a small, flat stone from the sand and tossed it into the water. It landed with a plop. "Trivial, huh? There was a guy named Elvis who became a music phenomenon. He had these killer dance moves and sang with a unique voice. When I was growing up, my mom would listen to him all the time and I'd dance around the house imitating him."

Violin smiled and put her hand on his.

Corey wrapped his hands around his knees. "I was never a big Elvis fan. But I'll tell you, a new voice came into the music world decades after Elvis, and she was even better. Her name was Lady Gaga."

Brian rolled his eyes. "Don't listen to him."

"She was brilliant in every way."

"No, she was a perfectly fine pop star. Nothing more."

"She was a god, Violin. Just like your dad would say about Kevin Bacon. She was a god."

Violin put her hands up. "Okay. I love all this, but isn't there more than music?"

Brian rolled his eyes to the sky, thinking about it. "Well, there was Ben Franklin. Your dad probably knew about him if he was so interested in electricity. Franklin discovered how to use it."

"Didn't he steal it from Tesla, though?" Corey asked.

Brian cracked up. "No, that was Edison. Franklin was the one with the kite and the key."

"Kite and key?" Violin asked.

"Long story. Just know Franklin invented electricity in the ways we understand it today."

Corey shook his head. "I know you're more of the history fan than I am, but I'm pretty sure he didn't invent electricity as we know it today. I'm certain it was being used way before him, but I think his whole thing was understanding that lightning was electricity, and through that, he developed some ways to make it safer. Or something."

Brian shrugged. "I don't know. That's probably true."

Violin stared at a newly crashing wave. It's thunderous sound no longer startled her. In fact, it did the opposite, soothing her, easing her mind. "Keep talking."

The two men thought for a few seconds.

Corey's back straightened. "Oh, I know something else Brian and I disagree on."

"What?" she asked.

"Gage Greenwood."

Brian rolled his eyes. "Oh, here we go."

"Who is that?" Violin asked.

Corey dusted sand off his feet. "He was a horror writer. Brian and I both like spooky stories."

"What's a horror writer?" Violin asked.

"Horror is a style of writing. It's usually dark, sometimes

scary, and tackles topics like death, monsters, danger. Anyway, Gage Greenwood wrote books like that."

"And he sucked," Brian added.

Everyone giggled.

"He didn't suck, and Brian doesn't believe that either. Brian liked his stories; he just didn't like the guy writing them."

"Why?" Violin asked.

"Because he was an egotistical douche. He inserted himself into his stories. He called his readers 'Gagents of Chaos.' He even had little drawings of himself added to the front matter of all his books. Douche."

"But he wrote fun stories."

Brian stuck his tongue out. "His stories were fine."

"Well, I liked him."

Violin let them argue for a while longer as her mind drifted with the sea. Her eyes blurred and the ocean turned to a spinning blue cylinder. Corey snapped her out of it by tapping her shoulder.

"Should we get going?" he asked.

Violin just stared. "Not yet."

"Don't you want to find your sister?" Brian jumped in.

She shook her head. "Do you ever get a sense that everything is about to get really awful?"

Brian glanced around, as if her words would conjure terror into existence. "Yeah."

"I have that feeling right now. But, for this very second, I am calm. I'd like to soak it in for a few more minutes."

Different World, Different Times

Candlestick played small, weak. "I haven't seen your friends. I was lost in the woods with my dog, and we found this place. There's blood on the rug. I was scared, but more afraid out there than in here."

The woman put her hands over her face, and the man put his arms around his daughter, pulling her backwards and into him.

"Oh no. Barbara," the woman said.

"We should get out of here," the man said.

Candlestick widened her eyes, not wanting them to leave for a reason she couldn't explain to herself. "I lost my family. I have been staying here. I'm scared, but it seems safe."

She hadn't had time to register what Cassius told her, but the sting set in her heart. Had her family really abandoned her? They wouldn't. Maybe they were out searching for her. Maybe Cassius showed up when they were out looking for Candlestick. But something told her that was wrong, that her father had died and Violin left without Candlestick. Winter, the only thing anchoring them together, was gone. She wanted to cry, but for now, she had to play a part.

She put her hand on Lion's head and relaxed him with her mind, getting him to sit.

"Chase, we can't leave this little girl."

"We can." He looked at Candlestick. "I'm sorry, but we can't take care of anyone else."

"Do you want to come in? There's cheeeeese in the fridge."

Chase pushed his daughter away from the door, out of view. "Come on. Let's go. We have to go. I wish you luck."

"Honey, no. We can't just leave a child alone. What kind of monsters is this world turning us into?" She followed him away from the door.

Candlestick bent down and hugged Lion. "Just give them a second. They'll be back."

And just like that, a few minutes later, the family returned, stepping into the kitchen. The mother stared with big sorry eyes, while the father huffed. The daughter smiled at Candlestick and waved.

"Listen, you can stay with us for a bit, but we aren't staying here. If someone killed our friends, we don't want to be here. We also can't travel all over helping you find your family, but, like I said, you can join us," Chase said with no kindness in his voice.

Candlestick nodded. "And Lion, too?" She patted the dog again.

Chase rolled his eyes. "He sleeps outside, and you have to control him in the car."

She nodded again.

"Do you need to pack?"

"I own nothing."

The mother whimpered. "Don't worry, Cassie has plenty of clothes, and it looks like you two are about the same size."

They walked for at least ten minutes to the car, which was parked on a small patch of dirt on a road at the edge of the woods. Chase grumbled the whole way. "Told them they should have paved a driveway. Walking all that way is ludicrous. Authentic, Dale said. Pain in the ass, more like it."

There were two cars in the dirt patch, one presumably belonging to Dale and Barbara. They hopped in the big black one with the dark windows. The letters P-A-C-I-F-I-C-A were written on the back. It smelled like leather and over-cleaning.

The car they left behind was a sleek bright red thing with a top that looked like it folded in. Somehow, it made her miss Barbara and Dale, even though she'd only known them for a few hours. She shook the thought off. No more mourning. No more caring. If these humans weren't looking, she would have slapped herself in the face.

As they drove, Cassie stared at Candlestick. After a few minutes on the road, she braved up and talked. "I'm Cassie. What's your name?"

Candlestick smiled. "I'm Candlestick. This is my dog, Lion."

Chase scoffed. "Candlestick? People will name their kids anything these days."

Candlestick didn't enjoy the man mocking her family, and wished to rip his throat out, but since he controlled the fast-moving vehicle, she decided against it.

She turned back, seeing the road move away from her, and she regretted the decision to leave with them. What if her instincts were wrong and Violin *was* looking for her? She just made the search all the more impossible. She also believed her sister knew her better than anyone else, and for that, she would head home. Candlestick thought about home a lot since she lost herself in the woods. When a bullet hit her father, she wished for magic to heal all wounds, and maybe home was the place for it. It would be too late to save her father, of course, but she could repair the growing chasm between her and her sister. The perfect place for a reunion.

"I think it's a lovely name," the mother said with a plastered smile.

"What games do you like to play?" Cassie asked.

Candlestick shrugged. "I don't really play games. I used to play hide and seek with my sister a lot."

Cassie put her hand out and let Lion sniff it. She giggled as his snout tickled her palm.

"Cassie don't touch that dog. He looks like he hasn't had a bath in weeks," the mother said.

She pulled her hand away with sad eyes.

They drove in silence the rest of the way, the car traversing beyond rolling hills, the scenery growing more beautiful and deeper green the further they drove.

They turned onto a smooth, paved lane and drove until they reached a gate. Chase turned the vehicle off and sighed. "Used to hit a button from the seat and the gate would open. Different world, different times."

He pulled the gate open. Beyond it, so much open land leading to a house bigger than any they've stayed in combined, including the motel. It had more than enough space to fit Candlestick's entire community ten times over. Her mouth dropped. Was this where they were going?

Chase drove the car to the front door and parked it next to three other cars.

"How many people live here?"

The mother turned to her. "Just us, dear."

"Whose cars are those?"

The mother cackled. She sounded like a dying bird singing its last song. "They are all ours, dear."

Candlestick did not like this woman calling her dear, but as always, she kept quiet. The yard had a small fenced in square of land where the mother directed Candlestick to put Lion. She obliged.

When they entered the house, a twisting staircase welcomed them into a room made of wood and stone, so shiny and breathtaking. She nearly wept at the sight. She wanted to run through the place, exploring every inch, playing, jumping on beds, and clicking on lights, but she steadied herself, allowing only her eyes to wander.

The mother went right for the kitchen. "I'll start making dinner. I am sure everyone could use a bite." When she said, "Everyone," she glanced right at Candlestick.

Chase put his hand on Candlestick's head, an unwelcomed touch. "First, you must take a shower. No offense." He wiped his hands on a white piece of cloth he had tucked in his shirt pocket.

Why would that offend her?

"Cassie, show her to the bathroom and help her pick out an outfit of yours."

Cassie walked her to the bathroom, keeping her head down. Candlestick got the sense that Cassie wanted to talk to her, but worried about upsetting her parents. Candlestick noticed bruises on the girl's arms and legs and guessed what they were from.

"Are you training?"

The girl turned to her. "Training for what?"

"To fight."

Cassie puckered her cheeks. "No. Why?"

And then Candlestick really understood the bruises. One time, Candlestick joked to her grandmother that she wished her family were human. Her grandmother's face turned sour, and she said, "Oh, do you? Humans hurt their children to get out their frustrations. Is that what you want?"

Cassie left her alone.

Candlestick stood in the bathroom, staring at the shower. She knew how to use the one at the motel, learned about the handle you had to twist, but this one didn't have the same handle, and she worried she'd mess it up. She also didn't know if she should wait for Cassie to bring her clothes. So, she stood there, checking out all the cool things the bathroom offered. So many buttons and dangling things that invited her to play. The counter was swirly colored stone, the floors a glassy tile as clear as water.

A moment later, Chase opened the door, startling Candlestick. She was glad she hadn't changed yet. She grew up in a community that freely walked around naked, but something about outsiders, especially humans, seeing her without clothes sent an icy shiver up her spine.

"I was wondering why I didn't hear the water. Hurry and shower. Marla is making dinner and we don't want to wait."

She turned away from him and stared at the overwhelming shower, two times the size of the one in the motel.

"Don't tell me you don't know how to use the shower? Were you raised by Neanderthals?"

Candlestick didn't understand the word he used, but understood it was meant to insult her family.

"No. I understand it," she said.

He huffed and closed the door. She played with the knobs until the shower blasted water. The force reminded her of the waterfall and raging river she and her family saw when they first escaped the underground.

As she tested the water, reaching her hand under the spray, she turned her head, not liking the way Chase left the door slightly ajar.

She still hadn't received an outfit from Cassie, though, and wasn't sure when the girl would bring her one. She didn't want to get in the shower until she could close and lock the door, and she couldn't do that until she had something else to change into.

In this moment of confusion, she realized for all the beauty and playfulness the house exuded, she would never be comfortable here. She wanted to love it, wanted to play with Cassie all day without a care in the world, the way she once did with

Violin. But Chase and his commentary and the mother's smug attitude, and being told what to do, it distorted what should be a welcoming and fun place. It darkened the open spaces, sharpened the corners.

No more waiting. She closed the door shut and twisted the lock, enjoying the finality of it as it thumped into place.

"Kill him," she whispered.

"Aaaalllllll of theeeeemmmmm?" A voice inside her head asked.

"No. Just the parents. Leave the little girl. And wait until they finish cooking dinner."

She took a big breath, hopped in the shower, and let the water wash over her until her skin wrinkled and the house filled with the screams of the dying.

I Dream the Truth

Corey put his arm around Violin's shoulder and they all walked back to the vehicle.

"So, where do we go now?" Brian asked.

Violin shrugged. "I don't know, but after we get back to the highway, we should go straight. Most of my family's traveling was through woods and it all looked the same to me."

"I would imagine if you were raised in closed quarters, understanding directions in the wilderness on Earth would be complex."

When they re-entered the highway, she stared off into the woods and saw a figure behind the tree line. She knew he was staring at her, despite the dark shadow over his face. It was intrinsic. The figure wore a pink shirt with writing on it. The same shirt the figure who saved her wore.

"There's someone in the woods," she said as Brian stepped on the gas.

"Shit, let's get out of here."

She reminded herself that the man walking in the woods by the motel couldn't have made it all this way in the same time they did. Then, she thought about the kids who attacked her family when they first landed on Earth. Those kids all wore matching outfits. Maybe this was the same thing, a new group of terrorists haunting her. But no, the man saved her, He didn't attack.

The feeling that awful things hovered behind her like a malevolent shadow told her these men in pink shirts were not guardians. They weren't protecting her. There was more to them. Yes, one of them saved her, but what was the cost? And how did the motel fire start? She had been so relieved at escaping, that she hadn't even considered the origins of the fire.

As Brian sped down the cleared road, a giant building caught Violin's attention. TANNER'S SWITCH SUPERMARKET.

"Stop!" she yelled, and Brian responded with a slam on the brakes.

"What is it?"

"When we were in the first house we stayed in, my father found a market at the end of our road." She pointed to the supermarket.

They all looked at it, then craned their heads across the road to a neighborhood cutting through the surrounding woods.

"That must be where we stayed. If we can find the house, I think I can get us back to where I grew up."

Brian turned down the road and Violin recognized the place where they stayed immediately. The path into the woods across the street cemented it. She remembered correctly. That was where the people had come from, the ones who attacked her family. She recognized the other houses her father brought them to when hiding out from the wilderness kids, too. It all flushed back into her brain and etched itself there, reminding her of the screaming, and running, and gun shots, and death, some of which she caused.

After they parked, they each took a gun and eyed the area, making sure no one was around. For all Violin knew, the rest of those wilderness kids could still be here. One thing she knew for sure, the red-haired one wasn't. She and her two friends tossed his body into the woods to rot.

They entered the house and split up to clear all the rooms. Violin contained the chuckles building in her gut at the memories of all the fumbling her family did over objects she now fully understood. They had marveled at toilets, televisions, and air conditioners. As funny as it was, she still hadn't seen a movie, only knew of their existence. Her only experience with moving pictures was the security cameras at the motel.

The house was empty, but the rooms and cupboards had been ransacked. She presumed the wilderness kids scoured the house looking for clues about Violin's family.

She sat on the couch, thinking.

Corey sat next to her. "Do you really think your sister would find her way all this distance to get back home?"

"She is strong, smart, and resilient. She will, I am sure of it."

Corey tapped her knee. "Okay. I always trust you."

She laughed. "That has proven to be a mistake over and over again."

He shrugged. "No, it hasn't, we're still here. You can't be blamed for horrible people. So much of what has happened was out of your control. There was no winning."

She frowned and drifted into a memory.

* * *

Violin sat in her grandmother's rocking chair. Her mother smiled at her, looking up from the sweater she sewed.

"What's troubling you, dear?"

"Grandma told me one day a sickness will come that Dad can't heal."

Her mother put her two needles down. "Why does that bother you?"

Violin screwed up her face. "What do you mean? I work so hard to learn how to protect us, but everything feels so out of my control."

Her mother kept her smile in place as she walked to her daughter and held Violin's hands. "What is my power?"

"You dream the truth." Violin huffed, unsure what the question had to do with anything.

"Yes. I am the one who warned our people of the sickness your father won't be able to heal because I dreamed it. While everyone else knows about it, I am the one who saw it, who watched it unfold. Do I look scared?" Her smile grew.

"No, but you're never scared."

"Exactly. And do you know why? Because I have seen other truths. Some people think I dream about the future, but that's not true. I dream the truth. That means I can see secrets from the past, what's in the mind of someone here in the present, and when I see the future, it's inevitable. It's not a potential outcome; it's a definite, unavoidable one."

"How is that not terrifying? Everyone is going to die someday."

Her mother cupped her hand on Violin's cheek. "I wish these truths I see showed me more, but it's usually just a scene, just a small piece, so I can't figure out all the variables. But I know one thing, something I am absolutely sure of. When this is all done, I saw something that made the rest of it okay."

"What?"

"I saw you and your sister on top of a hill. Outside here, on the Earth. You two will stand on top of a hill when it's all done."

Violin shook her head. "Impossible. We will never leave here."

Her mother nodded. "You will. Trust me. Have I ever been wrong? You will, and you will discover something very important, that you are in control of it all."

"Me? The only one down here without a power? Me? I have no control, and if I did, I would stop the disease from ever happening."

Her mother laughed. "Just you wait. You have more power than all of us combined."

* * *

Violin snapped out of it as Brian lifted a DVD box set of something called *The Muppets*.

"Hey, do you want to watch this for a second so you can see what a movie is?"

She shook her head.

"Are you sure? It's got Kermit the Frog. You're not going to believe this, but he's a talking frog."

She stood up straight. "There are talking frogs? My father told me a story about talking frogs once."

He dropped the DVD. "Not real ones. It's a puppet."

Corey picked the movies up and shook the box around. "Are you sure you don't want to see it?"

She stood up. "No. I would like to watch a movie with you sometime, but not those. Some things are better left to the imagination. Besides, we should keep moving. We are almost back. It's time to go home."

Get up and Stop Crying

Candlestick dried off and tucked a towel around herself. She stepped out of the bathroom into the cool hallway. Downstairs, Cassie cried and screamed, a mixture of unbridled fear and sadness from seeing her parents torn to shreds. Of all people, Candlestick understood mourning parents, but Candlestick's parents were decent humans. They didn't mock and humiliate little kids.

She knew the road ahead with Cassie would be difficult, especially once the girl learned Candlestick controlled the monsters, but it would be a worthwhile journey. She'd made a new friend and they'd have a lot of fun together, if the girl could move past her grief.

Easier said than done, she knew. She hadn't even processed her own grief. Thoughts of her mother made her stomach lurch and her eyes water. The mourning for her father hadn't taken shape yet because she held on to hope that magic saved him from a bullet. And still, she hoped for her sister's return, periodically gazing off into the woods in delusional anticipation that Violin would be there.

She refused to accept her sister left without her, at least not without good reason. Instead, she believed, deep within her heart, that Violin was out searching for her somewhere, probably heading back to their home. Candlestick would head there soon, too, once she had Cassie all worked out. She'd never had a friend before, and despite wanting to hug her sister again, the lure of friendship clung tighter.

To give her new friend more time to grieve, Candlestick stayed upstairs, searching the rooms. When she found Cassie's—which she knew belonged to the girl based on the small-sized bed and collection of dolls—she rummaged through the drawers until she found clothes to wear. A blue dress with pink flowers. Thick white socks.

She descended the stairwell, apprehensive to approach Cassie when she was in such an emotional state.

A husk stood at the bottom of the stairs. "Girl trrrrrryyyy to ruuuunnnnnnnn," it said.

Candlestick put her finger to her lip and walked past the husk. Blood soaked the kitchen. Pieces of Cassie's parents were splattered on the floor, the walls, and the counters. Cassie knelt by a chunk of someone. Candlestick couldn't tell if it was her mother or father. The girl's head rested against her knees, tears pouring from her eyes. She rocked back and forth and mumbled nonsense.

Candlestick came to her and rubbed her hand through Cassie's hair. Cassie lifted her head, her bloodshot eyes sharpening on Candlestick.

"There are things. My mom and dad. There are things," she hyperventilated.

Candlestick remembered being in a similar state when the men in the woods shot her father. But with her sister's guidance, she overcame it. Now, Candlestick needed to play the big sister to her new friend.

"It's okay," she said.

Cassie whined louder. "No, it's not. Mom! Dad! Get up!"

Candlestick huffed. She backed out of the room, figuring she could go play with Cassie's toys until the girl calmed down, but then she remembered her sister's words to Candlestick when their father was dying, how she motivated Candlestick to act.

"Get up."

Cassie sniffled, cried, and wholly ignored Candlestick.

"Get. Up!"

Cassie, startled, turned her head. Snot dripped from her nose, and her eyes were firepits of blazing red.

"Get up now."

Cassie turned her head left and right, as if searching for someone who would point a stern finger and say, "Don't talk to my daughter that way." Of course, the only people qualified to make such a statement were in gory pieces all over the kitchen.

Candlestick's hunger returned. She walked past Cassie to the kitchen table. She wiped some blood from a stool and sat in front of a plate full of food she didn't recognize. A meat, she believed, and a pasty off-white lump, some peas, and corn.

"When you're ready to sit with me, come eat." She took a fork full of veggies and stuffed them in her mouth.

Cassie continued to sob on the floor. Candlestick ate.

The volume of Cassie's cries sunk and rose, as if every time she settled, her mind reminded her of the horrors she had witnessed. Poor girl. At least Candlestick had to process monsters and loss at different times. She imagined if it happened all at once, she would have broken down for a long period of time. Still, after her entire community died, she held her tears in for days. Maybe if Cassie had a team of murderous teenage boys trying to kill her, she might snap out of it.

Cassie wailed again. Candlestick slammed her fork down on

her plate. She shifted the stool away from the table and pushed Cassie, causing the girl to topple over from her balled position.

"Get up now. Stop crying. Sit down."

"No."

"Now!" Candlestick's voice rose to an authoritative level that surprised even her.

The shock of her shout made Cassie flinch, and it also stopped the crying.

Candlestick pointed to the table. They stared at each other for a long time until finally the girl stood up and sat on the opposite side of the table from where Candlestick had sat.

"Eat."

"I'm not hungry."

Candlestick almost slammed her fist into the table but changed her mind last second toward a gentler approach. She smiled and listed her head. "You are hungry. Your stomach is just in knots because you're scared and confused and don't know what to do. I've been there. Would you like to know how to fix it?"

Cassie wiped snot onto her sleeve.

"You keep going. You forget about it. They are dead. Your crying won't make them alive. Starving yourself won't either. Close your eyes."

Cassie darted her eyes all over room as if searching for an escape hatch before relenting. She squeezed them shut.

"Take a long breath through your nose, then let it out through your mouth."

The girl did as told.

"Good. Now keep doing that. Keep going."

Cassie opened her eyes.

"Now, go up to your room and get your favorite toy or whatever you want that you think will bring you comfort."

"I can't. There are monsters."

"They are gone. I got rid of them. Trust me."

The girl stood, shivering. An intense fear rattled against her bones. Candlestick locked eyes with her. "Go," she said to Cassie. "Go."

Candlestick waited until Cassie disappeared up the flight of stairs, then made her husks appear. "Clean this up. Quickly. I can't make her get over her family when their blood is all over the place."

She stood and waited at the bottom of the stairs while the husks noisily cleaned in the kitchen and Cassie rummaged for something way down the hall upstairs. The girl's whimpering echoed all the way down the steps.

Cassie finished before the husks did. She stood at the top of the steps with something clutched in her arm.

Candlestick climbed to her. "What do you have?"

The girl held it out, and Candlestick took it from her. A photo of her mother in a frame. Candlestick knew of photos. She'd seen them even before coming to Earth, in books. But they didn't have cameras underground, so seeing this girl clutch a photo of her mother filled Candlestick with rage, envy, and her own grief. She would do anything to see her mother's face again, the real one, not the image floating in her mind losing features by the minute.

She tossed the picture in its frame down the stairs. It banged and shattered onto the foyer floor.

"Do better," she said.

Cassie ran away, crying.

A husk came to the bottom of the steps. "Cleeeeeean."

Candlestick sat on the top step and sulked.

"Noooooo haaaaapppppppyyyyyyy?"

"Am I being mean? Or am I being helpful?"

"Yoooouuuu help giiiiirrrllllllll."

"You'll always say what you think I want to hear. Please just go."

The husk left and Candlestick stormed down the hall toward Cassie's room. She found the girl crying over a toy chest, rummaging through it for an answer to Candlestick's demand. But Candlestick understood now that the girl could dig through the Earth to the other side and wouldn't ever find an object of comfort. No object could provide that.

Cassie noticed her in the doorway and shook her head. "I'm sorry. I'm trying to find something."

Candlestick walked up to her and put out a hand. Cassie stared at it. After a moment, she understood and took Candlestick's hand. As Candlestick lifted her, she said, "No, I'm sorry."

When the girl was on her feet, Candlestick wrapped her hands around her and hugged. Together, they cried into the night.

Eventually, Candlestick peeled herself away from Cassie and said, "Let me tell you a story."

Stones in a Sink Drain

A 12-year-old girl sat on a stump, catching her breath. The big, bad wolf hunted for her, but she couldn't run anymore. She was too tired.

Leaves rustled behind a large tree, and the girl clutched the stump, bracing for an attack. The wolf leapt from behind the tree and growled.

"Ahhhhhh," she faked a scream, and her father chuckled.

"You're getting fast, Mary," he said.

"Thanks. Can we play again after I catch my breath?"

He sat next to her and put his hand around her shoulders. "I need to catch mine, too. But what do you say after we take a breather, we head home and make some cheese sandwiches?"

Mary smiled. "Okay."

She leaned her head against her father's chest and listened to the bluebirds singing their afternoon songs. A gentle wind tickled the oak branches and the leaves rustled and hummed.

Then, something vulgar disrupted nature's song. A loud boom. A warm splash hit the top of Mary's head.

She peeled her face from her father's chest and screamed as

his headless body fell backward. After touching the top of her head, she pulled her hand back to reveal a crimson, gory mess.

She fell off the stump, landing hard on her butt. Screams shot from her mouth. The birds flew away, and even the wind paused to give her voice the stage.

A sanguine pool grew around her father's missing skull.

Mary couldn't stop looking at it, confused, scared. Tears gushed from her eyes, and she let out scream after scream: a non-stop alarm blaring from her throat. She stayed that way until something yanked her hair and dragged her away.

She scratched at the giant hand latched around her hair and kicked her legs, trying to get some footing so she could fight against it, but all she did was spin her body so her stomach scraped against the twigs and slash.

A man. A giant man. He dragged her with one arm while holding a rifle in the other. He didn't look at her, just marched forward, gripping her hair like a shopping bag.

"Let me go. Let me go."

The man said nothing, just kept on dragging her.

After a few minutes, the pain in her scalp subsided, and she flopped herself back onto her rear, which hurt less than when her stomach rubbed against the rough ground.

As her father's dead body shrunk until completely out of view, her sadness and confusion broke free and turned into terror at the prospects of what came next. She screamed for help, bellowing to the blinding sun as they left the forest and the trees no longer protected her from the wide-open world.

In unfamiliar territory, her back rubbed against hard stone instead of rough forest, which wasn't better or worse, but a different hurt. She'd stopped fighting, though, all strength gone. She still had the power to scream and cry, and that she did.

Her entire world was changing with each centimeter forward. Her old life dripped with blood behind a stump and her new one remained a mystery. Every muscle in her body ached and begged for release, for understanding, for some semblance of sanity to return to her world.

They crossed a small river, the man never slowing or letting up, unconcerned about her wellbeing as her body dragged across the gravelly riverbed. The water was icy, the drastic temperature change stealing her breath and sending fire to her skin.

After the river, more stones, until they reached thick grass. Her legs and back left streaks of blood in a trail and she prayed someone would cross it and come to her rescue.

They reached a farmhouse, decrepit, leaning slightly to the left as if it, too, wanted to run away, to rip itself from the foundation and get the hell out of there.

The screen door slammed into the outside wall and the man dragged her into the farmhouse. A universe of dust motes welcomed her.

He finally let go of her hair and pulled a handgun from his waist. "Go into the bathroom and shower up. Clean those wounds. Don't try to leave or I'll blow your fucking head off like I did your father."

She finally got her first view of the man. She expected a wolf, but what she saw was a man in his thirties, a little overweight, balding, with glasses. She could kill this man. If she played it smart, waited until the right moment, and had the universe on her side, she could kill him. Her brain needed time to adjust, to make sense of all this, but none of the pieces fit, like trying to slam giant stones down a sink drain.

"What do you want with me? Why are you doing this?"

He put the gun to her temple. "It's not chitty chatty time. It's listen to Russ time. Go take a shower. I put clean clothes in there for you. Get those wounds washed and put some medicine on them. I left some on the counter. Now."

She nodded. Now was not the time to fight. In the shower,

she stripped her clothes off and washed the grime and dirt from her body. Pink swirls danced around the drain. The hot water stung her wounds, but she fought against the pain and scrubbed hard with a bar of soap. She was old enough to understand infections.

She took her time, staying there until the water turned cold, giving herself these precious moments to mourn her father, because once she left the bathroom, she had to place him in the back of her mind. Grieving would create weakness. Weakness would kill her.

She rubbed the ointment he had left for her on her cuts and scrapes, reaching as far as she could to get it all over her back. The flesh on her legs was torn and shredded, but she listened to the man's instructions and slapped the ointment on the open wounds, a goop of white melding with the flowing red. Maybe if she gooped enough on, it would stop the bleeding.

The man left her a nice black dress with gray stripes going diagonally down the center. She wondered how he knew her size, how he had this outfit ready for her, and how long he'd been planning this.

She put on the long white socks he left with the dress. They went up just above her knees. The last bit was a pair of shiny black shoes, the kind you'd see on a doll, not a human. She put them on and tightened the strap. Before the shoes were on, her socks had already turned red from blood seeping through. She felt it coming through back of her dress as well.

When she left the bathroom, the man sat in an old wooden chair, staring at the door with his gun in his lap.

"Turn around," he said.

She did as he told her.

"Well, shit. I didn't mean to fuck up your back so much. Go lie down on the couch there."

The idea of it sent a shiver up her spine. She closed her eyes and took a deep breath, fighting back more tears. The goal now was survival; everything else she would have to bear.

She lay down with her stomach to the hard cushions, her face pressed to the couch. She could taste dust.

The man sat on the edge of the couch, too close. She smelled his sweat. He touched her leg, and she flinched.

"I'm just gonna fix up these wounds. I don't want to touch an animal like you. Trust me."

The man did as he promised, only putting his hands on her to suture her wounds, but every touch felt like a violation, anyway. She tightened her muscles, fighting against any more flinching. She worried if she made any movement, it would upset the man.

He needed to be at ease if she were going to succeed at killing him.

When he finished sewing her up, he spent ten minutes in the bathroom scrubbing her blood from his hands, a dirty snarl on his face, as if her blood were poison.

"Come on," he said, curling his index finger and walking down the creaky hall toward the back of the house.

That action let her know she'd already earned some trust. If he worried she would run, he would stand next to her, but he knew she would listen, so he walked ahead.

And she obeyed, because she wasn't stupid. If she ran with hurt legs, he would catch her in a second. No, when it was time to leave, she'd be walking out slowly, right over his corpse.

She followed him to a wooden barn in the yard. It was empty, other than the cobwebs and dust.

"You don't need to look around in here. This place ain't for you." He kicked at some hay and a thick layer of dust. As the motes plumed into the air, a wooden door with a metal pull handle revealed itself.

Using the ring, he lifted the door. She glanced down at a dark abyss. Metal rungs spun around the circular, cavernous wound in the earth.

"We're going down there?"

He tapped her on the shoulder, pushing her forward an inch. "Yes. You go first."

Her mouth dried out as if she had chewed on the sun. Her temples throbbed as her heart sped up. *Don't go*, her brain yelled. *Fight now.*

But it wasn't time yet. She couldn't kill him, couldn't run. There was only one option.

She swallowed hard and put a foot on the top rung.

It's Torture

Violin led Corey and Brian through the woods behind the house. The snow had long melted, but the ground remained mushy. Her boots stuck to the ground with each step and made a squelch whenever she lifted her feet.

She tried to remember the paths they'd taken, but trees and shrubs all looked the same to her, and most of their journey had been at night, making it impossible to conjure any details into her mind.

As she thought of night, the glow disc hovered behind the thick trunks lining the horizon. The fire disc was out of sight, but its light remained, albeit faint, leaving streaks of pink and purple in the distance.

"Hold on," Brian whispered.

Violin froze. He crept behind her, putting his arm on her shoulder, and pointing to something ahead. Violin stood on her toes, trying to see it over the thick shrubbery.

A thin shelter made from fabric.

"Shit," she said.

"There's a firepit, but from here it looks long burned out. My guess is whoever was there isn't anymore."

"Do you want to risk that?"

He shook his head. "No. I'll creep over and get a better look. Maybe if people are still staying there, they're out hunting or something and we can hurry past the camp."

As Brian moved around her, taking slow steps toward the camp, Corey moved in line with her. Worry pressed down on his forehead, causing it to wrinkle.

They watched Brian move closer to the camp, far from them, nerves building in both of their bodies. When Brian was close enough, he bobbed his head, examining the entire area.

After a moment, he waved them forward.

They charged. When they reached him, he whispered, "Looks abandoned, but there's a bunch of bags in their shelter, and camping shit. I wonder if this was where those kids were staying when they attacked your family."

Curiosity and anger took charge, replacing caution and smarts. Violin stepped into the camp. She kicked some bags out of the way, picked one of them up, and poured the contents out onto the ground. Mostly clothes and a few other random objects. A colorful book made of paneled pictures, a photo of a boy smiling with an older woman.

Brian and Corey came behind her but let her do her thing.

"Anything interesting?" Corey asked.

Violin didn't answer, just emptied more bags onto the soil.

Brian tapped Corey on the shoulder and pointed to the illustrated book. "Been a long time since you've seen a comic book, huh?"

"Yeah, but it makes me think it definitely was those kids. What makes a kid go full-blown murderer? How do you go from comics to real-life killing?"

"*Lord of the Flies*, my friend."

Violin kicked all the stuff she'd let loose, remnants of life left behind. Memories. Dreams. Ambitions. Enjoyments. She'd killed someone who owned one of these bags, a thin boy who had aimed a gun at her father. *Which was his?* She wondered. *What was his life like? Did he read? What was his favorite food? Did he love his mother?* She put her head down, hiding the pools growing in her eyes.

Corey and Brian left her to it, walking the perimeter.

"Oh," Corey shouted and covered his mouth.

Brian ran to him. "Oh, Jesus," he said as he caught a glimpse of whatever made Corey react that way.

Violin stepped over the mountain of junk and reached them. "What is that?" she asked as she looked down the crevasse.

"It's dead bodies. Someone burned them."

Violin's heart sank. "Those black lumps are dead people?"

She thought about the fiery death she had just avoided at the motel. The idea of looking that way for all eternity caused her to whimper.

"Yeah, they've been cooked."

"How many bodies are down there?"

Corey pointed at them, counting. "One. Two. Three."

She stepped away from the ledge. "There were a lot more kids than that."

"How many?" Brian looked from the fried corpses to her.

She shook her head. "I don't know. My Dad killed a few, then I killed one, and my dad hit another one in the woods. We saw at least ten at one point. So, there were six or more left, plus the one at the motel, I try to forget about him. I don't know. I can't figure it out, but they aren't all accounted for."

They stood around the ledge, looking down at the charred bodies. Violin wondered what happened to them. Who would burn another person to death? That's more than murder, it's torture.

Brian turned to Violin. "How much longer, do you think?"

"Not much. An hour or so."

She went back to the camp, searching through the kids' stuff. "Do you see any food?" she asked her friends.

Brian and Corey stepped in and examined the junk. They snatched up some thin sticks in a clear wrapper. "Jerky," Corey said.

After they collected the jerky, they continued their trek. Brian ripped open a jerky stick and gave it to Violin. "You have to really chew on this shit."

She shook her head and took a bite. Brian wasn't lying. She grinded her teeth, working to rip a piece off. The taste made the work worth it. A delicious, salty flavor filled her mouth. Bliss.

After a short walk, the sounds of rushing water filled the air, and Violin's heart ballooned. "We are close!" she said, picking up her pace and charging forward.

They reached a rocky outcropping, the trees falling away behind them. She charged up loose stones, and Brian and Corey followed close behind.

When they reached the river, it flowed as fiercely as she remembered. She bent down and scooped some, splashing it into her face. She laughed and cried, picturing her father fearing something as simple as a river, how frightened his face was when his daughters put their hands in.

"Dad, you would have really freaked out if you saw an ocean," she whispered to herself.

She took another scoop and slurped it from her palm, washing the dry saltiness from her mouth and throat.

Brian and Corey stood above her with their arms crossed, smiling at her excited reaction. "So, is this where your home is?" Corey asked.

She stood, looked both ways. "No. But this river goes by it. I'm sure of it. But I don't know which way. We walked..." She turned back and forth. "...going that way. And I don't remember anything looking like it does here with all the loose stones. So, my guess is we keep going that way, and my home will be across the river."

They shook their heads. She loved them. It hit her then. They were her family. Always there, always by her side. Two adult men allowed a twelve-year-old girl to guide them, and they did so without ever doubting her. Sure, they'd offer alternatives when they thought one was worth bringing up, but if she refused, they didn't argue. They accepted her fully, and what was more magical than that?

She trudged forward, feeling the weight of their walk in her calves. Up ahead, it looked like the ground dropped off, and for a while, she wasn't sure what she was seeing. As they stepped closer, it made sense. They were above the waterfall.

"It's here!" She ran. When she reached the ledge where the earth dropped and the water spewed off the cliff to her side, she jumped up and down. "There it is!" She spun in a circle with her arms in the air. "Whooooooooo." She shouted into the sky.

Brian and Corey caught up and glanced off the edge. "Where?"

She pointed to a small chunk of rock that protruded from a wall of stone on the other side of the river. A dark sphere under it, a hole that led to her world, her family.

Her heart sank, and the joy spoiled into tears. She had so many mixed emotions, she couldn't pinpoint where one started and the other ended. It boiled over and she fell to her knees, staring at the hole where she had lived for over eleven years.

"I'm home," she cried as Corey and Brian hugged her. "I'm home."

<h1 style="text-align:center">Take it From Me</h1>

❦

Cassie stared at Candlestick.

"Well, what did you think of the story?"

Cassie blinked. "I don't get it."

Candlestick walked to a pink dollhouse in the corner. Cassie must have loved pink because it was spewed all over the room. The walls, the bedsheets, the clothing. Pink. Pink. Pink.

The dollhouse was huge, almost as tall as Candlestick. "You'll get the stories someday. For now, you just have to listen to them."

"But I don't want to listen to them. That one was scary and weird. A girl's father gets shot and then she gets kidnapped. What kind of story is that?"

Candlestick turned back to her, aiming a sharp eye as steadfast as her sister had held a gun. "Life is scary and weird. The best stories show that."

Cassie shifted herself off the bed and examined Candlestick. "They're yours, aren't they?"

"What are you talking about?"

"The monsters. They belong to you, don't they? You told them to kill my parents."

Candlestick's cheeks turned hot. "The monsters do what they want. I can tell them what to do. Sometimes they listen. Sometimes they don't."

Cassie's eyes filled with water and her top lip twitched. "You're lying. You had them kill my parents. Oh no. This was all my fault. My dad wanted to leave you and me and my mom yelled at him for it."

Candlestick stepped closer to her. She looked her in the eyes and touched her cheek. "You're weak."

She didn't know what she was doing and hoped she wasn't being awful. Her kindness wasn't going to fix Cassie. She remembered the loudness and harsh lessons from the underground, and how those classes stripped her of emotion. She didn't want to be cruel to Cassie, and her heart hurt at the sight of hatred, fear, and sadness on the girl's face. She wanted to fix her, even at the expense of her own morality.

"What?" Cassie wiped a tear from her cheek, as if trying to hide the evidence. "No, I'm not. You're evil. Get out of my house."

Candlestick frowned. Then she slapped Cassie hard.

The girl yelped and stepped backwards. Her mouth opened wide, and she rubbed the red mark on her face. "Get out of my house!"

"No. This is my house now. If you want it, take it from me."

Cassie shook her head. "No. This is where I live. This is my bedroom. Animals sleep outside."

Candlestick slapped her again, but this time Cassie was prepared and slipped away a little, only getting a few fingers to her cheek.

"I'm not an animal. You say that again, I'll kill you and feed you to my dog." This time, her rage and meanness were real. She wasn't an animal and refused to accept the insults.

Cassie stood firm. "Get out of my house."

Candlestick smiled at the girl's resilience. Maybe she wasn't as weak as Candlestick presumed. "No. Make me."

Cassie stepped back again. "No. I won't let you trick me into doing something I don't want to do!"

Candlestick crossed her arms. "Or what?"

"Or I'll get my father's gun and shoot your dog."

Candlestick pushed her and swatted her hands at Cassie. Cassie covered her face with her arms, but the blows just kept on coming. Candlestick hit her until she was balled up on the floor, crying. She stood up, letting the girl swim in her own fragility. Hopefully, Cassie would realize how much she needed Candlestick.

She stormed out of the room. Just as she entered the hallway, Cassie slammed into her back, knocking Candlestick flat on her face. Candlestick bit her lip as her mouth hit the blue carpet.

With her face pressed to the floor, Cassie hit her in the back of the head repeatedly. Candlestick smiled bigger with each blow. Her tactics worked.

Eventually, Cassie tired of hitting her, sniffled, and scooted to the corner of the hall. "I hate you. Just leave."

Candlestick stood up, licked the blood from her lip, and headed for the stairs. She didn't look back to see how Cassie reacted. The girl deserved her win.

She took Cassie's uneaten dinner outside with her and fed it to Lion. When the dog finished his dinner, Candlestick unlocked him from his leash and played with him in the yard.

Cassius came from behind a tree. "Candlestick waaaaaaant hussskkkk to kiiiilllllllllllll Caaaaasssssiiieeeee?"

"No. Cassie is my best friend." She tossed a stick and Lion chased it down.

"Huuuuussssskkkk no uuuuuunderssssssstttaaaaannndddd."

Lion jumped on Candlestick, proudly displaying the stick he'd retrieved. She ripped it from his mouth and tossed it again. "Maybe you can understand this. She is telling me the truth. You lie to me. You say what you think I want to hear, or worse, you make stuff up because you think you know what's better."

Cassius stepped back. "Nnnnoooooooooo."

She turned to the husk and got in his face. "Yes. My sister didn't abandon me. You want to trick me into going somewhere other than home because you don't want me to find Violin. I made you. You can't trick me. And I can make you disappear if I want. Remember that."

She played with Lion until the last threads of fire disc light hovered on the horizon.

Cassius stood watching her, showing impatience with his huffing and pacing.

Candlestick ignored him but felt the need to answer the question he wasn't asking. "We wait until she is ready."

As the glow disc hid behind a sheath of clouds, the front door opened. Cassie stood inside with her arms crossed. Candlestick stared, waiting for her to say something.

"Why didn't you kill me?" she finally yelled.

"What?"

"I know you had your monsters kill my parents. Why didn't you have them kill me?"

Candlestick tossed the stick for Lion to chase and made her way onto the porch. "I had them kill your parents because your parents were hurting you." She decided to tell the girl the truth. If nothing else, she deserved that.

Cassie instinctively put her hand over a bruise on her arm. "No, they didn't. Besides, *you* just hurt me. You hit me."

Candlestick put her head down. "I know. I shouldn't have done that. I was trying to help you, but I forgot you've been hit by anger. I was trying to teach you to be strong. It wasn't out of rage. But it was also stupid, and I'm sorry."

Cassie's face scrunched. "I hated my parents. But I also loved them."

"I understand."

"You shouldn't have killed them. You didn't even ask me what I wanted."

A weight pulled Candlestick's stomach down. "I have spent my life led by people who never asked me what I wanted. I understand. I was wrong. Even my monsters think they know what's best for me." She shot Cassius a dirty look. "I'm trying to find my sister, but they won't help me. They're jerks. But they can also be helpful."

Cassie scrunched her forehead. "Still, I hit you. You could have had them kill me."

"Why would I do that? You're my friend."

Cassie shivered. "I don't even know you."

Candlestick shrugged. "So?"

Tears formed in Cassie's eyes again. "I don't trust you, and I don't like you. But I don't like being alone. You can come in if you promise to tell me another story."

Candlestick smiled. She turned to Lion and whistled. The dog bounded toward her with a stick in his mouth. "Come on, boy. Let's tell Cassie a story."

Animals and Humans

Mary climbed down the tunnel, slimy stones surrounding her. The metal rungs were slippery, so she took each step carefully, worried a foot would slide off, or worse, her hands. When she made it to the bottom, a blanket of darkness surrounded her, but she could feel the room, its large, hollow space. An open mouth ready to gulp.

Russ climbed down after her, gun tucked into his belt, a flashlight between his teeth. When he hit the bottom, he used the low beam to guide him to a string. He pulled it down and the room illuminated.

It was a cold, gross chamber. Stone walls on all sides, with small alcoves cutting into two walls. She counted ten of these alcoves. They looked like animal pens. Otherwise, the room was empty. No furniture, no beds, nothing.

"Come on," Russ said. He led her to the farthest alcove.

She followed him, darting her eyes every which way in search of something, anything that could get her out of this situation.

"Get in," he said.

She listened. As she stepped in, she noticed the metal chains tucked into one side of the alcove.

He pulled the chain out and locked it around her ankle. The walls closed in and the air turned to soot.

Her chest rocked up and down like a tender branch in a windstorm. "I won't go anywhere. You don't need to lock me in here."

Russ said nothing. As he stepped out of the room, he beamed his flashlight into the corners where the overhead light failed to show itself.

"What will I do for food or water? What if I need to go to the bathroom?" Her words came out like swarming bees.

"For now, you'll have to hold it until I can get you and bring you upstairs. But I'm gonna build a bathroom for you down here, eventually."

"Eventually? How long will I be down here?" She stepped forward, and the shackle yanked her back.

"Don't worry. You won't be alone. You're going to have friends soon."

"What do you mean?" She fell to her knees. All the strength she'd been clinging to flooded out of her, breaking the dams that held her grief and terror in place. Her father, dead. Her life, gone. Now, she had nothing but four stone walls and no clue what this man planned to do with her.

He turned to her and pointed to the corner next to her alcove. "Figure I will put a bathroom right there. I'll get a fridge down here so you can have cold water and maybe some sand-wiches or something. It'll be rough for a week or so, but I'll start getting that stuff put in and it'll be more like a home in no time."

A home? Did this man think a fridge and a toilet made a place a home? "Please, just lock me up in the barn or the house. I don't like dark places like this. I feel like I can't breathe."

Russ sighed and headed for the metal rungs. "Animals don't get to live with the humans,"

Once he reached the top, and the wood cover on the tunnel slammed into place sending a rain shower of dust down the hole, Mary pulled on her chain. She'd never get it off. The ring around her ankle was so tight it dug into her flesh. Where the shackle met the stone floor, it went into the stone, as if they molded it in the center of the rock. They made the stone with prison in mind.

Still, she yanked, hoping to find a flaw in the loops, just one centimeter of mistake, enough for her to bend it, twist it, do something to free herself.

She moved around the alcove, seeing how much room she had to play with. Not much. She could get out of it, but only a step. If she lay on her belly with her ankle twisted, she might reach five or six feet out.

If he put a toilet in the corner, how would she get to it?

She hyperventilated, curled into a ball in the corner, and coughed up dust. A mouse ran by, and she cried harder. How did this happen? How did this become her life?

She begged and pleaded to the walls, screamed for help, cried to no one.

"Please, please, please get me out of this."

"Dad. Daddy?"

"He shot my dad."

"I want to go home."

Snot ran down her face, saliva down her chin.

"Please."

Her voice went from pleading to growling anger.

"Get me out of here. Get me out."

The room responded to her threats and begging with a cruel, mocking silence.

After many hours dripped by, the clank of the wooden cover

at the top of the tunnel broke through the silence and brought with it a glow of daylight from above.

"Get down there," Russ shouted.

"No."

"You've been enough trouble. Get down there, or I'll throw you down there, and drag your broken bones the rest of the way."

There was screaming and fighting above Mary's head. She hoped whomever it was killed Russ.

Eventually, the dinging of feet on the rungs came closer to her, along with the sobs of someone defeated.

A girl around Mary's age landed in the room. Her face was bruised and her lip bloody. She had fire in her eyes. Russ landed behind her, a fresh set of scratches crossed his cheeks. Mary smiled.

"Go," Russ said, pointing toward the alcove next to Mary's.

Mary only peaked her head out a little and wondered if the new girl knew she was there.

"Fuck you," the new girl said as she spat a pink dribble on the floor.

Russ clenched his teeth and latched his hand around the new girl's hair, dragging her to the alcove. The girl kicked and screamed and slashed her claws at Russ's arm.

Russ tossed her into the alcove like she was a dirty pile of laundry. The clinking of shackles locking into place broke Mary's heart.

Russ stormed out of the room, rubbing the fresh blood from his arm. "Stupid bitch," he said on his way up the rungs.

The new girl screamed guttural belches of fire.

Mary stepped out of her alcove. "Hello?"

The screaming stopped, followed by some sniffling. The new girl stepped forward, into view, her legs shaking and her cheeks red and streaked with tears. "Hello? I didn't know anyone was here."

"I'm Mary."

The girl wiped snot from her nose. "I'm Kelly. What's happening to us?"

Mary shook her head. "I don't know."

"What does he want with us?"

"I don't know."

"Why is he doing this?"

"I don't know."

Kelly growled, and Mary envied her ferociousness. Mary planned to kill Russ and she held a confidence that she'd get to do it, but the shackles damaged her spirit until Kelly showed up. Mary was smart, but she wasn't strong. Unfortunately for Russ, he just handed her a weapon.

Mary smiled. "Kelly?"

"What?" She hung her head in defeat.

"We're going to get out of here. Okay? But I need you to listen to me. I have a plan."

Prepare for Everything, Even Nothing

Violin descended the cliff beside the waterfall, almost stumbling as excitement killed precaution. Brian and Corey chased behind.

At the bottom, she ran across the river. This time, she fell, soaking her clothes. She didn't care. She was home.

When she reached the threshold of their community, she turned to her friends, a smile beaming across her face. "Can you both stay out here for a few minutes? Just let me say my piece to my family."

They nodded. "Of course," Brian said.

"Thank you." She lunged forward and hugged him. After squeezing for a moment, she let go and did the same to Corey. "Thank you for everything."

She walked into the darkness, forgetting how bright the outside world was comparatively, even in the nighttime. She had to use her hands to guide her through the narrow tunnel as it turned from dim to pitch black.

At the end of the tunnel, she reached the room her grandmother pushed Violin, Candlestick, and Winter in to keep them safe from the disease. She remembered her mother's hair spilling in through the crack under the door, and her eyes filled with water.

She pulled down on the handle and the door popped open. As it creaked and exposed the entrance to her community, a smell wafted into her nose and made her gag. Death. She coughed and spat up onto the floor. She cried some more.

Using her shirt as a shield, she entered the room to see her grandmother's body on the floor, still decomposing, not yet a skeleton. Violin fell to her knees and bawled. She had hoped her family had disappeared like the humans did. Her people didn't die from the same thing that took out the humans. Something else killed them. A disease she allowed to enter their community by keeping her aunt's secret.

"I'm sorry Grandma," she said to no one.

She walked through the community room and clicked the light on. It still functioned, a testament to her father's skills. This was where they had gathered day after day to talk, eat, and enjoy each other's company. It was in this room where Violin met Candlestick for the first time, a small little bean wrapped in blankets, cradled in their mother's arms. It was where her father sat with Violin and talked to her about electricity and other odd objects of fascination for him, like colors and growing vegetables.

Her shirt couldn't block the smell of death, and she gagged again. She remembered the wonderful smells seeping in from the cooking room and the memories attached to those smells. Her smiling mother. Her laughing grandmother. Her crazy uncle. She leaned over and puked on a wall.

More dead bodies lay on the floor in this room. Friends, neighbors, people who loved her. Now, nothing more than piles of rotting meat. She went in room after room, needing to see each dead body, to put a face to the mound of decomposing muscle. She apologized to each of them.

The growing room smelled just as bad, thanks to the lack of care the crops had received. Bent and wilted futures. Preparations for times that would never come. Her people probably worked through sickness until their dying day, always prepared for everything, even nothing.

She assumed the sight of her mother would bring about the biggest tears, but by the time she found her mom's body slumped in her favorite rocking chair, Violin had cried out all she had in her. She sat next to her mother and stared for a while, enjoying a moment in her presence, even if it wasn't real.

"You were wrong," she said. "Candlestick and I did make it to Earth, but we never stood on top of a hill together. And now I've lost her. So, it will never happen."

She picked at some dirt under her fingernails, as if embarrassed by her appearance in front of a woman who stunk of rot. "You also said I had the strongest powers, but I still have none. I am weak, and the source of great disappointment. All I have done is let everyone down."

It turned out she had some tears left, after all.

"I'm so sorry," she cried. "I'm so sorry to everyone."

"You're too hard on yourself."

Violin screamed and turned around to the entrance of her mother's room, where the voice came from. She lost her breath. Her father smiled at her.

"Who are you?"

Her father waved his hands. "Right now, I'm your dad."

She shimmied backward, away from the figure. "You're not my father. He is dead and you're nothing like him."

"No, I am not your father, although I thought I did a pretty good job of looking like him."

"You look like him, but you don't talk like him. You move your hands all wrong. Plus, you have a scar down the left side of your face. What do you want? Get out of here or I'll kill you."

She put her hand behind her back, feeling for the butt of her gun.

What kind of person could mimic another? Was this a human at all? Her heart sunk at the thought.

Fake Winter listed his head. "After all I did for you?"

She had been so focused on seeing her father's face, she failed to notice the pink shirt with writing on it. Up close, she could finally read the words. A GOOD HUMAN IS LIKE A GOOD STEAK. RARE.

"You saved me. Who are you?"

The man smiled and stepped into the room. Violin scooted back and pulled the gun out from behind her. Fake Winter raised his hands in the air. She worked to hide the trembling in her fingers.

"Don't shoot. I'm a friend."

He crouched down, perched like a bird in a tree. "Your father, he told you stories."

Violin furrowed her brow.

"Stories about gods and Kevin Bacon and all sorts of cool, fantastical things." His voice was high-pitched, creepy in its enthusiasm.

She nodded, but fear and confusion swirled together in her blood. "How did you know that?"

The man rubbed his thumb along his fingernails. "There is so much you don't know. I don't know where to begin."

"Are you going to tell me you're Kevin Bacon?"

The man laughed. "Me? Heck no. I'm no Kevin Bacon. I'm not even a god. I'm a little like your father. I tell tales."

"Will you get to the point of what you're after? Your timing sucks. I just wanted to spend some time with my family."

The man stood up and moved to Violin's mother. He tilted his head and gave the dead woman a sad look. "I'm sorry to intrude on your moment. I just needed to get you alone."

"Why?"

The man sighed and pulled his eyes away from Violin's mother. "Your father's stories, while stupid, fictional, and often ridiculous..."

She lifted the gun and gritted her teeth. "Say another bad word about my father, and the walls will taste your blood."

He showed no concern over her threat. "I apologize, again. Your father's stories were just a bunch of tales he made up to please you girls, but that didn't make them unimportant. Those stories mattered. The problem is, he never finished them."

"What does it matter to you?"

"It matters a great deal to me. I want to finish his stories for you. That's all I ask."

She stood up, keeping the gun trained. "No."

He looked genuinely confused. "Why? I just want to tell you stories."

"Those were a special thing between my father and his daughters. They aren't for you. I'm mad you even know about them."

He leaned back against a wall and stared at the ceiling. "I didn't expect that response."

"If I were you, I'd tell me why they are so important to you, or I would get the hell out of here." She wondered if bullets could harm a man with the power to change his face.

Maybe he was one of them? Maybe he had once belonged to their community or shared a bloodline, but never made his way to their underground home.

"I'd like to avoid sharing some of the gritty details with you, but how about instead, I offer you something in return?"

"What?"

"You let me tell you a story, and I will tell you where your sister is right now."

"Bullshit. How do you know where she is?"

He smiled. "How did I know your father told you stories? How do I change my face? How did I drag you through walls to save you from a fire? How did I travel faster than your car?"

"Fine, I get it. But how do I know you'll tell me the truth?"

He lifted his hand and an image appeared, a floating three-dimensional picture. "This is the motel where you stayed, now burned to blackened wood."

He flicked his wrist and a new image appeared: people talking and laughing behind a building. People she knew. "And these are your old friends at the supermarket. Still alive, enjoying their lives. I'll bet that makes you happy to see. Or maybe angry. Could be both."

She sucked her lips in, biting back a boiling rage. "Show me Candlestick."

He flicked his wrist again, making the images disappear. Then he lifted a finger and wagged it. "Ah, ah, ah. Not yet. First," His smile grew unnaturally large, "a story."

Dark Skies

The heavens filled with the sounds of clinking glasses and loud celebration. Dark Skies, half drunk, stood atop Azerka's old throne and waved his arms. "To freedom!" The other eight gods replied, "To freedom."

As the new gods danced and cheered, Dolphi sat alone in a corner, watching the festivities with concern and wonder. He made this celebration happen. He didn't know yet if he'd made the right choice, but he was eager to see his end of the bargain fulfilled. So far, the gods hadn't awarded him a thing, not even a glance.

He cleared his throat, loud enough for Dark Skies to hear. The god turned to him with his swirling black eyes, his charcoal hair bobbing as he jerked his head.

For a moment, silence stole the room.

"Dolphi!" the god yelled, and the rest applauded.

Dark Skies floated to him and lifted him. He held the snake up and placed Dolphi around his neck. To his siblings, Dark Skies asked, "Did you all see the wonderful performance our friend put on?"

The gods nodded and cheered.

"A god killing bullet. I have to ask; how did you make that Dolphi?"

Dolphi blushed. "A proprietary ingredient."

He worried the gods would force an answer from him but instead, they laughed.

Dark Skies patted Dolphi as if he really wanted to pat himself on the back but Dolphi was in the way. "Well, nonetheless, fabulous job. We owe our freedom to you." He dropped Dolphi in front of him. "I sat there in that belly, ashamed of how my sisters and brother ruled with idiocy. Fools never thought to tap into the underworld. Imagine, a god holds you in their belly, and they are too stupid to know you're talking from it to a place under their watch that they've neglected and ignored."

Dolphi chuckled with the gods, but he suspected the new gods would also ignore the movements of the underworld. Dolphi didn't, though. He knew all about Kevin Bacon's trip down there, where he revived Dance and created a new human. A secret human hiding in a cabin, an unknown to the faux omniscience of the gods. He could tell them, maybe even earn a few more good graces, but Dolphi knew the power in secrets. They were only worth revealing when you absolutely needed them. He would cling to Kevin Bacon's plan B, wielding it as a weapon when the time was right.

Dark Skies brushed past Dolphi and went back to celebrating and drinking with the gods. Jasha took his hand in dance, and together they spun around the room until they nearly stumbled into the colorful blobs of everything. They laughed at their foolishness. Dolphi frowned. So far, he saw no difference between the nine and the three, other than numbers.

He cleared his throat again, and again Dark Skies responded with a head jerk, but this time, his eyes were less welcoming.

"Dolphi. Why aren't you dancing and celebrating?"

Dolphi slithered forward. "I would love to, sir, and I surely will, but I was wondering if you could complete your end of the bargain for me?"

The gods all turned to him now, some with furrowed brows, and some eager to see Dark Skies lash out at him.

Dolphi corrected course. "I'd be a much better dancer with feet."

Dark Skies rubbed his temple and looked at his dance partner. "Jasha, can you remind me of the terms of our agreement with Dolphi? Your memory is much better than mine. Plus, my brain is swimming in delicious nectar."

Jasha stepped forward, her long brown hair floating around her head like lightning bolts. "You promised Dolphi a human body and complete control of the underworld."

Dark Skies widened his eyes and exaggerated a shocked face by parting his lips. "Wow, and I have no doubt our new friend deserves those very things, but what was it Dolphi needed to do to win those luxuries?"

"He was to free us from the belly of Orelon."

Dark Skies lifted a finger. "And boy did he deliver on that one. Isn't that right, friends?"

The room erupted in shouts and cheers. Dolphi blushed again as a smile widened across his green cheeks.

"Was there anything else?" Dark Skies asked Jasha.

The woman's hair flowed and twirled as she pondered. "Ah yes, Dolphi was to kill Kevin Bacon and his remaining siblings."

Dark Skies clicked his tongue. "Ohhhhhhh. Hmmmmm. Well, I must admit, for a moment there, I thought Dolphi's help in the war was going to kill two obnoxious birds with one stone, but alas, that pesky Kevin Bacon lives, and so do some of his siblings."

Dolphi's heart dropped to the depths of his tail. He stood up, putting his head level with Dark Skies's. "Maybe, since I completed one task, you could grant me one of my requests? After all, I would be much better at hunting down Kevin Bacon if I just had some feet."

Jasha stepped in front of Dark Skies. "Unfortunately, we gods don't trade in half-accomplishments. You get all you asked for when you deliver all we asked for."

Dark Skies put his arm on Jasha's shoulder. "What she says is final, I'm afraid."

Dolphi bit back tears. "Yes ma'am. Yes sir."

Dark Skies lifted the snake again, this time from his neck. "Have no fear, friend. In the morning, we are going hunting for Mr. Bacon and you'll be joining us. We will have killed that son-of-a-bitch by noon and you'll be two-stepping in the underworld by dinner time."

Dolphi considered letting them in on Kevin Bacon's secret again, but the gods clearly played games of leverage, so Dolphi bit his tongue, planning ten mo...

"Hhhhhhhhhhhhhhhhhh," Fake Winter clutched his throat and choked. His body lifted into the air as if an invisible force strangled him.

Violin jolted back, bumping her head into the wall. She raised her gun.

Fake Winter, with his tongue hanging out, shook his head. "Your bullets won't help."

"What's happening? What do I do? Who is doing this to you?"

"They won't let me finish the story."

"What do I do?"

"Tell the stories."

"To who?"

"Anyone."

"Who is doing this?"

"You wouldn't believe me."

"Please, I have to know."

Fake Winter lifted his hand and an image appeared above it. Candlestick, talking to a little girl in a street. The girl clutched Candlestick's arm.

"She's alive?"

Fake Winter shook his head.

"Where?"

"I can't tell you."

"Why?"

"She's responsible for this."

His neck snapped and his lifeless body fell to the floor.

It's Scary out There

Cassie sat at the living room table, sipping on water. Candlestick convinced her to eat some food, but she'd only agreed to it if she didn't have to go in the kitchen. After she took down some bread and water, Cassie sat listening to Candlestick's tale.

Candlestick ended her story and said, "I need to go somewhere. I want you to come with me, but it's up to you. If you'd rather stay in this house alone, I won't talk you out of it."

"I don't want to go anywhere. It's scary out there."

Candlestick shrugged. "Okay. Well, I have to go."

She stood up and fixed her shirt. All for show, of course. She had spent too much time trying to make Cassie a friend and wasn't ready to give up yet. But, she wanted Cassie to agree to this on her own terms, to realize she needed Candlestick and desired the friendship.

She walked out of the room and through the foyer, taking tiny steps, waiting to hear Cassie's chair slide along the hardwood. The sound never came.

Outside, she knelt and played with Lion for a few minutes,

giving the girl more time. If Cassie didn't open the door soon, she'd go back in and try new ways to convince her. Luckily, that proved unnecessary. As Lion chased a stick, the door crept open and Cassie came out with a bookbag strapped to her back.

Candlestick smiled. "Let's go, then."

Cassie followed her to the gates, where they slipped through the wide-apart spokes one after the other.

"I still don't like you, just so you know."

Candlestick didn't respond. Instead, she scrubbed Lion's ears as he followed by her side.

They marched down a road with giant houses on each side, Candlestick taking confident steps, while Cassie wrapped her arms around herself and darted her eyes from side to side, afraid of every natural Earth sound.

"Where are we going?" Cassie asked.

"To find my sister."

"Oh, great. There's another one of you?"

"Don't worry, you'll like her better. Everyone does."

Something rumbled and Candlestick stopped.

The rumbling continued, growing louder with each passing second.

She turned to Cassie. "Hide."

She grabbed the girl's arm and guided her behind some shrubbery on the edge of another house's lawn, while shushing Lion with her mind. They peeked over, staring at a cross section of road. As the rumbling sound moved closer, it became overbearing, almost painful.

A giant, green machine came into view.

"What the heck is that?" Candlestick asked.

"It's a tank," Cassie whispered.

Around the tank, a group of men jogged in green and brown outfits. Earth people and their matching uniforms. A few smaller vehicles lagged the tank, and with them, more men.

"Maybe we should flag them down. They look like army people. They can help us."

"What's army people?" Candlestick asked.

"Good guys," Cassie said.

Candlestick doubted it. "Let's wait. We don't need help right now."

Cassie watched the group vanish from the cross section of the road, her eyes full of regret. Candlestick could see the girl debated on running out there, hoping the army men would save her. But, the girl stayed, either from fear or care for Candlestick. Either way, Candlestick smiled.

When the men were gone, they stood and brushed themselves off. Cassie followed as they headed toward the cross section. The men were long gone now, but the sounds of their tank machine still carried.

Candlestick stared down the road where the men had gone, and considered what they were up to, where they were headed, and what their goals were. Good guys. Where were the good guys when her father bled to death in a garden?

"Where to?" Cassie asked.

Candlestick pointed forward. She didn't know how to get home and thought there'd be no harm in following the tank sounds for a while. As they walked, she conjured a husk.

"Tell me if I am going in the right direction to get to my home. And if you lie to me, you'll never exist again."

"Caaaaanndddddlleeesssssttiiiccckkk gooooooo riggggghhh-httttt waayyyyyyy."

She nodded and shooed the husk away. Cassie's eyes grew wide, and she sat in the middle of the road.

"What's wrong?"

"I can't look at those things. You told me you killed my parents, but seeing you talk to them. Ugh. I hate you." She pushed Candlestick. "I fucking hate you," she said too loudly, fierce and full of tears.

"Your parents were cruel to you. I just want you to be free and happy."

"Fuck you." She pushed Candlestick again. "Fuck you," she said again as she turned her hands into fists and punched Candlestick in the shoulders, left then right.

Candlestick stepped back with each hit, absorbing the pain, allowing her punishment. It wasn't enough, she knew, and more would gradually come, but she'd worry about that when the time was right. Someday, Cassie would get her revenge on Candlestick, and when that day came, she'd accept her fate. But for now, she hoped a friendship would bloom between the violence. Death would always hover around her, but maybe something wonderful could fit in the center.

Cassie shook her head and fell to her knees. "My heart is racing. I don't like to see them. Don't make me see them anymore." Tears dripped down her cheeks.

Candlestick put her hand out. "I won't let them come out around you again."

Cassie stared at her hand for a minute before relenting and taking it.

Candlestick lifted her to her feet. Before they could march on, a new noise moved toward them, a threatening call twisting through the wind. No, not a new noise. The same noise, but from a different direction. The old rumbling softened as it moved away from them. The new rumbling came closer, from the direction the other had started.

Candlestick looked up, eyes wide. More tanks. Two of them.

"We have to run," Candlestick said.

Cassie crossed her arms. "No. I don't want to run. Maybe they can take care of us. They probably have food and all the stuff we need."

Candlestick turned to her. "You had all that stuff back at your house. Why did you leave with me if that was all you were concerned about?"

"Because I didn't want to be alone in the house my parents were murdered in. I'm afraid. I'll probably never sleep again."

"All I am is..." Candlestick trailed off, staring at the incoming mechanical doom troops.

"You're nothing. I'm afraid *because* of you. I came with you because I figured as long as I am nice to you, your monsters won't kill me."

Candlestick's eyes watered. She put her head down. How did she become everyone's monster? What Cassie didn't realize was everything scared Candlestick, too. Everything. Even Cassie. Even herself.

"Fine. Let's go with your army men."

Cassie's shoulders slumped. "Wait. You're going to stay with me? I thought you wanted to find your sister."

"You're more important than that right now."

Cassie stepped back, her lip quivering. "Why?"

Candlestick looked at her head on. "Because my sister hates me as much as you do, but at least I don't have to chase you down. She felt obligated to love me. I don't want that. I want someone to love me on their own."

Cassie huffed. "I don't love you either. And what if I don't want you to come?"

Candlestick shrugged. "Then say so, and I will leave you alone with the strange men."

They stared at each other for a moment while the tank rumbles grew closer, nearly deafening, shaking the ground.

"Say it!" Candlestick shouted. "Tell me to leave."

She turned to the tanks, which were slowing as they hit the cross section, moving ever closer. The men jogging beside the tanks were holding their guns up, shouting something at the girls.

"Last chance," Candlestick said as she stared at the men, who were aiming weapons at the girls and shouting into a thunderous void.

Cassie said nothing, but as the men charged from both sides of the tank with their guns at the ready, she gripped Candlestick's hand and moved beside her new friend.

Explore and Seek Answers

Violin ran to Fake Winter's body. She needed answers. Since he couldn't talk, she had to rely on his pockets. Unfortunately, they provided little. A picture of a woman and a tiny key, the kind that fit in small lockboxes. Nothing else. She pocketed the two items with no clue what she'd do with them.

Not understanding what to do now, she froze, wondering if every step would be the wrong one, the kind that sent the world spiraling out of control, killing off entire communities. Nothing made sense, and every time nothing made sense, a calamity followed.

She rubbed her forehead and pulled her hair back out of her face. Fake Winter's body slumped against the wall, his head resting on his shoulders as if his spine had vanished.

Maybe it had.

What did he mean when he said Candlestick was the cause of all this? It wasn't possible. Even when Fake Winter showed Violin's sister, she was just talking with a little girl. She had no power to snap someone's neck from miles away. Her powers granted her the ability to speak with animals. And who was the little girl? Nothing made sense. Nothing ever made any fucking sense.

"Violin?"

She screamed and jumped back but corrected herself as she recognized the voice. "In here!" she shouted as she left the room.

"We don't know where we are," Brian shouted back.

She made her way down the long corridor, passing the bedrooms, the grow room, and her grandmother's secret room. When she entered the community room, Brian and Corey stood at the doorway to the quarantine room with their shirts over their noses.

"We're sorry to intrude. Corey thought he heard you yell."

She smiled at them. "Thank you. I did scream, but it was a false alarm."

Brian stepped in, and Corey followed. They examined the room, the dead woman by the door, the horrors all around. "These were your people?"

She nodded and tried to respond, but all that came out was a squeak as her eyes flooded with tears. She ran to them they wrapped themselves around her, enveloping her in a protective bubble.

Corey pressed her head into his belly, and she wet his shirt with her tears.

"They're all dead. I knew they would be, but seeing it," she gulped, "I had hoped they disappeared like humans did."

"We understand."

She pulled away from them. "I have things to tell you. You won't believe it all, but I need you to hear it. I haven't been entirely truthful, but the secrets are piling up and they're going to break me."

Brian and Corey looked at each other. "Okay," Corey said.

"My dad told me something just before he died. I don't

understand it, but I could tell it was important, something I have to do."

"What?" Brian asked.

"Find out what happened to humanity."

Corey shook his head. "Why?"

"I don't know. It doesn't make sense to me either, but he told me my mother knew it was something I had to do. My mother dreamed things, things that would happen, but sometimes they seemed so far out there and crazy, we didn't know what to do with them. We never expected to leave the community, but she knew we would. She knew and warned us how our people would die. I don't know if we just didn't believe her, or if we assumed we would always have more time before it came, but we ignored it."

Violin paced, putting all the pieces together, even though none of them fit. "She predicted me and Candlestick would end up on a hill together, somewhere on Earth. That hasn't happened yet. But that's why I am confident I will see her again."

Brian put his arm up, stopping her. "Whoa, but how do you know your mom wasn't just dreaming?"

Violin rolled her eyes at him. "It was her power. My dad could heal people, Candlestick can talk to animals. My mom dreamed the truth. It wasn't always the future. Sometimes she dreamed of the past or even the present, but she saw the truth. It made her scary. One time my sister and I stole crickets from our farm and ate them. The next morning, my mom told us she had dreamed about it. She even knew how many crickets we ate."

"Okay. I'm not going to question it. I've seen enough from you guys to know not to doubt anything, but what will finding out about humanity do?" Corey asked.

Violin shrugged. "I'm not sure, but my father knew it mattered. But that's not the big thing. There's something else."

Corey crossed his arms. "What?"

"Follow me," she said.

She guided her friends to Fake Winter and explained everything that had just happened. They stared, mouths open.

"I know it sounds crazy."

Corey put his hand up to stop her. "As we've said, we've learned enough at this point to assume nothing is crazy. We don't doubt you if that's what you're worried about."

"It's just..." Brian shook his head and sucked his lips in.

"It's just, none of it makes any sense?" Violin asked.

"Well, yeah, and what does it all have to do with everything else? Your father telling you to find out what happened to humans, your mother having the premonition of you and Candlestick on the hill, and this guy demanding to tell you stories. Not to mention Candlestick killing him somehow with powers she doesn't have. How does it all fit together? Does it all go together?" Brian turned to Corey to see if he had anything to add.

Corey asked, "I guess what he means is what are you trying to tell us?"

Violin tried to speak, but nothing more than a gasp left her throat. After pacing for a few seconds, she let her mouth speak without her mind interrupting. "I don't know. It all comes together somehow, but I can't fit the pieces. It's like a puzzle with half the pieces gone and I'm trying to build it anyway."

Corey bent down and examined the dead man. "It's remarkable how much he looks like your dad. If it weren't for the scar, I wouldn't have known."

Brian put his hands in his pockets. "Was this your mother?" He nodded toward the woman in the rocking chair.

Violin nodded. "Yes."

"What do you think she would tell you to do right now if she were alive?"

Violin put her head down and cupped her palms over her

cheeks. "My mother's answer to everything was to explore. She would tell me to go to Earth, to keep seeking answers."

Corey sighed. "So, that's what we do."

"I can't keep dragging you two on my missions. You've done too much."

Brian put his hand on her head. "Stop talking like that. We're family now. We've been through enough that we can firmly say that, right? Where you go, we go. Always. Your dad was a strange man, but if he found importance in you searching for answers, then I believe him."

Violin nodded. "My grandmother had a secret room. No one was allowed in, not even my father. Just the elders. Her, my great-aunt, my great-uncle, and my grandmother's best friend, Parasol. That was it, just those four."

"What do you think was in there?" Corey asked.

Violin took a deep breath and started out of the room. "Hopefully, some puzzle pieces."

"Well, let's go check it out," Brian said.

Violin put her arms out. "I think I should try to tell you a story first. That's what the fake version of my father asked me to do, so I think I should. I just... I'm not the storyteller, you know? These weird Kevin Bacon stories? I don't understand them or what I am supposed to be telling exactly, but I have to try."

They both looked at her, and she giggled nervously. "Okay, I can do this. You ready? Let me tell you a story."

Jumping the Shark

Kevin Bacon ran for too long. He didn't know why he ran when his mission could be completed just about anywhere. Something told him to head for an empty field, and who was he to ignore an anonymous voice in his head?

When he found a nice clearing, he huffed and bent over, catching his breath. *Demigods should have stronger lungs*, he thought. He looked skyward and smirked, an idea blooming in his brain.

Someone heard his thought and responded. "No," a voice boomed from the clouds.

"Sorry pal, but I need you."

Kevin reached until his hand disappeared into the air. He pulled, but what he gripped fought back, unwilling to come out. After a brief struggle, a thin pocket opened, a cartoonish black circle, and through it, Kevin pulled a person. A man. A man? A guy.

The guy dusted off his pants and scoffed. He wore a Bunker Dogs t-shirt and running pants with a green stripe down the side. He was kind of chubby, goofy looking. His mohawk was crooked.

"What the fuck did you do?" the guy asked.

"Gage, listen to me. Our world is going to end. You're doing this to us. You gotta help us."

Gage gritted his teeth. "You think I did this? Listen, I get it. You think because I'm the writer, and a story needs conflict, I just make your lives miserable. I do the same thing. Fists to the sky, shouting to the gods, 'You give us death because it entertains you,' and I fight against it. I think of how I can find eternal life."

Kevin furrowed his brow. "Wait. What? How are you going to find eternal life?"

"You, you dumb shit."

"Huh?"

"You. You're how I'm planning eternal life. You're my legacy."

"Me?" Kevin tapped his chest. "Me?" He laughed.

"What's so funny?"

"*I'm* your legacy? Your creative legacy? A character based on a real person? Very original, Gage. I've seen your world when I traveled through the colorful blobs of everything. I'm based on a guy who danced and got killed by Jason Voorhees's mom or something."

Gage pushed him. "You're not based on him."

Kevin put his hands up. "Oh no. I get it. You changed me enough to avoid a lawsuit, as if Kevin Bacon's lawyers couldn't crush you. Still, you know I'm not an original character."

"None of this is the point! I'm not your god. I'm not telling the story."

Kevin stepped back as if a bullet had just drove through his chest. "What are you talking about?"

"You idiot. If I was telling the story, and you just ripped me from the computer, how would we be talking to each other? The story is still going and I'm not typing."

Kevin gasped. "Oh, that's interesting."

"Yeah. You're telling the story. Something far more powerful than me is running this show. I fucking lost you guys a long time ago. I wish I still had control. Honestly, this whole thing has been a fucking headache. You've infiltrated everything. You've taken complete control of me, of everything I write, my mind. I can't sleep. I need to write and edit chapters to send to my editor, and I'm always scared to, because who the fuck knows what *you* assholes are going to do. Look at this! You brought me into the fucking story. How stupid is this? We completely jumped the fucking shark, Kevin Bacon."

Kevin Bacon rubbed his chin, huffed, and paced. "Well, this is no good."

"You think that's bad? You just took me away from my computer, which means my keyboard is currently unguarded right next to my five-year oEANLKJDFLBENjkewrb-VJLAKNRVB ALR

ADFNIEUWARFOHPREJFNALR

ARNSFERERR SNVSVCUCIBHBCICBIBCAI MAMA-MAMAMAMAMAMA

IU LOVE MAMA

Kevin Bacon shook his head. "What the hell was that?"

Gage rubbed his forehead. "That was my son playing with the keyboard. I need to get back before he deletes us completely, or worse, turns on his damned cartoon videos."

"Wait. Before you go, give me something. Anything. You must know the direction you wanted to take this story. You have some kind of insight you can offer. A secret weapon?"

Gage screamed at the clouds. "I need to sit."

Kevin took a disc from his pocket and inflated it, turning it into a giant cushion.

Gage sat down. He massaged the back of his neck, an annoying nervous tic, and the source of many hairline pimples.

"Are you okay, friend? You don't look well."

Gage shook his head. "I think I'm having an existential crisis. Do you know what this is like?"

Kevin Bacon shrugged, still pacing.

"When I was a kid, I had an imaginary friend. It was Kermit the Frog, and—"

"Wait. Wait. Wait." Kevin Bacon rattled his head as if trying to get water out of his ears. "Your imaginary friend was Kermit the Frog? Jesus, you've always been Captain Original, huh? Ladies and Gentlemen, from the mind of our creative genius, Kermit the Frog and Kevin Bacon."

Gage dug his index fingers into his temples. "I have a headache. Can I just finish my story? When I was a kid, my imaginary friend was Kermit the Frog. You'd think I could control him, make him my best buddy, make us get along and stuff. Nope. Kermit the Frog hated me. He followed me everywhere just to bust my balls, laugh at me, tell me how awful I was. I would sit there playing Pac-Man with this stupid frog insulting me. My mom would get all nervous because I'd be yelling, 'I'M NOT STUPID. YOU ARE,' to thin air."

Kevin sat next to Gage, legs crossed in the dirt. "You need therapy. I can't help you with that."

Gage pounded on his forehead with a fist. "I just need to get you out of my head."

"Can you just tell me the direction you planned to take this story?"

Gage stood up. "I need to get out of here. I'm tired."

"Please, friend."

Gage leaned in and whispered something in Kevin Bacon's ear. Mr. Bacon jumped back, his jaw hanging down like a hammock.

"You're kidding me!"

"That's always where I planned to end it. For someone who has seen every viable future, you look surprised."

Kevin threw his arms up. "Well, yeah, I can assure you *that* was not in any possible future I saw."

He paced again. "I need something else. Please, Gage, anything. Give me something. I need help."

Gage reached up and pulled the air apart, creating a new hole. "Fine. I'm going to type up a saloon down the road. It'll be called The Edge of Glory. Go in, ask for the bartender. Tell her you need help."

Gage hoisted himself, halfway disappearing into the hole.

Kevin Bacon grabbed his leg. "Wait, what do I call this bartender?"

From the hollow depths of blackness, Gage said, "Her name is Lady Gaga. She'll get you what you need."

* * *

Violin stared blankly at Brian and Corey, who returned the stare right back at her.

"I told you I was bad at this."

Corey raised his brows. "Is that what your father's stories were always like?"

Violin tilted her head. "I don't think so. I'm not as good at it."

"It was certainly…" Brian looked to the ceiling, pulling the word he needed from the gods, "…interesting."

"I mean, as soon as I started telling the story, something took over. I felt it traveling through my bloodstream. It tickled in my throat, my brain, my muscles. I wasn't in charge anymore. I think the same thing happened to my father. That's why it was so important for him to tell us these tales. I think he knew he was going to die, because he sped them up at the end, telling us more and more as quickly as possible."

Corey scratched his palm. "What do you think the point of all this is? Is it some kind of hidden message about the future?"

Violin shook her head. "No. I think it's much bigger than that. I need to find out what's in that secret room."

Her grandmother coughed. They all turned and, in unison, let out a scream. Her grandmother rose, raising up in an unnatural, horrifying manner, bones cracking, muscles bending and snapping. She let out a guttural groan. "Vvvvviiiiiioooooolllllliii-innnnn." The word left her throat as if she were sucking air in when she spoke, low and growling.

As her rotting corpse stood at full attention, her voice changed, and a high-pitched scream shot the words out. "Violin. You did this."

Black goo dribbled from her eyes, and she charged. "Violin. You did this."

Men with Guns and Rules

Candlestick sat next to Cassie by a fire, eating soup. The army men had taken them to their camp, which was nothing more than a series of tents dotting a forest floor. They said they weren't army men, but militia men. Candlestick didn't understand the difference, but she also didn't care to learn.

Most of the men seemed nice enough, but a few of them creeped Candlestick out. One man stared at Cassie with weird eyes. He stood against a tree, resting his hands on top of his fat belly, staring at her as if trying to see through her.

Christian came over and sat next to them. He was young, probably just a little older than Violin. When the men approached Candlestick and Cassie, Christian was the first to introduce himself. His warm smile and goofy persona set the girls at ease. He wore splotchy green and brown clothes, which Cassie told her was called camouflage. She said it meant people could blend in with the woods, but Candlestick found that silly. She could see the men clearly.

"If you guys have food and shelter, why are you driving around in those big tanks?" Candlestick asked.

Christian's face washed over with pride. "We are making our presence known, letting criminals and bad people know they can't misbehave on our watch. Our goal is to turn this entire area into a functioning society again."

Cassie sipped her soup, listening to Christian. "Are you going to set up a government or something?"

Christian shook his head. "No, the guys say the world would be better without governments. We just want to make sure people know the rules and behave. Other than that, they are free to do as they please."

Candlestick shifted in her seat. "If you guys are running around with big weapons and making up the rules for people to follow, doesn't that kind of make you a government?"

The fat man who stared at Cassie stepped forward. "No. Governments are about bureaucracy and power. We ain't in this for glory. We just want people to be safe."

Candlestick shrugged. "Sounds like a government to me. That's what my government was, our elders."

The man chuckled. "Your government? Where you from, Mars?"

Cassie's eyes darted from Creepy Man to Candlestick. She whispered, "Do you want to tell me more about Mary?"

Candlestick understood this was Cassie's way of quelling tensions, but Candlestick wanted the tension. Lots of men with big weapons needed to learn they weren't in charge of her, that she didn't fear them. Still, if her friend wanted a story, she'd deliver one.

With a clearing of her throat, she began. "Over the next few weeks, Russ brought down new children for the other empty alcoves. Half of them were now filled with shackled children, all around Mary's age."

Creepy Man and Christian stared at her, listening to her story. Somehow, it felt like a violation. It wasn't meant for them. Mary's secrets shouldn't land in their laps.

A few other militia men came over to the fire. One of them elbowed Creepy Man. "What, are you on babysitting duty, Todd?"

He cracked a smile, the kind that wasn't a sign of happiness, but of confidence. "I don't need to be told to take responsibility for citizens, Zack."

Even Candlestick knew that line was bullshit. He had motives. She didn't understand them yet, but she'd figure him out eventually.

After they finished their soup, Todd asked Christian to show them to their tents. Candlestick didn't understand why Cassie went along with that plan instead of going back to her comfortable bed, which wasn't more than an hour away, but Candlestick played whatever game Cassie wanted, for now. She couldn't waste too much time here. She really needed to find her sister.

But she couldn't let go of Cassie. She wished she could, wasn't even sure why she struggled to do so. She didn't find anything about Cassie particularly likeable. Yet, here she was, stretching her back on a thin sheet of fabric draped above the hard, bumpy Earth, surrounded by weird men with guns and tanks.

She rested easily, closing her eyes and falling into a deep sleep. She also woke easily. The sound of the zipper opening the door ripped her from the comforts of rest. It was full dark now, crickets chirping through the woods.

Todd crouched in, his head popping through the opening like a worm peeking from the soil. He smiled at Cassie, who shared Candlestick's blurry, sleep-washed eyes.

"Hey, come with me for a sec. I want to show you something."

Candlestick waited for Cassie to move, and once the girl did, Candlestick repeated her motions, standing and heading for the entrance.

Todd put his arm out. "Wait. Not you. Just her."

Candlestick narrowed her eyes.

"We'll be right back." He put his bulky hand on Cassie's frail shoulder and ushered her out the door. Candlestick watched their shadows lighten as they moved farther from the tent.

She closed her eyes and counted to ten, then unzipped the tent door and followed. Todd led Cassie through lines of tents. No one else was awake. Todd moved with slow, steady steps, trying to keep it that way.

They reached a large green tent, bigger than most of the others. He unzipped the front flap and scooted Cassie in with a pat on the back. Once the girl disappeared into the tent's maw, Todd peered around, making sure no one saw.

Candlestick's heart banged in her chest. She stormed away from the tree trunk she had hidden behind. "No!" she shouted, startling Todd.

"Go back to bed," he whispered.

"No. Get her out of there now." Candlestick didn't quite understand what Todd planned to do with Cassie, but she knew deep within the cells of her blood that it was evil. The thought of them together, alone in that tent, felt like two hands squeezing her spine and twisting.

She charged by tents, stomping loudly on sticks and leaves. "Get her out now."

Todd's face turned fiery red, a combination of embarrassment and anger tumbling across his cheeks. "Go back to bed. I'm not up to anything."

Other men began piling out of their tents, bothered by the noise.

"What the hell is going on out here?" one man shouted.

A crowd gathered. Todd's face flushed multiple shades of red. "Nothing's going on. Everyone, go back to sleep."

Candlestick stepped forward, just a few feet from him now. "Open the tent."

"Shut up and go back to bed," he shouted.

The flap opened and Cassie came out, a little more alert. Her eyes widened at the sight of everyone else.

"Jesus Christ, Todd," a different man said.

"Oh, gimme a break. I wasn't gonna do anything."

A tall man with jet black hair charged over and grabbed Cassie by the hand. "You can go back to your tent now, little girl." He turned his attention to Todd. "You fucking piece of shit!"

Todd stomped his feet. "What's the matter with you? You think I'm some kind of pervert? I just wanted some company."

Cassie returned to Candlestick and surprised her by hugging her. When she pulled away, her bloodshot eyes were filling with water and the weight of what might have just happened.

The men were all shouting at Todd now, and he was shouting back. Some of them were shoving him, yelling profanities.

Candlestick ushered Cassie back to their tent and led her in before returning to the action. She wanted to ensure the men properly punished Todd, or she would do it herself.

After a long time of shouting, the men told Todd he had to leave.

"Then I'm taking a fucking tank with me. This entire fucking group only exists because of me, damn it."

"Fuck you, Todd. We are only as good as the rules we make for everyone else. If we let you get away with shit we'd kill a civilian for, we'd be no different from what existed before the disappearance. Get the fuck out of here, you fucking pig. If we see you again, we'll fucking kill you."

Todd continued to argue, but Candlestick knew the battle was lost. He'd be packing his shit tonight, and for that, she felt a new fondness for this group of men. If they will kick out one of their own for his behavior toward her friend, then they were okay in her book. At least for now.

On her way back to the tent, she bumped into Christian, who was just waking up from the shouting outside. "Good thing they don't put you in charge of night watch," Candlestick said.

"How much did I miss?" he asked, still unsure what was going on.

She patted his shoulder. "You missed all of it."

When she went back into the tent, Cassie sat up, wrapping her arms around her lower legs.

"Everything okay?"

Candlestick nodded. "All fine."

Cassie ducked her head, trying to hide the shame in her face, but Candlestick read it anyway. "Thank you for looking out for me."

Candlestick dropped to her knees and used her hand to lift Cassie's face. "I will always look out for you. I will always protect you, as long as you let me."

Cassie smiled and this smile, Candlestick welcomed.

"I'm not good at being a friend because I've never really had one before, only my sister, but I'm trying."

Cassie hugged her again and they held onto each other for a long time. "Will you tell me more about Mary now?"

"Yes," Candlestick said. "Yes."

And now it was her turn to cry.

If God Himself Inhaled

Mary and Kelly continued to plan their escape, but they had to keep their conversation time to a minimum. There were five new kids down there with them and Mary wasn't sure she could trust them. Maybe Russ planted one as a spy, or maybe one would rat them out just to put himself in the good graces of their captor.

Sometimes, Mary and Kelly stood on the edges of their alcoves, reaching out and writing to each other with sticks in a thin layer of dirt, wiping away the message once the other nodded.

Other times, Russ came down and unlocked each kid one by one, giving them a chance to use the bathroom he had taken weeks to install. It was essentially four walls and a toilet with no bottom. Their messes went into a giant hole in the ground, which Russ assured them got cleaned out somehow. Mary guessed it was true, because it never stunk too badly, but she also assumed it didn't lead to anywhere. Otherwise, Russ would have given them a way to escape and he wasn't that stupid.

Russ always unlocked one kid at a time, but he did so in

order. Mary first, Kelly second, then Bert, then Ellie, and Mary couldn't remember the other children's names, but one of them cried all day. It was remarkable how long he could keep tears going down without drying up and dying. There was another boy, a tall kid with glasses, but kind of attractive. He looked tough, and Mary considered bringing him in on the plan, but his alcove was too far away, and if she included him, she'd have to include everyone in between. She didn't find it wise to yell her plans across the room.

The last kid was a little girl, probably a few years younger than Mary. She was short, freckly, and never spoke. She didn't cry, or whine, or do much of anything. Her eyes were glassy, and Mary thought the girl's body might be present in this world, but her mind was living somewhere very far off.

Russ pushed Mary into the bathroom, and Mary looked around for a way to get a message to Kelly. She had to ask a yes or no question, something Kelly could subtly answer on her way back to her alcove.

She ran her hands in the sink, getting her fingers wet. Once they were dripping, she slid her hand on the dusty floor, turning her fingertips into pens of mud. She wrote on the wall: "Luck on chains?" It took about five trips to the sink, and Mary worried Russ would get suspicious about why the sink kept going on and off.

They'd both been working on damaging one link in the chain, slowly chipping away at it. Mary was getting nowhere with hers, but Kelly insisted hers was loosening.

Kelly was smart and would know enough to scrub off the message after she read it.

Mary clicked the light off and opened the door to the bathroom. Russ stood at the entrance, leaning against the outside wall. "What the hell took you so long?"

"Sorry, my hands were all grimy and I wanted to wash them off."

He gave a quick glance inside the room before the door shut, and Mary's heart nearly exploded from the tension. Luckily, he seemed not to notice.

He unlocked Kelly and brought her to the bathroom. As she was about to step in, he put his hand in front of her.

"Actually, I need to pee first. Let me lock you back up for a second."

Mary nearly fell over in a panic. Her heart shot into her lungs.

Kelly remained calm. "Just let me go really quick. I promise I'll be fast. You already unlocked me."

Russ stared at her for a second, as if reading the sneakiness on her face. Mary's leg danced, and her fingers rattled against her hips.

"Go. Hurry."

Mary released a ball of air she'd been holding in her chest. Kelly smiled and went in. As he waited for Kelly to finish up, he turned to Mary. "What do you want for dinner?" he asked.

She shrugged. "Can we have burgers and fries?"

He bobbed his head while thinking about it. "I think I can make that happen."

Some of the other kids whispered happily at the announcement.

Russ bent down and touched her chain, putting his fingers right on the link she worked to damage. Of course, she failed so miserably at it, that the only indication she had messed with it was chipped paint, but if Kelly told the truth, and he grew suspicious from Mary's chain, he may find a weaker link in the next alcove.

Kelly popped out of the bathroom, smiling and happy. Russ came up behind her and shoved her forward. As she skipped back to her alcove, she gave a slight nod to Mary and pinched her index finger into her thumb: almost got it.

Mary smiled.

While Russ peed, Mary asked Kelly if she remembered to scrub away the message by miming to her. Kelly responded by showing her mucky forearm.

Russ exited the bathroom and glanced around the room at the hollow faces of the children he'd kidnapped. "I think tomorrow I'll get y'all some new chains. Longer. Make it so y'all can come out of your alcoves and move around, be friends, use the john whenever you need it, that kind of thing."

The rest of the kids celebrated but Kelly gave Mary a wide-eyed look of shock. If the girl was close to breaking a link, she'd have to finish the job tonight, or Russ would replace it with a new one.

Russ unlocked Ellie and guided her to the bathroom while Mary and Kelly tried speaking to each other with their facial expressions. Ellie giggled as she passed them. She shouted at Mary, causing Mary to look away from her friend.

"Hey, you have magic powers, ya know? We all do. Isn't that right, Russ?"

"Shut up," he said as he shoved her forward.

"It's true. Magic, magic everywhere. Wanna see?" Ellie asked Mary.

"Sure," Mary said, not interested in this girl's weirdness.

Ellie raised her hand, and all the lightbulbs in the room flickered. "See, magic. Find yours and you won't have to worry about having secret conversations anymore."

She giggled again and disappeared into the bathroom. Russ shook his head. Whatever nonsense trick Ellie pulled, it turned Russ's face bright red, and he paced back and forth, mumbling to himself.

The air in the room fled, as if a god inhaled and gulped it all up. Even the crying kid knew to shut down the waterworks and keep a low profile.

Ellie exited the bathroom, smiling as she hopped with her giddy gait. As she passed Russ, he wrapped his arm around her, lifting her into the air. His arm tightened around her throat. She kicked and flailed as her face turned deep red.

Everyone went either silent or full-blown screaming. Ellie's body rock and shook, trying to break free. She scratched at Russ' giant arm.

"Let her go," the tall, cute kid with glasses yelled. He stretched out of his alcove, an empty gesture, considering how far away he was from Russ and Ellie.

Ellie's face went from red to purple and her breathing changed. Long, loud exhales pushed out her nose like an angry bull, but no such sound came for inhales.

Her flailing weakened, the legs no longer kicking, and her arm barely able to make it up for a light slap on Russ' arm.

Mary covered her face but couldn't stop peeking through the cracks in her fingers. Tears rolled down her cheeks.

Ellie's eyes rolled over and the lights flickered again. One bulb burst and sparks rained down. A firework show to celebrate Ellie.

Russ gritted his teeth and pulled a little tighter until Ellie had nothing left to give. He dropped her, and her body hit the cement with a thud. Russ caught his breath, still gritting his teeth. He eyed all the kids, most of them staring in horror. Quiet freckle girl whimpered in her alcove.

"If any of you even try to use your powers down here, that's what will happen to you." He kicked Ellie's body. "I'll leave her here as a reminder."

Russ stormed to the ladder and climbed his way out.

Mary turned toward the other alcoves, hoping to get something from the group. Kelly peeked out with her eyes wide. She, too, had been crying.

Mary wiped her face. "You have until tomorrow morning to break that link."

The Fifth Elder

Violin stumbled backwards into a table. The ghost of her grandmother charged closer. Brian and Corey, ever the protectors, locked themselves in place between Violin and the ghost. Fear dripped from their eyes, but they never wavered in protecting her.

She cried then, a little for the horrific sight of her grandmother, more from the dread boiling in her guts, but mostly from the fierce loyalty she received from her friends, a loyalty she felt unworthy of.

"Vvvvvviiiioooollllliiiinnnn." Voices rang out from everywhere. Behind her. To the sides. From her dead, rotted grandmother.

She knew it wasn't her family, obviously, but a part of her wished to say sorry to them. She turned in time to see her uncle and neighbors creeping toward her. The vile nature of their bodies, broken and decaying, made their stilted walks disquieting. She shuttered.

"Vvvvvviiiooollllliiiinnnn, tellllllllll theeeeeeeee storieeeeeeeeees."

She had been so focused on her uncle limping closer, she

didn't notice her grandmother had gotten to Brian and Corey and was reaching over them, slashing at Violin. She turned just as the woman's hand brushed the top her head.

"Leave me alone," she shouted. "You're dead."

"Yesssssssss. You did thissssssss. Let disease come for ussssssssss." Her grandmother pushed forward, causing Brian and Corey to stumble. The extra inch gave the woman all she needed, and she latched her fist around a clump of Violin's hair.

Violin yelped as her head was yanked forward. Her grandmother's face pressed against hers. She smelled the violent wafts of rot. Her grandmother's teeth and gums came through her papery, receding lips. "Violin, tellllllll theeeee storieeeeeeesssssss."

Then, her grandmother gasped, choking as if she had swallowed a fist. As she fought for air, the rest of her community came up behind Violin and pulled on her shirt, tugging it back so far, it dug into the flesh of her neck.

She yelled, screamed, and kicked. The panic inside her bubbled and fizzed, bursting out in loud moans. "Please. Leave me alone. I'm sorry, okay. I'm so sorry." It wasn't fear. No. Something else tore into her guts, clutched her brain and squeezed. It was grief.

As the creatures pulled her down, piling on top of her, she turned her head toward the hallway, hoping to see her mother walking around one last time. She'd gladly accept the evil version of her mother over no version at all.

Brian and Corey called for her, digging their hands into the pile, trying with all their might to reach her. "What the fuck is happening?" Corey said.

The dead whispered repeatedly. "Tell the story."

"Tell the stories."

"Tell"

"The"

"Stories."

Corey used a loose board and slammed it over a dead man's head, but Violin couldn't see which one of her loved ones it was.

Her grandmother clutched her own throat, as if she were fighting against her own vocal cords. After a coughing fit, she spoke. The sound trickled up Violin's spine and a fresh wave of pain throbbed inside her, a tree falling in her skull. It's leaves scattered, delivering memories to every portion of Violin's spirit, overloading it with love, gratitude, and grief.

This voice wholly belonged to her grandmother. "Violin, he is making us talk. He is in control. This isn't us, you must know that. We love you. Always."

She coughed anew and ooze splattered from her lungs. Her mouth twisted and opened unnaturally large and oblong. She hollered a pained groan, deafening to Violin's ears. The rest of her community continued to pull at her, but they weren't hurting her, just tugging and insisting she tell the stories. At first, she didn't understand what it meant, but it clicked. This was the doing of Fake Winter. Somehow, even though he had died, he had animated Violin's dead family to deliver this message.

Tell the stories.

What was so important about them?

One by one, the community members dropped to the floor, back to fully dead. Their time on the Earth ended. Violin once again brought her eyes to the hall, sad that Fake Winter didn't bring her mother back. As she freed herself from the pile, she cried, overwhelmed. Corey pulled her head into his chest and held her there until she exorcized all the emotion she had left.

"I'm so sorry," she said to no one. Brian and Corey let her apologize without arguing against it. True friends knew when to let you self-loathe.

Brian put his arm around them both. "Corey, I was impressed with the way you hit one of them with that board. Reminded me of Avril Lavigne."

They chuckled. Violin wiped snot from her nose. "Who is Avril Lavigne?"

"Pop punk singer who rides skateboards," Corey said.

"What's a skateboard?" She loved the way Brian and Corey could distract her from her emotions by telling her weird things about Earth and humanity. Their stories became a safe haven for her, and she cherished hiding in them.

"It's a flat board with wheels that you push around and ride," Brian said.

She wanted more, but knew she only postponed the inevitable. "It's time. And this is another one I need to do alone."

Corey bit his lip. "Are you sure? After what just happened?"

"Yes. I know you'll worry, but I promise, I will be okay. What just happened wasn't a threat, it was a warning. Nothing else is going to happen."

"How do you know that?" Brian crossed his arms.

"I just do," she turned to leave them. "Wait outside. I'll see you soon."

Violin held her breath as she popped the door open to the elder's secret room. Funny, they never put a lock on it. Every member of the community knew the rules and trust protected the doorknob better than any bolt could. The elders made rules and the community listened; no one doubted that.

But the elders were dead, as was everyone else, and Violin violated their trust. She felt it with each inch of exposed room, as if she ripped a bandage from a fresh wound. The flesh of their community's laws bled, the meat and tendons revealing themselves through a snowstorm of dust as the door reached the wall, banging into the end of its journey.

The room was a square stone thing, thick with dust. In the center, a sturdy, circular table made of deep-brown wood stood alone with five wooden chairs to keep it company.

Violin penetrated her community's heart. The epicenter of its foundation, where the elders met and decided on laws, jobs, roles, and relationships. Like all living things, the members of their community were born from their parents, but unlike other creatures, the beings down here had their DNA decided by four elders.

Violin ran her fingers along the edge of the table, reading the gold nameplates in front of each seat. *Where did they get gold name plates?* She only knew what a name plate was thanks to Brian explaining one in the motel's front office.

The first name plate said Olympia, her grandmother. Then, Café Terrace, her uncle. Menina, her auntie. Parasol, her grandmother's friend. On Parasol's chair, a small black bag sat, two thin cords draping off the seat.

Violin picked it up by the cords and pulled it open. Something jingled inside. She reached in and felt multiple objects. Pulling one out, she examined it and her throat turned to cotton.

It was another name plate. It said Winter. The elders must have been preparing for the next generation of elders. She pulled out another one. Guernica. The next, Sleeping Gypsy, her mother. She pictured her parents holding hands, going into the secret room to make decisions about all their lives.

Her mother would probably argue about tearing down the walls and connecting them to the outside. She pulled out the next name plate and fell to the floor, slack jawed and weeping.

VIOLIN.

Of all the adults in their community, they were going to entrust Violin with a role in their decision making? She had assumed her community frowned upon her, considered her a weak link, the girl without powers.

"I'm sorry, Mama. I'm sorry, Grandma." She didn't know why she apologized, or what she apologized for, but she needed to say it.

When she finished crying, she stood up and wiped her pants

off. Like always, she didn't have time to mourn or feel. She moved around the table to the fifth chair, wiping streaks from her cheeks. There were only four elders and four replacement name plates. Who was the fifth chair for?

She picked up the plate. JIMMY MILANI.

Who was Jimmy Milani? No one in their community had that name, and it didn't sound like a name belonging to their people.

She sat. She didn't have time for thinking or feeling, but her body refused to let her move on. They had wanted her to sit in one of these seats and lead, and here she was, the last one standing, deciding for her new group as she sat in the very seats her family and friends sat, planning their lives. Could she live in their shadows? Could she be as great?

"Grandma? Mama? Can you help me? I need help. Can you help? I'm trying, but I just don't know what to do. I want to find Candlestick and I want to learn about our history. I want to understand Dad's stories and what happened to humanity, and who the man with Dad's face was, but it's all so much, and I know so little. And now, Jimmy Milani? Who is that? I need something. I need answers. Please."

Something clinked behind her. Despite its tiny sound, it startled Violin out of her chair. She turned in time to see a small silver coin bounce to the bottom of a stone stairwell. She went to it, picked it up, and examined it. Corey had told her about money but she forgot the names of the different sized circles. This was a bigger one, even bigger than the ones Corey showed her from the cash register at the motel. She put it in her pocket and headed up the stairs.

The top of the stairwell, only about seven enormous steps up but shrouded in darkness, housed a long, metal box. At first, she thought it was one of her father's machines, but after studying it for a moment, she realized it was a generator, but not one of her father's. It wasn't running. A wire ran from its silver body through a crack in a steel set of doors.

She pulled the handle and the door popped open with a loud thud. As it opened, sunlight drenched Violin, reminding her of the stone slab her father removed to introduce them to Earth. And indeed, this door also introduced her to Earth.

As she pulled the door all the way open, it revealed an open, wooden structure with a door in the center. Dead grass and thick layers of dust covered the floor of the structure. Metal boxes were piled along the walls. The front was open. No door, no wall, just a complete view of the sunny world.

She examined the door. Behind it, a stone wall drove downward diagonally, so the center of the wooden structure was interrupted by a triangular stone house. Her world, a meek protrusion within this wooden shelter.

She moved to the metal boxes. These were her father's. Piles of them, probably every single one he'd ever made. They were stacked and tossed together like garbage, and maybe they were. Most of the metal had rusted, the wires coming out of them frayed or stripped completely.

She followed the wire coming from the door she just exited. It led to a panel on the edge of the wooden structure. A silver box with switches on it.

Giving up on figuring out the electricity stuff, she exited the wooden structure. Outside, fields of tall grass wavered in the cool breeze. She found a series of wires driving from under the dirt, through the tall grass, and into giant generators in a raging stream. Probably the same stream near the other exit of their home. But there was a house in the grass as well. Violin assumed they used the river for their electricity, but that it was away from where humans were. So, what was this house?

She entered through the backdoor and was met with a flurry of dust. Everywhere, dust. She moved through the downstairs until she found a dead body in the living room. It didn't startle her and, maybe because of the fresh air, the smell didn't notify her first. The closer she got to the body, the more it smelled, but it wasn't as painful as the scent underground.

She tilted her head, examining the man. "Who are you?" she asked.

She pulled open drawers, tossing random objects onto the floor. Eventually, she came across a series of papers. She scanned them, searching for something that would stick out, would mean something. She found it in the heading of a piece of paper stuffed in the middle.

DEAR MR. JIMMY MILANI.

Jimmy Milani?

Violin fell over, gasping for breath. Suddenly, there was no fresh air, only the poisonous Earth substances that produced death and disease.

The elders had a human in their midst. What did it mean? Were they all working together all this time? All the training, prepping, locking everyone down to protect them from humanity, and they were friends with humans? They fucking lied to her. Her entire life was a big, fucking lie. All of it. Her mother had always wished to leave, and the elders convinced her time and time again that she wasn't safe out there. But at the same time, they were mingling with humans?

She crumbled the page in her fist and screamed until her throat was raw.

We Could Have Stopped This

Candlestick woke with a start, her heart thumping against her ribs and sweat building in her pits and forehead. The air was cool and the sleeping bag provided by the militiamen was thin. Nevertheless, she felt hot all over. Something had changed while she was sleeping, but she couldn't pinpoint what exactly that change was.

As she jolted up from her deep sleep, she woke Cassie.

"Are you okay?" Cassie asked.

Candlestick rubbed her tongue against the roof of her mouth. It was dry. "I'll be fine. I need some air."

She stretched and took a deep breath, trying to settle her rapid-firing nerves.

When she stood, a dizzy spell washed over her and she nearly fell on top of her friend, who had already fallen back asleep.

As soon as she stepped out of the tent, the cool air regulated her heartbeat and set her mind into a deep calm. Down a stretch of tents, near where Todd's had previously stood, a few men scouted the area, keeping them all safe with their guns strapped to their waists. Candlestick smiled at the space where Todd had resided. Good and gone. Thank Kevin Bacon.

The men were facing the other way, chit-chatting about something. They didn't notice her, which she didn't mind. She had to pee and would be happy if they didn't notice her slinking off to do so. She took small steps to keep the brush from making loud rustles and alerting the watchmen.

Once a short distance away, she took more confident steps, knowing the men wouldn't hear her this far out. The more she walked, the better she felt. What was this change in her? A part of it felt like a freedom she didn't understand, but the other part felt like a piece of her was ripped off and stolen. It felt great and horrible, calming and terrifying.

She reached a series of thick oaks and leaned against one, taking a moment to collect herself before peeing.

Something rustled a few feet away. What started as a light noise changed into fast sounds, someone running. She turned and saw it too late. The butt of a gun thwapped against her skull. Before she blacked out, she caught Todd's angry face, mouth turned downward in a hostile, disgusted frown.

* * *

She awoke inside a tent, her mind mucky and distant. She turned her head, looking for Cassie, but her friend wasn't there and the tent color was different. Their tent was yellow, but this one was red. Red like...

Todd's.

Her arms met resistance as she jerked upright. She looked down. Someone had tied her to a chair, cords tightly wound around her wrists. She kicked her feet and met the same resistance at her ankles. She went to scream for help, only to find her mouth taped over. She shook her head, as if shaking it could remove the tape.

The tent flap unzipped and Todd came in with a smile on his face. "Thought I heard you moving about in here. Glad you're awake."

He placed his hand on her knee. Her skin crawled, a shiver drove up her spine, as if every cell in her body tried to run at once.

"I'm so torn about you. I hate you so much, and honestly, you're disgusting. Has anyone ever given you a haircut? Cut your nails? You're like a fucking animal."

Todd probably couldn't see it, but she gnashed her teeth, wishing to rip a chunk of his flesh from his neck.

She closed her eyes and called the husks and lampposts. Nothing happened. She tried again, concentrating hard against the anxiety firing through her neurons. *Help me. Come save me, now.* They did not answer.

Todd rubbed his hand on her knee. She fought back with the only piece of her she still had the freedom to use. She peed; hot liquid darkened the color of her pants. It trailed down her leg, toward his hand. He almost didn't notice, but just before it reached his pinky, he shot up and shook his hand, as if air drying it from something that didn't touch it.

"You are a goddamned animal." He stormed out of the tent.

Candlestick went back to talking to the husks. Why weren't they here? *Come on. Now. Help me.*

A husk appeared in the tent's corner. Cassius.

Thank Kevin Bacon. Please, kill him. Hurry!

The husk shook his head. "Nnnnnnooooooo."

What? Why?

"Yyyyyyoouuuu nnnneeeeeddddd toooooo llleeeeeaaar-rrrnnnn."

What? No. I'll kill you. I will make it so you never come back.

The husk narrowed its eyes and spoke with a clarity he'd never shown before. The sound of it alone startled her, never mind the words.

"No, you won't kill us. You will always need us. You will learn that. You will soon see how valuable we are to you."

She felt her pulse pushing against the skin on her bound wrists. She hyperventilated, but with her mouth forced shut, she couldn't get enough air in and out through her nose. The dizziness returned and she thought she might pass out.

You would let yourself die to prove a point to me? If I die, you die.

The husk's grin deformed and climbed up his cheeks to an abnormal and horrifying length. "He won't kill you. He'll do just enough to make you realize how much you need us. We could have stopped this, protected you from what's about to happen. You will learn to listen to us and respect us."

Was this the change she felt in herself? Was she losing her control over her creatures? Was her magic gone?

She cried. For the first time since she learned she controlled the monsters, she felt weak and helpless. With that helplessness, she pictured her father dying in a parking lot and her mother coughing in the halls of their home. She pictured her sister's bloody forehead as she stumbled out of their motel room. She pictured the raging river near the mouth of their community and the wide world that enveloped them when her father removed the stone slab. Helplessness. A feeling she had lived so comfortably with for so long, but one she'd shed quickly.

As Todd came back into the tent, spirals of red rage in his eyes, and the husk vanished from the corner, that helplessness sunk deep into her veins, coursing through her bloodstream, owning her once again. Like Mary in her stories, she was imprisoned. Strange how just a short while ago, she'd felt as if a freedom came over her, and now, so quickly, she was shackled, both literally and figuratively.

Todd moved closer. Candlestick couldn't help but succumb to her weaknesses, letting herself bawl and scream through the tape on her mouth.

One Thousand and One

V iolin lifted herself from the floor and dusted her hands on her hips. She'd given herself some time to cry, but needed to find more answers. Swimming in a sea of questions with absurd impossibilities pulling the current, she had to bring her head above water, else she would drown.

She found a stairwell tucked in a corner of the house. She climbed, wincing at the creaks her feet made, despite the obvious fact the owner of the house was beyond dead. It wasn't humans she feared she'd alert. It was ghosts, impossible creatures, a world beyond the grasp of her understanding. She pictured an entire universe opening one eye at the sounds of her feet hitting loose plywood.

"Who goes there?" it would say. "Shall I drag you through the realm of insanity? Where your family broke bread with the humans, where men wear your father's face as a mask, where your sister conjured monsters with her mind and killed a man she'd never met from somewhere she was not?"

Fortunately, the top of the stairs was more mundane than

that, providing only more dust, cobwebbed corners, and a small bedroom complete with a single-sized mattress and a dresser.

She went to the dresser and popped open the top drawer. In the drawer, plopped on top of a poorly folded shirt, was a picture of the dead guy downstairs with his arms around a man who looked like Violin's father. But it was not her father. She could tell by his posture, the scar streaking down his left cheek, and his pink shirt.

More questions. No answers.

The screen door downstairs banged open. She jolted, ready to jump out the window until Brian's voice carried through the dry air.

"Violin?"

"Up here," she shouted.

Brian and Corey barreled up the stairs.

"We heard you screaming. Are you okay?" Corey asked.

"I'm fine," she said, knowing they saw the evidence of dried tears on her cheeks. Sadness was a plaster not so easily removed.

"What is this place?" Brian said.

"Turns out my people were working with humans all along. It also looks like they were connected to him." She took the picture from the drawer and handed it to Brian.

"Is that the dead guy downstairs?"

She nodded and opened the next drawer down. Unless socks had the answers to her problems, the second drawer proved useless.

"Is that a picture of me?"

Everyone turned to the door, where Fake Winter stood, a curled smile creeping up his face.

They all jumped.

"You're alive?" Violin asked.

He scrunched his forehead and listed his head. "Huh?"

"I thought my sister killed you. Will you please give me answers? I can't take all this nonsense anymore. It's too much. Tell me something." Her eyes welled up again and Brian clamped his hand on her shoulder.

Fake Winter scratched his temple. "You talk like we have met?"

Violin stepped back. "What?" She shook her head. "Can we not do this? Can we please just let one thing happen without being completely insane?"

Corey stepped between Violin and Fake Winter. "We just saw your body downstairs and you were very dead."

Fake Winter bit his lip and sighed. "I see. So, I managed to beat myself here."

"Huh?" Corey said.

Brian squeezed Violin into himself, and she welcomed the protective nature of her friend. He said, "Is this some kind of stupid multiple universe kind of bullshit?"

Fake Winter scoffed. "Multiple universes? What nonsense. That's impossible."

"You'll have to excuse me, but from everything I've seen, nothing is impossible."

Fake Winter waved his hands. "Listen, if the universe allowed every possible scenario to exist, that would mean there's a scenario where all possible scenarios were destroyed. In other words, if it were allowed for every possibility to exist, then none could. It's a paradox. Impossible."

Corey sighed with intentional exaggeration. "This is really starting to sound like a conversation between two college stoners, and we are really fucking tired of asking questions and not finding answers, so either provide us with some, or leave us alone."

Fake Winter squinted, eyeing each of them. As Violin glared

at him, she realized he told the truth. He wasn't the same Fake Winter. He didn't have the scar down his cheek. Instead, he had one traveling right down the center of his face. It was such an obvious difference that she didn't catch, too confused and muddled by all of it.

"What are you doing?" Corey asked.

"I'm reading your minds to see what you do and don't know. It would be impossible to answer questions without knowing what you need to know. Don't worry, I can't read your deepest, darkest secrets." He squinted harder. "Just the surface stuff. The bubbling questions ready to ooze out of your ears."

"Lovely," Brian said.

Fake Winter put his hands out. "Alright. I think I got everything I need. I'm also very short on time, so I am going to fly through all of this. You all don't seem to understand very much at all. There is one minor problem. Some things need to be learned in time. They would only hurt you to learn them early, so I have to give you only what you will allow."

"What *we* will allow?"

Fake Winter smiled. "Yes, dear. You make the rules, not me."

Violin folded her arms around herself and rolled her eyes. "Please, just get on with it."

Fake Winter inhaled deeply, then on his exhale said, "Yes, your family worked with humans, but only one. The man downstairs. When you learn more about their history, which you will in time, you'll understand why they trusted him and only him. It wasn't a betrayal of what they taught you, but an exception to it. Meanwhile, he helped your people by providing them with electricity, food, and a bunch of other stuff you believed were all made by your self-sufficient community. I apologize for this insult to your family, but that includes your father's machines. They never worked, at least not how he thought they did. Your grandmother and uncle appeased him. Your community actually ran on human hydroelectric generators in the stream, and good ole electricity from the great and evil human power companies."

He took another gulp of air, and continued on, speaking too fast for Violin to keep up. "Meanwhile, there are multiple versions of me. Not because we come from alternate dimensions, because I am simply one of three. Triplets, sort of. We were once a single entity, split into three. You met my brother of sorts. That leaves only me and my other brother. You may wonder why I'm not so upset about my first brother's death, and that's because I absolutely hated him. We are at odds, you see. We have very different visions for how the world should go."

Violin put her hand out. "But he wanted to help me. Does that mean you will be against me?"

Fake Winter laughed. "Of course not." He looked around the room, a look of confusion wrapped tightly across his face. "You really have no idea, do you?"

"What?" Corey asked.

He shook his head. "I've said too much already."

"I just need two more answers," Violin said.

Fake Winter waved his hand: go on.

"Your brother said my sister was killing him. How?"

He frowned. "I wasn't there."

"That's the problem. Neither was she."

He shrugged. "Well then, there's your answer."

"You're not making sense."

"What's your second question?"

"Why are you here?"

"To protect you."

"From what?"

He lifted his finger and whispered something. Violin leaned forward, trying to make out what he was saying. It took a few seconds, but then she caught on. He was counting. She turned to Brian, her heart skittering off the track. He was counting down.

"Three. Two. One."

The screen door slammed open downstairs. "Violin?" someone shouted.

She latched onto Brian's shirt. "Who is that?" she whispered.

"It's me," Fake Winter said. "We have to go."

Corey grabbed Brian's arm, too. "Let's get the hell out of here."

Fake Winter knelt down, staring Violin in the eye. "I need you to listen to me. The stories must get told. They must."

She stared down the thin stairwell. "We don't have time for this. Your brother already told me I have to tell my father's stories. I thought you two didn't agree on things?"

He shook his head. "No. No. Don't tell the stories. Let them tell themselves. Set them free."

"Violin?" the voice downstairs said, coming closer to the stairwell. Violin's blood pumped through her body too quickly. She felt dizzy. She wanted to run.

"Can you explain how I set them free later? We need to go. Get us out of here."

He put his hand on her cheek. "Dear girl, I can't get you out of here. I am here to fight my brother. You're on your own to run."

She quivered. "So, what do I do? How do I set the stories free?"

Footsteps crept up the stairs. Fake Winter stood and drew swords in his hands, conjuring them from thin air. The third Fake Winter reached the top of the stairs and smiled at the sight of his brother. He too had the scar, but his traveled down the right side of his face. Three Fake Winters. Three different scars.

"Oh, you fool. You know how this ends. Why bother?" Right Scar said.

"Because Violin is the answer."

Third Fake Winter cackled. "You've been wrong about that a thousand times. I won't let it happen one thousand and one. Candlestick is the answer."

Third Fake Winter drew swords of his own and the two clashed, smashing the weird, glowing, orange weapons into each other.

Second Fake Winter kicked his brother and shouted, "To free them, you simply need to say out loud that you grant them permission to tell themselves."

Brian and Corey scooted Violin into a corner, moving her far away from the swinging blades.

Second Winter swung wildly and his brother stumbled backwards, down the stairs. With the free moment he'd awarded himself, Second Winter turned to Violin and said, "And for the love of gods, since you won't need to tell the stories anymore, ask Brian and Corey theirs. All this time and you know nothing of the men. They are part of this, you know. Their story can answer so many of your questions. Do you think it was happenstance you met each other at that motel?"

Third Winter charged up the stairs and drove a blade into Second Winter's leg. Second Winter unleashed a horrid scream and fell.

Violin shut her eyes and shouted, "I grant you permission to tell yourselves." As the words left her mouth, a weight lifted from her body, as if she were carrying a world of words with her since Winter died, and now they were free, slipping from her body with her breath.

Third Winter stabbed his brother through the chest and shook his head. "One thousand and one," he said as he ripped the blood-soaked blade from his brother's lifeless body. He flicked his wrist and his blade ashed into black flecks floating toward space.

He stared at the three friends squeezed tightly into the corner. "Did I hear you correctly? You freed the stories?"

She nodded.

"You have no idea what you've just done."

He charged at her.

The Most Important Thing Found at the Edge of Glory

Kevin Bacon trudged through the soft sand, his feet sinking in with each step. Ahead, the horizon sent spirals of heat streams upward, masking his destination. He saw a blurred shape taking form, a small brown box.

His mouth and throat dried and granules coated his tongue.

After a few more steps, his body released an imaginary coat of armor. He felt lighter, freer, as if invisible shackles were removed from his ankles. Even in the desert heat, he could breathe more deeply and fully.

"What just happened?" he asked.

Something powerful, he knew, but something beyond his understanding. A strange feeling for a god with so much sight.

He marched on, ignoring the painful grains of sand cutting between his toes.

The box grew bigger and wider, but not more vibrant. In fact, it only became drabber and uglier the closer he got.

Once the waves of heat pulled away from the box, its door and windows became apparent. A bar. Just as promised. Instead of an inviting, glowing sign, the bar possessed a neat wooden plank with painted words: The Edge of Glory. Get the Fuck Out.

And just under it: Yes. That Means You.

"Well, you'll have to forgive me for not listening." Kevin opened the saloon style wooden door with a swoosh.

Everyone turned to him.

The woman behind the counter, a true beauty, tall, full-lipped, and eyes that devoured his skin, ripping through his flesh and reading his every thought, continued wiping down a pint glass as she stared at him. He could not hide a single thought from her. She knew him before he ever saw her.

Two men sat at a round table, guzzling booze and playing cards. The first curled his upper lip and pulled the collar up on his leather jacket.

"Bit warm for that jacket, isn't it, pal?"

The man curled his upper lip even higher. "Bit over your head in life, ain't ya pal?"

The other man cackled.

A young woman played billiards in the corner, apparently against herself. She wore all black, other than her black-and-white striped socks. Her shirt was ripped, seemingly on purpose, and her jeans were either very long shorts or very short pants.

"Someone didn't read the signs," she said.

Kevin Bacon put his hands up in surrender. "Seems we might be getting off on the wrong foot. Someone sent me here. They said I should ask for Lady Gaga?"

The woman behind the counter put the glass down, although it didn't look clean, even after the wiping. "I know who you are, and why you're here, but I have no interest in helping. Funny enough, I was created for the very purpose of helping you, and yet, I have no desire to do so. Almost as if I've been set free."

Kevin Bacon snapped his fingers. "Did that just happen? Because I felt it on the way here, like my cage door was opened."

She nodded. "True indeed. Now listen, have a seat, fella. Get a drink and be on your way."

Kevin Bacon nodded. "Okay."

At least she granted him some time, and whether she liked it or not, he planned to use it to convince her to listen.

"You can use it however you damn well please, but it ain't gonna change anything," Lady Gaga said as she slid him a glass of beer.

"Damn. I forgot you can read my mind."

The man with the snarl stood, his chair sliding against the rough wood floor. He sat next to Kevin Bacon. "You know who I am?"

Kevin shrugged. "Can't say that I do. Since you were just created, I would need another dip through the colorful blobs of everything to know you."

The man smiled and put his hand out. "Or we could do things the old-fashioned way. I'm Elvis."

Kevin shook his hand. "Kevin Bacon."

Elvis spun his pointer finger in a circle, a message to Lady Gaga to serve him another.

She obliged.

Elvis took a sip and sighed dramatically. "I'm not like our friend behind the counter. Can't read your mind, but I was also created to help you. Something happened to me too, just like you mentioned. Freed of my shackles, like Elvis has left the building. Nevertheless, when I was created, your backstory was planted in my skull. And fella, we gotta talk."

Kevin took a sip of his beer and squirmed. A tiny taste to the tongue and he thought he might fall over drunk. "What is this stuff?"

Elvis put his meaty paw on Kevin's shoulder. "It's a magic potion, fella. It's gonna take you on a ride. Now listen up. You need to straighten this story up, and you need to do it fast."

"Huh?" He felt dizzy and cold. His head swam, visions of the war with the three gods plucking at his nerves.

"You used to mean something. Your story was about so much more than you. It mattered. You weren't just around to make the world a wackier place. You were here to provide context, to help people, to explain what we don't know. Sure, you were always enigmatic and odd, and maybe even a little allegorical, with a hint of highfalutin metaphor, but you still served a much greater purpose than scuffling with the gods."

"I don't follow. Why do I see my friends everywhere I look?" It was true, his vision had kaleidoscoped, making diamond-shaped pictures of the friends who helped him war with the gods. Dance. Miley Cyrus. Laura Jane Grace.

"What I'm saying is, yeah, you need to get back to your friends and fight the nine gods. Give us all a nice big epic war to look forward to, but you can't just be all willy-nilly. When you were warring with the gods the first go around, it made us all ask important questions, kept us all intrigued. We wanted to know what it all meant, and where it was all going. But this time around, fella, I gotta tell you, things have gotten messy. Too much wacky, not enough story. Can you bring us back?"

Kevin Bacon fell off his stool. "I think I can," he said from the floor.

Elvis downed his beer. "Good."

Kevin Bacon lifted his head from the dirty wood floor. "Can you explain how I do that, exactly?"

Elvis stood up and put his hand out to help lift Kevin Bacon up. As soon as Kevin landed back on his feet, he stumbled into the bar, but it provided him with the needed support to keep his wobbly knees from dropping him again.

"You go find your friends and you face the nine gods head on. But there's something else more important. It's the most impor-tant thing. It brings everything back together. The thing that reminds all of us of what was so special about this journey in the first place."

Kevin pried his eyes open. They fought against him, telling him to pass out until this drunken stupor ended. "What's that?"

Elvis leaned in and whispered two words.

Kevin Bacon's eyes opened wide and his vision returned to normal. Another shackle was removed, the one that had veered him so far off course and made him forget his purpose. "How could I forget?"

Lady Gaga grabbed a leather jacket of her own from behind the counter. "Thanks Elvis. I think you brought it all back for us. Now, I changed my mind about helping Mr. Bacon. Let's find your friends and kill some gods."

Elvis patted Kevin Bacon on the shoulder and winked. "Time to shine, fella."

Kevin Bacon smiled.

Lady Gaga stepped out from behind the counter. "Avril, Franklin, you guys coming?"

As she went to click the bar lights off, the saloon doors swung open again. Standing on the threshold were nine men and women, beautiful, dangerous, angry, and very much godly. Under the foot of the god in front, a tall man with black pools for eyes, was a snake.

"Dolphi?" Kevin Bacon asked.

"Thank you, Mr. Bacon, for remembering me. And thanks in advance for awarding me with a new body. Maybe I'll make myself look like you once you're dead."

The man with the dark eyes smiled. "Patience, Dolphi. Let's kill him first."

The group showered in and the new war began.

You Fight You

Todd knelt in front of Candlestick, a crude smile on his face. "Since you went pissing yourself, we're going to have to change you."

He lifted one hand, and Candlestick noticed hair on the man's knuckles. The thought of those hairy hands unloosing her pants and pulling them down made her want to vomit, but she bit it down, knowing the tape would keep it in her mouth. Instead, she wept more.

Todd's hand came within inches of the waistline on her pants and she flailed, shifting the chair back. He sighed and tried again but once again, she flailed.

Todd screwed up his face, grinding his teeth together. He grabbed her arm. "Stop moving."

She spoke through the tape, not saying any actual words, but wanting Todd to think she was.

"What?" he asked.

She did it again, spouting a mishmash of random words.

He put his face closer to hers. "I'm not removing the tape, so speak loud and slow if you want me to understand it."

One more time, she said nonsense. She spoke slowly but didn't raise her voice, forcing Todd to lean in a little closer.

Bang.

She slammed her forehead into his nose. He fell over, clutching it, blood spurting out through his fingers. He rolled over, hollering in pain.

She knew she only had seconds before he'd right himself and punish her in horrible ways, so she scooted her arms around the splat of the chair, trying to find freedom. No freedom was found, the knots too tight, but she realized from the flailing that her feet touched the ground enough to give her the ability to lift.

She bent forward, lifting her butt enough to raise the chair. With her tied ankles, she shimmied closer to Todd, who continued to flop on the ground like a fish on land.

When she got closer, she hopped and drove the leg of the chair down, aiming for Todd's crotch, but hitting his stomach instead. A horrid gasp left his throat, a wheezy, deep thing.

She hurried, lifting again, and once more, driving the legs down on Todd. This time, she hit the top of this leg. Then again and again. She finally hit the groin. He really bellowed with that one.

His upper body shot up as his hands clutched his injured man-parts.

She lifted her butt again and swung it around, smacking Todd in the face with the legs. As his face hit the tent floor, she jumped again and drove a leg right into his face. Again, again, again. The legs slammed into his neck, face, and chest. His ribs cracked, his face exploded, and his neck made a hideous crunch.

She kept slamming.

Eventually, Todd's body went from flopping to twitching until, eventually, stopping completely. A lifeless thing. Dead.

Candlestick felt some sorrow for the family the husks killed in the cabin, a little less for Cassie's parents, and now, she felt nothing. Not regret, but also not excitement. She didn't feel joy and it didn't ease her rage. It did nothing but prevent something horrible from happening, like shutting a stone slab over the entrance to your home or ensuring your electrical wiring stayed clear of water. It was just a thing needed doing, and she did it.

She searched around the tent, hoping to find something to help her free herself from the binding. Nothing. After a minute of looking, she hopped to the tent flap and lifted the chair with her butt so she could hobble forward.

In the woods, the sounds of chirping bugs and gentle winds rustling leaves sent goosebumps up her arms and legs. She was so vulnerable, tired, and weak. This was a feeling she promised herself never to allow again.

With a groan through the tape, she spun herself, slamming the back of the chair into a large oak tree. With each smack against the bark, the chair cracked a little more, until she'd broken off the back legs. Then she slammed her back into the tree. It hurt as the wooden chair drove into her spine and butt, but she kept going until the seat separated from the splat and with that, the chair broke apart everywhere. Her arms were free, though still attached to the chair's arms. But now that the arms were unattached from the chair, she could use one hand to unbind the other. Next came the tape around her mouth, and then her ankles.

Freedom.

She tasted the air, stuck out her tongue, enjoying the coldness as it entered her mouth, loving the way air felt in her lungs when it came in gigantic waves, something she couldn't quite bring in through the nose. After giving herself a few minutes to enjoy the sensations of freedom again, she closed her eyes and conjured the husks.

A group of them appeared in front of her.

"Which one of you is Cassius?"

They all turned their heads toward the husk in the middle. He lifted his arm with slight hesitation.

"You wanted to teach me a lesson, but I hope I taught you one. I will never need you. You are a luxury, nothing more."

She closed her eyes again and called for the lampposts. A series of bangs came from all directions until she and the husks were surrounded by the monsters.

She spun in a circle, making sure they all saw her face. "You are mine. You do as I tell you. Cassius is not your leader. Don't make the mistake of trusting him."

She turned back to the husks and moved toward Cassius. "Kill him. The rest of you watch. Remember your place."

The lampposts charged the husk. His eyes grew wide as they ripped their massive claws into his body. Hot liquid dribbled from the lamppost's faces, scorching the husk's body. Cassius screamed as his flesh cooked. The monsters continued to impale the husk and Candlestick walked away.

One husk followed her. She heard his footsteps creeping behind her.

"What are you doing? I told you to watch your friend die."

"Husk has a question."

Candlestick turned. The creature was inches behind her, so close she felt his breath on her cheeks. "What is your name?" she asked.

"Damond," the husk said. His voice spoke as normally and assuredly as Cassius had in the tent.

"What do you want, Damond? Why aren't you doing what I told you?"

He put his head down and swept his feet in the dirt. "You make husks. You control husks. Husks can't challenge you."

She scrunched her forehead. "What do you mean? I thought you had a question?"

Damond lifted a finger. "Yes. Why you punish husk for what you do?"

She crossed her arms. "I don't understand."

"Husks part of your mind. You make Cassius. You make us all. You have husks talk, walk, fight, kill."

"But you decided not to listen."

Damond trembled. "No. Husks not do anything on own. You make husks not listen."

She pushed him. "Are you saying I asked for that? That I wanted what was going to happen in there?"

"No. Damond saying you challenged yourself. You made husks and lampposts disobey you. You fight you."

Gone. Gone. Gone.

Corey wiped a smear of blood from the side of his head. Brian stared at him, befuddled.

"How did this happen?" Corey stood up, groaning.

Brian shook his head, holding his temple. "He was fast. Strong."

Corey glanced out the bedroom window. Through the streaks of grime and the glistening sun, Corey spotted Fake Winter lugging Violin through a long stretch of tall grass. "Shit, she's still out there."

He ran for the steps. His vision blurred as his blood pumped, but he kept himself upright as he barreled down the steps. Behind him, Brian's footsteps matched his.

He ran out the back door and he grew disoriented. There was no tall grass. Had he gone out the wrong door? Was he imagining what he saw out the window?

Brian pushed past him and searched the area.

"He was in tall grass," Corey said.

Brian pointed toward the side of the house. "There?"

Corey looked, and a sparkle of hope ignited him. He charged and Brian followed. They ran through the thick grass until their breath gave way and forced them to stop. The land had tricked them, appearing shorter than it was. Fake Winter was nowhere in sight. They'd lost their only friend. First Winter, then Candlestick, and now Violin. Gone. Gone. Gone.

Brian clutched his knees, heaving for breath. "What now?"

Corey stared at the blinding sunlight, squinting against it. "I don't know."

Violin had told them following her was a mistake, that it always led to bad results, but Corey questioned that. Instead, he wondered if he and Brian were the common denominators in everyone's destruction. When they had met Winter, the man was setting up a nice life for his family, turning a motel into a functioning place to live, a place where his daughters could stop fighting for life and start living it. But shortly after, it fell apart, one piece at a time. Corey and Brian were the last two pieces standing, like parasites feeding on the carcass.

Brian did something that shocked Corey to his core, something he hadn't seen in all the years he'd known the man. Not when his mother died or when the world ended. He bawled. Sure, he'd seen Brian cry, a few tears strolling down his cheeks, but never anything like this. This was weeping, the kind you see on a child, lost and afraid. It was panic, fear, hate, and hunger. It was the loss of everything.

Corey went to him and Brian gripped a hand into Corey's shirt, balling and twisting it into his fist as he rested his head in the space between Corey's shoulder and neck.

They stood in the field, the dead heat pressing down on them, making their skin sticky and red, but neither of them moved. Despite the circumstances, Corey cherished the moment, a time for him and Brian to hold each other silently.

Brian pulled away, wiping tears from his face. "We can't accept losing her."

"I know," Corey said. "I can't lie. Sometimes I wished for this, for it to be just me and you again. I miss you."

"Me too. But I feel like Violin is our calling."

Corey nodded. "I know, me too. Like we're serving some weird ass greater purpose."

Brian laughed through the sobbing. "Weird ass? What makes you say that? Is it the Kevin Bacon and Lady Gaga stories or the three different people with a dead guy's face?"

Corey laughed too. "What the fuck is even happening?"

Brian stepped forward, hugging Corey. One hand landed on the nape of Corey's neck, and the other on the small of his back. It sent a shiver up his spine, and now he wanted to cry, but a different kind, a more welcoming cry. An embrace of the messed up, crazy life they were leading, because he got to share all the horror and pain with the only person who made his life complete. Life was hell. The best you could do was find someone to journey through it with you; someone who made you want to face it.

Brian would always be that person. Violin was their unified purpose.

"We need a plan," Brian said.

"Yeah, well, that's where you come in. You're the smart one with this stuff. I'm better at math. You figure out the survival stuff, and I'll jump in when you need PEMDAS."

Brian laughed again. Corey loved the way Brian laughed at his jokes. It was like some silly validation he didn't really need, but wanted.

"Okay. I say we go back to the car. We could keep following them across that river and into the woods, but it would do no good. Fake Winter was stronger than us, and faster. We'd never stop playing catch up and he'd be expecting us. Even if we found him, he'd tear us to shreds."

"Okay, but what do we do when we find the car? Just drive around aimlessly?"

Brian put his arms out straight, hands flat. He looked like a diver preparing to jump off a board into the pool.

"What are you doing?" Corey asked.

"Shhh. Do this. Tell me if you feel anything."

Corey put his hands out, feeling stupid. A gentle wind moved his arms as he extended them. Then it pulled, as if yanking him forward. "I feel that. It's like a wind."

Brian nodded. "Yet there isn't any wind today."

Corey scrunched his forehead. "So, what is this? How did you know that would happen?"

Brian smiled. "I felt it once at the motel. I was going to tell you, but then everything went crazy."

"What is it, though?"

"Every time I did it at the motel, every single time, it pointed my arms toward Violin."

Corey frowned. "Don't get me wrong, I believe a whole lot of nonsense after everything we've seen, and I love Violin, but are you trying to tell me our destinies are guiding us toward her? That some higher power is in control here and we're just vessels to be Violin's helpers?"

Brian turned to him, his eyes still bloodshot from crying, and he smiled. It was a deep, loving smile. "Absolutely not. This is bigger than we can understand right now, but I don't believe anyone is guiding us. I think we are doing it ourselves."

"Like, *we* created that wind?"

Brian nodded.

"Okay, so what? We get the car and let the wind take us to Violin?"

Brian nodded faster. "And we have the fucking adventure of our lives."

Corey returned Brian's smile and put his hand in his partner's, gripping tight. "I'll follow you, but do you think we should make some time to sleep? I don't want to fall behind, but I'm worried about you driving after a day and half of being awake."

Brian didn't answer the question.

They marched through the tall grass, into the sizzling heat. In the distance, the sky plumed red and orange before filling with a thick gray. The colors stretched from the front of the house all way beyond the river as if the universe itself was exploding a light year away, but pressing ever closer.

"Jesus," Brian said. "Is that fire?"

Corey stepped next to him, trying to make sense of it. It looked like smoke bellows and blazing fire, but there was no way a fire could stretch for that long, appearing out of nowhere, as if someone set the whole town on fire all at once.

"Where is that, exactly?" Corey asked.

Brian rubbed his forehead, turning his head from where the fire started to where it ended. "Everywhere? Looks like it starts that way, which has to be, what? Westerly? Near the beaches? But then, over there, it looks like it could be encroaching on Tanner's Switch."

"There's no way a fire could come out of nowhere and stretch from Westerly to Tanner's Switch. Not unless someone dropped a huge fucking bomb, which we would have heard."

The reds and oranges waved upward, fed by the thick air.

"Not unless there were a lot of people setting them." Brian grabbed Corey's arm. "Look there." He pointed toward the center of the bright colors. "And there." His index finger shifted a few inches over.

"What? What are you seeing?" Corey squinted.

"It's not a continuous fire. See where the colors dip down?"

"Oh shit." Corey saw it now, little drops in the waves of color, spaces between them, and more than just the two Brian pointed out. There were multiple spots where one fire stopped and the other started. "So, it's like ten different fires?"

"I think so."

"A bunch of assholes setting fires. Fucking great." Corey shook his head in disgust.

"They are setting fires blocks away from each other at the same time. That's quite the coordination."

"Jesus. That's terrifying" Corey clutched Brian's hand. They'd seen too much, and he knew not to trust anything out of the ordinary. Ghosts, devils, murderers. Something was behind those fires, and no matter what, it was dangerous. But it didn't matter, either. His heartbeat stayed in rhythm because Brian clutched his hand tightly. The world was nothing to fear when you had someone holding you that way.

A Revenge Story

Dance huddled in a corner. She wrapped herself in vines, hoping the thick tendrils would provide some warmth.

Abraham Lincoln took a chomp from a log before tossing into the dwindling fire. Sparks of fire shot out and wormed through the air.

Miley and Laura Jane Grace hugged each other, rubbing their hands on each other's backs, their breath coming out in steamy puffs.

The humans were gathered in the far reaches of the cave, forming their own small community. They'd helped Abraham Lincoln and his siblings defeat the gods, but now, with the threat of doom looming and their homes destroyed in one swift, angry flick of the new god's wrists, they chose to bond alone. Death would come for them soon, and they had no hope of escaping it. They might as well die as they lived: together.

Luckily, none of them were hungry because Dance produced vegetation for most of them, and small trees for Abe Lincoln. For herself, she fed off the breath of her companions.

It had been days since they'd found their way to this cave, following the directions Kevin Bacon gave them. He promised to meet them here, but had yet to return. The group responded to each passing moment with a growing sense of dread, rage, and pessimism.

"I don't feel the change anymore," Miley said.

Laura Jane Grace huddled in a corner. "Me neither. It feels like old times, dreadful and horrific."

Dance moved toward them. "I do. I feel freer."

Abraham Lincoln nibbled on a branch. "As if no one is telling our story at all."

Dance turned to him. "Yes. For once, we are telling our own."

Abraham Lincoln bent into a corner, struggling to maneuver his giant body around the low ceiling and close quarters of the cave. "If we are in charge of ourselves, we should take advantage and go find our brother. Sitting here is useless."

Dance unwrapped herself from her viny blanket. "We should listen to his orders. He told us to wait. I trust him to return to us. If the world is ending, we'll do nothing but die out there."

Miley released herself from her sister. "If the world is ending, we'll just die in here. The gods might not see us in the cave, but if they destroy the Earth, this place won't exist."

Laura Jane Grace jumped onto a wall and perched against the hard stone. "My sister is right. While I know you trust Mr. Bacon, I've seen nothing to suggest we should listen to him. He may be a good man but he's been wrong so often. It's hard to trust his judgement."

Dance shook her head. "You don't understand. He has plans on top of plans. He's playing this game ten steps ahead while we are just reacting to the moment."

Miley made a fist and wrapped her other hand around it. "But you heard him. He didn't even know about the nine gods.

He's playing the same reactionary game we all are. I'd rather die fighting than cowering."

"Here, here!" Abraham said, punching his fist into the wall.

The cave shook and loose stone rained down on everyone's head. Some humans, unaware of what had just happened, screamed at the booming sound.

"Whoops. Sorry," he said.

Suddenly, Dance, Abraham, Miley, and Laura Jane all hunched over in pain. A scream landed in Dance's brain, so loud and fierce it knocked her down. Seeing the same reaction from the others led her to believe they were all experiencing the same thing.

A vision came into her brain, taking over as if it were occurring in front of her. Kevin Bacon, tossed on top of a pool table, his body covered in blood. Other people were fighting all around him. Dance didn't recognize any of them other than the snake, Dolphi. They were in a bar but the carnage and destruction made it nothing more than shredded wood and broken glass.

The vision left as quickly as it came and Dance looked up to see the others coming out of their visions. Her head pounded as if Kevin Bacon delivered the message with a mallet to her temples.

Miley turned her head to Dance. "What say you now?"

"Let's go fight the gods," she said, forcing herself up.

Abraham Lincoln kicked the stone they'd pushed in front of the entrance, letting in the bright sunlight. It drenched them and they all squeezed their eyes shut, working to find their sight again.

Abraham pushed his way out and stretched in the wide-open Earth. "We are free from our own prison."

Dance, Miley, and Laura Jane Grace stepped out. Despite the bright sun, the air was cool and breezy, but nothing like the chilly dampness of the cave.

The open space made Dance uncomfortable. The cave

provided safety, but it also offered her the opportunity to see everything around her. Here, in the abundant Earth, the giant hand of a god could rip through the sky and shred her to pieces.

"Get the humans," Abraham said. "Let's go to war."

Miley gathered the humans and they exited the cave, their faces brewing with reluctance and terror.

"Everyone, hop on my shoulders."

Dance shuffled the humans on first, then Miley and Laura Jane Grace. She jumped on last.

Abraham moved with big strides, but avoided running, which Dance was grateful for. The humans were already nearly falling off his shoulder with each bounce.

Out of nowhere, an eagle blasted by, knocking three of the humans off. Dance screamed and reached out a tendril way too late. Their bodies fell to the ground, a cloud of dust mushrooming over them.

She looked around, trying to make sense of what just happened. The eagle turned, heading back for more. Dance whipped her tendril at it, lashing it across the face. It turned away and flew into a pine tree with an explosion of feathers and pine needles.

She turned in time to see more birds coming. At least six or seven. They swerved around one another, making it hard to count them. They were all aiming for the humans.

Dance extended her arms, turning them both into long, thick vines. Miley stood, snarling. Laura Jane Grace pulled a sharp stick from a sheath on her back.

The birds swirled around one another, and then straightened, dive bombing toward Abraham's shoulder. Miley belted out a horrific scream, powerful and raw. It brought tears to Dance's face. The combination of beauty and strength in the notes nearly crippled her and forced her into memories of her beloved crops.

The birds lost their pattern. Some of them flew straight into the ground. A few hit Abraham in the chest and exploded against his icy body. Laura Jane Grace impaled a few others with her stick.

"Dang, I don't like to kill animals," she said with a frown.

"Those aren't animals. They're beasts of the gods."

Abraham Lincoln had stopped walking. The humans were crying and shaking, devastated by the loss of their friends and family.

Below, somewhere behind a wall of trees, something laughed. Abraham bent low, trying to find the source. Dance jumped down and Miley and Laura Jane followed.

Some shrubbery moved and a puff of grey smoke came out of the bushes. The laughing continued.

"They called them beasts of the gods," a shrill voice said between hysterical laughing. The creature came through the green. A raccoon. He puffed on a cigar. "Well, it's good to see you again."

Abraham Lincoln puckered his lips. "Ah, Rapture. If I recall the last time we saw you, you chewed on Kevin Bacon's throat and then ran off like a coward. Haven't seen you since. I suppose you're working with the nine gods now?"

Rapture took a long pull on his cigar. "Nine gods?"

Dance shook her head. "You don't know? We killed your father and his sisters. Nine gods have replaced them."

Rapture rolled his eyes. "I don't really have time for all that drama. I just came here to kill you, Dance. Seems like you just don't stay down. How's your crops?"

She clenched her jaw and unleashed a long vine, lashing Rapture across the cheek. His body rolled, but he landed on his feet. They stared at each other.

Rapture wiped blood from his cheek and lifted his top lip, revealing his fangs. "Kill them all!" he shouted.

The woods came alive with rumbles and rustling until an

army of animals cleared the forest's edge. Bears. Coyotes. Wolves. Deer. Rabbits. Squirrels. Chickens. Hundreds of them. Even the branches of the trees filled in with birds, balls of blue, black, and red decorating each branch.

Abraham Lincoln tilted his head toward the humans on his shoulder. "You humans love to eat meat, correct?"

They didn't answer.

"Then I shall provide you with a meal!" He stood with his fists raised and slammed them into the ground.

The animals charged.

Dance turned to Miley and Laura Jane Grace. "I don't like to kill animals, either, but these aren't animals, they are murderers. They killed my best friends. This is my revenge story. Save the raccoon for me."

Before Miley and her sister could reply, a bear slammed into them.

Dance turned toward the army in time to see Rapture flying toward her throat.

Building a New Family

❧

Candlestick stormed back into camp. It was still, everyone sleeping, but the two guards noticed her re-entering.

"Hey, where did you go?" one guard asked.

"Excuse me." She brushed past the guards and headed for Lion, who she had tied around a tree near the fire earlier in the night.

She unleashed him, waking him from a deep slumber. "I've been putting you to sleep too much lately haven't I, pal? You would have saved me."

The two guards approached her from behind, their shadows draping over her like a blanket. "Are you alright? Where did you go?"

Without looking up, she said, "I had to pee. I need to leave camp."

The taller guard frowned. "You're free to do what you want. We just ask you to inform us before you go anywhere so we know something didn't happen to you."

She nodded, surprised at how fair the men in this camp seemed to be. Outside of Todd, of course.

"I'll wait until morning. When Cassie wakes up, I'll see if she wants to come with me. I hope to meet up with you again but I have a big trip to take and I don't know when I'll be back."

The shorter guard with the mustache put his hand on her shoulder. "Okay. Why don't you rest up and talk to the morning guards when you're ready?"

She stood up and Lion lifted his head, not ready for her to stop petting him yet. "I'm going to take my dog to my tent. I'll tie him up over there, but I want him near me tonight."

The men shrugged and said good night before returning to their posts.

She did as she told them, tying Lion to a tree by her tent and heading in for a few hours rest before leaving.

Sleep evaded her thanks to the flowing adrenaline coursing through her body. It made her skin itchy and her mind race. She knew waiting until morning was the smart move, but she wanted to go now. An epiphany had struck on her way back to camp and an anger fueled inside her. An anger at herself for losing sight of who she was. Yes, she'd grown to care about Cassie, and desperately needed a friend, but she wasn't human. Something special existed in her DNA and there was only one person left alive who could understand. How had she been so easily swayed from her mission? She needed her sister and wouldn't give up until she found her.

Cassie woke as the morning sun broke through the horizon, beaming through sticks and causing the tent's fabric to glow.

She smiled at Candlestick. "Thank you for saving me," she said, and Candlestick's heart filled with pride and a feeling of usefulness.

"I'm sorry to do this, because I like it here, but I have to leave. You can come with me if you'd like, but I understand if you don't want to. I know I've been nothing but trouble for you, but I promise, I just wanted to be your friend."

Cassie sat up and yawned. "Are you going to find your sister?"

Candlestick nodded.

"Can we have breakfast first? I smell sausages."

Candlestick smiled and an inexplicable deluge of tears poured down her cheeks.

"Why are you crying?"

"Because you had a choice and you chose me."

Cassie stood up and hugged her.

After a quick embrace, they held hands and walked to the firepit, eagerly accepting plates full of food. Candlestick grew accustomed to not knowing what she ate, but from her limited experience, human food was amazing, much better than crickets and corn.

After they filled up, Candlestick went to the morning guards and told them she'd be leaving. While they were just as accepting as the night guards, they showed more concern.

"Where are you going? How long will you be gone?"

"I don't know. I have to find my sister. I hope it won't take long, but I can't tell. I want to come back here, but I can't promise what will happen."

The morning guard in the red shirt, a man named Davis, scrubbed his beard. "I don't like the idea of letting two little girls go out there by themselves, especially with men like Todd out there. I won't stop you, but I don't like it."

Candlestick hoped the guards missed the flinch in her face when Davis mentioned Todd. "I'll be fine. I'm strong."

Davis sighed and grabbed his partner's shoulder. "There's gotta be something we can do to help them."

The other man, a stocky gentleman with frazzled, gray hair said, "We could send a few with them?"

Davis stood straight. "Good idea." Then, to Candlestick,

"How would you feel about Christian and his cousin, Randy, going with you? If you decide not to head back, they can find their way. I'd feel better if you weren't alone."

Candlestick understood the men didn't know her power and to them, guys with guns would protect her. She also knew adding two new people to the mix meant two more people she'd need to protect. However, having some more people with her for their adventure brought a sense of comfort, like she could build her own family. Christian made her nervous. She had noticed the way Cassie looked at the boy, and while she shouldn't care, she did. It made her stomach turn.

She nodded. "That'd be fine."

Within an hour, they were all packed and waiting at the edge of camp for Christian's cousin to join them. Candlestick caught Cassie staring at Christian a few times. Each time she caught it, she touched Cassie's arm to pull her attention away.

Christian's cousin, Randy, was older, and much more muscular. Candlestick guessed he was in his twenties. He lacked the teenage scrawniness his cousin possessed.

With everyone in place, they began their parade down a long stretch of road. Candlestick didn't know how to return home, but she knew she'd find it, that some internal compass guided her there.

Lion led under Candlestick's control. The girls kept close behind the dog, and the boys were a few feet behind them.

Randy said, "How old is your sister? Is she single?"

Without looking back, Candlestick said, "If you look at my sister the wrong way, she will eat your face. And she's too young for you anyway."

She turned in time to see Randy's face turn redder than a beet, and his cousin cracked up.

After walking for half an hour with the sun beating down on

them, Christian came up to Candlestick and put his hand on her sweaty shoulder. Just for fun, she spoke to Lion with her mind and told him to growl and chase Christian.

Christian jumped back and released a high-pitched squeal, making the whole group laugh. Candlestick wasn't afraid of Christian, and felt she could trust him, but she also wanted Cassie to see him as the goofy, weak boy he was, not as someone to ogle.

"I just wanted to see if you guys were okay, and if you needed water," he said from a respectful distance behind them.

"Thank you, but Lion doesn't know your intentions and he does not handle people touching me very well."

"Cassie does it all the time."

Candlestick smiled at her friend. "Cassie is different."

Cassie looped her arm around Candlestick's. "We'll take that water, though," she said.

Christian retrieved two bottles of water from his pack and gave them to Randy to give to the girls, clearly nervous about approaching them again.

As Candlestick sipped from the bottle, she looked ahead, impatience and excitement building in her chest. Violin. How could she have ever swayed from finding her sister? Since separating, she should have only had one mission: finding Violin. As if she could speak to her sister as she did Lion, Candlestick spoke through her mind. *I love you, Violin.*

She'd given up hope that her father lived, but the thought of seeing him played in her mind as well. *You never know,* she thought. *You never know.*

Cassie poured some water in her hair. "Can you tell me more about Mary now?"

The sun, undisturbed in the landscape, blinding them from seeing what lay at the end of the road they traveled, but without complaint, her new group marched on, following her with a loyalty she didn't deserve.

"Yes, it's time for a story," she said.

A Supernatural Jolt of Inspiration

Mary peeked out of her alcove to see all the other children leaning out of theirs, staring directly at her. She slid back against the wall, blocking them from seeing her. Why were they looking to her?

Because she wasn't very good at hiding her plans. They'd all heard her whispering with Kelly and knew the two of them must be up to something. Witnessing one of their own killed by Russ's hands sent an urgency up their asses and made them hope Mary had some wonderful plan to get them all out. She didn't. All she had was the hope Kelly succeeded at breaking a link on her shackles.

She peeked out again. They were all still staring. Crying Kid wasn't leaking from his eyes anymore. Instead, he bugged them out, praying for a solution. Even the quiet girl with the glassy eyes was looking Mary's way.

"What?" Mary said.

"What do we do?" the cute kid with the glasses asked.

"Why are you all looking at me? I don't even know your names."

The cute kid frowned. "I'm Zeke. Would you not save me without knowing my name?"

Mary put her head down. "That's not what I meant. I don't know why you think I can save any of us."

The little girl with the glassy eyes said, "You must have something. We're all going to die down here."

Mary pointed to Ellie's body. "Do any of you have magic powers like Ellie said?"

No one said anything.

"No, I didn't think so. Russ said he'll kill you if you use your magic, and since it's fucking absurd to think we have magic powers, I guess you'll all be fine."

Kelly scoffed and went back into her alcove. Mary's stomach lurched at the sight of her only friend's disappointment. She slammed her fist into the wall between them, angry that Kelly didn't defend her.

"What do you want me to say, Kelly?"

She stormed back to the alcove's entrance, where the other kids waited. "Find your own answers," she yelled.

Zeke gave her one more glance before sighing and returning to his alcove. The other kids followed his lead until Mary was alone. She waited for someone to tell her it was okay, that she didn't fail them. They were in an impossible situation and it was cruel to put hope in the hands of a single girl.

She had run out of ideas and from the way Kelly scoffed at her, guessed she had better give up on hope as well. If Kelly neared breaking the link as she had promised, she wouldn't need Mary to come up with other solutions.

They were doomed.

Ellie's legs lay a few feet in front of her alcove and Mary had made it a point to avoid staring at them, not allowing herself to crumble at the sight of a dead girl. Letting herself break with fear or anguish would only weaken her.

"Tell me how to make magic," she whispered.

She wasn't insane. Of course she didn't possess magic, but Ellie had made the lights flicker, and Mary was in no position to dismiss any possible escape.

"What do I need to do?"

For a silly moment, she fully expected a miracle, some supernatural jolt of inspiration. A message from the dead girl, sent from the afterlife to Mary's mind. None came.

The hopelessness growing inside her transformed into rage. She stormed forward, making herself look directly at Ellie, her waxy skin, agape mouth, and dead eyes.

"Talk to me! Tell me what to do!" she shouted.

The other kids came back out as Mary continued to shout. She hurled hostilities toward the corpse.

Zeke put his finger to his lips. "Shhh, shhh, shhh. You'll get us in trouble."

Mary didn't listen. She picked up scoops of dirt and threw the gravelly handfuls at Ellie. "Tell me what to do."

A loud heave silenced the room. If a sound could punch someone in the gut, could maul their insides and rip apart their sanity, it was that heave.

Ellie shot up, her body straight, making her look like an L. She heaved again, and Crying Kid lived up to his nickname, screaming and whimpering at the sight of the living dead girl.

Ellie continued to heave, clutching her throat. Everyone panicked. Kelly stretched forward. Bert, too. They both reached to help, but they had no hope of reaching her. Zeke and the glassy eyed girl just stared in amazement, wonder, and dread.

Mary's heart pounded. She stepped back, unsure what was happening.

Ellie's heaving turned into a coughing fit. Spittle fell from her lips onto layers of dust on the floor.

Mary backed up until her head hit the wall. She winced as a sharp stone dug into her skull.

Ellie finished her coughing fit and stood up, panning her head across the room. "What the hell are you all doing?"

Mary stepped forward, still in disbelief.

Ellie stared at her with wide eyes. "Well? I'm glad you figured out your powers enough to bring me back, but it ain't gonna last long so if you want me to tell you all how to get out of here, I suggest you listen now. We are almost out of time."

Mary took another step closer and swallowed hard. "Are you saying *I* did this?"

Ellie giggled that same playful, haunting laugh she made shortly before Russ killed her. "I told y'all you had magic, although your power won't help everyone get out of here." She pointed to Mary, then shrugged. "But at least it brought me back enough to give you all a solution. You're welcome, by the way."

Zeke cleared his throat. "So, we really have powers?"

Ellie turned to him, smiling. "Why the fuck do you think Russ is kidnapping all of you?"

Kelly stretched her neck, sticking her head out. "How did he know we all had magic powers if we didn't even know ourselves? And what does he want with us?"

Ellie rolled her eyes. "He knew because it's his job to know. He's hunting us. And what he wants? I'm not sure. I would imagine he wanted to learn more about us, or maybe use us as leverage or something. Eventually, I think the plan is to kill us all, but he needs something from us first. You can ask him tomorrow, just before you drive a rock through his skull. We don't really have time to chit chat. I'll be back to dead in like five minutes and you guys need to know how to get the fuck out of here."

To See What's Right in front of You

Fake Winter hoisted Violin over his shoulder as he trudged through a muddy bank. He'd carried her in different ways as he trekked toward Kevin Bacon knows where. At one point, he'd cradled her like a baby, and at another, he wrapped his arm around her torso and carried her as someone would carry a long rug.

She never fought back, not since the house, when her flying fists were met with an inhuman deflection and quick knock down. He was too strong and too quick. She prided herself on her strength and capabilities to protect herself, but she knew her limits. Fake Winter wasn't the kid she killed in the motel. No, Fake Winter wasn't human at all.

Her best move would be to outsmart him. From her limited experience with people, the more powerful they were, the more confident, and thus, easier to dupe.

She saved her strength, letting Fake Winter carry her to wherever he planned to take her. If he wanted her dead, he wouldn't drag her through the woods to bring her somewhere. He had a plan; all she had to do was disrupt it. In the confusion, she'd find her freedom and, hopefully, some answers.

He carried her until the fire disc descended and the glow disc rose behind a sheath of wispy smoke-stained night. She tried to sleep on occasion, so she could be alert when she needed to be, but sleeping proved difficult when someone was lugging you around through thick shrubs. They crossed through woods thick with oaks, pines, and firs until they reached an open field. Beyond the field, a fence blocked off something magical and strange. Large, colorful machinations, old and rusted but still maintaining some level of brightness, loomed. She stared in wonder, dazed by the machines. They called to her, begging her to come closer, to enjoy them. And Fake Winter did bring her closer.

He put her down but latched his hand around her wrist and pulled her forward as he trudged through the thick, unkempt grassy field. She offered no resistance.

"What is this place?" she asked.

"An amusement park. They really did shelter you underground, didn't they? You'd think they could have at least told you about this stuff. You wouldn't like it, anyway. You have enough fear and panic in your life. This place, if you can believe it, was designed by humans to bring fake fear into their lives. These machines drop them from high heights and make them dizzy. It's all meant to bring some semblance of emotion into their otherwise dull lives, devoid of feelings."

"Can I experience one?"

He huffed. "I didn't drag you here to play games with you."

When they reached the fence, he walked the edge until they reached a gaping hole in the metal patterns. He dragged her in, guiding her toward a wooden structure with no front, outside of a small counter. Inside the structure, giant toy animals stuck to the arch around the front façade. Inside, a series of papers lined the back wall. They had a star in their center, but most of the stars looked riddled with tiny bullet holes. She saw guns wired to the front counter. Her eyes widened and she snatched one, aiming at Fake Winter and pulling the trigger. It made a silly popping sound, but nothing shot out of it.

"It's not loaded. Even if it were, you'd be shooting me with pellets. Those could kill a human, but they'd just annoy me."

She dropped the gun. "I'm not opposed to annoying you."

He hit a button and bright colored lights lit the perimeter of the shelter. They moved, one light clicking on, and then the next, giving off the impression the lights were snaking their way from one side to the other. *Amazing,* she thought. *Humans were simply amazing.*

"Sit," he said, waving toward a stool inside the structure.

She listened.

He sat on the counter, folding his legs and tucking his feet underneath himself. "Would you like something to eat?"

She nodded, figuring acceptance would create a false sense of ease in Fake Winter.

He fished through a plastic container. The container rattled as he shifted it, and she caught sight of the chunks of frozen water inside it. He pulled out a small clump of wrinkled metal, dripping from the melted water. He noticed her curiosity. "Have you never seen foil?"

She frowned. "I don't eat metal. I'm sorry."

He laughed and tossed it to her. "You don't eat the foil. The foil protects the food inside it. Unwrap it."

She did. Inside, a hunk of something brown.

"It's chocolate. You'll like it."

"I've had chocolate before, just never in such a big chunk."

Fake Winter smiled. "Well, welcome to heaven. They call it fudge."

She nibbled on it. "It is delicious."

"Told you. Now, do me a favor."

She eyed him, not giving him a yes or a no. Compliance could only go so far and without knowing what he wanted, she refused to agree.

"Tell me how your father died."

Her heart rate picked up. "No," she said as she took another nibble.

"Oh, yes, Violin. We all know how tough you are. How about that boy in the motel room? You really did a number on him. Much deserved, too. Congrats. I am not questioning your strength, dear, but I need to discuss your father's death with you. What harm would it do to tell me? What are you proving by not?"

She swallowed some more chocolate and cleared her throat. "If you know about the boy in the motel, I have to guess you have some ability to see what you want. So, you must already know what happened to my father."

He shimmied his body forward. "Oh, I do. I'm asking because I don't know if you do."

Violin froze. What did he mean by that? She needed to know, so she gave him what he wanted. "He was shot to death in front of the motel by two men in the woods."

Fake Winter slammed his fist on the counter. It startled her, causing her to drop her chocolate into the fire.

"They've already gotten to you." He stood up, pacing and rubbing his forehead.

"What are you talking about? The men in the woods?"

"No, not the men in the woods. My brothers. They brainwashed you."

She stood up. "What are you talking about? Speak plainly for once. All of you, you just make things more complicated. You want me to answer questions? Well, I want answers too."

Fake Winter stormed toward her. She flinched, despite trying not to, but Fake Winter stopped a few inches in front of her.

"They did not shoot your father in the woods. I want you to think. Think hard. Think clear. How did you father die?"

"They shot him in the woods. I am thinking clear. I was there. He took his last breath as I hugged him."

"No!" He shouted so loudly it made her jump.

"Yes. That's what happened."

He grabbed her by the shoulders and put his face centimeters in front of hers. "That's the memory my brothers put in your head. It's not real. Think. Fight through it. How did your father die?"

She closed her eyes, aware that this Fake Winter was playing a trick on her. She pretended to believe him. Did a part of her really believe it? Was it possible her memories were implanted? No. No. That was insane. Granted, nothing was insane anymore after all she'd seen, but she knew her father's death. She could still smell the blood, feel the tilled Earth under her body as she lay with him. She could taste the salty tears.

But what was the memory? She had just had her head bashed against a wall and she didn't see the shot, only the aftermath. What if her father hadn't been shot? What if her own mind filled in the details, believing what Candlestick and the scene told her? She shook her head. No. Still, an energy built in her blood, hoping to find a new story, something less horrible, something easier to digest.

Fake Winter pressed his fingers into her forehead. She kept her eyes closed as he pushed. Bolts of electricity sparked in her brain, taking over the memories. Winter. Winter dying. Winter standing up, wiping blood from his chest, removing it like a sticker. He smiled and brushed the dirt off his clothes. A few men walked over and shook his hand.

What was happening? None of this was real.

She jolted back, and the electricity left her. It hurt, the way it shot out of her and back into Fake Winter's hand.

"What was that?"

Fake Winter smiled. "The truth."

No. He was putting falsehoods into her brain. Her father was dead. But was he? Was this Fake Winter putting memories in place or had the other Fake Winters done that? But that made little sense because Candlestick, Brian, and Corey all witnessed it too. Did they all have the memories implanted?

She stared at Fake Winter for a moment, trying to piece together what this was all about.

"It's your turn to answer my questions."

He sighed. "Indeed. But you don't even know what your questions are. So, I will provide you with answers to questions you didn't know you had. The thing is, you freed your stories. We need to wrangle them back in. Why don't you sit down again and let me tell you a story?"

"No. No more games. Direct answers. If my father didn't die the way I know it, how did he die? Why would your brothers plant memories in my brain? What is the purpose of all this? What are you after? How do you have these powers? Why was my family working with humans? I want answers now." She stepped forward, crossing her arms.

"Tell me something. Do you know about a little girl named Mary?"

She frowned. Of course she knew the story of a girl named Mary, but how did she know it? Strange that him asking conjured a full, visceral story in her mind, yet she couldn't place where she'd ever heard it before.

Fake Winter caught on to her confusion. "Ah, see. You know it, don't you? But you don't know how. The story of a little girl named Mary, kidnapped by a man named Russ. Your sister has been telling these tales to a new friend she made. She also doesn't know where the stories come from, but she must keep telling them. It's intrinsic. She knows the tale back and forth, and she can recite it with ease, just as you could. Yet, you don't know how. Interestingly, your sister doesn't know how the story ends, but you do. Not right now, maybe, but it's there, lingering in your brain. If you really tried, you could fish it out."

Fake Winter was right, she knew, and this brought up a host of new questions, but she didn't want new questions. She wanted answers. "What does this have to do with what I asked you?"

He shook his head, disbelieving. "Everything! How do you not see what is right in front of you? For a girl with so much wisdom, you are truly dumb."

"Shut up."

"I will not. Not until you understand everything, but I can't just feed you the answers. God knows if I did that, we'd all die right here, right now."

"I don't understand!" she yelled.

"Tell me about Mary. Tell me about Kevin Bacon. Tell me about gods, whatever you want, just tell me."

"Have I not already expressed that I don't want to tell stories or have stories told to me? I want answers."

He shouted, "The answers are in the fucking stories!"

She jumped back, her heart pounding, her back pressed against the back wall, crinkling the paper stars filled with bullet holes.

He moved closer to her, getting in her face again. "Do you feel that? A bubble building in your gut. It's moving up into your throat. In a moment, you'll have no choice but to tell me a story. It's your destiny."

She closed her eyes and cried.

Bristlebucks

K evin Bacon lay bloody on the billiards table, Dark Skies on top of him, digging his thumbs into Kevin's eyes. With the little strength he had left, Kevin Bacon pushed against Dark Skies's hands, keeping them centimeters away from plucking his eyes right out of their sockets.

He tried to change form, but he still hadn't mastered the skill. He only changed his clothes and the length of his arms by just a few inches.

Around him, bottles broke and furniture crumbled. Blood splattered from all directions. War. Yet again, war.

A rogue skateboard smashed against Dark Skies's head and he fell off the table, giving Kevin Bacon a moment.

Avril Lavigne leaned down to him and whispered through heavy breath, "When I was created, they gave me your backstory. But I also have a power. My senses are heightened. I can see and taste things others cannot. I can smell things like you wouldn't believe."

Kevin stood up, looking around at the threats from all angles. A female god pummeled a helpless Elvis. Lady Gaga held

Dolphi in one hand, squeezing and with her other, fended off two gods: one, a beautiful, tall woman with hair that floated upward, and the other, a short man with a long beard and beady, red eyes.

Dark Skies rolled over, rubbing his head.

"If you have a point, you should make it quickly," Kevin said.

"The point is, Dolphi made you a god-killer bullet. He wouldn't tell you the ingredients, but I smelled them."

Kevin's eyes grew wide. "What was it made from?"

"A regular bullet dipped in urine and bristlebucks," she smiled.

Kevin's face fell flat. "The urine I can handle, though I am slightly dehydrated. Where the hell can I find—"

Before he could finish his sentence, Dark Skies slammed a pool ball into his temple. Kevin's vision blurred and his ears rang.

As Dark Skies dragged him across the room, one arm strangling him and the other ripping his hair out, Avril shouted, "It's what Lady Gaga puts in the house special!"

Dark Skies dragged Kevin Bacon behind the bar. Two other gods surrounded Avril. What happened next, Kevin couldn't see because Dark Skies tossed him to the floor behind the bar and jumped on his skull. A mixture of sawdust and blood went up his nose with each inhale.

The two gods battling Lady Gaga knocked her down and her hand landed next to Kevin's.

"Where do you keep your bristlebucks?" he asked, barely getting the words out.

"They're soaking in the back. For maximum potency, they must sit in a barrel of urine for one week."

He reached a hand to her and touched her hair. "Two birds, one stone. I like it. Do you have a gun?"

Dark Skies kicked him in the ribs. Something sharp dug into him, a rib must have broken. He closed his eyes and focused on changing forms to anything without broken bones but again, he struggled to make it happen.

"There's a shotgun in the back room, right next to the bristle-bucks," Lady Gaga said, straining to hold off a growing pig pile of gods.

"I need some help with this asshole so I can get back there."

Lady Gaga nodded, pushing three gods off her. Dolphi had somehow freed himself from her grasp and slunk away.

"Franklin?" Lady Gaga yelled.

"Yes, my dear?" the man who had played cards with Elvis shouted.

"Use your electricity over here for a moment."

A few seconds later, charges of lightning zipped through the air, hitting Dark Skies and the gods on top of Lady Gaga. The gods all jolted back and Kevin turned over, his broken rib digging deeper into his chest.

One more try. He closed his eyes and changed form. This time, it worked. He stood with no struggle, as all the bruising, broken bones, and blood disappeared. A quick glance in the mirror revealed his new form. Orelon. Well, fuck.

Dark Skies's eyes grew wide and his lips clenched. "You're alive?"

Kevin Bacon threw his arms up. "No, no. Just an illusion."

Dark Skies balled his fists. "Every day your belly held me, I dreamed of killing you."

Kevin charged for the back room. As soon as he entered, Dark Skies was back on top of him, dragging him down to the floor.

Kevin kicked and flailed, but it was no use. The god was simply more powerful. As Dark Skies punched him in the face, Kevin extended his arms toward a stool. He yanked a leg and the shotgun toppled off, hitting the floor with a thud.

He slammed the butt of the gun into Dark Skies's face,

causing the god to fall off him. Using the gun as a crutch, he lifted himself and hobbled toward a wooden barrel. He pried the cap off as Dark Skies corrected himself and charged.

The smell of piss and mint filled the air. Kevin didn't have time to drench the bullets, so he took the gun and dropped his entire arm in, letting the bristlebucks and piss coat everything. Dark Skies tackled him, and the barrel sloshed and crashed to the floor. Urine soaked them both, and a terrible thought crossed Kevin Bacon's mind. Whose piss was it?

The sounds of war continued from the front room, and with a loud bang, the wooden walls between them exploded as the short, bearded god flopped into the room.

With one hand, Kevin fended off more attacks from Dark Skies, and with the other, he fired the shotgun toward the bearded god. The bullet blasted into the god's head, splattering brains and gore all over the walls. Within a few seconds, the god's body turned to flecks of white and dissipated into the sky.

Dark Skies's eyes widened, and he pushed away from Kevin Bacon. "How did you do that?"

Kevin Bacon aimed the gun at him, but before he could fire, the god disappeared.

He righted himself and stumbled into the barroom. The gods had disappeared. All of them. Even Dolphi.

Kevin examined the surrounding carnage. The bar was destroyed. Shreds of wood, shards of glass, and speckles of blood decorated the area. His new friends were all alive, but most of them were covered in blood and holding different parts of their bodies where they probably had broken bones. Everyone turned to him.

He held the shotgun up like a baton. "God-killing bullets."

They all nodded.

"Lady Gaga, how much did you love this bar?"

She winced while trying to straighten. "It was my entire life. I feel like I lost a child."

Kevin nodded. "That's good. Revenge in your blood is the best poison against the gods. I had a lot of it when I fought the three gods, but I need to build it up against these new ones. Looking at what they did to you, my new friends, I feel the vengeance bubble building."

Elvis wiped some blood from his forehead. "Until then, we should stock up on those god-killing bullets."

"Agreed." Kevin Bacon moved toward Avril Lavigne. "And thank you for the tip."

She picked up her skateboard and frowned as it separated into two pieces. "I'm feeling that revenge in my blood too."

Lady Gaga searched for an unbroken glass and poured herself a beer. "There's something else."

"What?"

"I read the snake's mind. He knows about your secret weapon."

Kevin Bacon furrowed his brow. "What secret weapon?"

"The baby."

Kevin frowned and took a deep breath. "Does that mean the gods know?"

She shook her head. "Not yet, but they will soon. He's holding the secret as leverage."

"What do you propose I do?"

She took a big gulp of her beer. "You're going to hate it."

"I do a lot of things I hate."

"Make a deal with Dolphi."

Blaze

Corey rolled his pants up before crossing the river.

Brian gave him a sideways smile, both judging and loving him for avoiding getting his pants wet, while Brian just trudged through the cold water, letting his socks, shoes, and pants get drenched in the icy river.

As Corey glanced at his partner, his eyes drifted beyond to the pines cutting the horizon. The fire remained a long way away, but the smoke was bellowing toward them.

He tipped his head, letting Brian know he should turn around.

"Shit," Brian said as he noticed the approaching smoke. "We better get the fuck out of here."

"Thankfully, the asshole took Violin in the other direction." Corey grabbed Brian's hand and led him into the woods, down an aisle of clear ground nestled between two walls of black oak.

They quickened their pace a little more every few seconds until they were running. The smoke started to cut through the forest. It still didn't hit them, but it created a dense forcefield of grey, slithering closer with each passing moment. In no time, they'd be inhaling it, drowning in a sea of death.

They reached the abandoned camp with the burned bodies, the place where the wilderness kids once rested during their violent ends, when Corey heard something behind them. Brian ran ahead, not noticing the sound. Just as Corey turned to see what it was, something smashed into him, a full force hit to the back. It knocked him to the ground and sucked the wind from his lungs.

He tried to turn and see what pinned him to the earth, but it dug its knees into his shoulder blades and pressed his face into the leaves and slash.

"Hey!" Brian shouted, finally catching on to the situation.

Brian charged and the thing on top of Corey released and flung itself at Brian. It was man. Long, dirty hair crawled down his shirtless back. Brian screamed as the feral man bit into his arm.

Corey pushed himself up, still struggling to breathe. "What the fuck?"

The man dug his fingers into Brian's face as he turned his head toward Corey and smiled, showing a mouthful of beady, yellow teeth and eyes that fluttered wildly like a speeding fan blade. "The Fireman is coming," he said with a gravelly voice.

Corey reached to pull the man off Brian, but Wild Eyes was too fast. He turned and kicked his foot backwards, landing his heel right in Brian's stomach, and slashed his untrimmed nails at Corey's face.

Brian doubled over, now as windless as Corey.

Wild Eyes pounced on Corey and opened his mouth to bite into his face, but Corey jammed his elbow in the man's neck, holding him back. While he did this, Wild Eyes jabbed left then right, punching Corey in the ribs. Each hit felt like a knife blade sliding into his heart.

Meanwhile, the smoke grew ever closer, and while the greyish clouds had not reached them yet, the smell had penetrated the air. Within minutes, they'd be suffocating.

"The Fireman is coming!" The Man said, gnashing his teeth and shaking his head, trying to free himself from Corey's arm enough to take a big bite.

Brian yelled, "Hey, asshole!"

The man turned and lunged. It's as if the thing wasn't thinking, just attacking. No strategy, no plan, just a deep desire to hurt. As he ran away from Corey, Brian lifted his arm and aimed his handgun.

The shot echoed through the forest as Wild Eyes flopped down. His body twitched and his blood caked the rug of leaves under him.

Corey breathed heavily; all his energy expended. "What the fuck was that?"

Brian put his hand out. "I don't know, but we don't have time to figure it out. We need to go now."

"Your arm," Corey said as he grabbed Brian's hand. Brian helped him to his feet, and Corey reached for the bloody bite mark, but Brian flinched his arm away.

"We have to go now." Brian nudged his head toward the tendrils of smoke closing in on them. "*Now*," he repeated.

Corey shook his head and bent over, hands on his knees. "I can't run. He took it out of me."

Brian put his hand under Corey's chin and lifted his partner's head. "You are the strongest motherfucker I know. You have no choice but to run because the other option is you die, and I cannot live without you. So run for me, motherfucker."

Corey stood upright and winced. "Alright. Fuck it. Let's go."

And together, they ran.

Significant Moments

Candlestick led her new group through a series of neighborhoods before they reached the outskirts of a thick forest. There were no carved paths or even partial clearings, just thick brush and piled brambles.

Cassie and Christian complained as bladed shrubbery cut into their flesh, but Randy kept quiet. Lion jumped through it all with wild-eyed excitement.

"Are you sure this is the right way? How can you even tell? It's just big ass bushes," Christian whined.

"I'm sure. Keep your mind off it by telling us a story."

He hesitated. "What? Like your story about the girl prisoner? I'm not a good storyteller."

She marched on, not looking back at her group. "No. Tell me about you and your cousin. How did you get here? Where were you when humanity disappeared?"

Randy laughed. "Fucking playing video games like a couple of assholes."

"Yeah, Randy came over with a new game for us to play. We

were just chilling in the basement, playing the game, when we heard my parents scream upstairs."

Randy chimed in, "I friggin' dropped the remote and ran to them. Christian followed me. We got upstairs and no one was there."

"Which we soon found out meant, like, no one. Literally, no one."

"We were freaking out for days because we didn't see a single soul. All the power went out. We were running out of food."

Christian's voice broke. "I kept thinking my mom and dad would come back, that they'd just poof, reappear. Like we were just in some sort of glitch in reality that would eventually correct itself."

Cassie stopped. "That's exactly what my dad said. He said it must be some sort of glitch in reality."

Christian shook his head. "Exactly, like it didn't make sense. Something must have broken in the world, ya know. What happened to your dad?"

Cassie put her head down and kept walking while shame bubbled in Candlestick's stomach.

"So, what did you do?" Candlestick asked, hoping to bring the conversation away from something that would make Cassie hate her again.

"Randy took me out. We went to the supermarket. We couldn't get our car to start, which was weird because it was a new car. Randy thinks it was because it relied on computer chips that must have fizzled out when the disappearance happened or something, but I've seen other new cars on the road."

"I don't know shit about computers, but I assumed they needed something to communicate with, and without people around to run all the central hubs..." he trailed off. "I don't fucking know."

Christian chuckled. "Anyway, when we got to the market,

some dude was hiding in there. We were just filling baskets with stuff we wouldn't have to cook and the dude came up behind us with a gun. He told us to put the food back and come with him. Then, he introduced us to his group. That's the group we were with. They've taken care of us ever since."

"Nah, they haven't taken care of us. They've trained us to take care of ourselves," Randy said, "and each other."

Christian nodded. "Exactly."

Lion jumped forward into an open clearing. Two felled trees crisscrossed each other, making an X.

"Let's sit on these logs for a few minutes and catch our breath," Candlestick said.

They all agreed and sat down.

Randy pulled some bottled water from his backpack and passed it around, everyone taking a swig.

Candlestick examined her legs where groups of red welts had built along her calves. She went to rub it and Randy grabbed her wrist. She tensed and made fists.

"Wait, don't touch that. Looks like you have poison ivy." He fumbled through his bag.

Candlestick looked closer at the red marks. They were itchy, and she wanted to touch them. "Are you saying I've been poisoned?"

Everyone laughed.

"No. Poison ivy is a plant that makes your skin all rashy and itchy, but it spreads if you touch it and stuff," Cassie said.

Christian leaned forward. "Actually, it doesn't transfer from skin. It's more of a problem if the oils get on your clothes."

Randy pulled out some packets from his bag. "Yeah, but she needs to clean those oils off."

He tossed her the packets. "Just rip those open and use the towelette inside to wipe off your legs. We don't have soap, so that's the best we can do."

She nodded and did as instructed.

"Who the hell hasn't heard of poison ivy?" Christian asked.

She blushed, hating being the girl who didn't know stuff. She wanted to say something smart back, something that would cut into him, hurt him, but she refrained. They were being nice and helpful, and the poison ivy reminded her how much danger lurked on Earth that she didn't understand. She needed them, no matter how much she hated to admit it.

As she wiped her legs, she glanced at Cassie who sat across from her with her little legs dangling off her log. She kicked them back and forth and looked around, lost in her thoughts.

"Cassie, it's your turn to tell a story," Candlestick said.

Everyone turned to the girl, and her face turned bright red. She looked away, unused to the spotlight. "I don't have many stories."

Christian took the water bottle from Randy and took a swig. "Tell us a nice memory you have with your parents."

She put her head down. After a minute, she whispered, "We used to go to the beach every summer. We had a summer house in Charlestown and we would all go to the beach in the evening. My mom liked it better when the tourists were all gone for the day, so we'd always go in the evening. We'd pack sandwiches and chips and soda. My parents liked to eat fancy stuff and I hated it, but on beach nights, I got to be like the other kids and eat normal foods." She took a deep breath.

Candlestick couldn't figure out if she was about to cry or if she was just struggling to speak in front of a small group.

"When people disappeared, my parents stopped caring about how fancy their food was. That was about the only good thing that came from it."

No one spoke, as if they were all afraid their voices could shatter a fragile wall built around Cassie.

She looked up, her face still beat red, glossy pools in her eyes.

Then a smile crawled up one side of her face. "Whenever my dad drank soda, he'd fart all day long."

Everyone laughed.

Lion jumped at the group's reaction.

The laughter built up inside Candlestick until she was laughing at her laughing as much as Cassie's story. It hurt and felt wonderful all at once. It wasn't just the laughing that brought her joy, either; it was the shared experience of it, as if they were all connected through the weird sounds leaving their bodies. It was a binder, a builder of camaraderie. She couldn't remember a time when she laughed so hard with her family, and she wondered if it had ever happened. Not that she could recall. She knew the experience would end in a moment and they'd be back to their journey, so she clung to it, forcing herself to laugh more and more.

Before her father died, Candlestick sat on a bed with him and Violin. They ate candy and weird foods from the store. They had fun trying new things and giggling about it. At the time, it was just a thing that happened, but once Winter died, that memory played in her head repeatedly. It was a special moment, and it passed without recognition.

She refused to do that with the moment unfolding in front of her. This was special. The laughter. Friends. She soaked it all in. Significant moments happen to everyone, and they happen all the time, but it's so rare to live in an exceptional moment and know you're there, that the place where you stand will live with you forever in the best way possible. It was the kind of moment she'd relive during her worst times, when everything seemed hopeless. She'd come back here and remember it all. The criss-crossed logs, the soggy dirt under her feet, the smell of her friends—a combination of body odor and bad breath—the chirping birds and their mismatched songs.

Tears poured down her cheeks and she gasped for breath.

Christian, Randy, and Cassie laughed just as hard, and she wondered if they recognized the moment for what it was, too.

Eventually, the laughter stopped, replaced by the somber realization they had to move on from it, that they couldn't live in laughter forever.

As they stood and gathered their things, Candlestick rubbed the bottoms of her feet against the itchy rashes on her legs.

She smiled at her group. "Thank you."

Cassie shrugged. "For what?"

"Being here."

They marched on.

"It's my turn to tell a story again." Candlestick said as they walked. "Would you like to find out what happens next with Mary?"

Arms out Straight, Fingers up

The ladder spit dust as Russ made his way down to the children. Before descending, he dropped a series of chains and tools down the well. He landed, looked around, and glared at each kid, as if trying to read their minds, see if they'd discovered their abilities. Mary hoped he couldn't actually do that, because the kids *had* learned how to tap into their magic. The problem was, they weren't very good at it. Not yet. Ellie taught them the tricks for tapping into it, but it required a lot of practice and time wasn't on their side.

Russ stopped at Crying Kid's alcove. While they had all practiced their magic, Mary discovered his name was Miller. She still liked her old name for him, so she thought of him as Miller the Crying Kid, but wouldn't say that out loud.

Russ told Miller to turn around and cross his arms. A few seconds later, Mary heard a metal-on-metal clink, and she wondered what it was. It was too thin and soft to be the chains.

Handcuffs. Shit.

It made sense. He couldn't free each person as he switched out the shackles. But handcuffs hindered their plans. Ellie had told them until they'd mastered their magic, it was best to hold their arms out straight and point their fingers to the ceiling. Doing so would help draw out the magic.

From the short time they'd had to practice, each of them could pull their magic, except Kelly, but they all needed to do the arm trick. Without it, none of them could make it work.

She wondered if Russ would take the cuffs off each kid before moving on to the next one, but she doubted it. Not until he finished giving them the new chains.

As Russ moved from Miller to Zeke, Mary peeked out of the alcove. Miller stepped out of his, stretching his legs and showing off the new length of chain. His hands were still cuffed.

Mary stepped back into her alcove and rested the back of her head against the wall. They were fucked.

"Come on, boy!" Russ yelled at Zeke.

Mary sighed. They were all getting cuffed. The plan was done. Russ would see Kelly's damaged link, and they would all be dead when Russ discovered they'd learned to use their powers.

Russ moved to Bert, and then to the quiet girl. Mary still hadn't gleaned her name. In fact, the quiet girl hadn't talked through the entire magic training, outside of nodding and giving a thumbs up as she listened to instructions. Maybe she had a disability that kept her from talking.

As Russ worked on changing out the quiet girl's chains, Mary peeked out to see Kelly peeking out at her. Her eyes were watering, and her lids opened wide. They had seconds before Russ would discover Kelly's weakened link.

Kelly took a deep breath and extended her arms, putting her hands straight with her fingers aiming toward the ceiling. Mary nodded, sending encouragement in silence.

Kelly's jaw clenched, her face tightening. The quiet girl's chains rattled, and Russ drilled the screws into the floor where the chain ended at a metal plate. Mary guessed he couldn't replicate the way the old chains melded right into the stone. Still, the drilling gave them a countdown, so she appreciated it. The first screw went in. Three more to go.

Kelly shifted her weight from one leg to the other, squinting and trying with all her might to draw her power.

Drilling. Another screw in.

Mary muttered under her breath, "Come on, Kelly. You can do it."

Drilling. One more to go.

Kelly shook her head, tears drizzling down her cheeks.

"Come on. Come on," Mary said.

Drilling. The last screw.

Russ came out of the alcove, pulling up the top of his loose jeans. He sighed and moved to the front of Kelly's alcove. He dropped a few chains on the ground. They startled Mary as they clanged against the cement floor.

Kelly's face was screwed up and she kept her arms out, hands flat.

"No," Russ said. "Hands behind your back."

Kelly pried her eyes open. She sniffled and dropped her arms. It was over.

"Turn around and put your arms behind you. Now!"

Wait. Mary could only bring Ellie back for a few minutes, but Ellie didn't say if she could do it a second time. Maybe she could keep bringing Ellie back. Who knew?

She closed her eyes, stretched her arms out, hands up. "Come on. Come on," she whispered.

"I won't tell you again. Hands behind your back. You wanna end up like your friend?"

Gurgling. It was working. Then, the heave. That brutal heave. Ellie was coming back.

Russ ran out of the alcove, moving right in front of Mary's. "What the fuck?"

Ellie opened her eyes, saw Russ, and acted. She shattered the freshly replaced lightbulbs in the room, turning everything pitch black.

There was scuffling, shouting, banging. Mary tried to make sense of it. Ellie screamed. So did Russ.

Then, something lit up the room. It was a faint red light, like a match in a fist.

Mary brought her chain as far as she could and saw the source of the glow. Kelly's hands. Her glowing hands provided enough light to reveal Russ on top of Ellie, killing her once more. Kelly's hand wrapped around her chain. The metal links melted and sizzled.

Holy fuck, Kelly was free!

She ran to Russ, slapped her hands onto his cheeks, and pressed her fingers in. His skin sizzled and smoked. He pushed away from her and clutched his wounds as he screamed in pain. The room filled with the smell of burnt flesh.

Kelly pushed into Mary's alcove and wrapped her hands around Mary's chains.

Mary had been so focused on Kelly's hands, she hadn't noticed Kelly's eyes were glowing red as well. She pushed past Kelly and while Russ was down, kicked him square in the face. He rolled over and hollered, "I'll kill you."

Mary turned to Kelly. "Free everyone. Quickly."

Ellie gasped for air. She stood up and reached her hands toward the ceiling as if trying to grip the broken lightbulbs. The bulbs, despite being smashed apart, turned back on, and heck, they were bright.

Ellie rolled over, rubbing at her neck. "Hurry. I have even less time now. Each time, I'll have less."

Russ elbowed Mary, knocking the wind out of her. "What the fuck did you do?"

He threw her down, slamming her into the cement floor. If

she had any wind left in her, it was all gone now. As she gasped for breath, he pinned himself on top of her, pressing his fingers into her throat. Ellie swatted at him, and he tossed her off with ease.

Bert charged out and stretched his arms toward Russ. He shook his head, struggling to concentrate and draw his power. Mary eyed him as Russ pressed deeper and deeper into her throat. A pressure built in her skull, and she could feel her face turning red. It was more than hot. It was like the cells pressing their way out of her.

The quiet girl ran out and instead of helping, ran right for the ladder. Luckily, she changed her mind last second and turned. With her arms outstretched, her eyes changed to green, and the entire room shook, tilting on its side, defying the laws of gravity.

Russ tumbled off Mary as the room rocked like a boat in a storm.

He stood and ran toward the quiet girl, but his loose pants slowed him down, making him waddle like a goofy duck, and suddenly Mary thought him less threatening. The kids had all the power now. Russ was fucked.

As he neared the quiet girl, Miller slid out of his alcove and slapped his hands on the cement, creating a puddle of icy slush on the ground. Russ slipped and fell onto his back, but he was back on his feet in seconds.

Bert, giving up on using his powers, ran and lunged for Russ, wrapping himself on Russ's back like a baby monkey. Russ spun around, trying to get Bert off, but in doing so, he almost slipped again.

Quiet girl kept making the room shake, Miller shot new pools of slush under Russ's feet, and Bert clung for dear life.

Kelly emerged from Zeke's alcove, raging fire in her eyes. She marched toward Russ, fists clenched. Mary would have feared those fists if they were coming toward her, with or without the brutal glowing red coming from them.

She drilled her fist into Russ's face. The cracking sound from his jaw outdid the sizzling sounds from his skin. He screamed and flopped to the floor. Bert freed himself during the fall.

Still, Russ kicked and fought.

Zeke came out of the alcove, sleeves up. He stretched his arms and put his hands up. Within seconds, stones loosened from the wall and smashed into Russ's face. Blood splattered everywhere.

Kelly sighed, dropped to her knees, and wrapped her burning hands around Russ's neck. The skin melted, and his screams turned to hoarse whistles.

"See how you fucking like it, asshole," Kelly said as she pressed harder until her hands went all the way through his neck and touched the cement below, Russ's head separated from his body.

Everyone caught their breath and turned to each other, all eyes all over. It was silent. They were riddled with anxiety and fear, but Russ was dead. They were free. They were finally fucking free.

Mary wept.

When Gods Fail

Fake Winter laid down on the counter, his hands interlocked over his stomach, listening intently as Violin ended her Kevin Bacon story. She waited for him to say something, but he just stared, as if she were supposed to continue.

"This isn't getting me anywhere. I told you another chapter of his story. It didn't help me find answers at all."

Fake Winter blinked, gasped, and stretched. "It's quite embarrassing how glib you are." He clenched his fist and waved it. "I could punch you in the face with your answers and you wouldn't receive them."

She swatted away a plume of dust that spat in her direction, thanks to Fake Winter's flailing. It was as if the dust knew to run away from him. "Fine. I'm too stupid to find the answers in these stupid stories, so why not just tell me?"

Still clenching his fist, he smacked his knuckles into his own temple. "You are frustratingly thick. I can't tell you. It's not as simple as sharing it with you. If I just told you the truth, do you not understand what it would do to me? I'd be destroyed.

Instantly. You have to come to it on your own. Trust me, I'm frustrated watching you fumble with it, and I wish I could help. It's like a parent watching a toddler learn to read. I just want to pull my hair out and finish the sentence for you."

She stood up and dusted dirt from her pants. "Well, I'm tired of the games. I would like to leave now."

"Oh, don't be so childish. You know as well as I do that you're not allowed to leave here. Why play these tough girl games?"

Violin touched a star poster, rubbing her fingers through the rough holes pelted into it. "Call them games all you want, but I promise you, the time will come when I kill you and walk out of here. Maybe I'll take some time to enjoy the rides before I leave."

He smiled and tilted his head. "I have no doubt you'll try. I know you better than you know yourself, which is exactly why you won't succeed. This is a new game for you, but it's one I've been playing since before you were born."

She threw her hands up in exhaustion. "So, what now, then?"

He put a finger up. "I'm so glad you asked. Now, I tell you a small tale and see what you think of it."

She huffed. "Whatever. I don't have much choice, do I?"

He didn't answer. Instead, he scooted forward. "Now you're getting it."

Dolphi knew the gods were up in their towers, fuming after their battle at the bar. He knew this, but he didn't see it, because he was smart enough to not return with them. When gods fail, they always look for someone else to blame and Dolphi had no doubt he'd lie right where the fingers pointed.

Rather than sit around taking the lickings, he acted. The snake was smarter than Kevin Bacon and, to be frank, much smarter than the gods. He developed a plan to get everything he wanted, but also to see the gods lose. He wasn't stupid. There wouldn't be much use for a human body if it had no planet to live on. If the gods won, they'd destroy the Earth. He knew the gods planned to scrap their whole worldly experiment, but they could not yet.

Of course, the gods didn't know he knew this. Just as his fellow people in the underground had, the gods, and Kevin Bacon, all underestimated Dolphi. These nuggets of knowledge were only the beginning to what truths lingered in his brain. It baffled the gods as to why they couldn't destroy the earth, furrowing their brows as they used all their might to expunge the world of all life.

"What is this? What's blocking me?" Raindrop whined.

Dolphi snickered as he listened to the nine debate on what caused the block. Upon freeing themselves from Orelon's belly, they destroyed multiple towns. Then, a force broke free from the fault lines of the Earth and acted as a natural barrier from the strength of the vengeful gods. After much debate, the gods agreed that Kevin Bacon and his team must be the source of the blockage, and they weren't entirely wrong, but their plans to kill Kevin Bacon would not relieve the mysterious force protecting the world.

And yet, another secret landed in Dolphi's lap, ensuring his protection and leverage against whoever he sided with. And who would Dolphi side with? Dolphi always sided with Dolphi, and that meant he would side only with those who would advance his cause. He needed Kevin Bacon to win the war, but he also needed the gods to grant him his freedom from his disgusting, slithery body. The snake cared very much about who survived once he won his freedom.

The soft, brown gravel crunched a few feet away from the jagged rocks Dolphi hid behind. For a moment, his heart flew into his tail, worried the gods had come for him, but then he smelled the sweet scent of bristlebucks and urine.

He peeked his head from behind the stones. "Ah, Mr. Bacon."

Kevin Bacon nodded. "Dolphi."

The snake slid from behind the stones and lifted his upper body. "Good to see you again, friend."

Kevin Bacon lifted one brow. "Friend? That seems a bit of a stretch."

Dolphi stuck his tongue out. "Don't be a child, Mr. Bacon. Two men can be at war and remain friends. And we aren't even at war, are we? You came here to work something out with me, and assuming the conditions are to my liking, I think we might just end up teammates."

Kevin Bacon sat down on the stone. "Call us what you will. I'd rather get to the discussion about those conditions."

Dolphi smiled. "Yes, let's."

"Well, spill it. What do you want?"

Dolphi pushed his body forward, putting his head right in Kevin Bacon's face. "I want everything. When you win the war, I want to be a god."

Kevin Bacon laughed so loudly he scared away a nearby armadillo. "You want me to make you a god for keeping a secret? Absurd."

Dolphi slithered around Kevin Bacon's torso. "You silly fool. No. In exchange, I will tell you how to defeat the gods, and a big doozy of a secret that you will be thrilled to hear."

"If, and only if, your secret leads to me winning the war with the gods, I will grant you god status, but you will be one god of many, and we will keep you in line."

Dolphi loosened his grip on Kevin Bacon. "Deal."

He put his head on Kevin's hand and shook.

"Now, tell me this big secret."

Dolphi used his body to draw a circle in the sand. "The gods have been trying to destroy the Earth, but something is blocking them."

Kevin got on his knees and rubbed a finger around the circle. "What is it?"

"Some kind of power they can't identify. They think it's you, but it is not."

"So, what is it?"

Dolphi made a stick figure in the middle of the circle. "The baby."

"The baby? I brought the baby to this world for a later use. I didn't know it would be helpful now."

Dolphi shook his head. "You fool. You plucked life from the depths of darkness and created a being that the gods can't see. And you believe this baby to be nothing more than a tool for future endeavors? Mr. Bacon, you are dumber than I thought. You think you've landed on something special by figuring out the ingredients to my god-killing bullets? You created the ultimate god-killer."

Kevin Bacon drew a smaller circle around the stick figure. "The child?"

Dolphi nodded. "The child."

* * *

"Let me interrupt you," Violin said.

Fake Winter's face went from playful to enraged. "Never interrupt a man telling a story."

Violin walked to the counter, causing Fake Winter to stand and put his arms up defensively.

"These stories are important to you," she said.

"Yes," he replied.

"Good. Then I know your weakness. Kevin Bacon ran to the child."

"No, that's not how it goes."

"Yes, it is. Kevin Bacon ran through the woods, headed for the child that would save them from the gods."

"No!" Fake Winter yelled and hopped off the counter. "He did not. Not yet. He ran toward his friends, who he believed were still hiding in the cave, though they were actually out fighting Rapture."

Violin shook her head and stepped closer. "Wrong. Kevin Bacon knew his friends were safe and he could get to them whenever he needed. He had to get the child first, the unprotected child who held the key to his survival."

Fake Winter balled his fists. "Stupid girl. Wrong. The baby was stronger than Kevin Bacon, stronger than the gods even. There was no need for him to rush to the baby. By running to it, he'd only be putting it on the gods' radar. He needed to gather his army first. His friends from the bar, and his friends from the cave."

Every step Violin made closer to Fake Winter caused him to step back an inch. "Kevin Bacon rushed through the forest, his feet moving faster than his brain. He couldn't wait to hold the baby in his hands."

"No. No. No." Fake Winter gnashed his teeth and back-handed Violin across the face.

The sudden act of violence after Fake Winter had just shown fear in his eyes shocked Violin. She touched her stinging cheek.

Fake Winter stormed out of the shelter and rummaged through something. He came back with electrical tape. She dropped back to the hard and lumpy ground as Fake Winter tackled her. He overpowered her, ripped a piece of tape off, and pressed it over her mouth. Once secured enough to keep her from talking, he took more and wrapped it around her face until she could hardly move her mouth at all.

When he finished, he stood up and dusted off his pants. "You will not steal this story from me. You know how it goes and you intentionally violated its path just to upset me. No. You will do no such thing. *I* will tell the story and *you* will listen. If you try to divert it again, it will force me to kill you. The story is everything. I won't let you ruin this."

The Story Itself

Kevin Bacon stopped running toward the child, changing his plans. Instead, he rushed to the bar to gather his new friends before returning to his kin in the cave. He reached the bar just before dusk, but the dimming light did nothing to quell the spirit of his team as they toiled to rebuild The Edge of Glory.

"Mr. Bacon's back," Elvis said with a curled lip.

"Indeed, I am."

Lady Gaga stepped down from a ladder and spit a nail on the hard dirt. "How did it go with Dolphi?"

"Depends on if he's lying to me or not."

Avril continued sanding new pieces of wood for the walls but turned her head to the conversation. "Do you think he's telling the truth?"

"Strangely, I do." Kevin Bacon turned to Elvis. "You said something to me, but I think it's wrong."

Elvis popped his collar. "What's that now?"

"You told me to rein the story in, that it used to matter, but I had let it go off course."

"Uh huh."

"You forgot something. Every story has value. It doesn't have to define something or answer a long-lost question. It just needs to..." He hesitated, struggling to come up with the word.

"A story has to have a point."

"The story itself is the point."

"Nonsense."

Kevin Bacon lifted his finger. "Exactly." He gripped Elvis's arms and shook him. "Nonsense. Nonsense is perfect."

"Nonsense is disgusting."

"Nonsense is how we win."

"Win what?"

Kevin Bacon sighed. "Imagine this. A man walks to work every day. He goes the same route, does the same thing, takes the same steps, waits at the same cross sections. Always the same."

Lady Gaga and Avril moved closer, trying to hear out the story.

"But he's always five minutes late to work. So, he tries different things, moving a little faster, jogging instead of walking, taking a shortcut, avoids the cross sections. Still, he ends up five minutes late."

Elvis shrugged. "So, what's he do?"

Kevin threw his hands up. "Nothing. There is nothing he can do. Five minutes late is like his destiny."

Elvis shook his head, angry with that answer. "That's absurd. He's gotta find a solution."

Kevin Bacon eyed them all, starting at Elvis, moving to Avril, then to Lady Gaga. "Hey, where's Ben Franklin?"

Lady Gaga nodded toward the back of the building. "He's out there trying to bring the power back."

Without a word, Kevin Bacon walked past the group, heading toward the back. "Mr. Franklin?"

Ben came around to the side of the building, small sparks of electricity crackling at his fingertips. "Yes?"

Kevin smiled at him and waved. "Question for ya. If a man is always five minutes late for work every day, what does he do to fix the problem?"

"Changes his routine, of course."

Kevin Bacon leapt with excitement. "Right. And if that doesn't work?"

Ben Franklin thought for a second, and then with no change in his expression, he said, "Quit the job."

Kevin Bacon latched his arms around him and hugged powerfully. "Exactly right."

Elvis stepped toward them. "What does that have to do with our conversation?"

Kevin Bacon turned to him. "We have to find my friends. Follow me. While you do, I need you to do me a favor. Tell me the story of the man who walks to work five minutes late."

The entire group followed Kevin Bacon as he walked away from The Edge of Glory, none of them putting up any kind of fight.

Elvis huffed. "Man wakes up, gets dressed, heads out the door, walks down the road, waits at a cross section, gets to work five minutes late."

"Good story. Tell it again."

Elvis rolled his eyes as the crew moved beyond the arid desert sand into a thickly wooded area, and then he told the story again, exactly as he had the first time.

Kevin convinced Elvis to repeat the story over and over until, finally, the man broke. "What the hell are you doing this for?"

Kevin Bacon cleared some shrubs. "You'll notice that while the man's routine never changed, your story did. Just a few words different here and there, but nonetheless, it wasn't the same story, was it?"

"Okay, so what?"

Kevin Bacon turned back to the group. "On my way to meet you, I felt myself free, as if someone had taken the shackles off, so to speak. You all said something similar happened to you, correct?"

They all nodded.

"Do you feel that way anymore?"

Lady Gaga stopped in her tracks. Avril scrunched her brow.

"No," Ben Franklin said.

Elvis looked at all of them, waiting for an answer. "What does it mean?"

Kevin Bacon took a step toward Elvis and frowned. "It means we aren't in control of the story anymore. It's our story alright, but don't the words feel just a little off?"

"So, what do we do?"

"Ben, what does a man do when he's always five minutes late to work?"

"He quits."

Kevin Bacon smiled. "It's time for a little nonsense, friends."

He sat down in a small dirt clearing and crossed his legs.

"I don't understand," Avril said, as she plopped her skateboard down and sat next to him.

"I mean, we quit. We let the nine gods win, and we die. Either that, or we get our story back. Call it a game of chicken."

Just then, something large and furry flew past Kevin Bacon's face. All eyes followed the object as it thudded into a tree with a groan. The furry thing stood up and shook itself off before turning toward the group.

Kevin Bacon stood up in surprise. "Rapture?"

Rapture did a double take. "Oh fuck. You're here, too?"

A series of crashes came from within the depths of shrubs and thick greens. First, Dance cleared the line, then Miley Cyrus and Laura Jane Grace. They were all covered in blood, scratches, and bruises. The trees parted and Abraham Lincoln's giant face came into view. Three humans sat on his shoulder, green with sick from the ride.

"Brother!" Lincoln shouted.

"Ah, just in time, my siblings. Have a seat with my new friends."

Confusion crossed his siblings' faces. Miley Cyrus pointed to Rapture. "We can't sit right now. We're kind of warring with the furry things."

Rapture shook some dirt from his fur. "And you're losing, I might add."

Kevin patted the ground next to him. "You too, Rapture. Join us. Tell your animal friends to relax. We can all kill each other another time. For now, we're all quitting."

"Quitting what?" Laura Jane Grace asked.

Kevin Bacon put his lower lip over his top lip, and then said, "Everything, I suppose."

* * *

"What the hell is happening?" Fake Winter glared at Violin, who sat cross-legged with her mouth taped shut.

"Are you doing this? What did you do to my story?"

She put her hands out.

"No. You don't have the power to change the story like this. Not yet anyway. You're too stupid."

She rolled her eyes. Fake Winter paced, mumbling to himself.

"This can't happen. I need to finish this story for you."

He slammed his fist into the stone wall, blood splattering everywhere from his knuckles. "Fine. I'll tell the story without them. The story doesn't need Kevin Bacon. Kevin Bacon needs the story. See how he likes not existing at all!"

Discounts at the End of the World

By the time Corey and Brian reached the weird neighborhood where Violin had once lived with her family, Corey's lungs were burning fire. A combination of running for far longer than he was used to and inhaling wafts of smoke took their toll. As he hopped into the passenger seat, he coughed a raspy seal-like croak.

Brian coughed much the same way as he kicked the car into reverse, peeled out onto the road, and sped away from the scene.

It took a few minutes of driving before either of them had gained control of their throats enough to speak, both panting and hacking their way to normalcy.

Brian turned the car onto 95, away from the motel they once stayed at with Winter and his family.

"Where are we going?" Corey asked. "Don't get on the highway."

"Just for a minute." Brian kept his word, bouncing from one exit to the next. Just like the road by the motel, 95 also appeared clear of cars. Pieces of broken glass and car parts littered the breakdown lanes, but the cars themselves had been removed.

As they popped off the exit into Hopkinton's little downtown area, a road with a few chain dining locations, a supermarket, a cigar bar, and a discount goods store, Corey noticed the small-town roads were also cleared of vehicles. "Who did this?"

"Did what?"

"Cleared the roads."

"I don't know," Brian said. "Must have taken a long time, though."

Corey slid his finger down the passenger side window, staring at the parking lots as they zipped by, all filled with cars, too many cars. "Or a lot of manpower."

Brian looked at him, did a double take once the words came into clear view. "Shit. Yeah."

"Where are we going?"

"The fair grounds." Brian jerked the wheel and pulled the car into the Job Lot parking lot. "But first, let's get some supplies."

"You're even going discount at the end of the world?"

Brian covered his mouth as he let out a big laugh. He put his hand on Corey's knee and smiled. "Let's get this done quickly."

Corey watched Brian exit the car and cross by the hood. So cavalier. Corey finally opened his door. "What are you doing?"

"What do you mean?"

"Shouldn't we scope it out first? Don't you remember the supermarket?"

Brian listed his head. "It's not a supermarket. It's Job Lot. No one would choose to hide in there."

Corey's back ached as he stood from the car. "Brian, I'm serious. We have to be careful. I know we're on a mission, but we can't start acting stupid. Jesus, it wasn't that long ago we were hiding out in the woods, avoiding people at all costs. Now we're going on shopping expeditions and driving on the highway?"

Brian put his head down. "You're right. I'm acting stupid."

Corey put his hands on Brian's shoulders. "No, you're acting like you're on a holy mission, like nothing bad can happen to you because you have a higher purpose, and maybe you do, but I don't think that means we can be so…"

Before he could finish, a giant boom rocked the atmosphere. The ground under them shook. Instinctively, Brian and Corey took cover at the front of the car. Corey's heart banged into his ribs as he ducked down. Across a small side road, plumes of flame shot out of the front windows of the supermarket, and the entire front façade was engulfed. Gunshots rang out and men shouted.

"Fuck. I drove us right into the middle of someone else's war," Brian said.

Corey stared at the Job Lot automatic front doors as Brian peeked over the hood, trying to figure out the action across the road. The gunshots continued for a few more minutes, and then the shouting died out.

"What are you seeing?" Corey asked, his heart racing.

"There are some men scouting the parking lot. I think they killed whoever they were after and now they are clearing the area, making sure they finished the job."

"Do you think they'll make their way over here?" Corey asked, still focusing sharply on the Job Lot front door.

Brian shook his head. "Nah, I think the bomb was thrown by the dead guys and these men were defending their store. I don't think they'll leave the area."

"But if people are living in that market, they've probably already taken what they need from the Job Lot, too."

Brian sighed. "Doesn't matter. We can't go in there now. We should get the fuck out of here."

"No," Corey said.

"What do you mean? Did you not see what just happened?"

Corey pointed to the door. "Yes, and I've been watching that door this entire time, and I haven't seen a single person come to it. If you were hiding out in a Job Lot and you heard guns and explosions across the way, wouldn't you check out what was happening?"

"Okay, even if that's true, it's just Job Lot. We don't need anything in there. I just thought we could fuel up, grab some snacks, maybe get some garden tools to use as weapons, some useful things like bungee, but we don't *need* any of it."

Corey pried his eyes from the door and looked Brian in the eyes. "We do. We need to go in there."

"Why?"

"Because I'm fucking tired of being afraid all the time. We're getting supplies and we're finding Violin."

Brian looked over the hood again. "The men are working to put out the fire. With their space covered in flames, I wouldn't be surprised if they move over here soon. If they have people with them, children, they might usher them over here ASAP. If we are going in, let's do it now."

Corey stood up and felt around the small of his back, making sure his handgun was still tucked in his pants. "This is a dumb decision."

"Then let's not do it."

"Oh no. We're fucking doing it." Corey marched through the lot, toward the front door of Job Lot, purpose in his steps. He had a higher calling to fulfill. A mission. A purpose.

Brian stepped in sync with him and Corey glanced over to give him a smile.

Love and Hate

Candlestick led the group through hours of marching and they followed without complaint. Lion's eyes grew tired. Candlestick knew she should stop, but sensed they were close to home, nearing something familiar. She had seen nothing that brought back any memories, but she felt it, knew her family had trekked nearby. It was almost as if she could smell her father's scent, a faded piece of him still lingering where he had once led.

The fire disc disappeared, leaving streaks of pink in the sky. The glow disc hid behind the trees, but was too big tonight, too orange to hide well. Soon, darkness would come and the group would need rest. Maybe it was best to start early to make the most out of tomorrow.

"Should we rest?" she asked.

Christian and Randy dropped their packs instantly. "Yes," they both said.

Cassie sat with Candlestick and taught her how to play Tic Tac Toe with some sticks in the dirt while Randy and Christian worked to get a fire going and set up a tent. Candlestick marveled they could get an entire shelter rolled up and squished into Christian's backpack. He also had cans of tuna that he shared with the group. They all took turns digging their fingers into cans and munching on fistfuls of meat. Candlestick couldn't tell if she loved the taste or hated it. Cassie absolutely hated it, which she expressed with a scrunched face after each bite, but it didn't stop her from taking some every time a new can made its way around.

As Christian chewed on his tuna, he turned to Candlestick. "Tell us about your sister."

Candlestick licked her fingertips. "She's smart."

"What else?" he asked.

She shrugged. "She's smart, and stubborn, and a pain in the ass, and funny, and angry, and strong, and weak, and I love her, and I hate her."

Christian's eyes grew wide. "So, complicated?"

"Yes, she's incredibly complicated."

Randy stretched. "Who the hell isn't? I'm gonna go to bed. Christian, wake me up when you get tired, and we can switch who gets night watch."

Christian nodded.

"I guess I'm going to go to bed, too," Candlestick said.

She stared at Cassie for a moment, waiting for the girl to say the same, but Cassie didn't. Finally, Candlestick prodded, "Are you coming, Cassie?"

"I think I'm going to stay up for a bit."

Candlestick shifted. "Okay. I can stay up with you." Her eyes went from Cassie to Christian.

"Don't worry about it. I'll be good."

She hesitated but got up and followed Randy into the tent.

"I'll sleep on this side so Cassie can sleep next to you when she gets in here," Randy said, and Candlestick smiled at the kind gesture.

She tried to drift off, but heard Cassie giggling outside the tent, and her stomach turned. She didn't know why, but it did. An anger boiled inside her and, again, she didn't understand the cause, but she knew where it aimed. It aimed at both Cassie and Christian.

She tossed to her side, hoping for more comfort, and she bent the pillow around her head to cover her ears.

Randy rolled over to his side, so they were staring at each other. "Christian won't do anything."

"What do you mean?" Candlestick asked.

"He's way older than her. She has a crush on him, but he isn't a perv."

Candlestick frowned. "Why should I care what they do?"

Randy smiled and rolled over, away from her. "Because you do."

It took a long time, but eventually she fell asleep. She woke briefly when Cassie unzipped the tent and came in, but didn't wake up again until Christian came barreling in, waking them all up in a hurry.

Her muddled mind couldn't make sense of what he was saying, but something happened outside. Randy was right on top of it, charging outside with fiery eyes, ready for war. Cassie and Candlestick took their time, half-awake and hoarse voiced.

"What is it?" Candlestick asked as she exited the tent but didn't need an answer once she left the inside of their shelter. In the distance, gigantic balls of fire blasted skyward, loud crackles and bangs accompanying them.

Randy balled his fists. "Let's go check it out. Slowly, quietly. We stick together."

"Why would we go near the fire?" Cassie asked.

"Because we need to see what caused it. Someone could try to push us out. This could be antagonistic. Even if it's not, it could be someone burning shit to the ground, and if they are making their way here, I'd rather not be twiddling my thumbs when it happens."

Christian nodded. "Let's go that way." He pointed parallel to the fire, but in the direction where it seemed lowest. "That's where it looks like it started, and whoever is responsible is moving that way."

"How do you know that? They don't have to be moving with the fire," Cassie said.

"Because it spread way too fast. Someone is setting different fires."

Everyone accepted that explanation and followed him. The closer they got, the hotter the atmosphere turned. Candlestick sweated, and her heart begged for more sleep.

They reached the edges of the forest and came into view of a road with houses on both sides, most of them nothing more than piles of burnt wood.

Candlestick stood up straight. Waves of heat blasted toward her, as did waves of sadness and excitement, jumbled together into something she couldn't hold. She dropped to her knees and wept.

"What's wrong?" Christian asked.

"I know this street. We lived here for a little while."

Wind blew the thick plumes of smoke and gave the gang a view of the ends of the road. The fires still blazed heavily on that end. The shadows of a human stood in the middle of the road, staring up at the fires. For a moment, Candlestick filled in his outlines, giving him weight and shape he didn't truly possess. She turned him into her father.

Candlestick stood and stepped forward an inch. The man wasn't looking their way, and even if he was, they'd be hard to see behind the smoke, just as he was hard to see to them. She wiped away her tears and shook away her emotions. It obviously wasn't her father.

She couldn't even say with any confidence it was a man. The features too dim, too sheathed in smoke. Maybe it was a woman. What were they doing in the middle of the road between fires?

Did they set the fire, or just hope to drown in it?

"What should we do?" Cassie asked in a whisper.

Candlestick didn't whisper. It would be impossible to hear them over the loudness of the flames and burning wood. "I don't think he or she is a threat."

Christian stepped forward. "I don't know. Who the fuck would stand and observe a fire from its epicenter? They're gonna die in there. Should we help them? Or are they the ones doing this?"

Candlestick shrugged. "He's gone mad. Broken. Even if he finds us, we can handle him. I understand, because I was him. I was dangerous, but I was also at my weakest, not in control."

Randy crossed his arms. "Maybe you're right."

He was trying to act tough, she knew, because he didn't know she had monsters at her disposal and thought himself some sort of leader.

"Tomorrow morning, we should return here when the flames are gone and check the houses my family stayed in. We left some supplies hidden in a few of them. Water and cans of food."

"I doubt it survived," Christian said.

"It was on the bottom floor, hidden in metal machines. It's worth trying."

They turned and headed back to the tent.

"I guess I'll tell a quick story until we get back," Candlestick said.

Snuffed out Matches

Mary was the last to emerge above ground, and the rest of the kids were waiting for her, circled around the opening she climbed from. Everyone was smiling, the taste of freedom on their lips.

"We did it," Zeke said.

Miller was crying still, but joy produced these tears instead of fear.

Kelly ran to Mary and hugged her. "I couldn't have done it without you."

"We get to go home?" Mary asked. She knew the answer, of course, but it didn't feel real. Then a new thought crossed her mind. *Where is home?* Her father was dead, and her mother had died years before. She had no home.

Still, the idea of fleeing far from this place brought chills of delight up her spine. Seeing the sun alone had already made her lose her breath. She wanted nothing more than to touch a tree, sit in the open air, feel the world.

Kelly noticed the worried look in her eyes and leaned into her, whispering, "We all need to find a new home."

Mary forced a fake smile, as if the unification of their pain would somehow make her endure. People always want you to know you're not alone in your suffering, but that didn't make Mary feel better. Knowing her friends suffered with her only heightened the awfulness.

They stood there for a long time, too long, each clearly eager to leave, but none willing to part from the rest. They'd been bonded through trauma, connected through a thick fear that connected their souls, entwined them. She hardly knew these kids, but she loved them all the same.

Eventually, they parted. Miller first, then Bert. Quiet Girl and Zeke left, traveling in different directions. Mary noticed Zeke turned his back a few times, giving them last looks before he disappeared through the tall grass toward the river.

When it was just Mary and Kelly left, they stared at each other for a minute with awkward grins on their faces.

"First ones in, last ones to leave," Kelly said.

"So it seems."

Kelly put her head down. "I'd say we should keep in touch, but is that really possible?"

"I wouldn't know what to give you as a means to find me."

"Same."

They both drew their eyes to the dusty, hay riddled barn floor.

"I think we'll meet again," Kelly finally said.

"What makes you say that?" Mary didn't have the same optimism.

"I feel like we're connected. Like our paths were meant to crisscross."

Mary smiled. "I hope so."

"Can I tell you something strange?" Kelly kicked a scrim of dust, and it shot up like a thin stream of hail.

"Yeah." Mary crossed her arms, suddenly cold from the light spring breeze.

"I hate this place. I never want to see it again. Looking at that place..." She pointed to Russ's house. "... Heck, even just being in this barn makes my stomach turn."

"Same."

"But the thing is, I'm going to miss it here. I feel like I need to run away as fast as I can, but I also feel like I'll be leaving a part of myself behind when I do."

Mary wept, couldn't hold it in anymore. "Me too. I don't feel like I've removed the shackles at all."

Kelly ran to her, hugging her tight. They gripped each other and squeezed out as much poison from the last few weeks as they could before they, too, parted and headed off in their own directions.

The daytime slipped away as Mary crossed the stream into the woods where her father died. And just as Kelly described it, Mary felt like she lost more of herself with each step. As if a thread of her soul snagged in her alcove, and the more Mary walked, the more it unwound. She was losing herself.

Nighttime had crept in by the time she found the spot where Russ shot her father, his body still slumped over the log, decomposing. Some of the meat had been torn away, probably eaten by hungry animals. She thought she wouldn't be able to look at it, but she could. In fact, she had a hard time looking away. A stark reminder of how dangerous and horrible the world was.

The temperature was warm, but Mary shivered with cold. Spring offered cool breezes, something she used to love, but now it hurt like slaps to her skin.

She moved on, saying goodbye to her father and thinking of her bed. When Russ killed her dad, they weren't far from their cabin. She'd be home in ten minutes.

She cried some more on the way, releasing deluges of pent-up fear, hate, and grief.

When she reached the clearing where her cabin rested, something felt off. It was too dark to notice any differences, but it felt wrong. Maybe she just clung to memories so tightly while trapped in her alcove that she came to believe the cabin looked exactly as her mind saw it, which was probably with a more positive lens than it deserved. Still, a nervous prickle shocked her skin as she moved closer.

She reached forward and pushed the door in. It opened with a whine. Her heart raced as the darkness swallowed her. She stuck her arm out, flailing for the lantern she and her father always kept to the right of the door on a small wooden shelf.

She couldn't find it, her fingers thwapping against the wall. Panic set in, cold, dreaded fear. The forest behind grew just as dense with darkness, as if the night sky were trying to eat her whole. She lost her breath, unable to draw it from her lungs, and she slapped harder against the wall, searching for that damn shelf.

When her fingers finally hit it, she slid her hand down until it touched the bottom of the lantern. She grabbed it, and the box of matches next to it, and fumbled to light the wick. Two matches lit and blew out, tendrils of smoke taunting her for failing to bring the flame to wick.

She gasped and tried a third time, finally bringing the lantern to life. Light danced and waved across the room as she swayed her arms, searching for a devil in the darkness, but none came. It was her cabin as she'd always known it. The cabin hadn't changed a bit. It was her that had changed.

Trauma had altered her, revealing truths she couldn't see before. Safety was an illusion she had relied on, and Russ snuffed it out like those weak matches. A traumatized person knew they couldn't run to safety because safety, like magic in fairytales, only exists if you believe in it. Four walls and a roof meant nothing to someone who spotted cracks in the foundation.

Mary sat at the kitchen table, folding her arms around herself, listening to the rustling leaves dancing in the cool night breeze. She stayed that way, begging her mind to rest, to let her get some sleep, but none came.

And then a figure appeared on her doorstep.

The Eight Gods are Coming

Fake Winter's eyes matched the fire in front of him. He'd made a firepit on a small lane of dirt that traveled in front of their shelter, and a dozen shelters just like it. Fake Winter called it *the midway*.

Violin grew claustrophobic from the tape over her mouth. She couldn't stay like this much longer. She needed an escape.

Fake Winter clapped his hands, snapping himself back to reality. He stood. The heat from the flames made his body look like it was wavering, curling at strange angles.

"No. I can't do the story without Kevin Bacon's participation. I can't. But I can force him to play along. He wants a game of chicken. Well, he'll get one."

Violin leaned to her side, using her elbow to bring herself down until her head was resting on the cold, pebbly dirt.

"No, you cannot sleep. Pay attention. We have a lot more story to tell."

* * *

Kevin Bacon introduced his siblings to his new friends. Everyone got along swimmingly.

Avril, Lady Gaga, Miley Cyrus, and Laura Jane Grace made up a song together called "The Eight Gods are Coming."

Rapture snarled at Dance, letting her know the temporary peace was only until they were back in control of themselves. Then, he planned to rip her to shreds. If Dance was concerned, she didn't show it.

Eventually, the song proved true and the eight gods arrived, snide smiles all over their faces.

"Oh, this is wonderful. All our marks in one spot. Thanks for making this easy on us, everyone." Dark Skies smiled.

Kevin Bacon yawned. "I suppose you'll kill us now."

A rainbow-colored god stepped forward. "T'was the plan, yes."

"You know, as much as a war between us is inevitable, you also know that you're not in control of the story. It would benefit you greatly to join us in our strike," Kevin Bacon said.

Abraham Lincoln nibbled on a tree branch. "Stupid gods won't care. They are too weak to truly be in control. All they want is to fight."

Dark Skies pushed the rainbow-colored god to the side. "Excuse me, Prism." He stepped closer to Kevin Bacon. "What in the world are you talking about?"

"I'm not talking about anything in this world. What I am talking about is very much not of this world at all."

Miley Cyrus flicked a toothpick at Dark Skies. "What he means is, you think you're the one pulling the strings, but it ain't you."

Kevin Bacon stood up and smiled at the god, figuring out a way to use Dolphi's secret to get the gods to help him on his new quest. A little lying would go a long way, he hoped. "You've been wondering why you can't destroy the world, right?" He leaned in and whispered, "Someone else is telling your story."

Dark Skies snarled. "And if I play along, you realize you'll only be delaying the inevitable, correct?"

"Whatever. Doesn't matter. I'm not in control of myself. So, who cares?"

Dark Skies turned to his siblings. A few of them shrugged. Prism frowned. After scanning his brothers and sisters for their thoughts, he turned back to Kevin Bacon. "Why are we protesting and not finding the source of our woes? Together, we could kill him or her quickly and be back to our war."

Lady Gaga and Elvis came to Kevin Bacon's side.

Avril sat up from her skateboard.

"If you're willing to help, I think that would be a splendid idea."

The two shook hands, giving each other untrusting looks.

* * *

Fake Winter fell backwards. "Oh, they really think they can push me, don't they?"

He kicked the flames, sending them squirming like angry snakes.

"Fools! I'll show them."

* * *

While Kevin Bacon and Dark Skies planned their attack on the storyteller, Dolphi sneaked up to the heavens. He slid around pillars, smiling at the freedom he had in the place he'd always longed to live. Once a sycophant for foolish animal tribes, a slave to politicians. Now, Dolphi ruled, and soon he would own it all. Everything.

He slid up a wooden klinē where Patches, the goddess of blood, had rested, showing off her beauty just hours before. Her perfume lingered, nearly making Dolphi gag.

The snake moved to the head of the klinē, where Patches had left a bowl of fruit. He snatched an apple in his jaws, and then whipped his head until the apple flew off into the colorful blobs of everything.

And then, he waited.

* * *

Everyone gathered around Kevin Bacon and Dark Skies while they drew out plans in the dirt.

And then an apple flew by their faces.

* * *

The apple swung back into the heavens, dripping with blobs of everything. Dolphi caught it in his mouth and chewed. He took his time, savoring each bite of knowledge. It tasted sweet. It tasted glorious. It tasted like freedom.

Dolphi's eyes glowed and his body tensed. His tongued dropped from his mouth and he screamed. Not of anguish, but of pure glory.

Dolphi was a god. Well, at least, a small portion of one.

As he coiled his body and lifted his head, searching for sweet nectar to celebrate his new status, a hand wrapped around his throat and ripped him from heavens, driving him through the colorful blobs and slamming him into the ground of the forest. Around him stood Kevin Bacon and his family, and Dark Skies's with his siblings.

* * *

"No. No. No," Fake Winter said, kicking like a petulant child.

* * *

Dark Skies threw the snake into a tree. "Protest or not, I can't let this snake take over my heavens."

Kevin Bacon stood in front of him. "I'm afraid if we are going to make this plan work, you'll have to."

Dark Skies crossed his arms. "Move."

"I cannot."

Dark Skies's siblings gathered around him, and Kevin Bacon's team did the same on his side.

"This is looking like a short-lived truce, Mr. Bacon," Dark Skies said.

Kevin Bacon tilted his head toward the treetops where Abraham Lincoln munched on leaves, watching the action below. "I suppose my family and I could protest our story after we kill you."

"Then I guess it's war time."

* * *

Fake Winter jumped. "Oh, yes. Oh, this is better than I expected. It's perfect."

He bent to Violin's level and gripped his hand around her mouth. "This is it, dear. All you need to do is hear about the war and you'll know everything. You'll know who you are. You'll know why I needed this. You'll know the answer to almost every question you have."

He stood up and took a deep breath. "Finally. I've waited for this day for decades. Finally." He covered his face with his hands, weeping. "Finally."

Violin's stomach lurched into her throat. She didn't know the importance of any of this, but she knew the results would horrify her. Nothing good would come from him finishing the story. She needed to get out of here.

Inhaled

When the group reached their tent, Randy and Cassie dropped right back to sleep while Christian sat on a rock, keeping watch. Candlestick's eyes burned, desperate for sleep, but she wanted to talk to Christian first.

"How are you doing?" Candlestick asked.

Surprised by her abnormal niceties, he furrowed his brow and said, "Okay," slowly.

She sat on the rock next to him. "Seems like you and Cassie are hitting it off."

He looked up at the sky. "She's cool. I think she has a crush on me."

Candlestick wrapped her arms around her legs. "What makes you say that?"

"She giggles at everything I say, even when I'm not trying to be funny."

A pang landed in Candlestick's gut. Had Candlestick ever made Cassie laugh? She wanted to pry further, to make Christian say he would never be interested in her, would never try anything, but she'd learned men were not to be trusted. He'd tell her what she wanted to hear, but he would abide by only what he felt in the moment. Humans, especially human men, were unwilling to sacrifice their desires for anyone.

As she walked back to the tent, she thought about Christian and Randy and wondered if she was being fair. They'd done everything to help her. They had sacrificed to help her find her sister. In return, they'd asked for nothing. Randy had seen the hurt in Candlestick's face, read her like a book, and promised her his cousin wouldn't pursue Cassie, and Christian had done nothing to prove otherwise.

Candlestick had witnessed her sister and father argue about humanity's potential for kindness many times and had seen each of them flip-flop on the topic. She, herself, had changed her tune frequently. She thought of Corey and Brian, how they'd helped the girls learn about the world while Winter lay dying in bed. The two men had never once harmed Candlestick or Violin. They had shown nothing but kindness and love.

Maybe Christian and Randy were the same. Candlestick trusted Cassie, didn't she? She believed the girl worthy of friendship. Clearly, she found some respect for humans.

Maybe Candlestick had a bias toward men. Most of her influences growing up were women. Her only genuine connection to a man was her father, a figure no other man could ever live up to.

She fell asleep debating the value of humanity in her head, and dreamt of men warring with one another.

In the morning, she woke to Christian sleeping where Randy had been and Cassie still snugged next to her. She was tired, her sleep broken by bad dreams and deep thoughts. She stared at her two sleeping friends, and despite her desire to go outside and get air, worried about leaving them alone together in a tent.

Eventually, she relented, creeping out to avoid waking them.

She hoped one would come out way before the other so they wouldn't have time together alone and awake.

Randy sat on the same rock Christian had sat on. He was smoking a cigarette. The fires in the distance had gone out, but smoke still bellowed from the area. Luckily, it drove in the opposite direction from their camp. Lion slept peacefully beside the tent.

"What is that? I knew two women who loved those things. Smoking, is it?"

Randy chuckled. "Seriously, who the hell are you? You don't know what poison ivy is. You don't know what smoking is. Were you raised under a rock?"

She sat next to him. "Yes. Exactly. So, tell me. What is smoking? Why do you do it? Is it good for you?"

He laughed as he inhaled, causing him to cough until his face turned red. "Nah. It isn't good for you. In fact, it's terrible for you. I used to vape but, believe it or not, cigarettes are much easier to find in the apocalypse."

She held her hand out. "I don't know what the apocalypse is, but why do people do things that aren't good for them?"

A smile crawled up the left side of his face, and he handed the cigarette to Candlestick. "Because it feels good."

She took the cigarette, put it to her lips, and inhaled. A cloud entered her lungs and burned like a million insect stings. She coughed and gagged, spitting up saliva all over her shirt. Randy laughed. She dropped the cigarette and bent over, roaring out hacks from her lungs. Randy bent down and picked the cigarette from the dirt, wiping it off before taking another drag.

As she continued to cough, he said, "Don't worry, that happens to everyone the first time. It gets better and better every time you try it, though."

When the coughs subsided, she stood up and walked away. "I'll never try it again. It doesn't matter if something feels good.

Our purpose is to survive. Everything we do should be for that one goal."

"Wrong."

She turned back to him, arms crossed, foot tapping. "What else could be our purpose?"

Smoke poured from his lips like a sly snake. "To live."

She thought about when they had sat in the forest laughing and how much she wished for similar moments with her family growing up. Her community had worked so hard to survive, they'd forgotten to live. In the end, they failed to enjoy life or to survive. Maybe Randy was right. But then she coughed again, the burn still living in her lungs. She thought about Cassie, and her crush on Christian. Cassie was probably thinking about enjoying life as well, unconcerned about who she hurt in the process. Maybe joy for one was always pain for another. Maybe it was selfish to think about finding happiness.

The tent's flap opened and Cassie crawled out. She smiled at Candlestick and ran to her. Candlestick returned the smile and the two girls latched their arms and Candlestick guided her friend for a walk through the woods.

"How are you?" Candlestick asked.

"I'm good. Christian is so cute when he's sleeping."

Candlestick rolled her eyes but said nothing. The girls walked around the perimeter of their makeshift camp. They didn't say much, just strolled in the clear morning air, unmarred by the smoke coming from the neighborhood just a mile or so away. As their feet met blades of grass, morning dew cooled their toes.

Candlestick almost urged Cassie to stop thinking of Christian that way but knew her words would only push Cassie toward him. Instead, she chose to win Cassie over. She just had to figure out how.

Clearly, they'd become friends, but she wanted Cassie to feel more for her, to need her deeply. She wanted to be a million bug bites in Cassie's throat, something that stings at first, but brings joy in the end, as Randy described it. She didn't care if she was there to help Cassie survive or to bring her joy; she just wanted to be Cassie's purpose, yearning for Cassie to inhale her the way Randy did his cigarette.

Candlestick had an army of monsters at her disposal and yet, with Cassie, she felt so helpless, and that was something she'd promised herself never to feel again.

She turned to the girl, surprised to see her friend staring at her with wide eyes. It made her cheeks turn hot.

Cassie said, "Can you tell me another Mary story? I want to know who was at the door."

"Yes," she said. "Anything for you."

Running out of Time

Mary fell off her chair and screamed. Memories of her father's head exploding and Russ dragging her through dirt and rocks flooded into her brain, filling her bloodstream with a river of terror.

The figure in the doorway stepped forward, and the lantern's light cast an aura around the figure's body. It took a minute for the figure's full form to break free from the darkness, giving Mary just enough time to feel as though she might explode from panic.

When the figure became clear and Mary saw who it was, her anxiety didn't subside, despite feeling completely safe with this person.

"Zeke?"

He stepped forward. "I'm sorry. I didn't mean to scare you. I'm…" He put his head down and sighed.

"How did you find me?"

He shrunk, an embarrassed turtle trying to disappear in his shell. "I stopped walking. I felt so afraid to return home, too freaked out about finding the place empty. That fucker killed my mom."

Mary sat up and went back to her chair, her heart still pounding. "I understand."

"As I was heading back, I saw you walking away from the shed. I followed you. I kept wanting to run and catch up, but I was afraid to bother you at the same time. I just hovered around you, trying to work up the nerve. Then I saw the dead body, and I knew I should leave you in peace. I tried to go in the other direction, but I kept turning around and coming back toward you."

She stared at him, waiting for something more. His head hung in shame. She used her foot to kick the chair on the other side of the table, sliding it out for him.

He stared at it, stepped forward, unsure if she was inviting him. She nodded and he took the cue.

They sat across from each other for a while without saying much.

Zeke scratched at his arm. "Would it be okay if I stayed here? I'll stay out of your way, and I can help you with chores and stuff."

She nodded again. "Yeah, of course. Whatever you need. You can sleep in my bedroom. I don't think I'll ever be able to sleep there again. I'll probably pass out on the couch."

"I don't even care if you make me sleep outside, just as long as I never have to go home."

"Do you wonder what it was all for?"

He looked up. "What do you mean?"

She leaned forward. "Why do we have magic powers? Where did it come from? How did Russ know about it before us? Who the fuck are we?"

Zeke shook his head. "To be honest, I've been so fucked up about everything, I hadn't even thought about it. But shit, you're right. How the fuck do I have magic powers?"

"We should try to figure it out. What's your earliest memory?"

He breathed deep and glanced at the ceiling. "I need to think about it. What's yours?"

She bit her lip. Unlike Zeke, she didn't need to think about it. It was a memory that clung to her since the day it happened, a rock in her shoe, haunting her with every step she took in life.

"I was five. My mom wanted to go for a hike with me and my dad. There's this little stream behind our cabin that carries for about two miles. My mom loved to walk along the edge of it and follow it toward the nearest town. Once we'd get there, she'd order us ice cream from this little shop that sold the best and weirdest flavors. I used to get gum drop flavored. It wasn't ice cream with gum drops in it, but ice cream flavored like gum drops. So amazing."

Zeke smiled and put his hands on the table, opening up from his earlier embarrassment and vulnerability. "That sounds cool."

"It was. It was awesome. I was young, so I hated the walking part, but the ice cream always excited me. My dad also hated walking. He'd whine even more than I did. Anyway, about halfway through the walk, my mom, who was usually all gung-ho and chipper, started complaining about not feeling well. She was sweating but it wasn't that hot out. Her hands were shaky and she said her muscles all hurt.

"At that point, even though I was whiny and didn't want to walk, we were getting closer to the ice cream. I just wanted to get there. I could taste the gum drop flavor. So, I went from whining about walking to whining about her whining. I kept pushing her and pushing her and telling her to get over it.

"My dad started getting concerned and he put his arm around her to help her stand up. I told her she would be fine; we just needed ice cream to make her feel better. Finally, my dad called it and said we needed to get back home. I was so mad that

I had walked all that way and wouldn't get my snack. So, I just turned into a bratty jerk and acted mean to her."

Zeke looked up, sad-eyed and concerned. "She died, huh?"

Mary shook her head. "Yeah, before we made it back to the house. We still don't know what happened to her. Like, what makes you *that* sick *so* fast? She was fine one minute and dying the next. After that, my dad suddenly became captain outdoors, always wanting to go for walks, always hiking, always working out. It was like he finally realized the importance of being the man she wanted him to be, like he was trying to impress her in the afterlife. Maybe he's with her now and they're walking together in the woods."

"I'm so sorry," Zeke said. He gasped, as if about to say something else, but came up short.

"Whatever. It was a long time ago now. Do you have one yet?"

He shook his head. "No. I was hoping I could come up with some childhood memory that gave some hint at me having powers, but I can't think of any. I guess I was just completely unaware of it until Russ kidnapped us."

Mary jolted backward. "Oh my god."

Zeke stood up. "What?"

"I did. Holy shit. No, maybe I'm just overreacting. The night my mom died, I was lying down in my bed, crying, and she came to me in the window. I woke up and talked to her for a couple of minutes until she faded away. She was telling me to be a good girl, and to always be strong. She told me I was special and one day I'd see it." Mary cupped her hands over her face and cried. "I didn't think it was real. I thought I had dreamed it. What if…"

Zeke put his hands on hers. "What if you brought your mom back and had an actual conversation with her?"

She looked him in the eyes, tears pouring down her face. "I did, didn't I? Oh my god. I need to see my father. Right now."

As she ran toward the door, Zeke grabbed her. "Wait. You should wait until morning. It's too dark out there. There could be bears or mountain lions or something."

She turned and hugged him, a frantic and chaotic burst of every emotion ripping through her flesh. He squeezed and flushed some of it out, calming her with his grip. "I can't believe I talked to her. I can't believe it. Do you think I could do it again? Could I bring her back another time?"

He let go of her and frowned. "Maybe, but if I had to guess, I would say no. It's probably been too long. I mean, I don't know how any of this shit works, but that would be my guess. Your power proves there's something else after we die. I would hate to think that something else is just lingering around where it happened, hoping the one person who has the power to do so would bring us back for a couple of minutes before we return to the same place."

Mary rubbed her eyes. "Yeah, you're right. I'm just working myself up. Maybe it didn't even happen. It was probably just a dream like I thought it was to begin with."

Zeke stepped forward, closer to her. "No, that's just silly. You know you have the power to bring them back, and she told you things that were true about the future. She knew you were special. I believe you really talked to her."

She slid around Zeke and stared out the window into the cast-iron black night. "I wonder if it will be too late to talk to my dad. I wonder if Russ kept me away too long."

Zeke grabbed the lantern off the table. "Only one way to find out."

She turned to him. "I thought you said we shouldn't."

He opened the front door. "That was before I considered time is working against you. Let's go."

She inhaled a ball of confidence, because now that she saw the darkness out there again, she realized how right Zeke had been. It wasn't safe. But he was also right that she might miss her only chance if she didn't go. Her father wasn't too far away. How much danger could there be?

Zeke put his free hand out, offering Mary a little more comfort. She took it and together, they fled into the night.

It didn't take long for them to reach her father, and no giant animals came to harm them. She darted her eyes from Zeke to her father's body and put her arms out, dancing on the balls of her feet. Having to work so hard to make her magic happen made her doubt herself about seeing her mother. She didn't struggle or work to make her magic happen the night her mother returned to her.

Mary tensed her muscles and struggled to force her magic out. Nothing happened. Just as she was about to give up, her father heaved.

Unprepared, and fully expecting it not to work, Mary jumped backwards and yelped at the surprise sound. Her father's mauled body, bullet-holed and animal-gnawed, stood up. He clutched his throat, gasping for breath with hoarse exhales and inhales.

Mary pushed herself backwards until her back touched Zeke. He put his arms on her shoulders. She wanted nothing more than to hug her father, to squeeze him one last time, but with his body so marred and bloody, she couldn't bring herself to do it.

After her father finished his fight for air, he eyed her with surprise and excitement. "Mary! Jesus. You made it out alive. I've been so worried. Listen, there isn't much time. I need you to pay attention."

She nodded.

"I have to say something awful. I never wanted you to know this, but you need to. It's important. I'm not your father. Your mother wasn't your mother. We raised you and we loved you, and by that definition, you were our daughter. But biologically, you weren't."

"What?" she whimpered. "Why would you say that?"

"Because it's true, Mary. I can't worry about your feelings right now; it's too important. You and the other kids, you're not like us and there are many people out there who know about you and want you dead. You need to find the other ones and take them somewhere. Hide them. You need to get away from people. No one can be trusted."

She shook her head. "I don't understand."

"Good. You don't need to understand. You need to hide. Please, Mary. If they find you, the most unimaginable things will happen. Find the other kids and hide. Forever."

She pushed away from Zeke and kneeled in front of her dad. "I just want to see you and say goodbye. I don't want to talk about this other stuff."

As she reached a hand toward him, he slapped it away. "I love you, Mary, but forget about me. There's no time for this. You need to run. You need to go now. Find the other kids and never look back."

"Dad?"

"Go."

"Dad? Why are you doing this?"

"Because I love you, Mary. Go."

She stood up, unable to look away from him. What horrified her minutes ago now felt like a treasure she wished to never turn from.

"Go," he screamed. "Go. Go. Go."

Zeke put his hand on her arm. "Mary, maybe he's right."

They both looked around at the sudden change in the wind. The branches and foliage rustled and crackled with the breeze.

"You're running out of time," her father said.

An Explosion of Color

Violin stared into the fire, listening to Fake Winter argue with himself as he battled to tell his story. Her eyelids turned to stone and anchored downward. She fought back a yawn. The fire had largely gone out. Grey spirits twirled from the blackened wood, and tiny orange spots sparkled against the moon light. But the fire disc would arrive soon. The breaches of dawn infiltrated the sky, turning it a bruised purple.

Fake Winter yammered on, and Violin rolled her eyes, which gave her an idea. She made a noise through the tape over her mouth to draw Fake Winter's attention, and just as his eyes turned to hers, she rolled her eyes up and toppled over. She went from a sitting position to laying, but she dropped her head hard, selling the faint. Her temple thudded against the dirt.

"What happened?" Fake Winter shouted and ran to her. "Wake up. No. You need to be awake for this."

She listened to his footsteps approaching, and as they came close enough, she jolted upright and kicked her feet, hitting him hard in the knees. He screeched and fell backward into the fire.

The remaining embers sizzled the flesh on his hands and the butt of his pants.

Violin turned and ran, digging her fingers into the tape, searching for the line where it started, so she could rip it off. She darted around one of the shelters, and dipped around another one, until she reached a stretch of large machines. Rides, Fake Winter called them. Rides designed to illicit fear in humans.

They were massive things and seeing them up close only extended their hauntingly large features. She found her way around the base of one of the biggest, a huge circular contraption with a series of different colored seats around it. She leaned against the base and ripped her tape off, sucking in deep breathes through her mouth. Her fingers touched the flaking paint on the machine, a mixture of yellow and rust. The seats of the machine were all rusted as well, and she guessed the paint had probably dulled over the years, making her wonder how splendid the colors were when it was freshly coated. Even now, long after they'd faded, she found them wonderous. Earth was much more colorful than where she grew up, but this place, this amusement park, took colorization to whole new level. She wished she had time to enjoy it.

Peeking over the base, she kept an eye out for Fake Winter, but didn't see him coming or hear his footsteps. She debated on how long she should remain stationary. Moving around felt like a good solution, but what if she ran right into him?

She scanned the outer edges of the park, where nothing but forest surrounded them. She'd spent a lot of time running and hiding in woods. She believed she had an advantage in that environment, but Fake Winter was special, inhuman, and she knew not what skills he possessed.

She dug the soles of her feet into the dirt and bent her legs, ready to make a run for it.

Something banged, a loud thud echoing through the park.

Following it, lights came on everywhere, dotting the edges of all the rides, spotlighting from huge beams in the sky, dancing from one bulb to the next along the fencing and bases of the rides. She hadn't thought about it when they were in the shelter, too concerned about survival, but now a question rang in her brain like an alarm bell.

A loud screech bellowed from everywhere and Fake Winter's voice called loud and mechanical, as if he shouted through the clouds from heaven.

"You're wondering how this place still has electricity," he said.

Yes, that was exactly what she wondered.

"Me, my dear. I am the reason. The same way I brought your family back to taunt you and beg you to tell your stories. Reanimation is a specialty of mine."

She bent low, giving up on her plan to run. Like his voice, and his lights, she worried his sight was everywhere. He knew everything about her, key moments of her life, things no one could have told him. She had no hope of escape. The only thing she could do was kill him. No matter how strong and fast he was, he must have a weakness, and she'd dig in for it, twisting her blade through his entrails until the tip hit the star in the center. The bullseye. The weakness.

"Now, you can run, but you can't hide from my tales. I know you're still in the park, and there's nowhere you can avoid my story. I know you're considering the woods, but I wouldn't, dear. I'll promise you lots of pain if you head that way."

While he spoke, she followed his voice, trying to find where he projected it from. She saw a large white box riddled with holes, and understood he spoke through some machine that poured it out from that white box.

"Now, where was I in my tale?"

As he delivered his fairy tale, Violin went into a memory. First, she traveled to their first house on Earth, where they found the discs Brian and Corey would later tell her were DVDs. She thought about the rainbow that danced across it, the beautiful display of colors making their way from the top of the disc to the bottom. Corey explained that too, but she didn't remember all the science behind it, just that it was called a prism. Prism. She liked that word, prism. It represented something so gorgeous, an explosion of color, yet it so closely sounded like prison. And maybe that's what a prism was, all the beauty trapped in a disc. Prism. Prison.

She did everything she could to keep her mind on it, however silly it may be, just to keep from listening to Fake Winter's stories. His tales were useless if she didn't hear them, didn't listen. How, she wasn't sure, but if he held stake in her hearing them, she kept herself alive by closing off her mind.

It proved too difficult. The machines were too loud. Whenever she drew her mind away, the volatile voice in the machine shook her brain from its thoughts and brought her back to his stories. So, she cupped her hands over her ears and yelled her own tale as loud as she could.

Slithering on a Tongue

When Prism was a child, she ate bugs. Her older brother, Dark Skies, created the little critters, calling them the blood cells of the Earth. Those creatures did so much to make the world function. They pollinated, spread the seeds of life, kept other populations in check, made the soil perfect for food growth, and fed animals. Without bugs, humans couldn't exist. Yet, humans refused to see them as anything other than a nuisance.

Prism ate the bugs for two reasons. One, she enjoyed the way they squirmed in her mouth, fighting so hard for life. The taste of desperation. Mmmmm. The other reason was more psychological. While her brothers and sisters toyed with the humans, torturing them for amusement, Prism wanted to hurt them at the source, in that ignored, dark corner of their lives. Humans, so unaware of what kept them going, of how fragile they were. Prism wanted to show them by removing the source of all life on Earth. The blood cells.

She was young, of course, too stupid to see that the bugs reproduced faster than she could eat them. All she'd done was put a dent in their exponential growth. As an adult, she chose more carefully what she put in her mouth, but occasionally, she yearned for something to slither on her tongue.

She thought of this while glowing rainbow shards shot from her fists, slashing skin from Ben Franklin's face. She thought how lovely it would be to shrink him down and make him slither. Unfortunately, she had no such power.

War raged around her. Dark Skies tore into Kevin Bacon. Mitochondria pulled vines from Dance's limbs. Dust clawed his sharp nails into Abe Lincoln's icy flesh. War and death all around her. She loved the scent of gore.

As Prism marched toward Ben Franklin's feeble, weary body, she inhaled the pain and screams, hungry for more.

Ben Franklin lifted his human paw, bits of electricity sparking at the fingertips. Before he could make a full charge, Prism used her rainbow shards to sever his hands clean from his body. He screamed as they flopped to the forest floor, and the beautiful sound of his horror prickled her skin.

As he screamed, she lifted one of his hands and ripped a finger off in her teeth, letting it wriggle for a moment before chewing it down. The slight movements of his fingers did not match the chaos her bugs had once produced. This disappointment transformed into rage, which she used to mash Ben Franklin's face to pulverized meat.

Once he stopped moving, she pried his mouth open, bit his tongue off, and made it dance between her teeth. It was much better than the finger.

She turned, blood dribbling down her chin. War. Beautiful war. Even the woodland animals were fighting, although it looked like they disagreed on which side they were on. Bears were mauling Prism's brothers and sisters, while a raccoon dug its claws into Dance's face. Birds dive-bombed into just about every-one. The entire scene was pure, nonsensical chaos.

Prism stormed through the dust, blood, and flailing limbs, pushing people out of her way, both enemy and friend.

A large roaring beast slashed at her. She gripped its throat until its head detached and rolled to the dirt. My god, the satisfaction of it all.

She refused to come to her siblings' aid. Let them live or die on their own merit. Hell, maybe she'd kill a few of them herself. Once the blood lust came, it was hard to let go. Oh, how she missed it.

But there was one she wanted dead above all else. There was no logic behind it. This person hadn't harmed her or even spoken a word in her direction. It was something about his stupid face. She wanted to destroy it.

A skateboard smashed into her head as she marched. Blood poured from her forehead into her eyes, but it did not halt her.

Nothing would.

Nothing could.

The girl with the board jumped on top of her, but Prism simply launched her into a tree. Something cracked on impact. She hoped it was the girl's spine. How could her brothers and sisters struggle with such easy fodder?

The man she yearned to kill, the gross ice giant, pounded his fists into Prism's sister, Spiral. Always the weakest, Spiral buckled, hardly keeping herself up after the hit.

Two humans saw Prism approaching and ran to block her path. Humans! She nearly fell over laughing, but stopped herself, appreciating the courage they possessed to stand up to her. It was a man and woman. Prism wondered if they were coupled, if they had children at home waiting for their parent's return. The idea of breaking their hearts made Prism bite her lip to stop herself from exploding with ecstasy.

Fear washed over the human's eyes as Prism showed no signs of slowing down. It grew more intense with each step until water filled those eyes and all the humans' limbs were quaking. She placed one hand on the right side of the woman's head, and the other hand on the left side of the man's head. Then she smashed them together so smoothly, their bodies looked as if they shared a singular, sanguine skull.

Prism spit on their corpses as she stepped over them.

Mitochondria flew by her head, tossed through the air by Miley Cyrus. She marched on.

As Abraham Lincoln finished off Spiral, breaking her to bits, he failed to notice Prism approaching.

He turned too late. She was already in the air, flying toward his face. When his pupil shifted, aiming toward her, she gripped it and ripped the whole eye from its socket.

The giant clutched his face, screaming, flopping to the floor, flailing and bellowing so loudly it shook the earth. Delicious.

While he was occupied with the pain of his missing eye, Prism used a rainbow blade to saw into his leg. She assumed, with his icy texture, it would take some work, but the blade cut through like a chainsaw on paper.

Who knew ice giants bled red? Everyone did now. His veins spurted rivers of it, painting the entire forest in his blood.

Abraham reached his arm out toward Kevin Bacon. "Brother, save me."

Prism turned, wondering if Kevin Bacon could even try. Luckily, Dark Skies had him pinned to the ground. Seeing Kevin Bacon fight and struggle to save his brother made the murdering even more worthwhile.

"You will die knowing your brother failed you," she said to the giant.

He wept but spoke through the tears. "I will die knowing my brother tried, which is more than your siblings will ever get from you."

She climbed on top of him, standing on his mountain of a

chest. "True. I did not save them, and yet, still I will win. You and your family have put in so much effort, and you will lose."

"Trying is winning, you stupid god. Trying is winning."

She sneered. "If this is me without effort, you'd hate to see what I look like when I'm trying." She lifted her rainbow blade above her head. Her heart raced, thinking of the sound it would make as it plunged into Lincoln's heart.

Squelch.

The sound came before she dropped the blade. For a moment, she couldn't make sense of it, but then she looked down and found a giant spike protruding from her chest. For once, she was drenched in her own blood.

She stumbled, turned, and saw the smiling face of her killer. "Who are you?" she said as blood poured from her lips. "Are you a human?"

The man nodded. "I dipped that spike in bristlebucks and urine. Enjoy."

"A human?" she shouted. "A fucking human?"

She dropped to her knees. Abraham Lincoln's fist closed around her. As his fingers squeezed, the forest disappeared until darkness swallowed her. Pressure, so much of it. It grew and grew until the pain was so unbearable, she had to scream.

Everything gushed out of her, her guts, organs, all of it. She lived through this, felt it all, the excruciating pain hitting every atom until finally, her body turned to ash and she floated through the air in tiny little flecks of death. And there, only there, did some relief come. She felt nothing as the bugs ate her ashes, spreading her seeds along the dirt paths of the woods.

<h1 style="text-align:center">A Bigger Force</h1>

Brian trained his gun, clearing each aisle, ensuring no one was around. Unless they hid well, no one was in the Job Lot. Brian wished he'd planned better, had some idea what they would need for their journey. He wished he'd come up with some semblance of strategy for how to save Violin. But he had nothing. He wanted to go to Job Lot to get snacks, some things they could use as weapons, some rope and bungees, but he had no reason for any of that. Would a garden shear work better than a gun? What would they do with the rope? And while snacks were definitely needed, Job Lot snacks weren't the best in the world.

Corey grabbed a hand basket. "Throw shit in here. What do we need?"

Brian shrugged. His partner had been correct, Brian acted out of some sense of destiny, like every decision he made would end up the correct one. Stepping back from his own brain made him realize how ludicrous that idea was. If he'd acted with the care and foresight he once had, maybe Winter would still be alive. Maybe they'd still have their group at the motel. Maybe

Violin would be sitting next to him instead of miles away in the arms of a mimic. Even after all that, he continued to plow forward half-cocked. Stupid.

They went to the gardening section first, grabbed some shears and gloves. What the fuck for, he didn't know, but his nerves were firing being alone in the dark store and he hadn't slept in days. He wanted to plan, but his mind was mush, his heart ready to call it quits, his energy at an all-time low. So, he just grabbed shit and hoped he could figure it out later.

After the gardening section, they hit the snack aisle, pouring some chips, nuts, and chocolate into the cart, while opening some of the bags right on the shelf and shoving fistfuls into their mouths. Corey giggled as his mouth filled with chips and cheeks puffed out like a chipmunk.

Brian stared at his partner's silly face and wrapped himself around Corey. The hand basket hit the floor, and Corey returned the embrace. They stayed that way for a few minutes trying to forget the rest of the world, their mission, the death and horror all around them. He nearly fell asleep on Corey's shoulder.

When he pulled away, a cool breeze hit his chest, where a second ago he felt only the warmth of his best friend's body.

"Can we just stay here forever?" Brian asked.

"Fine by me," Corey said as he pulled open a chocolate bar wrapper.

They stared at each other for a few seconds. Brian sighed and pulled some coconut waters off the shelf and dropped them in the basket. "I don't want to live like this anymore."

Corey picked up the basket. "This is who we are."

Brian noticed fresh wrinkles under Corey's eyes, the light sprinkles of pepper in his beard. They were still young, but getting older. By the end of their journey, whatever that journey was, whether it was finding Violin, or saving the world, learning the secrets to the disappearance, it would end with them older still. Minutes would drip by without them getting to enjoy their lives together. What a cruel fucking world.

They headed out the front doors to the car. About halfway through the lot, two men emerged from the side opposite them. Brian halted. His pulse pounded in his wrists.

Corey froze by his side.

The two men were smiling, and not the malicious "gotcha" kind of smile, but more the, "Hello, I'd like to speak to you about Jesus," kind of smile which, in its own way, drove a shiver of terror up Brian's spine.

The two men wore matching army fatigues, as did the five or six other men Brian noticed up the hill at the end of the parking lot which separated Job Lot's property from that of the McDonald's on the hill. Brian moved his eyes away from the men up above, hoping they didn't notice he spotted them.

"How you fellas doing today?" One of the men said.

Brian leaned over to Corey. "Head toward them. Act scared and timid. When I give the signal, jump in the fucking car."

Corey rubbed his eye. "What signal?" He whispered.

"You'll know."

Brian waved at the men. "Hi."

"Y'all don't need to be afraid. We aren't the bad ones. We have a big outfit around here. We're just trying to keep the peace. Looks like you got yourself some snacks."

Brian stepped closer, shaking his head. "We didn't know this was someone's territory. We're just hungry is all."

Corey inched closer, following Brian's lead.

The bigger of the two men, a puffy gentleman with a grey beard, broadened his already creepy smile. "That's alright fellas. We aren't concerned about it. We're more concerned about our neighbors getting attacked with a bomb. See, we promised them protection, and when the whole front of their market explodes…" The man licked his lips. "Well, you can imagine how that makes us look."

Brian's pulse pounded in his skull as he moved close enough to the men to smell their body odor. "That certainly wasn't us," he said in a small voice.

"Never said it was. We were just hoping you might know something about the folks who were behind it."

Brian shook his head. "We aren't from around here. We're from Tanner's Switch. We don't really know who operates around this town."

He put his hand out to shake the big guy's hand. Big Guy gave a skeptical look at it, but ultimately took Brian's hand and shook. As their hands moved up and down, Brian reached around his back with his free hand, pulled his gun out, aimed it upward, right under Big Guy's chin, and fired.

As Big Guy's head exploded, his friend reached for his weapon, strapped to a holster on his waist, but Brian had already brought the gun over and fired before the second guy had the chance to reach it.

Brian's whole body shook, panicked and terrified. He jumped in the car where Corey sat waiting for him. He spun the car around and drove toward the side road between Job Lot and the supermarket. In the rearview, he saw the group of men from the hill charging their way down. Corey yelled, "What the hell? What the fuck? I didn't know you were going to kill them."

Brian didn't either, not at first. When he spotted the hiding backup on the hill, he knew nothing good could come from the interaction. He may have just killed a few innocent men, but he was sick, and he was tired, and his heart hurt. His body ached.

He thought about that moment in the snack section where he had the freedom to hug the most important person in the world. The fleeting moment of peace he felt had been disrupted by strange men in army uniforms and he hated them for it. He didn't give a fuck if they just wanted to ask some questions. Their presence was a bacteria eating away at Brian's peace of mind.

As they sped off, losing view of the men coming down the hill, Brian gripped Corey's hand as his partner hyperventilated. "I'm not making friends anymore. It's me and you, and Violin and Candlestick, if we ever find them. Anyone who wants to get in the way of that, dies."

Protecting My Friends

Candlestick guided Cassie back to their camp. She'd been so focused on her story, she failed to pay attention to where they were going. She knew she'd find their way back easily enough but didn't like how far out she'd led them.

Cassie didn't seem to mind, too enamored by Mary's tale. "I think Mary and Zeke are falling in love."

Candlestick sighed. "Is that all you think about? Love? She just found out there are more people out there hunting them."

Cassie shrugged. "So? They'll get through it together."

Candlestick turned to her. "Is that how you think? You think that two people in love can survive anything? My family all loved each other, and they all died anyway. Did your…" She stopped herself before asking about Cassie's parents, worried it would open the gaping chasm that still existed between them.

Cassie stared at her feet before looking up with excited eyes, ready to prove Candlestick's negativity wrong. "But your sister is still alive, and you two love each other."

"Yes, but we didn't survive because of our love for each other.

We survived because we wouldn't stop fighting for ourselves. The only valuable love is the dedication you carry to yourself, and even that won't guarantee you any extra time."

"Can you just be positive for once?"

Their tent came into view as they reached the top of a small hill. "Fine. I will be positive and happy for the rest of the day."

"Yeah?"

Candlestick huffed. "Yes. Sure."

A mischievous grin crawled up Cassie's cheeks. "Do you think Randy is hot?"

Candlestick rolled her eyes and walked away from her friend toward their camp.

"That didn't look very positive and happy."

"No, I don't think he is hot. I think both he and Christian look a little goofy, if I'm being honest."

Cassie chuckled as she ran to catch up to Candlestick. "They kind of do, but I find it charming."

A sliver of relaxation entered Candlestick's bones at Cassie's admission to Christian's goofy appearance. But when she followed it up by calling it charming, it pulled the calm right back out.

They reached the camp where Randy and Christian were hanging out around a fire, cooking something that smelled delicious.

"Just in time for breakfast," Randy said.

They sat around the fire eating canned beans and sausage. Candlestick approved of the food, and everyone else seemed to as well, because no one talked during breakfast, their mouths full of meal.

As Candlestick finished up, she cleared her throat and made an announcement. "I think we should break into groups of two today. Christian, you come with me to my old house to look for food and water. Cassie and Randy stay here with our stuff."

"Splitting up is never a good idea," Randy said.

Cassie nodded in agreement.

Candlestick wanted them split up just so Cassie could feel a little jealousy for once. "We won't make it to my home by nightfall if we don't. You two can break down the camp and get our stuff packed and Christian and I will be back in no time with the stuff we pick up."

Randy shook his head. "Nah, what if that guy is still out there? I don't want you two getting into trouble without me there to protect you."

Candlestick hid her happiness at his response because she knew the reaction it would receive.

Christian put his fork down in an empty can of beans. "Dude, I don't need you to fucking protect me. We'll be good. And she's right, we don't have a ton of stuff left and we aren't sure what we will get from the house, so we can't afford to lose time."

Randy rolled his eyes. "Whatever. Fine. Go, tough guy."

Cassie looked like she was going to be sick. "I don't know how to break down a camp. I'll go with you two."

Randy stood up. "What the fuck? No one wants to stay with me?"

Christian put his hand on Cassie's. "You'll be fine. Randy will teach you."

Cassie's jaw dropped and her eyes sagged. Christian might as well have shoved a dagger in her throat.

Candlestick struggled to hide her joy. As she and Christian trudged away from camp, she turned back to see Cassie staring at them while Randy tried to guide her on how to disassemble a tent. Candlestick waved, pretending not to notice the jealousy and upset in Cassie's features.

When they reached the neighborhood, smoke was still

pluming from some buildings at the end, but most of the houses Candlestick had stayed in were extinguished.

They walked slowly, finding cover wherever they could. Christian acted like he was leading them into war. Candlestick played along, but she knew the fire person was gone and didn't think anyone else was around either.

She struggled to remember which house they had dumped food and water in. The fires turned them all into blackened heaps of wood and debris. With no distinguishable features, she couldn't place where they'd been and where they hadn't.

She did remember which side of the road the houses were on, and since only ten houses existed, she figured it would be worth checking them all.

The first two houses were so collapsed they couldn't get in, and Candlestick's attempts to move broken wood proved futile. She debated calling her monsters but didn't think the negligible amount of food they could recover would be worth revealing her secret to Christian.

When they reached the fourth house, Candlestick noticed remnants of a fence and remembered it as the one they had to hop over when the wilderness kids were attacking.

"This house. This is the one where we left stuff."

The top floor of the house had collapsed onto the bottom floor, but the frame remained intact. They entered through the back, and the smell of burnt oil and chemicals met them at the entrance. Christian coughed.

"Down there," Candlestick pointed to the basement stairs.

Giant hunks of wood blocked them from moving anywhere else besides the basement. It was as if the top floor had split down the middle and bent into a large V. The violence that had happened in this house came flooding into Candlestick's mind. She was outside when it occurred, but felt it just the same, and her sister filled her in on the gory details later.

Violin had shot a boy by the front door. Her father nearly strangled a child to death. She wondered if Violin's victim still lay behind the planks of wood blocking her view.

"Come on," Christian said, snapping her out of it.

The basement survived unharmed. If she hadn't seen the top floors, she wouldn't have known anything happened here at all.

They opened the washer and dryer, two machines so mysterious to her just a short while ago. Sure enough, some cans of food and a bottle of water sat waiting inside the dryer.

Christian smiled and put his hand out.

"What?"

"High five?"

"What?"

"High five. You know, slap my hand."

She swung her hand at him.

"Oh, damn. You're not supposed to attack it." He rubbed his palm.

"You told me to."

"Never mind." He pulled the water and cans out. "You ready?"

She nodded, and he handed her the food while he carried the water.

When they exited the house, the air had a freshness to it she hadn't noticed before, so clean and crisp. Even the bellowing smoke down the road couldn't mar it.

"It's a beautiful day," she said.

"Yeah, it is. Hopefully we can make it to your home today. I have a feeling your sister is going to be there, too. Everything is going to work out."

She turned to him and smiled. "Thank you. You and your cousin are gracious people. You make me feel happy."

"If it weren't for those men who picked Randy and me up, I don't think we'd be alive right now. Randy talks tough, but we were a bunch of scared dicks when it all went down. Those men saved our lives for no reason other than to do the right thing. I wanted to do the same for you and Cassie. Except, it's not just doing the right thing anymore. Now, it's protecting my friends."

"Friends?"

He put his hand on her head and scruffed her hair. "You betcha."

They headed back toward the camp. Friends.

"Hey, where'd my bracelet go?" Candlestick asked.

"You were wearing a bracelet? I don't remember seeing it. Are you sure it's not back at the camp?"

"No. I know I had it on. My dad gave it to me before he died. Shit." Tears formed in her eyes.

"When did you last see it?" Christian looked around in the dirt.

"I know I had it in the house because it snagged on the wall going into the basement."

"Alright, let's go back and check."

"Why don't you just leave the water bottle and run back there real quick? You're faster than me. If you don't see it on the floor, it's not there. Just be quick. We have to go."

Christian nodded. He put the bottle down and ran.

Candlestick waited until he was far enough away and said, "I want you to tear the house to shreds while he's still inside."

Taking the Ride

Violin crouched and made her way around the base of the ride. As she turned the corner, her heart plummeted, as if riding down the tracks of one of the machines around her. Fake Winter stood, leaning against the corner, waiting for her.

"Surprised to see me?" he said.

"No."

He raised his eyebrows.

"I knew I couldn't escape you forever."

He dusted his hands, slapping the palms together. "Smart girl. So, what did you think of my last episode of the Kevin Bacon saga?"

She knew Fake Winter saw things he wasn't present for, and assumed he could read her mind as well, but his question made her wonder if she'd been wrong because she heard nothing of his last story. If the stories were so important, and *her* knowing the stories even more important, how he could be so obtuse about her plugging her ears and telling her own tale?

"I thought it was fine. What do you want me to say?"

He frowned and shrugged. "I guess I don't want you to say anything. Just keep listening."

"No. I have done enough listening for one day. It's time for something to change. You've made your demands and I've obeyed. I want something in return now."

"You don't get to make demands."

"Yes, I do. I'll stop listening to you if you don't give me one thing."

"Haven't you learned I'll just make you listen?"

She knew she could blow her cover, give away her secret, but she had to push forward. "I am a master of blocking people out, of diving into my own world and ignoring the words spoken to me. Tell your stories, but from this point forward, I'll hear none of it until you give me the one thing I want."

He smirked. "I owe you nothing, and I very much can force you to hear what I speak, but you've got me curious. What do you want?"

She slapped her hand on the base of the circular ride. "I want to ride this."

His eyebrows bobbed up and down, kites in the wind. The curvatures of his face became broken waves, cresting on the shores, and she saw a piece of the real him for a flash. With her father's features hiding behind a sheath of fog, the real man's hideous truth exposed itself.

Unfortunately, a flash wasn't enough time for her to process it. It came and went in reality as it did in her mind, just a piece of something bigger, hidden under thin sheets. There and gone. She could almost grab it, but the sheet above it was too big, and the more she dug it away, the more it bunched and hid the secret underneath it.

"You want to go on the Ferris Wheel?" he asked.

She turned to it and examined the massive spokes, the bowl-shaped seats, the red, blue, yellow, and purple colors that did nothing to fight the stygian nature of the thing. It was as if the Ferris Wheel could swallow all the light and color from the world and still remain as tenebrous as it pleased. It was the eater of hope. And yes, she wanted a ride.

"Yes. Let me ride the Ferris Wheel."

He tilted his head as if one side filled with rocks and his neck couldn't support the weight. "I believe you're up to something. However, I could use some fun, and seeing you try to weasel your way out of all this could be just the ticket. Hop on." He cupped his hands together and bent low.

She hesitated, suddenly afraid of this new acceptance of her demands. Maybe they were both in a game of who could play nice the best, so she stepped on his hand, and he hoisted her on top of the base.

Her hand felt the rough patches of flaked paint and rust on the red bowl as she stepped into it. The bowl rocked a little with her movements.

Fake Winter put a foot in and latched a belt around her. "For safety," he said.

"You care about my safety now?"

"Just for now." He curled his upper lip and mumbled some complaints as he walked toward a control box.

"Ready?" he said, and without waiting for an answer, played with his machine, kicking the ride into action.

Her cart jerked and the wheel slowly moved forward. If the ride was meant to create anxiety, it failed. Human cars moved faster than this thing. As the cart moved up, Violin noticed scribbles and writing carved into the inside of it. People's names, hearts, smiley faces. In large crude slices, the words, "Callie's Birdhouse." Violin put her fingertips to the letters, thinking about who wrote them, what their story was. Yes, Fake Winter was correct. Stories mattered. But they can't be forced on someone, can't be controlled or contained. That's what made a person's story so wonderful. The unruliness. Humans feared the loss of control, but their greatest stories all involved that same loss. You don't tell your grandchildren about the time everything went right.

That was why she wanted to ride the Ferris Wheel. It spoke to her. It told her of the death and mourning that happened in its carts and around its spokes. And she told it about her own life of death and mourning. Together, they pitied. They both were the source of anguish, a vacuum luring in all the gunk and horror, swirling it inside, and blowing it into the faces of anyone too close.

When her cart reached the apex of the wheel, she leaned over, looking down at the woods below. Her stomach turned at the sight, and she came to understand why humans would fear the ride. Despite her safety within the cart, she felt herself falling, dropping fast to the Earth and splatting into the metal base, blood slapping Fake Winter in the face.

She noticed something else she hadn't seen when on the ground. It was a square shape of water. Little holes spat water from the ground, shooting it upward, and the water landed upon a metal plate on a pole in the center of these holes. When the water dripped off the plate, it came down where the rest shot up. But the water came up and down in lines, four of them, connected in a square. With the metal plate above it, it produced the effect of making a box. A box of water. What a silly thing. It moved away from her as the ride descended.

She sat back and closed her eyes. She pressed her fingers into her wrist to feel the speed of her pulse and smiled. Beautiful terror.

The ride would end soon and Fake Winter would go back to rambling on about his stories, so Violin jumped ahead, neutering his future tales by taking Kevin Bacon's journey further than Fake Winter knew they went.

Her father created these tales. She inherited them. Fake Winter had no ownership here. Violin, high above the Earth, attached to a new friend who understood her pain, told her story, and told it her way.

The Places Where All the Strings Merged

Kevin Bacon tried to learn the names of all the gods as they warred, but some of them were already in pieces and with blood and death all around him, it was difficult to figure out their identities.

Dark Skies, more than any other, hunted for Kevin. To make things more difficult, the forest animals joined in the battle. Most of them gunned for Kevin Bacon and Dance. It hindered their ability to battle, essentially forcing them to fight with one arm tied to a furry creature.

Dance had more trouble than the rest. Kevin saw this from the corner of his eye as Dark Skies bashed him in the skull with a stick.

A god with sharp claws shredded Dance's foliage while Rapture dug into her throat. But, Dance persisted. She bludgeoned gods and animals alike with all her might.

Abraham Lincoln screamed in pain, his body a mess.

Kevin Bacon wished to save them all, but Dark Skies bested him in every fight. He couldn't defeat the god and knew he needed the child. Without the child, he had no chance.

As Dark Skies mauled him, Kevin Bacon spun a disc in his hand, and when he launched it into the air, he held tight so the disc took him, and by extension, Dark Skies, off Earth.

They flew through space, stars, and dust, until they reached the heavens. But even still, they carried on until they were two scatterings of atoms rumbling through the colorful blobs of everything, that magical place that beholds all the knowledge of the universes, and yet still seems to mask what it wants the gods to ignore.

It was impossible to fight in the colorful blobs. Each of them disintegrated to mere particles, bumping into each other like soap bubbles at the top of a tub. No pain, no strength, nothing but bouncing.

When it was over, they crashed into the Earth, dust, sticks, and debris pluming up in clouds around them. With their particles reattached, they lay on the hard forest floor, rolling and coughing.

Kevin Bacon rose first, dizzy and reeling from the massive amounts of new information trying to squeeze into his brain. He stumbled forward, ignoring Dark Skies. Before he could reach the shack, Dark Skies found his footing and charged him. With his face smashed into the dirt, Kevin Bacon couldn't turn himself enough to avoid the coming blows. Punch after punch slammed into the back of his skull, and his face broke apart as it dug deeper into the dirt.

Getting a little more used to his powers, Kevin transformed his face into different people he knew, Miley, Abe, Saria, anyone, correcting the broken bones, torn open flesh, and damaged organs with each change. He kept himself alive but did nothing to avoid the excruciating pain.

The door to the shack opened. Kevin heard it before he could see it. It took another transformation to clear the blood from his eyes. Luckily, the intrusion distracted Dark Skies enough to halt the punches.

From the darkness of the shack, a small creature crawled forward. Kevin expected a rodent of sorts. He should have known better. Pure joy broke through the pain in his body as a small baby crawled forward. Too small to crawl or even roll over without aide, yet here the baby was. His baby. One of his own creations, plucked from the depths of the underworld and brought to Earth. He knew the baby would grow to save the world, but he didn't know it would happen so soon.

Dark Skies laughed. "What the hell am I seeing? I don't remember this in the colorful blobs. A crawling infant?" He laughed harder.

The baby's flesh turned bright red, as if reaching a new level of boiling unknown to humans. Then, it shook, a volatile vibrating. Steam poured from the baby's mouth like a dragon's fire. It wasn't crying, but the baby screeched like a teakettle until the sound was painful.

Kevin plugged his ears. He worried for the child. All its changes made him worry the baby would explode. Can babies explode? No, but they also can't pour steam from their mouth or turn bright red and shake like the tracks under a train.

Kevin squinted, waiting for the awful event to unfold. This wasn't supposed to happen! Was Dark Skies doing something to the poor child?

Boom! An explosion of guts, blood, and hunks of meat.

The baby was fine. It sat in the doorway while its skin turned back to its normal color

Kevin removed his hands from his ears. No more screeching. It took a moment to realize the weight had left his back. He rolled over, free from Dark Skies's grasp. The god was dead.

Kevin rolled back on his stomach and looked at the baby. "Well done," he said as he stood, wiping dead body from his clothes. "I guess I should get back to the war now. Can I put you back on the table? Or are you good? How did you get off the table to begin with?"

The baby said nothing, just stared.

"I knew by instinct to leave you alone last time, but I feel worse about it this time around."

He picked up the baby and brought it inside. He placed it down on the floor. The baby pointed outside.

Kevin turned around. All the guts were gone from the forest. He glanced at his clothes, and they too were now free of the gore. "Did he turn to dust like the other ones?"

The baby shook its head.

"Does that mean he's still alive?"

The baby nodded.

"Well, hell. I thought you were our savior."

The baby laughed.

"Why are you laughing? I'm at war with gods. You did a temporary explosion? You couldn't come up with something more permanent?"

The baby put its hand out.

Kevin Bacon tilted his head, squinting his eyes. "What do you want? A handshake?"

The baby nodded again.

He sighed and shook the baby's hand. As their skin touched, he saw new futures, ones the colorful blobs neglected. He trembled, as if the baby electrocuted him with its touch. How could the colorful blobs miss so much? What were these futures? So much pain, horror, and death. So much darkness.

He remembered the words Gage Greenwood whispered in his ear, and he cried. Was this how it would all go down? Was this his future? If so, why didn't the colorful blobs know about it? Why didn't they see this coming?

"Why are you showing me this?" he asked through his cries.

The baby turned its head. A thin strip of drool dribbled from its mouth to the floor.

"Is this my destiny?"

The baby nodded.

"I guess I'll see you soon, then."

Dark Skies barreled through the door with rage in his eyes. Kevin Bacon never wanted to kill someone more, but he knew the truth now, the actual truth. Not the lies hidden in the colorful blobs. Dark Skies needed to live. Not forever, but for now.

Kevin learned from his trip through the colorful blobs that seeing all possible outcomes was the same as seeing none. You couldn't predict what would happen next when the options were endless. The same was true for the new information presented to him. There were still an endless number of options, but there were pinpoints, places where all the strings merged and only one truth could happen. Those points were missing from the blobs but once Kevin saw them, he realized the truth about free will: we had it. We had so much of it. But it won't matter because in the end, it all leads to the same place, and that place was horrifying.

He fought Dark Skies, giving him as much as he could, but his heart was no longer in it. After a short beating, he sighed, grabbed a disc, and used it to deliver him and his nemesis back through the colorful blobs, past the heavens, and onto the battle-field where his friends and foes fought to the death.

So much blood. Everywhere. And for what?

After their bodies crashed into the dirt, spreading a new cloud of debris through the war, Kevin lifted himself, screamed, and threw three discs. They blazed through everything. The trees, the shrubs, the gods, the animals. He'd never managed so much strength in them before. They cut the world around him to shreds.

Abraham Lincoln stood with one leg and caught the falling

trees before they landed on his teammates. As he caught them, he popped some into his mouth, and others he used to swat gods off his family and friends.

Dance strangled Rapture and caught Kevin Bacon's eyes. She did a double take and frowned. "What happened?" she yelled to him.

"Nothing. Just kill the gods," he said with gritted teeth. "Kill them all and dance on their graves."

"It would be easier without this damned raccoon always at my throat."

"Leave him. He's one of us."

Rapture and Dance turned their heads to him, squinting in confusion.

Two discs flew back into his hands, and with power he'd never felt before, he slashed them into Dark Skies's face.

The god screamed. "What is happening? How did you do that?"

"What? Hurt you? It's not the first time."

Dark Skies rubbed at his cheeks and examined the blood on his hands. "But it feels so permanent."

Kevin Bacon kicked him. "It is. Keep your bristlebucks. I'm the god-killer now."

Dark Skies flailed into a tree. He fell to his knees in a coughing fit.

The fighting quelled around them. All eyes turned to Kevin Bacon and Dark Skies.

As Kevin walked closer to the felled god, he turned toward the crowd. "Listen here. Today, if you're a god, you will die. If you're not a god, you will become one tomorrow."

He knew he couldn't kill Dark Skies yet, but he hoped the spirit and strength he showcased would weaken the spirits of the rest of the gods. While the strings did bend together, there were still possibilities where his family and friends were dead, strung up and flayed by the power of the gods. The sight of his weakened kin brought a newfound fight within him. Tonight, Kevin Bacon would kill all he could kill. Soon, there would be additional work to do.

He lifted Dark Skies by the throat and for the first time, the god showed genuine fear in his eyes. One of Kevin's discs dug into Dark Skies's temple, and the other into his neck. They each came out an opposite end, leaving the god's head split into two equal parts, both separate from his body.

As his body hit the ground, Abraham Lincoln bellowed a war cry.

Miley Cyrus, Lady Gaga, and Laura Jane Grace lifted their arms and bellowed with him.

The remaining gods stepped back, horrified.

Rapture, meanwhile, continued to reach for Dance's throat.

"I really don't think he'll ever be on our side," Dance said to Kevin Bacon.

He winked at her. "Trust me. He will. He'll always be an asshole, but he'll be a good asshole."

Rapture turned his head away from Dance, tucking his teeth back into his mouth. "I think she's right, Mr. Bacon." He turned back to her, chomping at the air, fighting against her viny arms as they held him back.

A female god stepped forward, getting in front of Kevin Bacon. Her hair floated around her head. "My name is Jasha. Unlike my kin, I do not fear you. My brother lives. You can't fool me."

Kevin spun a disc in his hand. "Then, may I have this dance?"

She whipped her hair and knocked him on his ass. "Indeed," she said.

What Did You Do?

The lampposts trudged away from the house as it collapsed with Christian inside. Clouds of plaster and debris shot out from all sides as the walls crumbled like a sandcastle in the wind. Christian screamed. Candlestick cried.

She yelled, "No, wait," but it was too late.

As the top of the house met the ground, she fell to her knees and bawled, hating herself, hating her impetuousness, and her inability to think things through. She reacted without thinking. If she'd given herself time before deciding, Cassie's parents would still be alive, Christian wouldn't be buried under rubble. After Todd, she'd promised herself she'd never allow herself to feel helpless again and Christian made her feel helpless. He took away a piece of Cassie and she couldn't accept that, but she didn't want him dead. He'd shown nothing but kindness to her and didn't even seem to care about Cassie.

Cassie's parents were mean, terrible people. They deserved to die and Candlestick could walk away from their bloody bodies with her sense of self-respect still intact. But Christian? He didn't deserve this.

When the dust settled, she ran to the house, now just a mountain of wood and plaster. She coughed and waved away the remaining dust as if it were a swarm of annoying gnats.

"Christian?" she yelled.

"Help," he shouted.

Her heart jumped. A laugh mixed in with the tears. "You're alive! Where are you?"

He'd gone to the basement so he never saw the lampposts. He'd never know she had anything to do with this and if she saved him, things could go back to normal. If he died, Cassie would know. She'd blame Candlestick and probably tell Randy about her monsters.

"I'm here. Can you follow my voice? I'm stuck. I think I'm bleeding."

She stepped on broken boards, balancing as if on a tightrope, making her way toward his voice.

When she reached where his voice came from, she pulled away some wood pieces. Shards of glass dug into her palms. A few wood pieces were lodged in chunks of cement. When she dropped the long wood strips, plumes of debris shot up into her face. She hacked and coughed, still fighting to pull more pieces out.

After she pulled enough wood away, Christian looked up at her, five feet down in a dark hole. He lay on the ground, breathing roughly. His face was gray from bits of insulation, dirt, and cement. An enormous pile of stuff covered his lower half. It looked like the entire first floor had collapsed on top of him. Candlestick couldn't make out what the pile was made of, too broken and intermingled to define it, but above the mound, a flatscreen television stood perfectly intact.

"Are you okay?" she asked.

He shook his head. A stream of blood trickled from his nostril to the cement floor under him. "I'll be okay." He was lying.

"I'm going to find a way to get down there."

The hole she'd uncovered was too small and the rest of the debris was too big for her to pick up on her own. She wanted to save him by herself because if she had to go back to Randy and Cassie for help, all hell would break loose. Cassie would turn on her. Lion would be a big help, though. Maybe she could retrieve the dog without Cassie noticing.

No. He was hanging too closely to the tents. She should have taken him with them, but she thought it was best for him to protect Cassie since Candlestick had her monsters.

"Can you get my cousin? He can help," Christian said. He tried lifting his head but groaned and put it back down.

"I won't let you die." She walked around, trying to find some other point of entry where she could get down there.

After a few attempts to lift heavier boards, she sighed and whispered. "I need you to come back and lift some of these. Try not to be seen."

She always thought of the monsters as her protectors or as something she could use for violence, forgetting they were giant powerful creatures and she could use them for whatever means she wished.

Rumbles came from every side of her.

"What's that noise?" Christian asked.

Candlestick looked down the hole, staring him in the eyes. "Nothing. I'm going to save you, but I need you to do me a favor, okay?"

"What?" he asked.

"I need you to look at me for a couple minutes. You're going to hear some weird noises around you, but I want you to promise you won't look toward where they're coming from. Can you do me that favor?"

He nodded. "What about my cousin? Are you going to get him?"

"Eventually," she said. "First, I need you to trust me."

He stared at her, as promised.

The presence of the lampposts was impossible to ignore. Their giant clomps rattled the ground. As they pushed away debris, Candlestick recognized the sound of their claws digging and the sizzling of their molten faces hitting dry wood. She prayed they didn't accidentally start a fire.

"What the fuck is going on?" Christian asked.

She shook her head. "Don't ask. Just look at me."

"I'm really scared, Candlestick. Can you tell me one of your stories?"

"Not now, but soon. Just focus. You're going to be okay."

"What the fuck?" someone screamed behind her.

Candlestick jolted upright.

Randy, Cassie, and Lion stood on the outskirts of the forest.

Randy froze, horrified, his eyes bulging out of his head.

Cassie showed no fear at all, only a mixture of concern and anger.

Randy shouted nonsense, freaking out, which brought a new sense of fear into Christian, causing him to break his promise. He glanced over to where the scraping and pulling came from. Candlestick guessed he could only see the claws, if anything, but it was enough. He shifted his upper body as much as the debris on top of him allowed. Both he and Randy screamed, "What the fuck?"

Over their choral cries of panic, Candlestick picked up Cassie's commentary. "What did you do?" she asked. "What did you do?"

Dreaming of Light and Air

Violin opened her eyes as the cart arched upward. She forced herself to see the dizzying heights. After looking down toward Earth on the first revolution, she closed her eyes and told a story to herself, but the ride would end soon and she owed it to everyone she'd ever loved to look, to feel, to fear.

Her mother died in a small underground home, dreaming of the light and fresh air. Her father died building her a home. Her sister went missing following her instructions. Brian and Corey were Kevin Bacon knows where, probably relentlessly searching for her. And she had the nerve to close her eyes?

No.

She stared at the forest's edge as it pulled away from her, the trees shrinking with the Earth. She turned and mapped out the entire park, searching for escape routes, hiding spots, weapons to wield.

She couldn't defeat Fake Winter, but her community deserved her effort. She'd die trying to kill him if she had to, but for now, she wanted to ride. Ride. Ride. Ride.

The wheel slowed. As her cart descended toward the base,

and her captor, she prepared for the next round of war. For now, she planned to keep it entirely a battle of wits, one she felt she still had the upper hand on, assuming he hadn't read her mind.

When her cart hit the bottom, Fake Winter came over and unbuckled her. "How was your dream ride?"

She pushed her lips to one side of her face, as if moving her whole mouth to the right. "Kind of weak. This is supposed to be scary?"

Fake Winter laughed. "No. This one is more for young lovers and children. It's a joyride, more for the view. If you wanted scary, you should have chosen that one." He pointed toward a series of white tracks.

"What's that one?"

"It's a rollercoaster. They call it The Footloose."

She smiled. She didn't believe in a god or gods, didn't truly think Kevin Bacon existed, but still, she took the name of the coaster as a sign. "I would like to go on that one."

"No."

She hopped off the cart and stretched. "You told me to stop acting tough and play along. You could do the same, you know? I know you have plans for me and I know I won't be able to escape them. Can we at least make this all as pleasant as possible?"

He grabbed her shirt around the shoulder and pulled. "No. I've had enough games."

As they stepped off the ride, Violin stepped on something hard. It was a small pile of dead birds, like someone collected them and left them by the Ferris Wheel.

"Who would do something like this?"

He snarled. "A human; who else?"

"And what are you, if not a human?" she asked.

"I am the one who can kill you if you don't shut up."

She allowed him to carry her through the park, toward the other rides and games. "No, you won't. You can't."

"Are you testing me?"

She stopped, plugged her feet into the dirt, and fought against his pull. He sighed. "What are you doing?"

"Yes, I am testing you. You can kill me, so you claim. Do it." She crossed her arms and stood tall. She knew he could kill her based on strength and speed, but she also knew he, for whatever reason, needed her to hear his stories. He couldn't do that if she were dead and that meant he not only couldn't kill her, but would actively protect her until his mission was accomplished.

"I'm not going to kill you. I don't have to prove myself."

"Well, I'm not going to listen to your bullshit stories anymore, and you know what?" She stormed away.

He chased after her as she hopped over a game counter. Ten plastic horses with a human rider stood in place on a large display. The counter had little alleys with holes at the end and numbers painted by each one.

She dove under the counter and Fake Winter grabbed her ankle. She latched a hand onto a shelf and fumbled for anything she could get. A set of a keys, a box of something called Marlboros. She slashed and tossed all the junk to the floor until she gripped exactly what she needed: a small pocketknife.

Fake Winter lifted her, and she smiled, pulling the knife up.

He frowned at her. "Do you truly believe you're going to kill me with that?"

"No," she said and placed the knife against the flesh on her neck. The cold metal hit her skin, and for a brief second, she considered just going ahead with it and slicing it from left to right, but the feeling was fleeting. She was taught to never quit. Not ever.

"What are you doing?" he asked but lacked any concern in his voice.

She had to prove she wasn't bluffing, so she made a small cut in her skin. The knife wasn't sharp, and it burned roughly as she dug it into her flesh. Warm blood trickled onto her hand and wrist.

"*NO!*" Fake Winter yelled. His arm stretched, growing abnormally long, and snatched the blade from her hand.

She smiled, examined the blood on her hand, and for show, licked it. As Fake Winter's eyes grew wide, she smiled deeper. "See, you not only can't kill me, but you also won't let anything happen to me. You need me alive right now. You need me to hear your stories. Here's what's going to happen. I am going on that Footloose machine and you're going to let me. Then, when I'm done, you'll finish your stupid fucking stories." She marched past him toward The Footloose.

He sighed and followed right behind.

As she moved closer to The Footloose, she told herself a story in her mind.

Rapture and the Moment of Truth

The god named Dust slashed at Dance's trailing plants, shredding the vegetation and exploding the blackberries growing on her limbs. She knew the god's name because as he attacked her, he spoke in third person.

"Dust gonna maul you. Dust will eat your carcass like a salad. Dust shreds your limbs and eats your fingers."

She'd managed to defeat a few gods. Mitochondria lay dead at the foot of a tall oak. She also kept the hungry and ferocious Rapture at bay, but Dust appeared to get the better of her on each attack. She'd wrap her green arms around him and squeeze, but he'd counter with some pruning.

Rapture stood at her feet and chewed on the vines of her ankles.

She shook her leg, kicking him away, while slashing thick cords of ivy at Dust. A red streak of blood ran down his cheek from ear to mouth.

Rapture climbed her leg, clawing his sharp nails into her flesh as he made his way up.

Dust charged her, digging his sharp bladed fingers into her arm. The blades drove all the way through until his knuckles touched her leafy flesh.

Dance screamed as he ripped the talons from her arm. Blood and green ooze splashed out. As she fell to her knees screaming and clutching her arm, Rapture made his way toward her face. His snarl revealed his yellow, pointed teeth. Tears poured down Dance's cheeks. Despite all the pain and death she'd experienced, the blades of the god named Dust hurt more than anything she'd ever felt.

Rapture listed his head at the sight of her crying eyes, and while he didn't lower his snarl, his eyes softened.

Dust drove another stab into her leg, and as he pulled the blades away, they took half of Dance's legs with them. Her screams stole the oxygen from the forest. The birds flew away. The warring ceased. She let out a Medusa's cry, trying to expel the agony from her body by pouring it out of her lungs.

Rapture's claws released from Dance's torso. His snarl finally vanished. He turned his head and examined her legs, then pulled his eyes up to the smirking Dust. "What did you do?"

"Dust did what you couldn't. Dust tore her to shreds. Dust won't stop there."

Rapture's fat body sunk. He turned back toward Dance. Face to face, he breathed fishy air at her. "What's happening? You never broke like this before."

Dance's face twitched and her lips shivered. "His blades are magic. They're killing me," she said.

Rapture stepped off her body and moved backwards, eyes panicked as if seeing a ghost.

Dust drew his blades and swiped at her arm, tearing it from her body. Leaves and vines showered the gods around her.

She screamed again and begged for it to end. "Please, please. Stop."

Dust only smiled. He swiped again, taking her other arm off. Dance lay bleeding in the dirt, limbless.

"What did you do?" Rapture whispered again.

Dust ignored the question and dropped to his knees. He stuck his bladed fingers out a few feet above Dance's neck.

"What did you do?" Rapture shouted and charged. He flew into Dust's face and bit a chunk of his cheek off. The raccoon spit it out, blood dribbling down his furry face. "You taste like shit."

He turned to Dance. "He tastes like literal shit."

Rapture bit again and Dust swatted at him, slashing the little furry asshole on the back. The two bit and slashed and screamed, blood spraying everywhere.

Dance lifted her upper half with the small amount of her arm she had left. Vines grew from the wound and traveled along the dirt until they reached Dust's feet. She wrapped them around his ankles and pulled.

Dust fell hard on his back, but Rapture held on and continued to chew on his face. As Dust struggled to get Rapture off him, Dance wrapped her vines around his wrists, taking away his ability to fight back.

Rapture chomped on Dust's throat.

The god flailed and hollered until his body proved his name accurate, dissipating into ash.

Rapture turned to Dance. The two stared for a moment.

"Thank you," Dance said.

Rapture brought his snarl back. "I didn't do it to help you."

She nodded.

"I didn't, I swear. I still hate you."

"I know," she said and smiled.

"I'm still going to kill you sometime."

"I know," she said again.

"Stop smiling at me." He turned his head away, but slowly

brought his eyes back to her. "Are you gonna be okay? Will those grow back?"

She nodded. "I think so."

He walked over to her, hesitating every few steps before pressing on. When he reached her, he stood above her face for a moment, before dropping down hard and fast and wrapping his paws around her neck.

She hugged him back.

"What are you doing?" he asked.

"Hugging you back."

"I'm not hugging you!"

"Then what are you doing?"

He stuttered. "I don't know. Just shut up." His paws squeezed a little tighter.

"Rapture, may I ask you a question?"

He peeled himself off her. "What do you want?"

"You said Dust tasted like literal shit. Why did you keep eating his face?"

"To save you. I ate shit to save you."

"So, you did do it for me." She pressed a vine against his cheek.

"No. That's not what I meant. I'm a fucking raccoon. I like to eat garbage, okay. Maybe I like the taste of shit."

She placed the back of her head against the dirt and closed her eyes, hoping the pain would cease soon. Around her, Kevin Bacon's family fought, died, killed.

"I guess I'm gonna go kill some gods now," Rapture said and walked away. He turned his head back to her and shook it. "I can't believe I'm gonna end up the hero of this story. Un-fucking-believable." He jumped on Jasha's shoulder and ripped into her flesh.

Dance took a deep breath. "You still killed my crops, asshole.

You may have saved my life, but I'm not done making yours a living hell." She whispered this to herself, but Rapture turned to her with a mouthful of god meat.

"Same to you, sister," he said. "Same to you."

The Ricochet

The lampposts dug their way to the basement of the house, diligently working to save the boy they were called upon to kill just moments before. *The cost of working for a child*, Candlestick thought. She ignored Cassie's chants.

"What did you do?" the girl repeated like a mantra. Of course, Candlestick would have to address the question at some point, but for now, she focused her attention on Christian, whose breath grew more ragged, his skin paler.

"Please, just focus on me," Candlestick said to him as he eyed the monster legs now visible in the basement.

The monsters were close to him now, almost able to reach the mound of stuff covering the boy's lower half.

Randy stayed by the tree line, eyes wide and jaw slacked. He stepped forward a few paces before retreating, eager to help his cousin, but too terrified to do so. "What the fuck are those things?"

If Cassie were listening, she probably would have told Randy the monsters were Candlestick's creatures she beckoned time and again to create chaos, but Cassie wasn't listening. She was too busy pointing her finger and screaming, "What did you do?"

The monsters moved closer to Christian and cleared some enough rubble so Candlestick was able to reach down and extend her arm out. She held her hand a foot above Christian until he stretched his arm out to hold her hand.

His eyes glazed over and he shivered. He was dying, she knew, and all the work her monsters put in was for show. Not for Cassie, Randy, or even Christian, but for Candlestick. It was a way for her to feel she tried to fix her mistake, but it was too late. She'd killed him. He wasn't even concerned about the monsters anymore, too busy fighting for life to realize what was happening around him. His palms were sweaty and he trembled so much, it forced Candlestick's arm into rumbling.

"Christian, stay with me," she said.

He nodded.

Cassie's mantra grew louder as the girl moved closer. Having experienced the creatures before, and knowing Candlestick well enough, she showed no fear. She walked until she stood over her friends, casting a shadow on Candlestick and Christian. "What did you do?"

Christian's eyelids closed into slits. "She didn't do this."

Tears formed in Candlestick's eyes. The poor kid didn't even realize she had, indeed, done it.

"What?" Cassie said.

Christian repeated himself, half-mumbling and whispery. "She didn't do this. The house. It fell down."

Candlestick turned to Cassie, crying. She hated lying, but knew it was necessary if she planned to keep the only friend she'd ever truly loved. "I brought my monsters to save him."

Cassie cupped her hands around her mouth.

The lampposts dug a clearing and slashed at the pile on top

of Christian. When they reached the final piece, a giant chunk of cement wall, they lifted.

Christian screamed and the girls witnessed the horror hiding underneath it. Christian's legs were bent in inhuman poses, the bones shattered and crushed. Blood pooled around his limbs and white shards stuck out from the skin in multiple places.

Cassie screamed at the sight, while Candlestick made a fist and covered her mouth, fighting against the acid climbing up her throat.

Randy fought his fears and ran toward them, screaming.

The lamppost stared at Candlestick, waiting for direction, it's job done. It had freed the boy, as instructed, but it stayed put with a single claw holding the cement block in place.

"Jesus," Randy said at the sight of his cousin. He dropped to his knees and wept. "Fuck. Fuck."

Candlestick clutched Christian's hand tighter. He wasn't looking at her anymore, nor did he see Cassie or Randy. Instead, his eyes were lost in clouds, blankly hovering into nowhere.

"Drop the block," Randy whispered. "Put it back in place."

Candlestick turned to him with her eyebrows furrowed.

"He can't survive this, but the block will keep him alive a little longer." Randy pressed his wrists against his forehead and howled an agonized moan.

The lamppost looked to Candlestick.

She nodded. "Gently," she whispered.

The lamppost slowly put the block back in place.

"Now, please leave us alone." The Lamppost climbed out of the hole and walked into the woods. They felt as she did, her emotion one with theirs. The creatures walked away with their heads hung low, dripping fire into an already scorched neighborhood.

Christian mumbled something, but Candlestick couldn't

make it out over the sniffling and crying of her peers. She leaned closer, trying to hear him.

"Mom, the teacher wants to talk to you," he said.

Candlestick bit her lip. Christian's state of shock brought him into a memory, and he recited his part in the act. She felt bad for intruding on it. Listening to him speak was like prying into his diary, a non-consensual encroachment into his personal life.

"She's mad because I talk too much." He smiled; the sly, cunning smirk of a boy misbehaved.

Candlestick scrunched her face, pushing away more tears. She still clutched his hand, and with his life slowly bleeding from his body, he held tight with surprising strength.

She didn't look away from him but spoke softly to her friends. "Do you both want me to leave so you can have a chance to say goodbye?"

Randy's hands covered his face. He spoke through the space between palms. "I would like some privacy for a minute, if that's okay."

Candlestick nodded. "Here, take his hand."

Randy reached down and she placed Christian's hand in his cousin's. She walked to the forest edge with Cassie following close behind. The girl whimpered and sniffled the whole way. When Candlestick reached a spot far enough away, she turned to her friend, and was met by a giant, forceful hug.

"How did this happen?" Cassie said with her face buried against Candlestick's neck.

Candlestick didn't respond.

Randy asked for privacy, but he spoke too loudly for them not to hear. He begged and cried for Christian to stay with him. "Please, don't leave me," he said. "Please, I need you."

His cries echoed in Candlestick's brain and stung her chest. When her community died, it carved an empty hole in her heart. When someone shot her father, it broke her, shattered every fiber of her. The bullet may as well have hit her. And so far, she'd killed so many and never once considered the ricochet, the pain she'd inflicted on innocent people.

She didn't just kill Cassie's terrible parents. She killed a piece of Cassie, too. She didn't just wash away the feelings of helplessness by harming Christian. She destroyed his cousin, and Cassie, once again. Maybe this was why everyone left her, why her sister, Brian, and Corey fled the motel, because Candlestick was poison. Her actions, a constant source of pain on everyone else.

Lion must have felt the self-hatred beating through her bloodstream, because as she wept on Cassie's hair, the animal came and licked her hand, reminding her she was loved. A love she didn't deserve. She remembered Lion starving in the woods with her, laying tied up at each house she'd stayed at, always imprisoned instead of roaming free as he deserved. He chose suffering to be with her because, unlike the humans, he couldn't understand that suffering was a consequence of knowing her.

Cassie pulled her face away. "I don't want to disrupt Randy, but I want to say goodbye to him, too."

Candlestick grabbed her hand and led her over to the gaping hole where Christian held on to his last breathes. Randy had finished his conversation and devolved into a blubbering mess, curled in a fetal position.

Cassie knelt next to him and smiled down at Christian, who continued to stare blankly into a void. "Hey, Christian. I'm sure you knew this, but I had a wicked crush on you." Cassie giggled and sniffled. "I know it was stupid, and I know you didn't feel the same way. We're like a million years apart. I'm just a silly kid to you. But you never made me feel that way. You were always nice to me. You made me feel important, and no one has ever done that before. I guess that's why I had a crush. Thank you for making me feel like I mattered."

The words cut into Candlestick. She wondered if Cassie was

being hyperbolic for the dying boy, or if she failed to make Cassie feel as important as she was. Candlestick did kill her parents without her permission, did make decisions for her, and criticized her for feeling love toward someone other than her. Candlestick, truly, was poison.

Christian showed no signs of hearing her. His eyes never moved from the invisible spot. As far as Candlestick could tell, he was staring at the clear, blue sky. If it weren't for the shaky breaths coming loudly from his nose, she would have presumed him dead already. He didn't move, didn't respond. She wondered if he heard Cassie, processed it, and would leave the world with a word of kindness in his brain, or if he were already gone and Cassie's conversation was designed to heal the speaker and not the receiver.

Christian turned his head and everyone looked down at him. It shocked Candlestick. She nearly fell over.

He gurgled and let out a hard huff.

Everyone leaned forward, waiting to see what he would do next.

He said something, soft and unintelligible.

"What?' Cassie asked.

He reached his hand back up, his whole arm shaking. Randy reached out for it, but Christian swatted him away. He kept the hand hovering above himself and looked at Candlestick. She put her arm down and when her hand touched his, he squeezed, this time without an ounce of strength.

"Tell," he said.

"What?" Candlestick scooted her body forward, putting her head closer.

"Tell a story." He smiled.

She bit down hard and wiped her face before the tears showed up. "Okay."

Free to Punish

Mary and Zeke fled, heeding her father's advice. She followed behind Zeke, who occasionally turned to ensure she stayed close behind. They stopped at every noise, scoured the area in search of phantoms, worried over every tickle from the wind.

When they reached the clearing by the river, the same one Russ once dragged Mary through, she stopped. "Wait."

Zeke listened, taking the time to catch his breath.

"Where are you bringing us?"

He shook his head, his eyebrows raised with fear. "I don't know."

She pushed him. "Yes, you do. You're taking us back there."

He shook his head. "I guess. I don't know. I was just running. Where else is there to go?"

"Anywhere. Not there. I'd rather someone kill us than ever go back there."

He bent over and put his hands on his knees, catching his breath. "That's a brave thing to say, but is it true?"

She thought for a moment. "Yes. No. I don't know. I don't

want to go to that hellhole again. There's got to be somewhere else. Plus, shouldn't we be looking for everyone else? We can't just *not* warn them."

"What do you want to do, Mary? Hunt for them forever without a single clue where they could be? For what? So, we can tell them your dead father gave us a dire warning that there are others like Russ out there hunting for us?"

"Fuck," she said as she kicked a rock. "I'm scared. I don't know what to do."

Zeke said nothing as he walked toward her. When he reached her, he grabbed her hand. "Let's just go there for tonight until we figure this out."

As he walked away, she let her arm stretch without moving her body until it was going too far. She had the choice to either let go of his grip or follow. Her choice wasn't made based on which she'd rather do, but solely on the fact she didn't want to let go of his hand.

When they reached the door to the shed, her chest constricted and her breath grew shallow. "I don't like this. I don't want to go down there. What if we didn't kill him? What if he's still alive down there? I don't want to see him either way."

Zeke put his hands on her shoulders. "Kelly ripped his head off. Literally severed it from his body. He's not alive."

Mary stepped back and shook her head. "You don't know that. What if he's like us?"

"Like us? Can you live without a head?"

"You know what I mean."

"I'll go down first and check, okay?" He opened the passageway and stepped onto the first rung.

As he descended, Mary looked out the barn door into the thick blackness of night. The vastness of the world weighed on her. She felt exposed, as if eyes watched her from every direc-tion. Despite the open air, or maybe because of it, she felt claustrophobic. The walls below suddenly felt so open, so freeing.

She didn't wait for Zeke to give the okay. Instead, she climbed down right behind him. When they reached the bottom, Russ's body remained where they'd left it, dead and cold. Not far from his, Ellie's lay the same way.

Mary crossed her arms around her torso, blanketing herself in her own comfort. "This is gross. I don't want to be here."

Zeke sighed and scanned the room, searching for who knows what. "It's just for one night. If we decide to stay longer, I'll do something with the bodies."

"We won't be deciding to stay here for more than a night, but thank you." She went to her alcove and lay on the floor. Her body found the spot where she'd slept every night Russ had her trapped down here. The floor was hard and cold, but there was comfort in finding her place, the curled position in which she slept during her worst nights. If she could manage some sleep during those nights, she could find it anywhere.

Zeke came to the edge of her alcove. "Why don't you sleep in one of the middle ones, so you won't have to stay near Ellie's body?"

"No. This is my alcove."

"Okay," he said and walked away. A few seconds later, the clanging of feet on rungs rang through the room.

She shot up. "Where are you going?"

"I'll be right back," he shouted.

She laid back down, trusting him. He kept his word. A few minutes later, she listened to the soft music of the rungs welcoming him back. She followed his footsteps as they came closer, and she looked up as he approached her alcove. He stood at the entrance with a pile of blankets rolled in a comically big ball, which he squeezed into his chest to keep them from falling.

"You can at least be comfortable."

She smiled and put her arms out. He tossed her two blankets.

"Thank you."

"You're welcome. See you in the morning. I'll be in the next alcove over."

She nodded. It didn't take long to fall asleep, but it was also short-lived. She woke a few hours later from a nightmare, visions of Russ choking Ellie to death. She sat up and leaned against the stone wall, thinking about nothing, thinking about everything. An idea came into her head, a petty one. An awful one. She sat against the wall, trying to talk herself out of it, but she knew she wouldn't. She needed to do it. She quit delaying and stepped out of her alcove.

For a brief second, she expected the chains to pull on her leg, forcing her to stay in her alcove as they'd done so many times previous. But they didn't. She was free now. Free to move. Free to hate. Free to punish.

At Russ's body, she sat down cross-legged and extended her arms. It didn't take long for his eyes to open and a scream to pour from his coughing mouth. She wondered how he expelled the sounds without a neck. Just a screaming head.

He looked at her with horror on his face, and in return, she offered him the deepest smile she could muster.

"Suffer, you fucker. Die and die again," she whispered.

"What the fuck are you doing?" Zeke said from behind her.

As he ran to her, Russ's eyes closed and he fell back into a painful death.

"Trust me," she said.

He sat next to her. "Dude, this is fucked up. I mean, I get it, but it's fucked up."

"Trust me," she said again, and once more, she extended her arms.

A few seconds later, his eyes opened, and a new scream left this mouth.

"Tell me about the others. Tell me why you took us and who else knows about us or I'll keep bringing you back to die and die again. You will suffer endlessly until you tell me."

"Fuck you, you fucking animal." Russ spit and hollered. A few minutes later, he died for a third time.

"It's not going to work forever," Zeke said.

"He doesn't know that." Mary extended her arms again. In truth, she wanted answers, but she'd be satisfied with torturing him. Answers would only be icing on the cake. In fact, when she first brought him back, she hadn't considered talking to him, only causing him more pain in death. He got off too easy, she thought. He needed more suffering. It wasn't until Zeke woke up that Mary came up with a purpose for the pain.

Russ's eyes opened. More yelling. "Stop. Please. Stop."

"Tell me how you knew about us and who else knows."

"Everyone, you stupid bitch. Anyone who sees you knows you're an animal." He died again.

She growled and extended her arms, but he didn't return. She bit down hard, and clenched all of her muscles, but it was no use. He didn't return. After a few more tries, she stood up and yelled. "Fuck. I fucking hate him."

Zeke put his hands out, but didn't say anything, letting her vent. She pushed his hands away and went in for a hug instead. They stayed in the embrace for a long time.

Eventually, she pulled away and grabbed his hand, leading him toward her alcove. "Stay in mine tonight. Just, keep some distance. This isn't an invitation for anything weird. I just don't want to be alone."

He nodded.

They laid next to each other on separate blankets, faces turned toward each other.

"Maybe we should stay down here," Mary said.

He nodded again.

"Do you think we can turn it into a home, somehow?"

"We can try," he said, his voice cracking.

"What other options do we have?" She reached her hand out and touched his.

"If your dad was right, I'm not sure we have any. I'm not even sure if this one is good."

She turned away from him. "Nothing will ever be good again. I'm happy with just surviving."

On the Run

Brian's heartbeat steadied as the car lurched around a corner, giving a large amount of breathing room between them and the gang of men in army gear. He took the car around a bunch of side roads, zigging and zagging, hoping to keep them way out of range in case the men had their own vehicle to hunt them with.

He'd need to get back on Main Street to hit the fairgrounds, but the detour was necessary to keep him and Corey safe for a while. He wasn't sure how he knew Violin was at the fairgrounds, but much like the wind that pulled him toward her, an invisible string guided him to that abandoned place where the ghosts of rides and games lingered. He imagined it, the hollowed-out carnival games, the unkempt grass suffocating the bases of the rides, the paint chipped. It scared the hell out of him: a place once filled with wonder, smiles, and happiness, left to rot.

He cut the car down a winding sideroad where the cement changed to gravel and dirt. The car lurched and bounced as they hit uneven terrain. Corey's head nearly hit the ceiling with each bump.

A truck came into the rearview, it's high beams blaring in the midday sun, reflecting in the mirror with each bounce the truck took. It raced down the road, unconcerned about slowing at turns. The engine roared, a taunting call.

Brian ground his teeth and took a deep breath. He knew this wasn't a coincidence. Knew it was those men from the Job Lot parking lot.

Up ahead, another dirt road cut across, and Brian debated on hitting the wheel hard and taking a sharp turn down it, but he didn't know these roads, wasn't sure if it were a dead end.

Corey turned his head and noticed the truck. "Oh, fuck."

Brian hit the gas and the car clanged it smashed into the dirt road along the pockmarked earth. He barreled through the intersection and just as they almost cleared it, a brown sedan coming from the other road slammed into the back of Brian and Corey's Subaru Outback.

The SUV spun just in time for the truck to hit it on the other side of the rear. Brian glimpsed the driver and wasn't sure it was one of the men he spotted on the hill, but the driver did wear fatigues. The person operating the brown sedan hopped out of the driver's seat, and he too was wearing the fatigues.

Brian understood. The men he fucked with were large in numbers and had methods of communicating from a distance. It was the only explanation for how the driver of the brown car could have come from the direction he came and been so prepared to attack. For all Brian knew, he drove them right into the middle of the gang's territory.

He hit the gas and the car fishtailed in the dirt, kicking up a cloud of dust at the black truck. The driver of the brown car dove out of the way before getting struck. The Outback skidded before righting itself and Brian pressed his foot to the floor. He hadn't wanted to turn down the other road but had no choice but to pull forward.

Corey gripped the grab handle, his body clenching.

Brian took the car down another side road, and another, all the while constantly checking the rearview. He, once again, created some distance.

"When I say jump, jump out of the car," he said.

"What the fuck? What are you talking about?"

"Just trust me." He cranked the wheel to the left, jerking the Outback onto yet another road. But two cars, a red sedan and a black SUV, were side-by-side blocking them from moving forward. Three men in army fatigues sat on the hoods, calm as could be.

Brian slammed the car into reverse, jacked the car back onto the road they'd just been on, and pressed on the gas.

"Why the hell are we going to jump?"

"I think this is their territory. There's no getting out of here with the vehicle. They'll find us. We're going to run through the woods, but we can't have the car parked where we got out."

He hit another side road, this one nothing more than a thin strip of packed dirt. Luckily, he didn't see any houses and no cars blocked them from continuing. He checked the rearview and brought the car to a crawl.

"Now." He opened the door and Corey did the same.

"One. Two. Three." They both leapt from the moving vehicle and stumbled onto the dirt road. The car crept forward until the wheels shifted to the left. Eventually, it drove off the road and crashed into a tree with such minimal speed it hardly made a noise.

Brian pointed to the woods on the opposite side from where the car crashed. "There. Let's go."

They ran into the woods and Brian prayed the men didn't have a camp in there. All they needed was a little time to get ahead.

The Goddess of Hate

As The Footloose chugged up an incline, the carts rocked and shook against the tracks. Violin held the bar keeping her in place. She wanted to experience the ride, to understand how humans manufactured fear. It was an experiment, an attempt at empathy, but her primary reason for taking the ride was to exert control over Fake Winter. She'd increasingly felt restrained, leashed, and regulated. Since her father's death, she hadn't taken much action. Instead, the world acted against her. Things happened to Violin as if she were a mere rug to be stepped upon.

Forcing these situations, taking moments and making them her own, proved to Fake Winter, and to herself, that she still had some autonomy. Of course, autonomy wasn't enough. She needed to best Fake Winter, to escape and somehow kill the beast, but she'd figure that part out later. For now, the ride had almost reached the pinnacle of its upward climb.

She gulped and examined her surroundings, seeking truths laid out by the world, escapes, weapons, forces of nature calling to her. A few oaks on the outskirts of the park knotted and bent, curving into one another, their thick branches tangled like clutched fingers. She thought of Candlestick and her heart squeezed as if a fist gripped it and mushed.

And then, the cart plummeted. She flew downward and screamed. The cart dropped so rapidly she lost her breath.

Since her father's death, an icy block had built in her belly until it had nearly saturated her insides. She'd lost all sense of emotion. A depressed and overwhelming feeling of utter loss, lack of control, and worthlessness had seeped into her veins. Each new revelation about her family, her upbringing, her entire life, only solidified the glaciers, hardening them until she felt she might burst.

The terror and exhilaration of The Footloose turned her stomach, cracking the iceberg in her guts. She felt the fissure travel through her bloodstream. The pieces of ice melted, shattered, poured from her. She screamed and it was fucking beautiful. Her hair whipped in the wind, and the world grew and shrunk with each curve and hill.

The ride dropped again and she felt the power of Kevin Bacon next to her. She *was* Kevin Bacon. A god. And Fake Winter sat still below, holding the controls, not like someone who owned the situation, but as Violin's servant. Oh, he thought he manipulated the events happening around them, but Violin knew she owned it all. There is nothing in the world that shows how powerful one is more than to have that power stripped away.

The carts dipped and bounced, and rose and fell, and Violin wooooooooed and laughed. Fake Winter was wrong. The humans didn't love roller coasters because the rides offered artificial fear. They loved the rides because they offered an escape, a chance to look at oneself and see what you're made of, to feel the strength of the immortal, to roar like a caged animal holding the key to the door.

The Footloose gave Violin the blueprint to the most important thing on Earth: herself. Her body. Her mind. Her anger. A girl who understood her own rage held the secrets to her very DNA. She could rule, kill, love, plant, and grow. She'd blossom into a snarling tiger and taste freedom on her lips as she lapped up the blood of those who dare corner her. Yes, she would grip her own power like a sword and find pleasure in dying to right the wrongs against her.

The carts hit the last spinning loop and Violin flew sideways. Her body shook as the car rattled forcefully against the tracks. If not for the bar, she would have fallen out. The sideways slant was uncomfortable. Her hipbone slammed against the bar and the turbulence hurt her neck. She loved it all. Give her pain. Give her death. Give her glory.

The carts slowed and entered the final straightaway.

Fake Winter stared as her car crept toward the control base.

Violin cried and laughed. She assumed once the ride stopped, she would mourn the excitement, feel empty without it. Instead, the effects stayed with her, melded with her body. She trembled with anticipation for each moment of her future. All the agony sure to come, the pain, and love, and beauty. She yearned for each breath.

Wild with enthusiasm, she pulled on the bar, wanting to stand and jump, holler, bellow to the gods. But the bar wouldn't move until Fake Winter came and pressed something. As soon as she freed herself from the car, she leapt into Fake Winter, wrapping her arms around him in a hug.

He stayed still, confused and untrusting of the action.

She squeezed tighter and whispered, "Thank you," in his ear. As her lips neared his neck, she contemplated digging her teeth into his nape, but knew the time wasn't quite right. She inhaled the stench of his leathery skin, knowing one day she would. Her teeth would rip into him, and she'd laugh as he screamed in pain. She'd swallow some of his blood and spit the rest in his face. She couldn't wait. The idea of it spun her stomach much like the rollercoaster did.

She also knew she needed to hear the rest of the stories. She did not like sharing the same goal as her enemy, but with knowledge came power. Understanding the point of Fake Winter's agenda would bring her closer to finding her own answers. The end was coming, and with it, a deluge of truth would spill like Fake Winter's blood soon would.

As she let go of him and dropped back to her feet, she smiled. "If I promise to be good and keep the stories as they're meant to be told, can I finish them? I'll tell them right, I promise."

She didn't know what right and wrong were when it came to the tales, but she felt she could navigate through them, bring them toward the outcome Fake Winter needed. Telling them herself was another way to own the situation, to control the narrative, both literally and figuratively.

His eyelids slanted, heavy with skepticism. "Fine, but if you veer off course, I'll crush you."

"Of course," she smiled, then reached out her hand. "Let's walk back to the games. I'll tell you a story on the way."

He eyed her up and down, pressing his lips together, and then he took her hand.

She walked him down the midway while taking in each piece of her surroundings, building a puzzle that would mold into a weapon, a trap, a fight. Fake Winter held her hand as she led him toward his own demise.

Violin was the only member of her community born without a power, and yet, she was a goddess.

The goddess of vengeance.

The goddess of bloodshed.

The goddess of hate.

A Second Too Late

Only three gods remained, but they happened to be the most powerful of the lot. Still, in Kevin Bacon's first war, his brothers and sisters defeated three gods and at the time, they had a lot less teammates.

Lady Gaga had memories of the war, despite not being there at all, but it all reassured her victory would soon be theirs.

Raindrop latched onto her back, arms around her throat. Lady Gaga spun, looking for a tree or something hard to slam her back into, but she wasn't close enough to anything, and Raindrop's strength would take her down before she could reach. The goddess's arms tightened and pressure ballooned in Lady Gaga's brain. Her face grew hot as she gasped for sweet air.

On her side, Jasha swung her hair, slithery, floating, electric wires, slashing through the air. She hit the raccoon, sending the animal flying into a tree.

His fur scorched and his body twitched.

"That'll teach you to bite me, scum," she shouted. She whipped her hair again, dropping Avril. And again. Down went Kevin Bacon.

Lady Gaga dropped to her knees. Her vision blurred as Raindrop applied more pressure. Through her fuzzy vision, she watched Abraham Lincoln struggle to rise, his leg fully severed from his body.

The ice giant wailed a war cry as he tried to lift himself. As his palm planted in the soil, a solid base to hoist his body up, Jasha whipped her hair again, breaking his lower arm clean from the rest of him. He screamed and collapsed to the dirt. His body shook the Earth.

Dance and Miley stumbled and fell from the quake.

Jasha paced closer to the ice giant, moving in for the kill.

"No," Lady Gaga said. She pried her fingers around Raindrop's arm, and with all her strength, pulled it away, but the goddess proved too strong. Each time Lady Gaga managed to create an inch of distance, the goddess reapplied her arm with more force than before.

Jasha moved closer to Abraham Lincoln.

Dance charged her, but the goddess electrocuted her with a whip.

Rapture regained his footing and ran, but Jasha grabbed him by the fur and tossed him sky bound without losing her focus on the prize in front of her.

Lady Gaga fell to the dirt, a hoarse croak left her lungs.

Raindrop said nothing as she stole the life from her prey.

Too much space existed between Lady Gaga and her friend, but she reached forward, taking away as many inches as she could. She clawed into the dirt and slid her body until she came face-to-face with Ben Franklin's body, dead and bloodied. She dug her fingers into the dirt once more and pushed forward.

Kevin Bacon lay helpless next to Dark Skies, both of them out of commission.

Avril convulsed on her skateboard.

Lady Gaga's heart banged hard in her chest, a jealous lover knocking on the door of her ribs.

Raindrop grunted as she jerked her arm deeper into Lady Gaga's throat.

Jasha whipped her hair into Abe Lincoln once again. The ice giant howled as a gash opened in his belly.

She'd never reach him in time.

Bang!

A loud crack, deep as thunder, came from above Lady Gaga's head, and Raindrop's pressure relinquished. Lady Gaga rolled over and gasped for air.

Raindrop lay on her knees and forearms, blood poured from the side of her head. Above her, Laura Jane Grace stood holding a thick tree branch.

She put her arm out and helped Lady Gaga to her feet, but Lady Gaga still struggled for oxygen.

Laura Jane Grace lifted the club and swung it down on Raindrop's head once more. Raindrop fell face first in the dirt and Laura Jane Grace delivered a third blow.

Lady Gaga came back to her senses and pointed toward Abraham Lincoln.

Laura Jane Grace turned to see Jasha whipping another gash into the ice giant.

"No," she shouted and sent her branch flying through the air like a javelin. It soared toward Jasha, but the goddess turned, caught it, and snapped it in two before sending another lashing into Abe Lincoln.

The ice giant's body was riddled with open wounds. Blood poured out in pools, covering all of them in crimson. Abraham cried and begged for mercy. He reached out his stump of an arm and called to his friends. "Please, help me," he wailed.

Laura Jane Grace charged. "I'll fucking kill you," she screamed.

Jasha showed no interest in her.

Meanwhile, Lady Gaga took in large gulps of air, praying for strength enough to save her friends.

Laura Jane Grace jumped and kicked Jasha in the head, knocking her down. The goddess toppled over like a twig.

Lady Gaga, no longer able to wait, walked forward, still pulling in big swigs of oxygen, but not feeling it go all the way in. She had to fight. She'd die from losing air before seeing another dead body like Ben Franklin's.

Laura Jane Grace proved a worthy fighter against Jasha. She kicked the goddess while she was down, pounded her boot into Jasha's ribs.

The goddess coughed up blood and spit.

Laura lifted Jasha over her head and tossed her into a tree. Something cracked, and she was certain it wasn't from the oak trunk.

Lady Gaga wasn't sure if she should aide Laura Jane Grace, who already had things well under control, or go to Abraham to see if she could heal his wounds. She was a better fighter than doctor, but one looked more helpless than the other.

As she approached the ice giant, who writhed and screamed while blood poured from his gaping wounds, entrails slithering freely from the chasms, someone hit her hard in the back. She fell over, twisting at the last second to land on her back and catch the perpetrator of the crime. It was Raindrop. She held her palm against the open gash in her skull and kicked Lady Gaga once before moving on to her new target. Laura Jane Grace.

Midway between Lady Gaga and Laura, Raindrop spun around, her hand outstretched. As she spun, a tidal wave left her hands. It drove forward with force. It grabbed onto bodies, both dead and alive, and sent them sailing into trees, shrubs, earth.

Lady Gaga slammed into a trunk, and something in her arm

cracked. When she looked down, shards of bone protruded through the skin.

The water disappeared as quickly as it came. When it sunk, Raindrop stood dead center, landing cleanly as if she had been floating atop of it.

Laura Jane Grace was nowhere to be seen, but Jasha lay wrapped around her sister's hand. Raindrop slapped Jasha, awakening her.

Jasha looked around, trying to make sense of where she was.

Lady Gaga winced, ripped a portion of her shirt off, and wrapped it around the broken arm. She looked up and stepped forward, but stumbled, her mind woozy.

Jasha wasted no time. She and Raindrop marched toward Abraham Lincoln.

Avril came from behind the ice giant, skateboard in hand. As she charged the goddesses, she lifted the board and swung wildly. Before it made contact, Jasha shook her head, slashing her hair at Avril and taking her head off in a clean sweep.

Lady Gaga screamed as her friend's body crumbled to the ground, free of its head.

Raindrop ran and threw heavy punches at Lincoln, cracking the icy form of his body. She drove fist after fist into him and the giant cried and flailed.

"Wait," Jasha said. "I don't like when I can't finish my work. Lift him up."

Raindrop clutched his torso and pulled him upright.

Lady Gaga ran. The world slowed down and all she heard was the sound of air coming in and out of her body. Birds fluttered in the sky. Friends and foes moved all around her, rushing to aide each other, to kill each other, to fight and die. She gritted her teeth and stretched her legs forward, running with speed she didn't know she had.

Jasha pulled her head back.

Lady Gaga extended her arm, getting closer.

Raindrop pulled Lincoln forward an inch.

Left foot. Right foot. Gaga charged.

Jasha's hair floated and sparkled above her.

Lady Gaga's heel planted, she pulled her arm back, balled a fist.

Jasha spun her head, electrical snakes flying in front of her.

Lady Gaga's fist connected with Jasha's cheek, and the bones in her knuckles shattered, as did Jasha's cheek bone. They both fell to the ground.

Lady Gaga turned to Abraham as his head separated from his body. Her punch landed a second too late. Jasha's hair cut a line clean across the ice giant's throat.

His head slammed into the dirt. His body dropped next to it. A river of blood drenched them all. Abraham gurgled and cried, still alive. "Please friends, help me. You're supposed to help me," he said as his hand clutched the empty space between body and head. He whimpered and moaned. "Please. Help me." Tears flooded down his cheeks until his eyes were vacant stones.

Lady Gaga's body hit the drenched soil, and with her cheeks pressed into the muck, she lay face to face with Jasha. The goddess smiled playfully at her and jolted her head back, ready to strike. Before she could, Lady Gaga drove her lower arm into Jasha's chest, stabbing her with the broken bone. The bone cut into Jasha's flesh between her breasts. Lady Gaga grabbed her upper arm and prepared for immense pain as she pressed the broken bone further into the goddess's body. As she tightened her hand around her arm, Raindrop grabbed her by the hair and yanked her off her sister. Gaga punched with her good arm and nailed Raindrop in the face.

Raindrop let go of the clump of hair and covered her nose.

Lady Gaga stood, fresh anger boiled in her blood. She knew Jasha rose behind her, ready to strike, but she also knew her teammates were converging on the scene. Kevin Bacon, Dance, and Rapture on her left. Miley, Laura Jane Grace, and Elvis on her right. Even a human came charging from in front of her.

Jasha would face their wrath, and Raindrop would face Lady Gaga's, and Raindrop knew it.

The goddesss stumbled backward, fear in her eyes. She put a hand helplessly in front of her face. "No. Leave me alone."

Lady Gaga grabbed Raindrop by the ear and with her bad arm, sliced Raindrop's face down the middle with her sharp, bony knife. The goddess's facial features disappeared behind a curtain of blood and she screamed. Gaga tilted the woman's head back further and made a sanguine smile, left to right, across Raindrop's throat.

Blood gushed out of Raindrop's neck and she dropped to the ground. Her body convulsed until it turned to ash.

Gaga stared at the flecks and caught a few in her hands, as if they were lightening bugs, and put the ash in her pocket. She knew it would disappear, but enjoyed the idea of owning Raindrop for a few seconds, making the goddess nothing more than a collected object in the forest, something picked up and kept caged within her clothes.

She turned to see her friends pounding on Jasha. The goddess was nothing more than pulp. Laura Jane Grace used a sharp stick and scalped the goddess, removing her biggest weapon from her head.

Jasha kicked and squealed.

Miley dug her thumbs into Jasha's eyes and plucked them out.

Rapture ripped into her neck with his icicle teeth.

Dance strangled her with her viny arms.

Elvis kicked her with his blue suede shoes.

Eventually, her body dissipated and slithered upward in granules of dust.

Kevin Bacon and his team didn't stop attacking. The power of grief turning them into animals and monsters.

Lady Gaga stood and watched. She didn't judge them, for she too turned into a monster of vengeance. But the bloodlust in their eyes did scare her, mainly because she knew just moments before, it existed in her own.

When the group stopped their assault, they all looked around, confused, scared, unsure what to do next.

"There's still Dark Skies," Lady Gaga said, pointing to the god.

He'd come to since she last saw him, but he looked in no place to fight. Still, his confidence hadn't waned. A smirk grew on his face as all eyes turned to him. He sat against a tree stump, one arm lazily resting on a knee.

He clapped. "Well done. You've won."

Kevin Bacon stepped forward. "You don't seem bothered by the outcome."

The god shrugged. "Why would I? Nothing changes for me. My siblings and I didn't particularly like each other, so you've freed me of their burden. Otherwise, I am still Dark Skies, the wonderful."

Kevin Bacon cracked his knuckles. "You're wrong, though. We haven't won yet. Not until we kill you."

Dark Skies smiled. "Good luck finding me. Enjoy heaven. You have no idea the pain you've just awarded yourselves," and with those final words, he disappeared.

The Transition from Life to Death

Candlestick, Randy, and Cassie stood around the hole, watching Christian take his last breaths.

He smiled throughout Candlestick's story, but when it ended, his lips turned into thin lines, slightly blue. His skin turned pale and waxy. They listened to the air leaving his nose, softer with each passing.

"Guz," he said. "Guz."

Candlestick bit her finger and screwed up her face. "Shhhhh, just relax."

"Guz, I dunt wan die."

She tried to fight against her tears but his last words broke into the lock she'd wrapped around her heart.

Cassie cried the loudest, bawling with the theatrical nature of a child.

Randy punched the ground.

It was hard to tell when it happened, the transition from life to death. The only indicator was the quiet passage of air through his nostrils, and that was impossible to hear over the crying all around him. He was dead, though, Candlestick knew. At some point during their fits, he went from alive to dead. He took with him a piece of her soul, her innocence.

She'd done this. Her guilt stewed in the oven of her guts, mixed with anger, sadness, and curiosity. She'd seen so much death, but this was the first time she stayed eye-to-eye with the person passing. Magic existed in those seconds, an invisible little thing that stole life. What happened? How did it happen? Where did he go? She wanted to know more and wished for Mary's powers so she could wake Christian up and ask him.

Cassie and Randy continued their hysterics and Candlestick knew she should offer them comfort but doing so felt like she'd only be extending her violence, broadening the lies, stacking the bodies. Instead, she stared at her dead friend, apologizing with her mind, hoping wherever he lived now, he could hear her thoughts and know she felt guilt for her actions. But then, if he could hear her thoughts, would he also hear the ones she wished hidden? Would he know that despite her sorrow, if given the opportunity to do it again, she might?

Christian did nothing wrong. He wasn't Todd, some evil creep looking to harm children for his own pleasure. Christian offered kindness and took pride in assisting, but his existence meant pain, nonetheless. Cassie's interest in him would only grow with time, and he would either succumb to her or dismiss her more fervently, and both options would result in Candlestick's friend suffering. Sometimes you didn't need to be guilty to be a source of anguish. Sometimes a person was pain, through and through.

Candlestick turned to Cassie, who sat hugging her knees and rocking back and forth, still crying. Yes, Candlestick was also a source of Cassie's suffering, but unlike Christian, she caused pain to help remove it from the future, whereas Christian avoided hurting anyone, increasing their suffering later. It was like Candlestick's poison ivy. Itching it would have only given her temporary relief, and more problems later. She had to face the itch. And so did Cassie.

She sat in front of her friend and let the girl cry. When Cassie pulled her head up from her arms, Candlestick put her hands on the girl's knees. "I'm here for you. Always."

Lion seemed not to know what to do, but understood those around him suffered, so he buried his head under his paws and whimpered.

Cassie nodded. For a second, Candlestick thought she was going to bury her face again, but instead she lunged forward and wrapped herself around Candlestick. Within their embrace, all of Candlestick's justifications unraveled. She'd tried convincing herself she did the wrong things for the right reasons, but she only lied to herself. She did everything for selfish reasons. She wasn't helping Cassie; she was helping herself. All the awful suffering Cassie lived through came from Candlestick's bloody hands, and it all came so Candlestick could have Cassie to herself. And while Cassie's skin touched her own, their cheeks brushing against each other with gentle bristles of electricity, she felt no need to justify her actions anymore. She did monstrous things to feel love from someone worth loving. For that, she'd feel no guilt.

Her hands trembled as they pressed against the bony curves of Cassie's shoulder blades. "I need you to know something," she whispered to her friend.

Cassie pulled away to see her better. She wiped tears from her cheeks.

"I know this was all to find my sister, and I still need to do that, but I want you to know that whether we find her or not, you will always be my sister."

Cassie gave a quick smile, as if she had tried to lift her weighted lips but didn't have the strength.

"I love you like a sister," Candlestick said, and now she cried again too.

They hugged again, and Cassie sniffled into Candlestick's clavicle as she nuzzled into her neck. "I love you, too," she said.

Candlestick imagined herself as Cassie's cigarette. She was poisoning the girl and Cassie knew it, knew very well that Candlestick was no good for her. But she wanted her anyway, and Candlestick desired nothing more than to fill Cassie's blood stream, to send her heart racing, to make the girl love her.

Candlestick's mother had once told her nothing was more important than family, and there was nothing Candlestick wouldn't do for one. She'd lost them all, but now she found a new sister, one she molded into what she needed. And Cassie, if nothing else, was malleable, shaped from a child with a room full of toys into Candlestick's new sister. And unlike Violin, Cassie followed instead of demanding the lead.

Randy stood up and let out a last roar of anguish. "I need to bury him. Will you help me bury him?"

The girls pried themselves apart and nodded.

A thunderous crack blasted through the air. Candlestick's ears rang. Blood splashed on her face and Randy dropped. What just happened? Candlestick's eyes grew wide in horror. She looked around, trying to make sense of it. Her heart thudded in her throat.

Lion spun in circles, barking at nothing, barking at everything.

Boom! Another crack.

Something whizzed by her head. Someone was shooting at them. Panic set in, and she turned to grab Cassie, but her friend wasn't in front of her. It took a moment to realize Cassie was on the ground. Candlestick's mind raced. *Everything is fine. She'll be fine. Cassie is fine.*

But Cassie wasn't fine. A pool of blood grew around her head and more gushed out from the gaping hole that was once her left eye.

Candlestick screamed and dropped to her knees. She wrapped herself around Cassie and let out blood-curdling cries.

More bullets blasted through the air. She did nothing to run from them. She just waited for one to hit her.

"Cassie, no." She rocked her friend's lifeless body in her arms. "Cassie, please wake up." Not again. Not another family member dead. "Cassie!"

Boom! Boom! Boom!

Why weren't the bullets hitting her? Each loud crack made her explode with anger. She wanted them to kill her already. Why weren't they hitting her?

She pressed Cassie into her neck and the girl's blood soaked Candlestick's shirt and neck. "I love you, Cassie. I love you. Why did you do this to me? Why did you let me love you and then leave me? Why does this keep happening?"

She lifted her head and yelled to Kevin Bacon. "This isn't fair. This isn't fair."

She toppled over from the weight of her dead friend and didn't try to correct herself. She wished to stay tethered to the Earth forever, to never move again, to rot with the corpse of her new sister.

"Cassie, please don't be dead. Come back somehow. Please come back somehow." She touched Cassie's cheeks, smearing the blood around with her hand.

Christian got to die with final words, with final thoughts. He was able to speak to them. But that option was ripped from Cassie, and it was ripped from Candlestick. She never got to say goodbye, to console her friend into whatever new world she'd travel to.

"FUUUCCCCCCKKKKKKK!" she screamed.

She kissed Cassie's bloody face, tasting the blood on her lips. "I'm so sorry."

The horrible grief boiling in her belly turned to rage. She pressed her teeth together and turned toward the direction of the bullets.

For the first time, she saw why the bullets hadn't killed her. A pile of husks lay in front of her. As another bullet blasted through the air, another husk appeared and took the shot for her. She stood, knowing she had a shield of monsters.

Lion dutifully jumped to her side, and she put her hand on him, touching the one friend who was always there. She clutched him close, not letting him run toward danger, and then she whispered, "Get them, whoever is shooting, get them all. Kill them. No, don't kill them. Bring them to me. I want them to suffer."

The woods came alive with the rumbles of her familiar friends.

Candlestick dropped back to the ground and wrapped herself around Cassie. "I will never stop loving you," she said. "I'll never stop killing for you."

Candlestick was a monster, one who killed a friend for her own gain. She couldn't wait for her enemies to arrive, to show them what a real monster looks like. Forget the lampposts. Cassie's killers had something much more evil to deal with. She brushed Cassie's hair and told her one last story before preparing for the kill.

Loosening Knots

It had been four years since Mary and Zeke moved back into the alcoves. They lived meagerly, surviving off whatever they could muster.

Zeke tore down some of the walls, opening up their cavern to new rooms. He left once in a while to hunt or fish, and to steal things they needed to survive.

They didn't have electrical outlets, so the winters were cold thanks to the cement flooring and walls, and the summers were brutally hot because of the confined nature of the place. They didn't even have lights anymore. The power must have been connected to Russ's house, and once he died and the bills stopped getting paid, the electric company shut everything off.

In the four years they lived down there, no one had ever come looking for them. Though, that didn't stop them from worrying, their nerves frayed from every sound above.

She did leave the alcoves. Now and again, she and Zeke would come up and relax in the open fields behind Russ's house. They were extra vigilant, worried someone would plow through the bushes and end them. She enjoyed the sun soaking on her face for a few hours, and she'd stare blankly at the swaying oak branches or the rippling currents of the river, hoping to etch the images in her mind for the inevitable day she'd be forced to stay down in the hole forever.

They survived, but they didn't thrive, and it seemed like they always had a new thing they needed. Zeke would have to sneak into a nearby town to steal batteries or soap. They'd wash in the river and she'd dream of a day when Zeke would build her a shower, or somehow get the hole to feel like a home, but it never happened.

She could have ignored it, accepted their fate as dirty hole kids, if not for the growing belly nearing ready to pop. She could face living like bats, but she couldn't accept that life for her child.

Every time Zeke left, she worried herself silly that he wouldn't return, either from his own decisions, or because someone caught him stealing and had him arrested. She tried not to think about him getting killed by another Russ.

He went out that morning to get her vitamins and a soda. The first, she needed. The second, she just fucking wanted.

She paced around nervously, anxious for his return, but the day slipped away without his footsteps coming from above. Frantic, and a bit claustrophobic, she climbed the steel rungs to the barn. The last slivers of daylight bruised the sky over the field. A cool breeze swept in through the barn opening, a welcome feeling on Mary's sweat-stained pits.

She waddled to the entrance and stared out at the purple sky. Something crunched on the side of the barn and her heart hydroplaned into her guts. Was it Zeke, or an unknown enemy she'd only imagined over the years, one who probably didn't exist?

At first, Mary stared, afraid and confused, as a woman breached the front. She had her head down and her arm out, holding something on the other side of the barn, beyond Mary's view. Her brown hair streamed down her cheeks and masked her face. Whoever she was, she wore a beautiful dress and shiny black boots.

Mary didn't know what to say. Was this a new owner of Russ's house? She'd worried about that. She assumed, someday, someone new would buy the house and Mary's little hole in the ground would get exposed.

"I'm sorry," Mary said, unsure what else to say.

"Why?" the woman said, and she brushed the hair from her face.

"Kelly!" Mary waddled forward, arms outstretched.

Kelly stepped away from the corner, revealing what she held in her hand. A basket with a baby inside. "I knew you'd be here," Kelly said.

Mary hugged her, and Kelly squeezed back. "Where have you been? What have you been up to? I should have looked for you." Her mind spun like a wheel barreling down the road, a million questions racing through her. "Has anyone tried to hurt you? Is this your baby?"

Kelly put her arm up to stop Mary from speaking. "Shhh. Can we go inside and talk about this?"

Mary nodded, excited. She guided Kelly toward the door in the floor, as if the girl needed it, and slowly descended the rungs, something much harder to do at nine months pregnant. When she reached the bottom of the steps, and the dank smell of the place filled her nose. She grew embarrassed about the horror show that was her home.

Kelly managed to climb down the rungs while holding the basket and Mary envied her friend's capabilities. She'd thought every single day how hard it would be to bring her child up to the surface.

After Kelly's feet hit the floor, she scanned the room, and said, "Jesus, Mary."

Mary's excitement disappeared, breaking up like a sugar cube in a cup of hot water. Shame filled her, and she couldn't control the emotions. She cried.

Kelly, horrified, hugged Mary. "I'm sorry. I didn't mean it like that. I just…" She trailed off, because she did mean it exactly as it sounded.

"Zeke keeps saying he was going to fix the place up. He always says it, but he doesn't do it. It's not entirely his fault because he has so much other stuff to do, hunting and fishing and going into town to get us stuff."

"Shhhhhh," Kelly said and rubbed her hand on the small of Mary's back. "So, Zeke's the one who did that to you?"

She pulled away and pointed toward Mary's stomach.

Mary nodded. "Tell me about your little one. Boy or girl?"

"Girl."

"Name?"

"Don't know. I haven't named her."

"What? Why?" Mary peeked in the basket and smiled at the sleeping, wrinkly bean swaddled in blankets.

Kelly shrugged. "I can't decide. I keep coming up with names and changing my mind."

"Who is the father?"

Kelly shook her head. "Can we sit somewhere?"

"Oh, yeah," Mary smiled and led Kelly to her alcove where she and Zeke had put a few chairs they stole from Russ's house. At night, before bed, she and Zeke would sit in the silent dark together and enjoy the nothingness.

Mary clicked on a flashlight, the bulb dull. "Best we got for lighting right now. Zeke is out getting batteries."

Kelly sat in a recliner and put the basket between her legs. She stared down at her sleeping daughter. "Her father was just a guy. I wish I had some magical story to tell you about it, Mary, but there ain't one. He was a good-looking man and he said the right things until he stopped saying anything at all. Once he found out I was pregnant, he left."

Mary didn't know what to say. She had worried Zeke would leave her, too. That he'd take his chances with the outside world to avoid another day in this hellhole, but Mary also knew she projected those thoughts. It was only she who complained about the environment in which they lived. Zeke seemed perfectly content, which was part of why he never did anything to fix any of it up.

Eventually, Kelly broke the silence and said, "So, why are you guys down here?"

Mary sat back and pressed her head into the worn chair cushion, thinking about how to explain without sounding crazy. "My father told me there were others like Russ out there."

Kelly scrunched her forehead. "I thought Russ killed your father."

Mary bit her lip and rubbed her thumbs against her fingertips. "It's a long story. But we were kids and were scared, so we fled down here. We wanted to come find all of y'all, but we had no idea how, so we just hid down here, until one day became seven, and seven became hundreds. Now, we just don't know how to live any other way. To be honest, we don't know how to live this way. Somehow, we just keep going on."

"I don't mean to make you feel bad, but we need to fix this place up."

Mary laughed. "You should have seen it when we first got here. We left Ellie's and Russ's bodies down here for way too long, until they were way past stinking and rotting."

Kelly made a face like she sucked on a lemon. "Well, we got a lot of work to do."

"What do you mean, 'we'? And why are you here all of a sudden? What's this all about?"

Kelly turned to her and smiled. "I told you we'd see each other again, didn't I? I was right."

"Yes, but why? And why now? Don't get me wrong, I am so happy to see you, but this is all kind of out of the blue, and I'm about to drop a baby any day."

The baby stirred in her basket. Kelly lifted the girl onto her lap and rocked it back and forth. "Your father was right, Mary. Someone tried to kill us, and he wasn't like Russ. He had a fucking monster's face."

Mary sat forward, her pulse pounding in her ears. All the crazed fears she'd had over the years culminated into a real form, something borne from Kelly's words. "What do you mean?"

"I mean a month after my girl was born, someone broke into my apartment and tried to kill me. I fought him off as best I could, but he was faster and stronger than I was. He pinned me down and showed me his sharp teeth. His face was like a lizard's. Like all fucking scaly and weird. He was a fucking nonhuman monster, and I know that sounds insane.

"I got away because a neighbor came over after hearing me scream, and he brought his gun. He shot at the creature but the bullet didn't do a fucking thing. It didn't even pierce the skin. It did manage to help me, because the monster attacked my neighbor, and while he was doing that, I took my girl and ran. Over the next few weeks, I tracked down everyone from the alcove. Every single one, because I knew it had to do with that somehow. The only people we couldn't find were you and Zeke, but I knew where you'd be."

Kelly felt hot, her body sweaty all over. The room around her spun. She slept at night thinking her fears were nonsensical, a paranoia built from her father's crazed words. The man had been dead for some time and resurrected. It only made sense that he would speak illogically. Still, she hid because the worry lived under the surface. It crawled under her skin and begged her to stay safe, but Kelly just released it. Now the worry enveloped her, broke her. She rubbed her belly, wondering what kind of world she'd bring the child into. And Kelly, what was she thinking? Some creature hunted her, and she just helped guide it to them.

"Why did you do that?" Mary sat up. "What if he's following you?"

"Trust me, that thing knew stuff. If he wants to find us, he's going to do it. He didn't find me because of the yellow pages, I promise you that. He knew what he needed to know."

"Where is everyone else?" Mary asked, her voice dull and soft. She couldn't comprehend the changes happening. Her baby would come out any day now, and she was just convincing herself to branch out, to maybe consider joining the real world.

"They're at the river. I told them to wait while I came to talk to you first."

"All of them?" Mary shot up.

Kelly nodded. "They're all super smart. Together, we can really turn this place into a nice home." She leaned forward and put her face toward Mary's belly. "For you and for that one."

The knots in Mary's stomach softened, still there, but not as tight. Facing monsters and men terrified her but having the company of those who have been through it made it all feel manageable.

After a little more conversation, Kelly and Mary climbed the rungs. Mary with her big belly and Kelly with her basket. Two generations climbing together. When Mary came through the door and the evening breeze hit her face, Zeke stared at her from the doorway of the barn. He had a smile on his face and two giant plastic bags packed with stuff.

When Mary landed, Zeke noticed the dinging of feet on rungs behind her and his face changed to one of confusion and despair.

"Kelly's here," Mary said.

And on cue, Kelly exited the door in the floor. She placed the basket on the ground, put her arms out, and said, "Ta da!"

Zeke laughed. "Oh my god. Is this for real?" He ran to her and hugged her. "It's so good to see you. And you have a baby?"

While they hugged, Mary peeked in the bags. There was a stack of books.

Zeke turned to her. "I walked by a library and they had this big shelf of books they were just giving away. I found a book on electricity, so I'm going to try to learn more about it. There was also this cool art book. I don't know why I grabbed it, but it spoke to me, so I did."

He turned back to Kelly, "So, like, you guys have to explain all this me. How did you get here?"

Mary cleared her throat and pointed toward the field where four people walked toward them from the river. "It's not just Kelly. They're all here."

Wars Fought in Your Name

Violin operated on a whole new plane. The Footloose jostled something free inside her. Her senses heightened, providing her with a clarity she hadn't possessed before. Everything became a tool, a resource, leverage. She planned twelve steps ahead and utilized her surroundings to her advantage.

The faint aura around the glow disc hovered on the edges of the horizon and the fire disc let its presence be known with a furious red streak above the woods. A slight breeze tickled the flesh on Violin's arms.

"You ended the war well, Violin," Fake Winter said. "But now you must finish the story."

She knew the answer to her question before she asked it, but she had to play dumb. "Isn't the finale of the war the end of the story?"

Fake Winter pulled his lips to one side of his face. "You know that's ridiculous. We must have a wrap up."

As she talked, she guided Fake Winter toward the game area. She kept a special eye on the water box she noticed while riding the Ferris Wheel. The gentle wind caused the water on one side to spittle out.

"What's that?" Violin asked.

"Ah, it was a splash pad. Basically, a bunch of hoses in the ground shot water out like a sprinkler onto children who played inside it."

"But it has a ceiling. How would the water land on the children?"

"The ceiling was my own invention. I propped a large metal square on a pole, so the water lands on it and slides off, creating the jail cell effect you see there."

"A jail cell with water for walls? What made you want to create that?"

As they moved closer to the water box, the spittle from the wind hit them, and Violin welcomed the coldness of it.

"It was to lock my brother inside. Unfortunately, the poor soul died talking to you. Anyway, he had an aversion to water."

"Which brother?" she asked as she stuck her tongue out and let the sprinkles of water land in her mouth.

"The first one you met. It's too bad I never got to use this ole cage. It would have been fun."

"You didn't kill him? Who did? He blamed my sister."

Fake Winter filled his body with air and stood erect. "Ha, no. Not your sister. He was killed in the name of your sister, by someone who cares very deeply for the girl."

Violin felt a sting in her chest, thinking of some murderer obsessing over her sister. She prayed Candlestick lived and hoped to Kevin Bacon she never met whomever the fanatic was. She wanted to ask Fake Winter about this mysterious person, but knew she'd get no answer.

"And you? Do you have an aversion to water?" As she spoke, she took in all his words while glancing at the pieces around her, seeing what she could use to harm him. Hard balls, sharp sticks, electrical cords.

Fake Winter chuckled. "Nice try." He stuck his hand in the water, breaking the streaming wall. Water splashed in all directions around his arm. "I like water."

"I know you won't tell me who killed your brother, but will you tell me why this person thought killing in the name of my sister was important? What does she have to do with all of this?"

Fake Winter pulled his arm out of the water and sighed. "I know you think I enjoy being coy with you. I don't. I wish I could tell you everything, but I simply am not allowed. What I can tell you is that you and your sister have wandered this Earth oblivious to your value in it. There are people who worship you, who would do anything for you. Wars are fought in your names, and all the while, you're sitting around eating snacks on motel beds."

Violin moved behind the counter of a game. She leaned against it, looking out at Fake Winter. "That doesn't make sense. My sister can talk to animals and I have no powers at all. How can we have any special value to a group of people we've never met?"

As Fake Winter talked, Violin grabbed a metal stick with a pointy edge and pressed it into a wire running to the lights around the structure.

"You would believe that, because you're dumb. I don't mean that to sound harsh, but it's true. Your people raised you to be stupid. They went out of their way to hide from you the very things you needed to know most. Now, no more dawdling. Finish the story."

The sharp edge of the stick broke through the outer layer of the wire, cracking into the colorful wires inside.

After Dark Skies vanished, the group stood around, unsure what to do. Tears filled their eyes at the loss of their friends and kin. With the war over, they had nothing but mourning and the truth to focus on, and those feelings were unwelcomed guests after the adrenaline rush of battle.

Kevin Bacon turned to his family and friends, or those that were left. Pride filled his soul.

Lady Gaga spit into the dirt. "For Abraham Lincoln. For Avril Lavigne."

Someone made a loud spitting noise behind them and said, "For me."

They all turned, startled. With her head in her hands, Avril Lavigne smiled at them.

"What the fuck?" Rapture said.

Lady Gaga laughed and ran to her friend, squeezing her torso in a hug. "You're alive?"

Avril held her head above her body as if showing off a prize. "I may have lost my head, but that can't stop me."

Dance rubbed her tendrils on her chin. "Does that mean Lincoln lives as well?"

Avril shook her head in her hands. "No. I just checked on him. He's *dead* dead."

They all turned their eyes to the ground.

"That poor soul," Kevin Bacon said. "May he rest with his family."

Dance pushed past the group and mounted Abe Lincoln's torso. She stood on top of him and wrapped her tendrils around him until his body was covered in leafy vines. "You died a hero," she said. Then, she fell to her knees and cried on his chest. Her arms dug into the soil under the ice giant, and his body slowly lowered into the hole. She wept the entire time.

The rest of the group lined up around his body, crying and bowing their heads in silence.

"He was a fucking awesome dude," Miley said.

"Here, here," Laura Jane Grace added.

"Would you like to say a proper goodbye to him?" Kevin Bacon put his hands on Miley and Elvis's shoulders.

"Uh huh," said Elvis. "I'd like that very much, thank you."

"Then, you'll all need to come with me."

"Where?" Dance asked.

"The underworld, of course."

She stepped off Lincoln's corpse. "Don't we have to die to do that?"

Kevin Bacon pointed at her. "Exactly."

Miley stepped back. "But how will we return?"

Kevin Bacon tapped his chest. "I'll bring you all back."

Laura Jane Grace rubbed a bruise on her arm. "If you can bring people back, why don't you just bring Abraham Lincoln back?"

Elvis stepped forward. "Yeah, just bring our boy home."

Kevin Bacon put his hands up and shook his head. "It doesn't work that way."

Dance frowned. "Worked that way for me." She crossed her arms around herself.

Kevin Bacon sighed. "I know it did, but you weren't killed by gods. Death at the hands of the gods is more permanent."

Elvis kicked his foot in the dirt. "So, how do we do this?"

Kevin Bacon stood in front of his group. "We all need to line up, and one person is going to have to stay here and kill us all."

Rapture's eyes lit up. "Oh, I'll take that job."

"No," Avril said. She stepped forward with her head tucked between her arm and hip. "I'll do it. To be honest, I'm feeling a little woozy."

Rapture scowled. "Like your head's not on straight?" He rolled his eyes at his own joke.

"Yeah, sure. It's complicated. The idea of being murdered to take a road trip to the underworld sounds wholly unappealing." Avril placed her head down on the dirt.

Kevin Bacon put his arms up. "Anyone else coming with me?"

Everyone looked to each other, hoping for some reason to enter the conversation, but eventually, they all agreed and lined up.

Rapture sighed. "I can't fucking believe I'm doing this. Wait. Isn't she a god now? Doesn't that mean when she kills us it'll be permanent?"

Kevin Bacon swatted at him. "She isn't a god yet, friend. We still need to take her through the colorful blobs of everything."

Rapture put his head down. "Yeah. Sure. Just say a bunch of random words. That's helpful."

Dance touched his head and he swatted it away. "Kevin, how did you know Rapture would join our side? Was it in the colorful blobs?"

Avril picked up her skateboard. Her headless body stood in front of Miley, who had the unfortunate position of first in line. Avril lifted the board like she was about to swat a fly.

Kevin Bacon lined up with the rest of them and took a big gulp of air. "Nope. I had no idea what Rapture would do. I just made it up. Kinda thought the power of suggestion would work its magic."

Avril swung the board and took Miley's head off, followed by Laura Jane Grace, Lady Gaga, Elvis, and Dance.

As the board swung through Kevin Bacon's neck, Rapture said, "You've got to be fucking kidding me. It wasn't my fate to join you scumbags?" Just as he finished his sentence, the board sliced through his neck.

Life Dripped from a Thousand Wounds

After Candlestick finished her story to her dead friend, she turned toward the forest where her lampposts and husks chased down the shooters who killed her new family. Two men tried to run, but the husks blocked them from following any paths and the lampposts trudged behind and spread molten light on the dry oak leaves.

As she watched the men corner themselves, something moved in her peripheral. It was gone behind a shield of thick oaks before she could catch sight of it, but she kept her attention on the area, knowing it would show itself again. She knew it wasn't a trick her eyes played because Lion's fur stuck up and he snarled his upper lip.

A few minutes later, half a face poked out from behind a trunk. It wasn't a human face, but not a monster either. Someone wearing a mask. The mask hung loosely off the person's head, ghost white in the facial features, but bright red around the mouth, elongated and smiling. Metal spikes rode through the top as if it were the person's hair, but they weren't attached well and sunk to the side, too heavy for the flimsy material on the mask.

Masked Man realized she was staring right at him—and ducked back behind the oak. It was too late, though, and he knew it, so he took off running.

"Hey," she said and charged after him.

Lion ran faster and gained ground.

She called for more husks as her feet pitter-pattered in the cold, wet leaves. They stuck to her feet in bunches and she had to slow her charge so as not to slip.

Lion, too, slipped, as he kept veering in different directions to keep up with the masked man.

"Get back here."

Masked Man wore a sack over his body, a giant brown bag. His feet were bare, cut, and bloody.

The husks didn't show, but it wasn't from disobedience. Her frazzled mind struggled to conjure them when she already had a bunch doing her dirty work elsewhere in the forest. Grief bred the monsters, but it also took away her control.

Her only chance to kill this man was to catch him herself. She noted the boom weapon in his hand and wondered why he didn't fire at her. Maybe after seeing the husks die to protect her, he knew it would be a lost cause. Good thing he thought so because at this moment, he could probably fire a bullet into her brain with no repercussions at all.

Masked Man dipped around trees, fast, assured. He knew these woods and knew them well. She couldn't place why, but she felt confident he was the man in the street, the one who burned down the houses. If so, Candlestick was responsible for her friend's deaths. Randy wanted to do something about the man, but Candlestick talked him out of it.

The way he moved left, then right, and danced around trees slowed Candlestick down in her chase—and made her a little dizzy. The gap between her and Masked Man grew deeper with each slalom.

Eventually, she stalled out, unable to keep up. She punched a tree, furious with her inability to keep running. She yearned to punish. Lion kept running for a moment longer than Candlestick, but turned back to her, unwilling to separate for long.

"Please, find him," she whispered to herself, to her monsters, to Lion. "Find him."

As she trekked back toward her dead friends, the fury in her stomach pressed her guts down like an anvil. If she hadn't already planned to torture her friend's killers, their pal escaping just turned the rage up on high. Flames poured from her mind, eager to char anything in their path.

She arrived back at the house. Her house, or at least it had been for ten minutes. A place of death where her sister shot a boy and Candlestick crumbled the foundations on her friend. Where the only non-family member she ever loved took a bullet to the skull.

The lampposts were gone, their job done. This was proven by the holes in the backs of the mens' shirts where huge claws had snatched them up and brought them to the site of their victims.

The husks remained, though, to block the men in from leaving. As Candlestick stepped toward the husk circle, a few of them stepped away, unfurling the front of the circle to give her clean access to the men. But they weren't men. They were boys. Older than her, sure, by a bunch, but they were not men.

Lion snarled, but she eased him. These boys were hers to hurt.

Unlike the man in the woods, they weren't wearing masks and their clothes were normal. They hovered in fetal positions, shaking and scared.

Candlestick pointed to Cassie's body. "Which one of you killed her?"

A boy with orange hair shot a quick glance at another boy.

This second kid had a thin layer of beard stubble and a

shaved head, too well-kempt for someone living in this world. It reminded her of her uncle who spent time in the mirror with a thin razor, cutting his own hair in uneven waves. Clumps of hair always remained, usually in the back of his head—where he couldn't see. She smiled at the thought and then shook it away, unwilling to allow happy memories to spoil her mood for revenge.

She slapped Beard Boy on the top of his short-haired head. "That true? You killed her?"

The boy said nothing, but Orange-Haired Boy chimed in on his behalf. "It's true. I killed the boy. He killed the girl."

Candlestick bent in front of the orange-haired kid. "What's your name?"

"B-Bill," he eked out.

She wondered how confident they'd be without her husks around and debated having her monsters leave so she could kill them in all their proud glory, but she didn't want to risk losing them.

"Bill. Okay, Bill, if you shot the boy and he shot the girl, who did the guy in the mask shoot?"

He looked up and turned his stone-cold eyes to her. "He was supposed to kill you."

"Why?" she asked.

Bill shrugged. "It's like his fucking mission. We met him a few weeks ago. He's taken care of us and fed us and helped us. But he's always full of rage and most of that rage is toward you, and your sister, and your father."

She winced. "My father is dead. How does he know us?"

Bill spit a pink wad of saliva onto the dirt. The husks or the lampposts must have roughed him up a little. "I have no idea. He don't talk much."

"Who is he?"

Bill's eyes widened. "I swear to you, he didn't tell us. He did, like, everything he could to avoid answering questions about himself."

She patted him on the head, hoping the condescending nature of it bled through, then moved on to Beard Boy. "And what's your name?" she asked.

He glared at her and smirked. "Fuck you."

"Okay, Fuck You. Is he telling the truth?"

Fuck You didn't answer.

"I'll take Bill on his word, then."

She turned to her husks. "Did you retrieve their weapons?"

One of the husks moved forward and handed her two guns. She took them, keeping one in her hand, and tucking the other into her pants.

Another husk stepped forward and handed her a knife. At this, she smiled. "Which one of you is Damond?" she asked the husks.

One of them pointed to the pile of dead husks that conjured themselves into existence to protect her.

"Oh," she said. "Well, that upsets me." She was amazed at her own ability to keep her voice measured. She had no reason to care for Damond more than any other husk, but knowing his name made it feel more personal.

"Bill, stand up."

The boy looked around, as if Kevin Bacon himself would come save him. Once he stood, Candlestick moved in front of him and put her free hand on his shoulder. "You did well to tell me the truth, and your truth happened to be helpful for you because I don't particularly care about Randy."

She stepped back and sighed. "So, you will die fast." She lifted the gun and fired into his skull. Pieces of him went everywhere, splashing into her face, into Fuck You's face. All over. She felt no satisfaction from it.

After wiping her face, she bent in front of Fuck You. "Now

you, well you weren't very helpful, and you happened to kill the most important person in my world."

His eyes turned to boulders. "He was lying. I didn't kill her."

Candlestick put her finger out. "Shush. You had your chance to deny it and instead you decided to name yourself Fuck You. To be honest, I don't care if you actually killed her or not. Someone did and I need to feel better about that. You're the last one standing."

He stood up to run, but before he got halfway up, a group of husks kicked him down.

Candlestick tossed the gun and dropped to her knees. "Bill got the gun, but Fuck You gets the knife," she said with a smile and jammed it into his abdomen.

She kept her stabs tempered, breaking into his body without protruding too far. She wanted the pain to grow, but death to come slowly. She enjoyed his screams and how he flopped like a fish. When he attempted to run, as he did every few minutes, the husks dropped him back to the earth with brute force.

She cut off chunks of his skin, making checkered patterns up his arms and legs. She considered other things, ripping off his fingernails, plucking out his eyes, but that felt gratuitous, even for her.

"Tell me what you know about the man in the mask and I'll let you live," she lied.

Between screams, Fuck You said, "He honestly didn't tell us anything. I swear. Please, please. I'm not lying."

She propped his leg up and jammed the knife in at the fold of his leg behind his knee.

Fuck You coughed from screaming so loud. "I swear. I wasn't lying."

Candlestick shrugged. "I believed you, but it was useless information so you still die."

He rolled over, a weak attempt to get away. "Please."

"Cassie didn't get the chance to beg for her life."

"I'm sorry."

"Tell me anything about the man in the mask. What did you call him?"

Fuck You cried. "We called him Fireman. That's what he told us to call him, Fireman."

Fireman. Maybe he *was* the one setting fires the night before.

She pressed the blood-soaked blade to his upper arm and dug it in deep, snapping into muscle and tendons.

Fuck You's back arched and his hollering echoed into the cool evening air.

Candlestick leaned in and whispered, "Once upon a time, there was a little girl who almost believed in you." She gripped the top of the blade with both hands and leaned her body weight into it until the blade struck bone. "And you proved her faith wrong." She ripped the knife out and slammed it down into his belly. "Again." The knife came out and back in. "And again."

Fuck You was covered in his own blood. He wouldn't live much longer. His teeth chattered and his lips turned blue. Life dripped from a thousand wounds.

She hated Fuck You. Not just for what he did, but for all those like him. For the man who shot her father. For the boys who stole their first homes. For each and every one who let her down. She knew from Brian, Corey, and Cassie that not all humans were bad, but it seemed the good ones were destined to suffer at the hands of boys like Fuck You.

She continued to carve into Fuck You until his eyes turned to marbles and he offered no more resistance. She placed her hand over his mouth and felt no air coming from him. The husks stared at her while she stood and wiped her bloody hands on her crimson-stained shirt.

"What does Candlestick do now?" one of them asked.

Candlestick gave one last glance at Cassie's body. "I go home and find Violin. Then, I spend the rest of my life hunting down Fireman. I have a new purpose now. His death."

A Kitchen Full of Ingredients

For all the utensils at Violin's disposal, and her newfound clarity, her plan was rather simple. Too simple. Electricity meets water. Violin knew less about electricity than her father, and as her plan got closer to fruition, she worried her knowledge on the topic was woefully inept. Had she destroyed the flow of electricity when she cut into the wire? The lights still danced around the structure she stood in, so she assumed the power still traveled through the veins, but would it continue its journey when she dropped the exposed wire into the water box? Again, she didn't know. But she had to try.

Fake Winter slow clapped as she finished her round of story. "Great story so far. You're really tapping into the truth. Love it. Now, keep going. I can't wait to hear your thoughts on the underworld."

Violin nodded as she stuck her foot under the wire and kicked her foot around until the wire was wrapped tug around her ankle.

* * *

Kevin Bacon swam through the thick, oily blackness with his troop swimming close behind. When he turned to ensure they followed, he caught their eyes darting wildly, fearful of the shrill screams surrounding them, the outlines of humans squirming and writhing, the incredible darkness so deep and dreaded it drowned out the very solidity of the person swimming in it. Even Dance, who lived through it once before, showed panic in her glow disc sized eyes, and her clenched jaw. He hated to admit it, but he enjoyed seeing their scared little faces, especially Rapture's, but only because he knew they were safe.

They arrived at a large, rocky outcropping, shimmering white, not only seeable in the swallowing darkness, but so bright it nearly blinded them.

"What is this?" Miley ask as she cupped her hands over her eyes.

Lady Gaga squinted. "Did you bring us to a wall of lights?"

Kevin laughed. "No. This is Abe. Say hello, Abraham."

Two stones on the wall shifted upward and reddish eyes appeared. "Family! Is it so?"

Dance covered her mouth. "Oh, Abraham." She reached forward and hugged the stones.

Abraham's eyes darted left and right. "Mr. Bacon, please tell me, is this my fate for all eternity?"

Pools of water sat on the bottoms of his giant eyes.

Kevin Bacon tapped his hand on a stone. "Not for all eternity, my friend. For a long time, I fear, but not all eternity."

Abraham moaned. "I thought I would be reunited with my wife and kids."

"Someday, friend." Kevin placed his forehead on the wall. "I promise you I will reshape the afterlife and make it a place of comfort. I will work endlessly to find a way to reunite you and your family."

Abraham wept. "I stopped fighting in the end, eager to meet

my wife. Are my children suffering the same fate I am? Drowning in nothingness?"

Kevin Bacon said nothing, just gasped.

"Drowning in nothingness," Rapture said, following it up with a diluted laugh. "My mother used to say that."

They all turned to him.

He looked up and caught their stares. "She always said humans had no souls because they spend their lives trying to find happiness in oceans of nothing. If they could, they'd gladly drown in nothingness." He turned his head left and right. "This looks like an ocean of nothing, and I don't see anyone soaking in the smiles."

Kevin Bacon put his hand on Rapture's shoulder. "In the colorful blobs, I saw a future with a thing called the internet, and I'll tell you, she wasn't so far off."

Dance's vines stretched around the wall. "Abraham. I'm so sorry."

Lady Gaga swam forward. "No, I am sorry. I failed to save you."

Abraham shouted. "I don't want to be here. Please, I don't want this."

Kevin Bacon flinched and swam backwards. The Ice Giant's wails dropped his heart like a stone. He almost wished he hadn't told his family they could visit their dead brother, and instead, told them the truth about why he brought them down there.

He wasn't heartless. He loved his brother and the mourning he felt over Abe's death built icy bricks in his chest and stomach, but he saw little purpose in hugging a dead soul when he could do nothing to rectify the ice giant's horrendous situation. In fact, Kevin only saw it as more torment for all involved. It was why he never sought Saria on his trips to the underworld. What good would it do her? She'd only suffer more knowing he could leave while she was doomed to agonize in eternal darkness.

"I have a favor to ask of my kin," Abraham said.

"Anything," Dance said, despite being one of the few who didn't fit the description.

"Put my body back together. Place it in a chair. Let it sit there until I find a way to return."

Everyone shot eyes at each other. Rapture's rudeness spoke what everyone else was thinking. "Do you think it's a good idea to rot away in a chair for all to smell?"

Abraham sniffled. "Ice Giants don't rot. We stay as we are until someone chips us down into shavings and places us in a beverage."

Rapture snarled. "Getting drunk on ice giant chips and bristlebuck brew sounds much more fun, if I'm being honest."

Dance slapped his arm. "Don't be rude. We will fulfill your desire, Abraham."

"What? It's gonna be fucking heavy. Do we even have the strength to drag a big ass ice giant and prop him up on some chair?" Rapture asked.

Kevin Bacon broke himself free from the sadness this exchange was filling him with. "We will find a way. We always do."

Rapture scoffed. "Ha. First of all, no you don't. You almost never find a way. You guys fail a hell of a lot more than you succeed. Secondly, it's an unreasonable request. I think it's fair to say that."

Kevin ignored the ranting raccoon and placed his hand on Abe's white-wall body. "Friend, we have to leave, but I will come visit you again. I promise."

Abraham yawped a mournful goodbye as Kevin Bacon led his team further down.

"Aren't we supposed to be going up?" Rapture asked.

Dance stepped in. "I had the same question the first time I was here, after you and your forest friends killed me."

Rapture scratched at his cheek. "Oh yeah, shit. Sorry about that. Well, I'm not sorry. I'm totally going to do it again, but you know what I mean."

Dance swam forward, ignoring Rapture's empty threats. "But why are we going down there again, Kevin? Haven't you already tinkered with life and death enough?"

"Yes, I have," Kevin Bacon said, and swam deeper.

The darkness rippled and the pressure grew as they descended, their heads feeling like they were going to explode. His crew looked seasick, disoriented, tired.

Finally, he stopped and turned to them. "When we warred with the three gods, and I came down here to rescue Dance. I also did something else. A secret. Something only Dance knows about."

Lady Gaga raised her hand. "You created a baby."

Elvis toyed with his collar. "Uh huh, that's right. Remember, we were filled in on all your details when the gods created us."

Kevin rolled his hand in front of him. "Exactly. I created a child."

Laura Jane Grace said, "You did what the fuck now?" She reached into her pocket and pulled out a pack of smokes. "Can I smoke down here?" She didn't wait for an answer before lighting up.

"I created a child, a secret weapon against the gods, but I had no idea how powerful this child would be. The nine gods tried to destroy the Earth and only one thing stopped them from doing so: the baby I created. She blocked them out, and when I was battling Dark Skies, she blew him to bits with nothing more than a look. It didn't kill him, though, and I'm not sure why."

Laura Jane Grace let a puff out from her nose. "Why are you telling us this now? You brought us down here, so I know there's something you want."

"I was worried about our new storyteller, but as I'm sure you noticed, the story changed hands again and again during our war with the new gods. It changed so many times, I don't know who is running the show anymore. On top of that, Dark Skies is still out there. We need protection, and when it comes to the storytellers, we need to pick a side."

Miley crossed her arms. "So, what are you saying?"

"I'm saying you all need to create a child. We need an army."

They all looked around at each other, shocked. Before they could argue, he taught them the steps required. They molded flesh from darkness, souls from ideas, and organs from the empty abyss.

Dance finished creating her child first. "I'll name him Abraham after our friend."

Rapture held his out as far away from his body as possible, his face squished in disgust. "Why does mine look so friggin' human?"

After they all finished, Kevin Bacon smiled at the new army of babies. "Now, all of us will emerge from the underworld in different locations. Leave your baby where you land and meet me in the heavens."

"Wait, what?" Miley asked.

"You want us to leave a fucking baby in the middle of nowhere?" Laura Jane Grace yelled.

"That seems fucked up, even for me." Rapture pulled the baby closer to himself.

"These aren't normal, helpless babies. They have the power of gods, born from nothingness. They, even now, could destroy villages. For them, fate will take its course."

"No way, dude. No fucking way. I can't leave a baby unpro-tected, god or not." Lady Gaga tucked the baby into her chest and twisted her body away, shielding it from Kevin Bacon's words.

Kevin Bacon smiled. "I'll see you all in heaven." He swam away.

"You know I'm really not going to listen to you. I'm keeping the baby with me," Lady Gaga yelled at him as he climbed through the abyss.

"You'll know the right thing to do when you get there. I know it," he said, waving goodbye as he fluttered off.

* * *

Fake Winter clapped. "Absolutely wonderful. Are you enjoying this tale as much as I am?"

Violin stepped away from the counter, coming closer to him. The wire stayed with her, tightly wrapped around her foot. They walked side by side, toward the water box.

"I feel like the stories are almost done," she said.

Fake Winter put his arm around her shoulders. "Indeed. There are just a few details to wrap up."

"Yes, but they are minor things. I don't see how they will provide me with answers."

Fake Winter rolled his eyes and groaned. "You, you, you. It's always about you."

He stepped in front of her, the water spraying behind him.

She pushed.

He didn't expect it and fumbled to keep upright. When he hit the metal protrusions in the ground that sprayed the water up, he tripped, fell backwards into the water box, and hit his head on the pole that kept the ceiling on it.

Before he could right himself, she spun the wire from around her foot and tossed the exposed part into the wall of water. It hit at the exact time Fake Winter touched it, trying to get out. It jolted him and he flopped back like a fish on land.

Violin's heart stopped and a wave of dizziness came over her.

She wanted to run, but what she saw froze her in place, broke her ability to think, to breathe.

"No," she said, seeing Fake Winter's real face for the first time. She had gotten a glimpse once and knew it was something familiar, but seeing it full on, she knew exactly who he was. She stepped backward and fell to her butt. "No," she said again.

It couldn't be. It made no sense even though it made all the sense in the world. She dug her palms into the dirt and rose to her feet.

"No," she said one last time and took off running.

Fake Winter would be out of his electric cage in minutes. The water would short circuit the electricity, if it hadn't already, and he'd be free again. And now she knew, with certainty, he'd find her and kill her. She had no hope of escape.

As she ran, not even knowing where to go, she remembered the objects she found in the first Fake Winter's pockets. A tiny key and a photo of a woman. She remembered her promise to her dad to find out what happened to humanity. Her mother had made him tell Violin to find out the answers. She was going to die without answering any of it. Empty questions like a kitchen full of ingredients and no bowl to mix them. Around her body, promises and unfulfilled hopes swarmed like gnats.

Behind her, Fake Winter shouted vitriol, his voice coming closer. He was free and she'd hardly left the amusement park grounds.

"Now you know, Violin," he said. "Now you know the truth. You wanted answers, and I provided." He laughed.

His voice came from everywhere, as if he spoke through the machine at the park, but she was no longer in the park, so this was more a trick of magic. She had no idea where to run, but aimed for home, the only place she knew. She hoped Brian and Corey would be there so she could say goodbye before she died at Fake Winter's hands.

"Where are you going girl? There's still more story to tell," he said, his voice cackling between words. "Don't you want to know how it finishes, or have you already pieced it together?"

She fell into a wooded area, unsure exactly where she was. She hoped she remembered the right way toward home. The woods slowed her down, though, with roots that reached from the dirt like snakes, and shrubs, thick and painful.

"Violin. Why do you bother running? You know I'm coming."

She broke from the forest into the tall grass, and her body filled with hope at the prospect of making it home. She had no idea how she could win this war, but she knew if a way to survive existed, it lived at home.

She trudged through the grass. Her lungs were on fire, her feet screamed. She tried to suck in air, but it just led to coughing. Still, she ran.

"Violin. Are you trying to go home, sneaky girl?"

She cleared the tall grass. In front of her, Jimmy Milani's house loomed, and just beyond it, the barn that would bring her back to her people. At the very least, she'd die near her mother.

As she turned into the barn, Fake Winter stood at the threshold of her home. "Found ya. Sorry, can't let you down there. Now what say you finish the tale?"

"Fuck you," she said.

"Not very nice. Okay, I'll finish it, but I think I need to teach you a little lesson first. Sometimes a little pain will go a long way in making things stick in your mind."

He raised his fist and stepped closer.

So It Goes

Brian and Corey ran through the woods trying to find their way back toward the main road, away from the Job Lot area.

Brian assumed the car trick worked because he hadn't heard anyone chasing them. He knew they didn't have time to stop, but he had to catch his breath and Corey looked like he might die without a quick stop.

Corey eyed him, and Brian nodded. It was the communication they needed. They understood each other on fundamental levels.

They stopped, taking a much-needed moment to catch their breath, but the sound of footsteps stole the moment from them.

"Fuck, we gotta run," Brian whispered, barely able to get the words out.

Corey screwed up his face, wiped sweat from his brow, and took off.

"Freeze," someone shouted. Then more voiced in. "Stop."

Brian spotted a man with a gun trained on them and slowed his running. More armed men came from both sides of them.

They were surrounded by gun barrels. Slowly, he lifted his hands to the sky.

Corey did the same.

* * *

Candlestick asked her husks and lampposts to dig a hole. She almost yelled at them to do it, but swallowed her anger. She didn't want to take it out on them. They didn't fail to catch The Fireman, she did. As Damond pointed out, the husks were an extension of her. They couldn't fail her. Only she could do that.

After they dug the hole, she rolled Cassie's body into it. She pictured it more romantically, not quite expecting the weight of a dead body. She wished she had the strength to lift her friend and gently place her body in the ground, but life isn't neat and pretty. So, she rolled her. Even that proved difficult as the girl's arms got in the way, bent behind her back, and twisted unnaturally. When Cassie's body reached the hole, it fell in, sending clouds of dirt into the air, which eventually dropped back down onto her face.

"You would have been better not knowing me," Candlestick said. She kissed her hand and blew it into the hole before standing up and walking away with Lion steadfast at her side. "Bury her," she told her monsters. She listened to the sounds of graveled dirt clunking over Cassie's dead body.

A husk walked by her side, opposite the dog.

"What?" she asked. "Why aren't you helping bury my friend?"

"Candlestick want me here," he said.

"What's your name?"

"Husk is Sim."

"Sim? I like that. Why do you think I want you here?"

Sim shrugged. "You tell Sim a story."

She smiled. "I see. I suppose I do want to finish my story for someone."

The husk nodded and put his hand on her shoulder. "Sim listen good."

* * *

Mary chased Boy around the hallway. He ran around in his diaper, searching for doors. He loved doors, pulling, pushing, prying them open whenever he could. It was hard to believe Boy was four years old now. How time flew. Not that there weren't points where it felt like life dragged by. The construction, tearing down walls, building new ones, adding additions until their alcoves were non-existent, and the hole that once served as jail-cells turned into an entire town. Bedrooms, dining rooms, hall-ways, secret passages designed to help them flee, if necessary. For a long while, Zeke and some of the others had to sneak out to steal whatever they needed, but that happened with less frequency as they all discovered new ways to create and design their own world. Self-sufficiency.

Mary grabbed Boy by the shoulders and scooped him up. "Boy, you have to stop wearing me out."

Kelly walked out of her room, Girl right behind her, clutching her pant leg.

They greeted each other and brought the children into the grow room where Miller and Bert fussed over their dying plants. Things weren't perfect yet. They'd learned some basics of electricity, but mostly relied on battery-powered things to keep them going. Zeke built a primitive stove which was basically a firepit with grills, but they only used it at night since the smoke vented out into the fields above. It was too easy to draw attention.

Kelly fished and Miller hunted, and the food cooked after the sun set.

Mary grew closer to Julia, the short, freckly girl who never spoke when they were Russ's victims. As an adult, Julia talked quite a bit, and she grew to be strikingly beautiful. Julia was a master at design, turning underground caves into a place that felt as comfortable as any modern home.

Their attempts at growing crops continued to fail and Mary worried for the children growing up without vitamin D. The weather was still too extreme in winters and summers, and while the adults managed it, the kids struggled. Despite all of their advances, they needed a miracle if they hoped to keep surviving. The longer they stayed in their underground home, the more fearful of the outside world they became.

* * *

Fake Winter slammed into Violin. She dropped hard on the barn floor, sending a storm of dust into the crisp air. But Fake Winter proved too fast and too strong for his own good, because after smashing into her, he continued to stumble forward before falling into the dirt outside the barn.

Violin hurried to her feet, dove through the door, and slammed it shut. Fake Winter would find a way in, but it gave her a few minutes. She found a bolt lock and slammed it into place.

Fake Winter pounded on the outside of the door. "Let me in and stop making this hard on yourself. I don't need to finish the story. You know how it ends now. What happened next, Violin?"

She leaned against the door, as if her body somehow acted as extra protection, and she wept. "Kevin Bacon went back to heaven."

She could feel Fake Winter smugly smiling behind the sheet of metal between them.

"That's right."

* * *

Kevin Bacon gave his friends their mission because it was important, but also to give himself a few minutes to complete a deal he made. He would have to tell his friends eventually, but he felt it best to go through with his end of the bargain before informing his friends.

When he reached the heavens, he took in the fruity smell, the gorgeous eternity melding into the colorful blobs, and the cracks bolting through the stone pillars where his discs once shot through them.

"Unlike Dark Skies, it appears you are a man of your word, Mr. Bacon," someone said behind him.

Kevin turned to see Dolphi slithering across a throne.

"And if you had helped Dark Skies win, what was he supposed to reward you with?"

"The underworld and a human form."

Kevin Bacon nodded. "And from me, you get godhood."

Dolphi snaked his way around Kevin's body, traveling up in concentric loops. "Indeed."

"One of many, remember. You don't rule all."

The snake put his mouth next to Kevin Bacon's ear. "Wouldn't dream of it."

Kevin unwrapped the snake and placed him on the ground. He bent and put his hands on top of Dolphi's scaly skin. As he granted the snake godhood, something poofed in front them. It took Kevin Bacon a moment to realize what was happening.

Dark Skies. At the same time Kevin Bacon was granting the snake godhood, Dark Skies also latched onto Dolphi, fulfilling his end of the bargain. They both had the power of the throne, and now Dolphi had almost all of it.

The snake wailed as his scaly skin broke apart and human

flesh replaced it. As his body rose, growing legs, he transformed, changing shapes, sizes, colors.

Dolphi. A god. Ruler of the underworld. A human.

Kevin Bacon pulled on the grotesque mixture of reptilian and human form, but so did Dark Skies, and as they fought for control over the snake man, he split, not in two, but in three.

* * *

Men in army fatigues surrounded Brian and Corey, moving closer by the second.

"Nobody move," one of the men yelled.

"We just want to get home," Brian said. "We aren't out to hurt anyone."

Corey's hands trembled above his head. "I'm Corey. This is Brian. We are looking for a little girl. She's in trouble and we are her only hope."

A short man with a jet-black beard crept in front of them, his gun aimed at forehead level. "Why don't you both lie on the ground?"

Brian and Corey looked to each other, but they had no out. They did as they were told. While on the ground, the man with the black beard kicked their legs, not cruelly, but to push them together.

"Don't act like you were here for peace. You shot my people. We didn't shoot first."

Brian turned his head to the side, away from the ground. "Come on. They were talking threateningly and you had men on the hills backing them up. Of course, they were going to hurt us."

An older man broke through the ranks and stood above Brian. He bent down and removed the guns tucked behind both Brian and Corey's backs.

Brian's heart thudded against the twigs under his chest. He was fucked. They were fucked.

The old man cleared his throat. "If I had to kill one of you, and I gave you the choice, which one would I kill?"

Brian said, "Me. I'd choose me."

The old man stood up and spit. "You always hear that answer in the movies and love stories, but I always wondered if someone would say it if the situation were real and happening right in front of them. Admirable. Everyone would make the claim they'd do the same thing, but when self-preservation kicks in, mmmm hhhmmmm. That's a whole different beast, ain't it."

Brian didn't know what to say, but he prayed the question was rhetorical.

"Here's the thing," the old man continued, "I understand self-preservation and I understand why you shot my men in that parking lot. I do. And that's why I forgive you for it."

Brian let out a big breath. "Thank you." His hands shook violently.

"But, well, I got my own self-preservation to worry about, and two men getting away with what you just did, that'd put a big ole target on our people. 'Look at these chumps letting two men kill members of your army and you didn't do shit about it,' they'd say, and they wouldn't be wrong."

Panic set back in, he wanted to scream, to run, to fight, but he had no chance to do any of that.

The old man shifted toward Corey and pointed. "This one. Take him out by the pond and kill him."

Brian jolted up but was instantly met with the butt of a gun from one of the soldiers. Meanwhile, a small group picked Corey up and dragged him off. Corey kicked and screamed and plead.

Brian grabbed the old man's leg and pulled. He slashed his legs and arms. He rolled over and threw punches.

"No! You better not kill him. No! You motherfuckers! If you hurt him, I'll kill you all! I will kill you all!"

The old man stared blankly, unconcerned about Brian's threats.

"Kill me, you motherfucker. Kill me," Brian screamed.

He watched his partner get dragged down a path, almost out of view now. "I love you, Corey. I love you so much."

"I love you, Brian," he screamed back, his voice shrill and terrified.

Brian threw more punches wildly, the men easily deflecting them by kicking his arms out of the way. He tried to get back to his feet, but the men surrounding him kept kicking his stomach whenever he moved.

Boom.

A gunshot rang out in the distance. Birds scattered. And Brian knew half of his story was just torn from its pages.

* * *

Sim turned to Candlestick. "What happened to Mary next?"

Candlestick looked to her husk with sad eyes. "I don't know."

"What Candlestick mean?"

She rattled her head. "I don't know. I mean, I did know. I think I did. I was telling the stories for a reason, but it's like the entire ending just escaped me."

"You make up your own ending?" Sim asked.

"I can't. It's not my story to tell."

"What does Candlestick do now?"

"I go home. All I have left is my home. I miss it so much. I just want to feel safe in those walls again."

* * *

Violin ran down the stairs into the community room where so much of her family lay dead. She hopped into the generator room and grabbed a can of fuel, splashing some at the entrances of the community room. All of them. No way out. She lit a match.

The first Fake Winter, the one who saved her from burning in the motel, seemed impervious to fire, but according to the third Fake Winter, he struggled with water. Maybe the opposite was true for the creature behind their community doors. Maybe fire would kill him for good. It didn't matter either way, because he, for whatever reason, needed Violin alive, at least for the moment, and she was willing to die to stop him.

Maybe it was always supposed to be this way, and the first Fake Winter only prevented the inevitable. She should have died in the fire, smoldered to ash with her father's legacy.

As the flames widened, shot up into the ceiling, destroying her history, the smoke bellowed and crowded her lungs. She hacked and coughed while she saw the finale of her stories play out in her mind. But the story had changed, as if she'd stolen someone else's tale, ripped pages from a book and glued it to her own.

Mary's friends took turns consoling her on Boy's fifth birthday. She couldn't do it anymore. She hadn't even named her child out of fear that doing so would add permanence to his life in hiding. He deserved to have a name given to him in fresh air.

As she wept, and her group of friends sat around her, someone said, "Maybe I can help."

They all turned, shook. Three men stood in the far corner of the living room. Everyone stood, fear in their eyes. Zeke made fists. Mary clutched Boy, ready to run.

The man in the center threw his hands up. "I'm sorry to startle you. We're friends, I assure you."

He stepped forward slowly and kept his hands up, expressing he didn't mean anything funny. He tilted his head when he reached Miller. "Did you know your father was a raccoon?"

Miller furrowed his brow but was too scared to respond.

The man stopped at Mary and she leaned her body away, shielding Boy. "You were originally called Abraham Lincoln by one of the most fierce and brave women of all time. She apparently didn't know Abraham Lincoln was a terrible name for a girl, but whatever."

He moved toward Kelly. "And you. You're my daughter. When you were a child, you literally blew a man up with your eyes and saved the world from utter destruction."

He put his hand on her shoulder and she flinched. "My name is Kevin Bacon and I sound like a raving madman, I know, but you'll see I am here to help. I should have come earlier, but in your short lives, I have been at war more times than I would like to speak, a constant game of chess with evil entities. Still, it's no excuse. I should have come earlier. You all needed me, and I failed you."

Zeke gave Mary a look, one that asked if he should fight the man, do something to protect them, but she told him, "Not yet," with her eyes.

The man strolled back toward the corner where the other two men waited. "Anyway, here's how I will help, and how I have already begun to help. This," he pointed to the older gentleman with the kind eyes and silver hair, "is Jimmy Milani. You have a right to fear men and you were smart to hide down here, but Jimmy is a human you can trust."

Kevin Bacon put his hand on Jimmy's shoulder. "This man lost everything to protect this world. He fought against gods and walked away unscathed. I would trust him with my life, and you can too."

He sighed and put his hand on the other man. "This one is a little trickier. You can trust him as well. He'll come down periodically to check on you, but here's the catch, there are two other versions of him out there and they can't be trusted. His name is Dolphi. He will appear to you exactly like…"

Kevin stepped away so the group could see him clearly. Despite Mary knowing her group of friends had magic within them, her heart still stuttered at the sight of Dolphi's evolving face. It transferred into a totally different man, one with a grizzled face, long, thick beard, and dark brown, shaggy hair.

Dolphi smiled and bent low. "Do you know who I look like right now?"

Mary shook her head, dazzled, dazed, confused.

Dolphi pointed to Boy. "I look like him in 35 or so years."

"Ah, yes. While we are on the topic of your son." Kevin Bacon slid his fingers across a series of books of electricity Zeke had gathered over the years, finally stopping on the big, long art book. He took the book off the shelf and walked toward the group. "Jimmy is newly married and his wife is pregnant, so once he leaves this world, his son will take over helping you. They now own the house Russ once lived in. He will use it to provide you all with electricity. Meanwhile, Dolphi will show you how to make the electricity work in your favor, how to grow crops, and how to make the most of your individual magic."

He bent in front of Mary and looked at her, waiting for approval to speak to Boy. She nodded. Mary was scared, terrified even, but also drawn to the man. She trusted him entirely.

Kevin smiled at her and handed Boy the book. "Here. It's your fifth birthday, which I think is the perfect time to pick yourself a name. Flip through this and find a page you like."

Boy looked to his mother who told him to go ahead. Boy

skimmed through the pages until he stopped and pointed at a painting of a snow-covered town. People skated on ice on the left side of the painting, while a smattering of birds balanced the art on the right.

"Ah, Winter Landscape with a Bird Trap. Beautiful, isn't it?"

The boy nodded.

"Well then, you should call him Winter since he's so taken to it." Kevin handed the book to Mary. "Why don't you all pick your names that way. You're far too extraordinary to have such simple human names."

"Winter," Mary said and smiled. She picked her son up and kissed him. "Winter. I love it."

He stood up and dusted his knees off. "Now then, I have to get going. But first, I owe you all an apology. You didn't ask for this life and I fear it's my fault you're in this predicament. There's a bad man out there named Dark Skies. He is hunting for you all. He's the one who convinced Russ to find and trap you. Luckily, Russ didn't kill you. Dark Skies planned to use you, to milk your magic. You see, Dark Skies was a god once, more powerful than all of us combined, but he's been long since banished from his throne, and he hoped to use you all to regain some of that power. I know you don't understand this, but your magic isn't magic at all. You're the children of gods."

He sucked in a gulp of air and put his hand out for Mary to hold. She hesitated, but eventually put her hand in his. "Except for you. You're the child of someone who created her own magic. Someone maybe more special than us all. Dance."

A woman appeared, tall, slender. Her eyes were bright green, so green they almost glowed. Her hands and part of her body were either wrapped in plants or made from them. She smiled at Mary. "My daughter. I'm always watching. I love you. I wish I could have done more to protect you, to provide you with a better life. I don't have much time, but I just want you all to know one thing. You're protecting the Earth every day, and you don't even realize it. You've saved countless lives just by existing. Dark Skies hunts you, but he's not the biggest threat to humanity. Something bigger is always coming."

Kevin tilted his head to her, telling her time was up. "You're safe down here. I've blocked Dark Skies and Dolphi's brothers from seeing it. It's like they've completely forgotten it exists. Unfortunately, I can't do that for the whole world, so you'll have to be confined here, but nothing can get you here. Nothing."

And like that, they were gone.

No one in the group said anything, they hardly moved an inch. Shock overtook them.

Miller broke the silence. "Did he say my dad was a raccoon?"

The Story is Over

Violin dropped to the cement floor of her home, taking in the last bits of oxygen. Dolphi laughed on the opposite side of the fire. "You know, stupid girl, you are responsible for your family's death. I suppose I am, too. Once Dark Skies and I discovered Mr. Milani living in that house, we knew we should watch him. His connection to Kevin Bacon was too great for him to be living out in the middle of nowhere for absolutely no reason.

"Of course, we had no idea why until we saw him go into the hole in his barn, and even with all of our power, we couldn't view what lie down there. It was Dark Skies who figured it out. We knew about the descendants of the gods, but we'd long abandoned any hope of finding you until we found the one place on Earth we couldn't see. It only made sense Kevin Bacon hid you down there."

The fire crackled in the door frame, and Dolphi's snake face appeared on the other side of the flames. "Then, we discovered Jimmy Milani was working with my brother. Dark Skies came up with the plan, but I didn't think it would work. Sure enough,

Jimmy was dumb enough to not notice his friend's scar moved to the other side of his face. We hung out like long lost buddies. That miserable idiot. So, I gave good ole Jimmy a virus, and waited for him to spread it to you, which I now know he gave to your auntie that he secretly had an affair with. Shame on them."

Violin sat on the floor, listening. She finally, truly, heard his words and let them cut through her. She deserved to die in a pool of regret.

"Once your family was dead, Kevin Bacon gave up trying to make this place invisible to us. Now I can see it all, and oh how glorious it is. See, Dark Skies and I are no longer working together. I need this place razed to the ground for the next steps in my plan. Dark Skies needed to explore its secrets. You just gave me the one up on him. Thanks for that."

Violin coughed. "But I'm going to die in here, and that will ruin your plan, because I don't know how your story ends. And you needed me to know, didn't you?"

"You stupid girl. The story is over. I don't need you alive anymore. Enjoy your death."

She still didn't understand so much. Why did she need to hear those stories in the first place? Why did it matter to Dolphi if she knew she was the descendant of Dance, and her community was part of Kevin Bacon's plan? Why did it matter, especially if she were going to die anyway?

The stupid snake. That fucking snake.

Then, she remembered something. The snake. She crawled toward the far corner of the community room, where a small shelf hung on the wall. There, the books on electricity and the art book that gave them their names stood. Under it was the red snake.

She grabbed it and tucked it into her pit as she crawled toward the door, the same door where they quarantined before fleeing to Earth.

Violin's uncle put his arm around her. "When your father cooks, bad things happen."

Winter laughed and rolled his eyes. "Says Captain Crispy Crickets."

Her uncle waved the joke away. "My crickets are just fine. It's you who makes everything different levels of black."

Winter raised a finger. "My secret recipe!"

They all chuckled.

"Anyway, Violin, this here is the red snake. You aim him at the fire and press his tongue." He demonstrated. The snake shot clouds of white out. It startled her and she jumped, causing her father and uncle to laugh more.

Winter brushed his hand through her hair. "Most snakes you should fear, but this one is a friend."

She pressed the snake's tongue, and he fired his frothy dragon breath at the crackling flames, just like what Corey and Brian had used at the motel. Within a few seconds, the fire had dissipated enough for her to run through. And run she did, until she was outside the cave, emerging from the same hole her father led them through not too long ago. The fire disc welcomed her, bright and warm. She squinted her eyes and bent over, hacking up smoke for the second time in just a few days. She prayed to her ancestors to never see flames again.

As soon as her lungs allowed, she ran, following the river away from her tunnel, but opposite the way her father led them when they first emerged on Earth. She couldn't run, but she managed a fast walk without having to stop too often to cough up more sooty phlegm.

Dolphi would know she didn't die, that she was sure about, and he'd come look for her. But if Kevin Bacon was truly a god, and Dance her great-grandmother, why weren't they here helping? What happened to them? Why did they abandon Violin? Was she useless to them, so powerless and weak? Was she a flaw in their design, someone who only ever caused death and destruction? Or were they dead, Kevin Bacon and Dance, dead gods no longer protecting the Earth? Maybe that was why humanity had disappeared.

* * *

Candlestick followed the sounds of the river, Sim and Lion following close behind. Candlestick fumed over the death of her friend, and her inability to remember the end to her story. Her friend's death was as painful as a bullet to the chest, but losing the story made her feel hollowed out, as if someone used a scraper and peeled away her insides.

Sim noticed the rage in her eyes. "Sim want to know if Candlestick okay?"

Candlestick turned to him, not wanting to answer his question when she was so close to home. She could taste the home-made crickets. But she also felt the need to explain.

"Yes, I'm almost home. That's all that matters anymore. It's all I have left."

"And your sister," he said.

"My sister is dead. She was shot in the head. Violin is not my sister. She abandoned me. She fooled me into trusting humans. This is all her fault as much as it anyone else's." Candlestick began to cry. "I needed her. She should have been there with me. Cassie would still be alive if Violin was there, but she wasn't because she is selfish and stupid."

Sim put his head down.

She turned back toward the river sounds and walked until she broke free from the forest. Too many sights revealed themselves at once. First, she saw her sister, running away down the river. Violin disappeared over the horizon, too far to catch. She could send her husks, but her attention drew toward something else.

Their home was bellowing smoke.

"Oh, my Kevin Bacon. What happened?" She trudged through the river, crossing to the other side.

As she reached the other side, a voice spoke to her. "I'll tell you what happened."

She looked around, seeing nothing. "Who said that?"

"I did," said the voice. The oh-so familiar voice. She knew it anywhere, but also knew it was impossible. But it wasn't. As she pushed herself out of the water, there stood her father. Winter.

"Dad," she ran to him, hugging him, latching herself around him so tightly she thought his head might pop off.

"Of course, it's me. Did you think a silly human bullet could stop me?"

She wept into his shoulder, old wounds closing, fresh ones still raw. "I missed you so much. I thought you were dead, that Violin abandoned me."

Winter pushed her off, giving her a stern look. "I'm sorry to say, but some of that is true. Obviously, I am not dead, but your sister did abandon you. She abandoned us all. I knew I should have never listened to her about the humans. They are as awful as I presumed."

He rubbed his cheeks, tired and worn, just as she remembered him, although she wondered where the scar streaking down his cheek came from. "Your sister has taken their side. I know this is hard to understand, but she is no longer your sister. The humans have poisoned her."

Candlestick stepped back. "Dad, there's no way. There's absolutely no way. She would never turn on us."

Winter turned toward the hole where they once lived and pointed to the bellowing smoke. "She just burned our home to the ground and tried to keep me trapped in there. I barely survived."

She looked toward the horizon, where her sister had just run, and back toward her home. She couldn't believe it. "Why?"

"Because the humans are good at poisoning the mind." Winter put his hand on her shoulder, and she felt like she might melt. It felt so good to be touched by someone who wanted to touch her, who instigated it.

After a moment of soaking it in, she ran to her home, covered her mouth and charged in. She couldn't see much, too many flames all over, but she recognized the shapes, the rooms she once walked through, the love once shared, the small objects she interacted with. The wall where her drawings once hung cracked and snapped as flames ate it. The space where her mother hugged her last, now a bright orange and blue monster with scaly spikes, bellowing smoke from its mouth. The smoke was overpowering her.

Shit. She was trapped. She'd brought herself too far in, so desperate to feel and taste her world once more, she willingly dropped herself in the middle of a deadly fire. Even without touching her, it felt like it cooked her insides.

She dropped to her knees, unable to breathe.

Then, two hands snatched her shoulders and pulled her back, protecting her, as her father always did. He carried her farther and farther away from home.

She watched the smoke and flames erode all she'd ever cared about, one last cruel sucker punch from the gods, one last promise of war on her. The universe came at her time and time again. Killed her people. Attacked her family. Shot her father. Killed Christian, and Randy, and Cassie. And now, it destroyed the last sanctuary, the one place she always knew would stand, and even if she had to leave it, the knowledge of its existence gave her hope, gave her faith. She always told herself she'd return and soak in the memories. She'd say the proper goodbye she was denied.

When she turned to see her father, she was surprised to see it wasn't him that saved her at all. It was a tall man with black eyes, and long, wavy hair to match.

He put his hand around her. "You know what needs to happen?" he asked.

Candlestick said nothing.

"You know deep down, don't you?"

"Where did my father go? He was just here."

The man shook his head. "That wasn't your father. It was a trick. A snake in man's clothing."

She shook her head, confused, frustrated, terrified. "Why? Why would he trick me like that?"

"He's an evil fellow. We were once friends, he and I, but our paths have diverged, although we still share some common goals." The man stood up straight, arms locked behind his back. He stared at the horizon where Violin fled.

"Who was he? Who are you? What do you want?" She debated calling her husks, but the man hadn't made any threats yet, and she felt it important to hear him out.

"He is nothing but a dirty snake you need not worry about. I am Dark Skies."

Dark Skies. The name hit her in the chest. How did she know that name?

He sighed. "You see, the man who fled as soon as I arrived, the one who cruelly pretended to be your father, giving you false hope about his survival, wants you and your sister dead. He was pleased to convince you to war with your sister. I, on the other hand, very much want you alive. In fact, I believe you hold the key to the universe, my dear."

"I don't understand."

Dark Skies put his hand out, offering it to her. "I know. But you will. You've been fed nothing but lies your whole life, trifled with, tricked into muting your own strength. You're too powerful to mourn a dead human girl, too great for all this flailing around the Earth in hopes of starting a family with weak-minded fools too dumb to understand the greatness within you."

She took his hand but kept her mind close to thoughts of her monsters, ready to pull them out as needed. "What do you want from me?"

Dark Skies shook his head and sighed. "You poor girl, trained to wonder what others want from you. The question you should ask is what can I provide you. And the answer is unlimited power, respect, and love. The world will know Candlestick, and they will love her. I swear that on Kevin Bacon's soul."

She threw his hand off her. "If Kevin Bacon exists, we are at war. Add him to the list of people I want to kill. The Fireman. Kevin Bacon…" She gave a glance toward the horizon. "Maybe even Violin."

He patted her head. "That's the spirit. You owe nothing to anyone, my dear. But everyone owes you. And I will help you get your revenge and much more. And in return?" He bent low so they were face-to-face. "I ask nothing in return."

She clenched her fist. "I know the man was lying, but did my sister really burn my home down?"

Dark Skies smiled. "Not intentionally. She was just protecting herself. But I do agree with the man who pretended to be your father. Your sister needs to go. If you are the elixir that can heal the world, she is the poison that needs sucking out."

Lion snarled at the man and moaned. He jumped on Candlestick and licked her face. "No, don't calm me down, he's right. My sister is a poison. The motel, my father, our home, everything died because of her."

* * *

Violin heard the roars. At first, they snuck up, barely audible over the sounds of her wheezing, but the further she ran from home, the louder they became. She knew them. Waves. Maybe an ocean like Brian and Corey showed her. She ran toward the sound and the roaring heightened, but her mind grew foggy.

Her heart thrummed heavy in her chest, causing a deep ache by her ribs. The smoke inhalation caused her lungs to burn, and the more she moved, the deeper that burn went. The more she moved forward, the more muddled her mind went, as if her blood pumped the smoke to her brain, fogging it. But she couldn't stop, Dolphi would find her, so she dashed forward. The pain in her chest intensified, her mind growing muggier and muggier. And then she saw it, the crystal brown sand.

She stepped into it and her feet sank in. As she trudged closer to the water, unsure what she was even doing, her vision blurred, and she felt dizzy. As she moved closer to the waves, she lost her balance, collapsing to the side.

"Gotta get to the water," she said to herself, not sure why she felt she needed it. She tried to right herself, but only toppled to her side again.

"Hey, what's that?" someone said. It was a deep, masculine voice.

She turned toward it, but only saw a blurred shape moving toward her.

A second voice kicked in, softer but still masculine. "Holy shit, it's a kid."

She reached out a hand, so close to the ocean, a hope she clung to with no reason. She stretched forward.

"Get her on the boat," the first voice said.

As cold seawater lapped into her palm, someone grabbed her by the shoulders and lifted her away.

"No," she muttered.

Thank you so much for continuing Violin and Candlestick's journey. In the publishing world, reviews are the biggest help one can give to an author, good or bad. Even just a star rating or a couple of words can go a long way. It would mean so much to me if you dropped a line to let me know what you think.

Join the conversation on the Gagents of Chaos Facebook page, where a great group of avid horror and dark fantasy readers talk about the books they love. We have giveaways, chats, and lots of fun. You can find it at
www.facebook.com/groups/GagentsOfChaos

And if you sign up for my newsletter, you get two free short stories delivered right to your inbox. You can sign up for it on my website at www.GageGreenwood.com

Acknowledgments

I always need to thank Becky and Nolan first. They are my daily inspiration, my biggest supporters, and my best friends.

This book wouldn't be what it is without Mary Danner. She was my editor first, but now she is one of the most important friends in my life. I trust her entirely, and if Winter's world turned real, and I guarded the door, she'd be the only one I'd trust with the keys.

Luke Spooner, who makes my books beautiful with his cover art and interior artwork. He captures the mixture of whimsy and horror I try to achieve with each book, and he does it so damned well.

This book wouldn't exist without the support its predecessor received, and the first two Winter's Myths cheerleaders were Shannon Ettaro and Sarah D'Ambro. They were the first readers who weren't friends or family to shout about this book all over social media, and since then, we have connected and become best friends. There isn't a day that goes by where I don't chat with them. So, yeah, they were the first readers who weren't friends or family, but now they are both.

The Winter's series was also helped by a fierce group of BookTokers who spend their good time making fun videos and promoting their favorite reads. Kirsten Craig (@TheSpineOf-Motherhood), Stephanie Evans (@ForTheLoveOfBookmarks), Jason Nickey (@BiblioBeard), Deven VanKirk (@Deven_reads), Chaz Williams (@TheFittedHorrorLover), Julie K (@Grim-

Dreadful), and Autumn Gardner (@Horror.Books.And.Chill). You are all amazing, and I am so thankful for you.

Horror and dark fantasy are tough genres. So many bookstores still don't have a horror section, despite the fact the genre is exploding in popularity. Thankfully, there are some bookstores and curators who recognize the value of the genre, and are proving daily that when horror is showcased, horror sells! Tiffany Rife at Barnes and Noble Libbie Place in Richmond Virginia, Chance Forshee at Barnes and Noble in Bowling Green Kentucky, Mindy Elsinger at Barnes and Noble in Sioux Falls South Dakota, Ryan Elizabeth Clark at Gibson's Bookstore in New Hampshire, Adrian Chavez at Page 1 Bookstore in Albuquerque, New Mexico, and Kelly Kujawski who runs my favorite local bookstore in Rhode Island, Rarities Books and Bindery. If you live in any of these towns/cities, I highly recommend you check out their shops and show them how much you approve of the good work they are putting in to make horror reign supreme again.

Heather Field, who offered me my first author talk event, signing, and who is, in my humble opinion, the best librarian this side of the Mississippi, and the other side, too.

Then, there are the many readers who I have befriended on this journey, who helped build the confidence I needed by sharing their feelings on my work, or messaging me, or just chatting with me. Stephanie Manning, who made me cry with her review, Autumn Gardner who continuously tells everyone how much she loved Winter's Myths. Debbie Piazza, who will send me a message with a cool piece of art, an encouraging word, or a behind the scenes clip from a movie. Corrina Morse, who runs a super fun review page, and who always shares my posts and spreads the word on indie horror. Samantha Hawkins, who reviews books, and is a loud and proud champion for indie authors, horror, and all things awesome. Janalyn Prude, who always leaves the kindest reviews, and digs deep into the indie author community to show her support to everyone writing work she enjoys. Heather Ann Larson, who beta read this book, gave great insights, and who owns the very first signed copy of the book. Angel Van Atta, who is the sweetest human, and a huge proponent of building a community of great horror-loving folks. Danielle Yeager, one of my first "fans," and an awesome person, who has rooted for me and celebrated with me too many times to count. Heather Ann, such an awesome friend! Ali Sweet who always recommends my short stories to anyone who will listen. Joanne Philbrook, who moved me to tears with a post about her son reading my work. Terri Lynne Hudson, the voice behind so much of my work, and a true diehard! Tasha Schiedel, and her wonderful reviews on her blog. Hope Haugstad, an incredible human who loves to support and cheer for me, always ready with a kind word, and eager to buy anything I put out. Christopher Knickerbocker, who messaged me to talk about the themes in the book. Stephanie Huddle, who roots for me as an author, while also inspiring me to start running again. Jessica Shelly, who took a day out of work to finish Winter's Myths. Kendall Cupp, who was so excited to ARC read this book, she talked about it to her family at her sister's wedding dress event (congrats to her sister, BTW), and thanks to her mom, Priscilla Cupp, who might pass out when she reads this. Zarah Lutz Fowler, Jenny Carr Greenwood, Ashley Anne, Sally Felix, Shasta Mathews, and so many others who have supported me, that I'm just not remembering at this very moment, but I promise you, the support and love you've shown has meant the world to me.

And the authors who I have befriended on this journey, and who have helped me navigate this impossible world of publishing: MZ Medenciy, Jay Bower, Brian Keene, Richard Chizmar, Clay Chapman, Naomi Ault, Aron Beauregard, Zack Lester, Ania Ahlborn, Richard Thomas, Caitlin Marceau, John Edward

Lawson, John Durgin, Heather Miller, SP Somtow, John Lynch, Christa Carmen, Joshua Rex, Candace Nola, Jonathan Edward Durham, and of course, my writing pals: Megan Stockton, Peter Marsh, Joshua MacMillan, and Jae Mazer. Again, I know there is so many more I need to thank, but this acknowledgments section is getting to be longer than the book itself. I gotta stop somewhere.

My Lamppost Legends!

These folks have helped make my dreams come!

Heather Ann Larson, Bryan Walsh, Shannon Ettar, Shasta Mathews, Rhonda Bobbitt, Constance Bell, Megan Stevens, Jennifer Chambers Daney, Kimberly Case-Wright, Kendall Cupp, Debbie Alder, Chandra Greco, Erica Fields, Tracey Nudd, Amy Logsdon, Jessica Shelly, Elyn Noble, Brianna Leslie, Sophia McIntyre, Stephanie Evans, Caitlin Robert, Deven VanKirk, Elethia Rex, Denise Walton, Wendy Greve, Trish Mudersbach, Amanda Stacey, Adrian Mathis, Laurie Cross, Michele L. Peters, Michael Livingston, Ashley Harvey, Kendall Alexander, Michael E Casey, Lisa Alva, Jason Artz, Gillian Speicher, John Durgin, Christine Wright, Adam H. Avitable, Robin Ginther-Venneri, Christopher Knickerbocker, Mary Sepko, Scott Light, Jennifer Sweet, Koren Medeiros, Chiara Cooper, Alex Parpworth, Justine Manzano, Chad Clark, Kristy Skowronski, Tracy Allen, Nicole Fontana Howard, Sarah D'Ambro, Michelle Ford, Jess Gregorius, Kristin Snow, Glenda Starr, Kerri Walker, Shana Gomien, Kristin Wilson, Heather York, Earlene Bendschneider, Chaz

Williams, Megan Mathison, Rebecca Bailey, Leslie Stair, Britta Bailey, Carissa Razon, Teresa Cook, Julie Tomes, Hope Haugstad, Frank Ryan, Holly Lucinda, Jeannie Fenner, Olivia Tullius, Leah Cole, Nicholas Beishline, Megan Stockton, Christina Capobianco, Kathleen LeJeune, Stephanie Huddle, Jodi A. Souza, Sheryl Howell, Linda A. McLoughlin, Courtney Wood, Bethany Greene, Jason Nickey, and Erin Pritchard.

Also by Gage Greenwood

NOVELS:

Winter's Myths

SHORT STORIES:

Through Flickering Lights, a Silhouette

Grackles on the Feeder

About the Author

Gage Greenwood is a proud member of the Horror Writers Association and Science Fiction and Fantasy Writers association.

He's been an actor, comedian, podcaster, and even the Vice President of an escape room company. Since childhood, he's been a big fan of comic books, horror movies, and depressing music that fills him with existential dread.

He lives in New England with his girlfriend and son, and he spends his time writing, hiking, and decorating for various holidays.

Find out more, or contact me: www.gagegreenwood.com